Starmont Studies in Literary Criticism #44
ISSN 0738-0119

**Cryptical Secrets
from the
"Crypt of Cthulhu"**

Edited by
Robert M. Price

Starmont House, Inc.
1992

Robert M. Price has written critical articles on Lovecraft, Howard, Ligotti, and others for *Lovecraft Studies, Dagon* and other journals and for anthologies including *Discovering Modern Horror* and *An Epicure in the Terrible.* He edited *The Horror of It All, H.P. Lovecraft and the Cthulhu Mythos,* and *Black Forbidden Things* (Starmont House), as well as the fiction anthology, *Tales of the Lovecraft Mythos* (Fedogan & Bremer). He has been the editor of the journal *Crypt of Cthulhu* for a decade.

Published and copyright © 1992 by Starmont House, Inc., P.O. Box 851, Mercer Island, WA 98040. All rights reserved. International copyrights reserved in all countries. No part of this book may be reproduced in any form, except for brief passages quoted in reviews, without the expressed written permission of the publisher. Printed in U.S.A.

Cover art © 1992 by Bruce Timm

Contents

Introduction	1
Who Wrote "The Mound"? by S. T. Joshi	3
H. P. Lovecraft and *The Dream-Quest of Unknown Kadath* by S. T. Joshi	7
The Sources for "From Beyond" by S. T. Joshi	18
Lovecraft and the *Regnum Congo* by S. T. Joshi	24
Tentacles in Dreamland: Cthulhu Mythos Elements in the Dunsanian Stories by Will Murray	30
Self-Parody in Lovecraft's Revisions by Will Murray	34
The First Cthulhu Mythos Poem by Will Murray	37
Prehuman Language in Lovecraft by Will Murray	41
H. P. Lovecraft's *Fungi from Yuggoth* by David E. Schultz	46
Lovecraft's New York Exile by David E. Schultz	52
E. R. B. and H. P. L. by William Fulwiler	60
Randolph Carter, Warlord of Mars by Robert M. Price	66
The Pseudo-Intellectual in Weird Fiction by Robert M. Price	69
August Derleth: Myth-Maker by Robert M. Price	72
"Lovecraftianity" and the Pagan Revival by Robert M. Price	74
Cosmic Fear and the Fear of the Lord: Lovecraft's Religious Vision by Robert M. Price	78

Chariots of the Old Ones? by Robert M. Price and Charles Garofalo	86
The *Necronomicon*: The Origin of a Spoof by Colin Wilson	88
The Diary of Alonzo Typer by William Lumley	91
A Sacrifice to Science by Adolphe de Castro	97
The Automatic Executioner by Adolphe de Castro	114
The Tower from Yuggoth by Ramsey Campbell	120
The Ringer of the Doorbell by Jim Cort	138
The Slitherer from the Slime by Lin Carter	143
Limericks from Yuggoth by Lin Carter	147
Mildew from Shaggai by Robert M. Price	156
Shards from Shaggai by Robert M. Price	161
Famous Last Words by Robert M. Price	165
Screwtape's Letter to Cthulhu by Robert M. Price	167
Mail-Call of Cthulhu	168

Introduction
Robert M. Price

"They were the black, forbidden things most sane people have never even heard of, or have heard of only in furtive, timorous ,whispers; the banned and dreaded repositories of cryptical secrets and immemorial formulae which have trickled down the stream of time from the days of man's youth, and the dim, fabulous days before man was."

This passage from H. P. Lovecraft's "The Haunter of the Dark" belongs to the scene in which the interloping Robert Blake stumbles upon a cache of antique tomes abandoned many years before by the Starry Wisdom Church in their hasty departure from the premises. Yet do the words not apply with equal force to the mad revelations mercifully cloaked behind the cheerily hued covers of *Crypt of Cthulhu*? It is with the latter that the present pages are taken up, for better or for worse. Two previous collections of *Cryptic* reprints have proven sufficiently popular as to justify a third, and the mindless, tenebrous forces of the blindly reeling cosmos have predestined you to buy it!

The opportunity to collect a third "Best of . . ." volume is something of a relief, as the selection of contents for the previous two volumes was inevitably somewhat arbitrary, leaving much good material dangerously at large. But with the appearance of *Black Forbidden Things* most of the scholarly and speculative gems from *Crypt of Cthulhu* are available in a more convenient and abiding form.

It will be noticed immediately that *Black Forbidden Things* showcases the work of a handful of today's prominent Lovecraftian researchers, S. T. Joshi, Will Murray, David Schultz, William Fulwiler, and myself. These tortured souls have contributed much of the splendid scholarly analysis that has distinguished *Crypt of Cthulhu* from other fanzines during its decade of existence. Two items here did not appear in the pages of *Crypt*. One is my study "Randolph Carter, Warlord of Mars," which forms a sequel of sorts to Fulwiler's essay, "E. R. B. and H. P. L." My essay first appeared in *Tekeli-li* #1 in 1991. Similarly, I have also taken the liberty of borrowing (from the second issue of the same magazine) my controversial essay "Cosmic Fear and the Fear of the Lord: Lovecraft's Religious Vision," as a natural adjunct to my earlier "'Lovecraftianity' and the Pagan Revival."

One of the things that *Crypt* readers always seemed to appreciate most about the magazine, and a trait which served to distinguish it from its venerable predecessor and inspiration, *Lovecraft Studies*, is the element of humor. There are few things as generative of cringing disgust as fannish humor which degrades the very idol which the fan slavishly serves. So we always sought to provide a more offbeat type of Lovecraftian humor. The present collection features a bit of it. Here's hoping that it may provide a bit of relief from what is otherwise at times heavy going.

Fiction, a frequent visitor to the pages of *Crypt*, is not

1

unrepresented in these pages, either. Ramsey Campbell has graciously allowed us again to reprint his early draft "The Tower from Yuggoth," strictly for purposes of comparison with his later version, "The Mine on Yuggoth," which appeared in his collection *The Inhabitant of the Lake* (Arkham House, 1963).

A similar scholarly purpose is served by the inclusion here of three draft stories Lovecraft received from the hands of his revision clients. De Castro's "The Automatic Executioner" became HPL's "The Electric Executioner," while "A Sacrifice to Science" became "Clarendon's Last Test" or simply "The Last Test." William Lumley's "The Diary of Alonzo Typer" turned out surprisingly well as Lovecraft's rewrite of the same name. Here, then, are three of his revision tales in the case of which we may be precisely sure what role Lovecraft had.

One of the most important criticisms of the previous *Crypt* collections was that we failed to include any of the letters the magazine received. Indeed, these were some readers' favorite portion of an issue. More than once we read the comment that someone would not mind if the occasional issue were to be devoted entirely to letters! One of the magazine's chief services to the Lovecraftian community was this provision of a forum where fans, critics, and authors could express their opinions about and to one another. If a reader cared not for the fiction of Lin Carter or Brian Lumley, why, he could tell him so and know that Carter or Lumley would read it and probably reply! One thinks of the party-line telephone system of rural Dunwich. At any rate, here is a generous sampling of some of the more substantial letters, several of them virtually constituting mini-articles in their own right!

Once again, to all who contributed to the magazine, and all who wrote for it for ten years: thank you! And if you are just now discovering *Crypt of Cthulhu*, I cannot say you haven't missed much, but if you will add to this volume its two predecessors, *H. P. Lovecraft and the Cthulhu Mythos* and *The Horror of it All: Encrusted Gems from the Crypt of Cthulhu*, you can pretty well catch up with the rest of us!

Robert M. Price

Who Wrote "The Mound"
S. T. Joshi

In Zealia Brown Reed Bishop's oftentimes fantastic memoir, "H. P. Lovecraft: A Pupil's View,"[1] she declares expressly that Frank Belknap Long helped to revise a lengthy tale that Lovecraft ghost-wrote for Mrs. Bishop, "The Mound." Yet both Long and Lovecraft were and have been ceaselessly stating that Lovecraft, and Lovecraft alone, wrote the novelette. As recently as 1975, Long stated categorically: "I had nothing whatever to do with the writing of *The Mound*."[2] Who actually authored this tale, a major Lovecraftian opus fully as long as "The Whisperer in Darkness"?

Evidence shows that, although Long did indeed have a hand in the process of revision (or ghost-writing) of "The Mound," he is nonetheless fundamentally correct when he states, "That brooding, somber, and magnificently atmospheric story is Lovecraftian from the first page to the last."[3] However, behind this statement lies a wealth of detail which even yet is not completely unraveled. Indeed, the published versions of "The Mound" are certainly not Lovecraft's in every respect.

Mrs. Bishop had given Lovecraft the task of revising or ghost-writing "The Mound" in late 1929. R. H. Barlow states that "*The Mound* was . . . written by Lovecraft . . . from a late synopsis [by Mrs. Bishop], something like 'There is an Indian mound near here, which is haunted by a headless ghost. Sometimes it is a woman.'"[4] But Lovecraft found this plot-germ far too tame, and began expanding it, incorporating into it many elements of his myth-cycle. Lovecraft wrote to Elizabeth Toldridge: ". . . everything pertaining to the Mayan & Aztec civilisations is interesting, & I fancy I shall use the theme more than once. Indeed—my next revision job will give me a chance to practice, since it will require the introduction of this theme in such a way as to involve wholly original composition on my part."[5]

We next hear that the ghost-writing of "The Mound" is "proving to be rather an incubus, for the idea is spinning itself out into a veritable novelette."[6] Evidently Lovecraft finished the entire tale in early 1930. It appears that Lovecraft now handed on his autograph version of the tale to Long for typing, and that Long actually prepared the typed version: the typewriter face of the typescript and carbon copy (still surviving in the John Hay Library) is identical to that of letters by Long for this period. Moreover, Long seems to have made certain transcriptional errors in the text due to his inability to read Lovecraft's handwriting; one word is rendered on the typescript as "atariousness," and I have still not been able to ascertain what Lovecraft's intention here was.[7] (Lovecraft's handwritten manuscript has of course perished.) After the typescript was finished in 82 pages, it was submitted—either by Long (who at this time was Mrs. Bishop's major literary agent)[8] or by Lovecraft—to *Weird Tales*, but Editor Farnsworth Wright rejected it, presumably on account of its length; Long writes to Lovecraft (c. 19 March 1930): "It was incredibly asinine of him

[Wright] to reject The Mound—and on such a flimsy pretext" (ms., JHL).
 The decision was then evidently made (probably by Mrs. Bishop, who desperately wished to sell this story and any other of "her" works) to revise or abridge the story so that it would be more saleable to a pulp market. Frank Belknap Long was entrusted with this task. All that Long did, however, was to abridge the text, and this is indicated by the fact that the pages of the surviving typescript (but not the carbon) are renumbered in pen, apparently by Long. In all, the text was shortened by about twenty pages. Long may perhaps have provided suitable transitional passages for the abridged version (although there are none such on either the typescript or the carbon), but this is the extent of his role in the tale. When Long completed this "revised version," he apparently made some attempts to sell it, but these efforts came to nothing.[9] Both the abridged and the unabridged versions of "The Mound" lay in manuscript (or, rather, typescript) for years.
 When he visited Barlow in De Land, Florida, in the summer of 1934, Lovecraft evidently made mention of this lengthy ghostwriting effort; Barlow, with his eye ever toward publication (amongst his many book ventures were Lovecraft's *Fungi from Yuggoth* series; possibly the essays written to the Transatlantic Circulator in 1921 defending the story "Dagon"; another collection of poems by Lovecraft; and several other projects, all of which came to naught), expressed a desire to publish the tale, either in magazine form or as a separate chapbook. Lovecraft wrote to Mrs. Bishop informing her of the plan, and she in turn wrote to Long and asked him to send the *original* version to Lovecraft and Barlow in Florida. Needless to say, Long did not think he had the full version, for although he had "preserved the sheets [he] omitted in making the revised version . . ., . . . they [later] sank from sight." Long rightfully complained to Lovecraft: "Did you actually imagine that I could store MS rejects for more than *five* years in perfect safety?"[10] Long did, however, send this abridged/revised version to Lovecraft.
 As noted, the original typescript of "The Mound" was the one Long used in making the "revised version"; but the carbon was still with Mrs. Bishop, although it was missing the first three pages.[11] Barlow (on Lovecraft's suggestion) asked Mrs. Bishop to send him this copy and she complied in mid-July 1934.[12] Barlow evidently decided that the original, unabridged version by Lovecraft should be the one published. In the meanwhile Long had managed to locate the pages that he had removed in his abridged version and sent them to Barlow. Barlow now possessed two complete typescripts of "The Mound," save that the carbon lacked the first three pages. He forthwith typed them himself.
 In the unabridged text, Lovecraft had made slight revisions and corrections in pen; but the text was almost precisely the same as that written in 1929-30. Plans for publication were apparently carried on, but soon foundered and were abandoned. In early 1937, a month before Lovecraft's death, Barlow sent the original typescript back to Lovecraft,[13] keeping the carbon himself. After Lovecraft's death both copies were deposited in the John Hay Library.

Thus ends Frank Belknap Long's involvement in the affair; but the saga of "The Mound" is not yet over. A few years after Lovecraft's death, August Derleth acquired the typescript (probably borrowing it from the John Hay Library) and "touched [it] up . . . for sales purposes."[14] This involved radically altering Lovecraft's punctuation, deleting passages (a total of about 150 words), and rephrasing sentences. It was this adulterated version of "The Mound" that was published (in still more abridged form) in *Weird Tales* for November 1940 and (unabridged) in *Beyond the Wall of Sleep* (1943). The text was later reproduced in Mrs. Bishop's *The Curse of Yig* (1953) and in Lovecraft's *The Horror in the Museum and Other Revisions* (1970). All published versions of "The Mound," therefore, while not being "by Lovecraft and Long," can certainly be regarded as "by Lovecraft and Derleth"; the tale is certainly more a "collaboration" than are any of the sixteen so-called "posthumous collaborations" of Lovecraft and Derleth, from *The Lurker at the Threshold* (1945) to "The Watchers out of Time" (1971). The quest for the scholar would be a restoration of the text of "The Mound" as it was written by Lovecraft (and Lovecraft alone) in late 1929 and early 1930.

It is, then, not surprising that, amidst the bizarre circumstances surrounding the writing and attempted selling of "The Mound," all parties in question (save, of course, Lovecraft) should be confused as to the authorship of the tale. Barlow, indeed, wryly records an amusing comment on the affair by Lovecraft: "L[ovecraft] perceived that Belknap had written [on the typescript] By *F.B.L. & Z.B.R.*—'the two people who had nothing to do with it' —& thereupon suggested that I call it *The Mound, by R. H. Barlow!*"[15] One can well understand Lovecraft's irritation at being robbed of credit for this story, "in view of the labour I put into it back in dear old '29"[16]—and especially in view of the fact that its cosmic scope and brilliant social criticism of the underground mound civilisation can make it rank even with the best of Lovecraft's later narratives.

NOTES

[1]In her *The Curse of Yig* (Sauk City, WI: Arkham House, 1953), pp. 139-51. It contains the claim that Lovecraft knew several African tongues.
[2]Frank Belknap Long, *Howard Phillips Lovecraft: Dreamer on the Nightside* (Sauk City, WI: Arkham House, 1975), pp. xiii-xiv.
[3]Ibid., p. xiv.
[4]Note by Barlow on the title page of one of the T.Mss. of "The Mound," John Hay Library, Brown University (hereafter referred to as JHL).
[5]Lovecraft to E. Toldridge, 26 November 1929 (ms., JHL).
[6]Lovecraft to E. Toldridge, 20 December 1929 (SL III.97-98).
[7]This word is simply omitted in the published versions of the tale and the sentence containing it amended accordingly.
[8]Sonny Belknap [was] . . . her main literary agent": Love-

craft to R. H. Barlow, 12 July 1934 (ms., JHL).
   [9]Frank Belknap Long to S. T. Joshi, 17 May 1977. Lovecraft himself seems to have doubted Long's efforts in this regard: "I assumed that Sonny Belknap . . . *had* done so [i.e., tried to market the story]; & am astonished to find that any stone was left unturned." Lovecraft to R. H. Barlow, 12 July 1934 (ms. JHL).
   [10]Frank Belknap Long to H. P. Lovecraft, [28 May 1934]; ms., JHL.
   [11]Mrs. Bishop writes to Lovecraft (26 May 1934): "Do you suppose Mr. Barlow would be interested in reading Medusa's Coil? I have it and a carbon copy of The Mound except for the first three pages" (ms., JHL).
   [12]Cf. Zealia Bishop on R. H. Barlow, 11 July 1934 (ms., JHL).
   [13]Lovecraft to Barlow, 3 January 1936 [i.e., 1937; misdated by Lovecraft]; ms., JHL.
   [14]Barlow, note on title page of one of the T.Mss. of "The Mound," JHL.
   [15]Ibid.
   [16]Lovecraft to Barlow, 3 January 1936 [i.e., 1937]; ms., JHL.

[A restored version of Lovecraft's original tale appeared, since the publication of this article, in the new edition of *The Horror in the Museum and Other Revisions*, textually corrected by S. T. Joshi.]

H. P. Lovecraft and
The Dream-Quest of Unknown Kadath
S. T. Joshi

The Dream-Quest of Unknown Kadath is one of the longest of H. P. Lovecraft's fictional works—only the two novels, *The Case of Charles Dexter Ward* and *At the Mountains of Madness*, are longer —and it is also one of the most autobiographical of his works. Although much of it is written in a witty, humorous style, its conclusion makes it clear that Lovecraft intended to convey a very serious message with this dream-fantasy. It would be wise for us to look into certain aspects of Lovecraft's life, and to see what incidents and sentiments find an echo in *The Dream-Quest*.
One commentator has written that Lovecraft's life was "almost entirely without incident, yet rich in detail"; and this is true enough. Howard Phillips Lovecraft did not lead a very eventful life: he was born in Providence on August 20, 1890, and died in Providence on March 15, 1937. In those 46 1/2 years less than five years were spent away from Providence, while only two years of his life were spent outside of New England. Those two years, however, are vital to our understanding of *The Dream-Quest*, as shall later be seen.
Lovecraft came from a comparatively well-to-do family which lived in a huge Victorian mansion at 454 Angell Street on the East Side of Providence. (This house no longer stands, having been torn down in the late 1950s to make way for an apartment house complex.) When Lovecraft was three his father, a traveling salesman, suddenly went insane and spent the last five years of his life in a mental institution, dying when Lovecraft was eight. His fatal malady was diagnosed as paresis, which is vaguely related to syphilis; although it is quite rash to believe—as one Lovecraft critic has done—that Lovecraft himself was congenitally syphilitic, having inherited it from his father. At any event, the upbringing of the young boy fell to his mother—a neurotically overpossessive woman who herself died in a mental institution in 1921—and his maternal grandfather, Whipple Phillips. This grandfather spurred Lovecraft's early studies in literature and science. When Lovecraft was six his maternal grandmother died; the subsequent gloom into which the household was plunged affected Lovecraft tremendously, and inspired horrible nightmares where faceless "night-gaunts" attacked him and bore him off into space. (These night-gaunts play, of course, a significant role in *The Dream-Quest*, and they show how Lovecraft incorporated details from his own dreams into his fiction.) Lovecraft continued to have very vivid dreams throughout his life, some of which he directly transcribed into stories.
Lovecraft's early readings and writings are of the utmost significance in our understanding of *The Dream-Quest*. Some of his earliest readings were fairy tales, particularly those of the brothers Grimm; this may have ignited a taste for fantasy, for not much later Lovecraft was poring over the *Arabian Nights*, imagining himself a Moslem and giving himself the name of Abdul Alhazred. (Alhazred later becomes the author of Lovecraft's invented book of magical

lore, *The Necronomicon*.) Not long after he discovered classical antiquity, and began reading translations and paraphrases of the Greek and Roman classics. He was particularly enamoured of the *Odyssey*—which, as we shall see, cast a rather strong influence upon *The Dream-Quest*. Lovecraft even began writing verse translations and paraphrases of the classics himself: in a work called "The Poem of Ulysses" (dating to his seventh year) he tells the whole story of the *Odyssey* in 120 lines of rhyming English verse. He had mastered Latin sufficiently that at the age of ten or so he produced a literal verse translation of the beginning of Ovid's *Metamorphoses*.

But while these literary pursuits were being carried on, Lovecraft was becoming fascinated with the sciences, particularly those of astronomy and chemistry. I mention this because if one reads nothing by Lovecraft but *The Dream-Quest*, one may gain the impression that he was some strange mystic who lived perpetually in a dream-world and wrote about curious little beings who don't exist. Nothing could be further from the truth. Lovecraft was a stolid materialist (in the philosophical sense), and did not approve of any form of mysticism or occultism, much less believe in it. Most of his tales occur in a very meticulously described real world, where the intrusion of monsters—which must not be taken literally, but symbolically, as representations of all that is unknown to men—is graphically and intensely described. In this sense *The Dream-Quest* is quite atypical of Lovecraft's work—it is one of the few tales which takes place wholly in a dream-world, and we shall see that this device was intended to convey a very exact philosophical meaning.

It is also important to know that Lovecraft had, as early as the age of twelve, shorn himself of any religious belief. The combination of his interests in science and in classical antiquity had made him wonder whether the Christian religion was any more true than that of the Greeks and Romans—particularly when there was little scientific basis for a belief in Christianity or, for that matter, any sort of deity. Throughout his life he remained a staunch atheist, and, with Bertrand Russell (whom he read and admired), agreed that the Christian Church had probably done Western Civilisation more harm than good. We can feel this atheism in the generally pagan or even pantheistic atmosphere of *The Dream-Quest*—all his creatures worship not one god, as do the Christians, but many gods.

Lovecraft spent his entire adolescence in the East Side of Providence, becoming fascinated with its antiquity. In later life he liked wryly to imagine himself as a gentleman of the eighteenth century, sporting a periwig and wearing colonial attire. Lovecraft had read vastly in eighteenth-century literature, and felt that that century somehow represented his true home. By the time he was 25 he had begun to write prolifically for amateur presses. He had no occupation as such, since he relied on the family inheritance to support himself. Most of the money he earned in his life was through the process of professional revision-work, where he would revise or ghost-write books, articles, stories, and poems—most of them of the most wretched quality—for a rather low fee. Among his revisions were a psychology textbook, a history of Dartmouth College, and horror tales by would-be authors and authoresses.

It was through his work for the amateur press that he met the woman whom he would eventually marry. He first met Sonia Greene, a widowed Russian Jew some years older than he, in 1921, when he was 31. After a three-year romance they married and settled in Brooklyn.

One commentator has written that "it is difficult to imagine a couple more ill-matched." Indeed, it is difficult to believe that such a man as Lovecraft—reclusive, caught up in his own activities, not at all a ladies' man—would marry at all. Needless to say the marriage was not a success. At first the couple's difficulties were financial: Lovecraft could find no regular occupation in New York, while his wife, who ran a hat-shop, ran into similar difficulties; the hat-shop went out of business, and she had to go to Cleveland to work, leaving Lovecraft alone in New York.

Lovecraft had first been captivated by New York, but it was not long before he came to hate the place. He lived in a rather squalid part of the town—the area of Brooklyn called "Red Hook" (during his New York stay he wrote a story called "The Horror at Red Hook"—it is not a pleasant tale), and among the incidents of his two-year stay in New York was his being robbed in the night of all his clothing. He began seeing his literary friends less and less, ashamed of his threadbare clothes. Finally he became tremendously homesick for Providence, as one letter written to his aunts testifies:

> I will be dogmatic only to the extent of saying that it is New England I *must* have—in some form or other. Providence is part of me—I *am* Providence . . . Providence would always be at the back of my head as a goal to be worked toward—an ultimate Paradise to be regain'd at last.

Now, before one laughs at these sentiments, put yourself in Lovecraft's place. Here is a man who had spent his entire life in Providence and New England, such that they had become his haven and his refuge. Then, suddenly, at the age of 34, he is uprooted and placed in an environment—New York—which is radically different in character. Lovecraft's "sense of place" was extremely pronounced—he reacted very keenly to his surroundings, and if they were not congenial, then he could hardly function. He lived in the age before technology had allowed travel to be simple and omnipresent, and like most of the human race before one or two generations ago, he felt very close to his native soil. I quote again from the letter to his aunts:

> To all intents and purposes I am more naturally isolated from mankind than Nathaniel Hawthorne himself, who dwelt alone in the midst of crowds, and whom Salem knew only after he had died. Therefore, it may be taken as axiomatic that the people of a place matter absolutely nothing to me except as components of the general landscape and scenery . . . My life lies not among people but among scenes—my local affections are not personal, but topographical and architectural.

Finally Lovecraft's aunts invited him to come back to Providence, which he did in April of 1926. Only a few months later, at the end of 1926 and the beginning of 1927, he wrote *The Dream-Quest*, in a period of about three months. Let me read you another letter which describes his coming home from the hated New York:

> The train sped on, and I experienced silent convulsions of joy in returning step by step to a waking and tri-dimensional life. New Haven—New London—and then quaint Mystic, with its colonial hillside and landlocked cove. Then at last a still subtler magick fill'd the air—nobler roofs and steeples, with the train rushing airily above them on its lofty viaduct—*Westerly*—in His Majesty's Province of RHODE-ISLAND & PROVIDENCE-PLANTATIONS! GOD SAVE THE KING!! Intoxication follow'd—Kingston-East Greenwich with its steep Georgian alleys climbing up from the railway—Apponaug and its ancient roofs—Auburn—just outside the city limits—I fumble with bags and wraps in a desperate effort to appear calm—THEN—a delirious marble dome outside the window—a hissing of air brakes—a slackening of speed—surges of ecstasy and dropping of clouds from my eyes and mind—HOME—UNION STATION—PROVIDENCE!!!!

Clearly Providence was at the center of Lovecraft's heart.

The eleven years of his life following his return to Providence can be told briefly. Having now a settled home, he began traveling widely for short periods of time, as far as New Orleans and Key West. He was fascinated by the colonial sites in Charleston, SC, as well as Richmond, VA, and other sites along the Atlantic seaboard. He obtained a divorce from his wife in 1929. He wrote many of his greatest stories in his final ten years, including *At the Mountains of Madness*, "The Shadow out of Time," "The Colour out of Space," *The Case of Charles Dexter Ward*, and others. In late 1936 he became critically ill with cancer of the intestine, and died a few months later. He is buried in Swan Point Cemetery, and recently a marker has been set up on his grave which bears the inscription: "I AM PROVIDENCE."

Lovecraft was astonishingly well read in many fields of literature, particularly that of fantasy. In fact, his long essay "Supernatural Horror in Literature," has been called the best survey of imaginative fiction, from antiquity to his time, ever written. Lovecraft was understandably influenced by a large number of writers, and it is these literary influences upon *The Dream-Quest* that I now want to touch upon.

The most obvious—and in some ways the most superficial—influence is that of Lord Dunsany. Lovecraft wrote that he received an "electric shock" when first reading Dunsany in 1919, and soon afterwards he wrote a number of short stories which imitated Dunsany's elegant, solemn, lyrical style, which is founded largely upon the King James Bible. But by around 1926, when Lovecraft wrote *The Dream-Quest*, the Dunsany influence had fairly well worn off, and it could be said that *The Dream-Quest* is Lovecraft's final trib-

ute to the Irish fantaisiste. Lovecraft's earlier Dunsanian stories are quite derivative and somewhat unoriginal in style—though not in concept—and Lovecraft was content to do no more than to attempt as faithful a pastiche of Dunsany as he could manage. But he was not very good at imitating Dunsany's sublimely simple lyricism. *The Dream-Quest* reveals an assimilation of Dunsany's style. Lovecraft's work is far denser than most of Dunsany's, and is packed more with adjectival description. It could virtually be said that *The Dream-Quest* is a novel-length prose-poem, for although Lovecraft never revised the novel—it lay in manuscript until after his death—his careful choice of language is evident on every page. Certain particular passages do remind us of Dunsany, however: Lovecraft mentions that the walls of Thran were "wrought in one solid piece," which reminds us of a passage in Dunsany's "Idle Days on the Yann" (in *A Dreamer's Tales*), where a throne is carved from one solid piece of ivory. Randolph Carter's voyage on the galleon also reminds us of "Idle Days on the Yann," which describes a languid journey through a fantasy-world on a boat.

One of my colleagues, Peter Cannon, has revealed another important literary influence upon *The Dream-Quest*: William Beckford's eighteenth century Oriental novel, *The History of the Caliph Vathek*. Lovecraft admitted in a letter that he wrote *The Dream-Quest* in a continuous narrative without subdivisions into chapters in imitation of Beckford's *Vathek*. There are other particular features in Lovecraft's work which also hint of the debt in *Vathek*. Both *Vathek* and *The Dream-Quest*, of course, are derived in part from the *Arabian Nights*, which, as you will recall, Lovecraft read at a tremendously early age. Lovecraft's exotic descriptions of towns and gardens and other sites quite strongly evoke *Arabian Nights* atmosphere.

Some of Lovecraft's descriptive passages seem to owe their genesis in part to the work of Oscar Wilde, particularly his fairy tales. Wilde uses vivid description, much as Lovecraft does, to lend a shimmering exoticism and beauty to his works. Here is a passage from the fairy tale, "The Young King":

> After some time he rose from his seat, and leaning against the carved penthouse of the chimney, looked round at the dimly-lit room. The walls were hung with rich tapestries representing the Triumph of Beauty. A large press, inlaid with agate and lapis lazuli, filled one corner, and facing the window stood a curiously wrought cabinet with lacquer panels of powdered and mosaiced gold, on which were placed some delicate goblets of Venetian glass, and a cup of dark-veined onyx. Pale poppies were broidered on the silk coverlet of the bed, as though they had fallen from the tired hands of sleep, and tall reeds of fluted ivory bare up the velvet canopy, from which great tufts of ostrich plumes sprang, like white foam, to the pallid silver of the fretted ceiling. A laughing Narcissus in green bronze held a polished mirror above its head. On the table stood a flat bowl of amethyst.

Lovecraft read and admired Wilde's fairy tales, calling them "exquisite" in his study on "Supernatural Horror in Literature."

These are the basic literary influences, although other minor ones appear. Lovecraft was vastly enamoured of Edgar Allan Poe, whom he first read at the age of seven, and there occurs a (perhaps unconscious) echo of "The Pit and the Pendulum" in *The Dream-Quest*, when Carter is trapped by the slant-eyed merchant in a dungeon:

> The odour of the place was intolerable, and when Carter was locked into a chamber and left alone he scarcely had strength to crawl around and ascertain its form and dimensions. It was circular, and about 20 feet across.

It could be asked whether Lovecraft was influenced either by William Morris or E. R. Eddison, but I think the answer in both these cases is no. Lovecraft alludes to Morris only twice, to my knowledge, in his thousands of letters, and then only to his poetry and to his political activities. As for Eddison, Lovecraft first encountered his *Worm Ouroboros* only in late 1927, several months after finishing *The Dream-Quest*.

One very crucial influence that I have not touched upon— and, indeed, which few commentators have ever mentioned—is the influence of classical antiquity upon *The Dream-Quest*. Remember that Lovecraft had read and become very fond of the Greek and Roman classics at a very early age; and throughout his life he was fascinated by ancient history, literature, and mythology; to the point that he once wrote: "To me the Roman Empire will always seem the central incident of human history." This classical influence manifests itself in a number of ways. Let me mention particulars before I discuss more general features.

Many of the characters in *The Dream-Quest* behave as if they were living in the classical world. For example, when the cats have defeated the zoogs, Lovecraft writes the following about the peace treaty:

> Terms were discussed at length . . . and it was decided that the zoogs might remain a free tribe on condition of rendering to the cats a large annual tribute of grouse, quail, and pheasants.

Those of you who are versed in ancient history will know that it was common in ancient Greece and Rome for the defeated party in a war to render tribute to the victor. The Athenians of the fifth century B. C. maintained their empire through quadrennial tributes, while the Romans also exacted tribute, though less often (they relied more on direct taxation).

Indeed, many of the battles in Lovecraft's novels—between the cats and the zoogs, the ghouls and the moonbeasts—are quite reminiscent of an ancient Greek work—a parody of Homer—entitled "The Battle of the Frogs and Mice." Lovecraft owned a copy of this work—in Alexander Pope's translation, since he never mastered Greek —and it is not unlikely that he was imitating this amusing parody of epic style in his own tongue-in-cheek military accounts.

One passage early in the novel—where the galley that Carter is on suddenly flies into space and goes to the other side of the moon—seems borrowed rather directly from a work of the late Greek writer Lucian called the *True History*, where a ship is swept up by a typhoon and is borne into space, landing upon an "island hanging in mid-air."

Greek and Roman mythology and religion seem to have played a role in shaping *The Dream-Quest*. One passage describes the use of omens from the gods, another describes a people who erected "several rude altars" to propitiate their gods, while another makes a distinction between the great gods (that is, the Great Ones who are the gods of earth reigning in Kadath) and what Lovecraft calls "modest gods." This differentiation is similar to the Roman division of gods: on the one hand there was the pantheon of gods represented by Jupiter, Venus, and the others on Mt. Olympus, while on the other hand the Romans also had what they called "Penates," or "household gods," who guarded over each family. Indeed, the castle of the Great Ones at Kadath is quite reminiscent of the gods' home on Olympus, particularly as described by Homer at the beginning of the fifth book of the *Odyssey*.

The *Odyssey* can be shown to have had a significant hand in influencing *The Dream-Quest*. Randolph Carter's journey more or less falls into the category of the *Odyssey* theme, but the goals of Odysseus and Randolph Carter are subtly different: whereas Odysseus is trying to return home to Ithaca, Carter wants to find his "sunset city"—which he realizes only at the end is his own native land. Other particulars in *The Dream-Quest* point to its derivation from the *Odyssey*: Carter, when stopping in an inn at Ulthar, declares that "Ulthar would be a very likely place to dwell in always, were not the memory of a greater sunset city ever guiding one toward unknown perils"; similarly, Odysseus enjoys Calypso's isle for nine years because of its loveliness, but finally returns home to Ithaca, knowing that that is where he belongs. The scene in *The Dream-Quest* where the slant-eyed merchant drugs Randolph Carter with wine echoes a passage in Book Ten of the *Odyssey*, where Circe drugs Odysseus' men with "Pramnian wine." There is a passage, admittedly, in Beckford's *Vathek* where the central character is given a potion which is later suspected to be a poison, but the passage in Lovecraft's novel seems closer to the *Odyssey* than to *Vathek*. Moreover, Lovecraft's description of the huge gug sentry vaguely reminds us of the Cyclops in the ninth book of the *Odyssey*. Toward the latter part of the novel, Randolph Carter encounters a jagged rock which emits a "dull and ceaseless howling": this seems to be an echo of the island of the Sirens in the *Odyssey*, Book Twelve.

In parts of the novel there occur passages which bring not the *Odyssey*, but Vergil's *Aeneid* to mind. In the beginning, when Carter is trying to find those people who have the blood of the gods in them, he notices the features of the god carved on Mt. Ngranek, and afterwards:

> Carter questioned all the mariners closely about those whom they had met in the taverns of Celephais, asking the names and ways of the strange men with long narrow eyes, long-lobed ears, thin noses, and pointed chins.

Here Lovecraft reflects the common belief among the Greeks and Romans that the gods and their progeny always have some distinguishing feature, even when disguised as human beings. Vergil has a stunning passage in Book One of the *Aeneid* where he describes Venus walking in disguise as a huntress. Vergil writes:

> Dixit et avertens rosea cervice refulsit, ambrosiaeque comae divinum vertice odorem spiravere; pedes vestis defluxit ad imos, et vera incessu patuit dea. (I.401-05)

> (Thus she spoke, and turning around she shone from her roseal neck, and her ambrosial hair sprinkled divine perfume from her head; her clothes fell to her feet, and her true divinity lay revealed by her walk.)

Toward the end of Lovecraft's novel is a significant passage where Nyarlathotep tells Carter:

"You have not come as one curious, but as one seeking his due, nor have you ever failed in reverence toward the mild gods of earth."

This remark reminds us of Aeneas, whom Vergil frequently calls "pious"; that is, paying due reverence to the gods. Aeneas, like Carter, is seeking his due—namely, the foundation of Rome. In this way Lovecraft has fascinatingly combined details, themes, and elements from the two greatest of classical works--the *Odyssey* and the *Aeneid*--for both of which, as we learn in his letters, he had a vast admiration.

But Lovecraft's novel is far from being merely a retelling of other writers' works. It is basically a very personal and autobiographical statement, in spite of its borrowings of particulars from other sources. What is the "message" of *The Dream-Quest*? It is revealed in Nyarlathotep's speech at the end of the novel: "For know you, that your gold and marble city of wonder is only the sum of what you have seen and loved in youth." Remember Lovecraft's attachment to Providence and New England; remember his semi-banishment for two years in New York; then his ecstatic return to Providence, upon which Lovecraft wrote this novel in a burst of energy. The extent to which Randolph Carter is intended simply as a Lovecraft *persona* is clear throughout the work.   Carter was born and raised in Boston, Lovecraft in Providence.   Carter was an experienced dreamer in strange lands; so, too, did Lovecraft dream and write about exotic places. Indeed, there is one place in the original manuscript of the novel (housed in the John Hay Library) where Lovecraft, writing about Carter, wrote not "*He* did such-and-such a thing," but "*I* did such-and-such a thing." This unconscious mistake reveals unmistakably the degree to which Lovecraft identified with Carter.

The *Dream-Quest* is full of autobiographical elements which require a detailed knowledge of Lovecraft's life fully to appreciate. Carter is particularly fond of small black kittens; so, too, was Lovecraft. One of his associates tells the tale that Lovecraft stayed up all night in a chair because a cat had fallen asleep in his lap. When asked why he never got up and went to bed, he replied with perfect sincerity, "But I didn't want to disturb kitty!" The genial humor of the entire story (save the conclusion) also shows that his work was a very personal one for Lovecraft.   There are many "in-jokes" in the novel: Lovecraft refers constantly to other of his own stories (as shall be explained more detailedly later on):   the characters Richard Pickman, Atal the high-priest, King Kuranes of Celephais, and others had all appeared in earlier stories of Lovecraft's.

By revealing that Carter's long-sought-for "sunset city" is simply the memories of his childhood and the places where he was reared, Lovecraft was clearly making a personal *credo*. Lovecraft always looked with longing to the time of his childhood--to the point of declaring in one letter that "Adulthood is hell"--and was never happier than when reminiscing about his boyhood. Like Carter, Lovecraft visited many places which were exotic and exciting—New York, New Orleans, Florida—but in none did he find that familiarity which only Providence could provide. Similarly, Carter travels through dream to many enticing lands, but keeps moving on to his "sunset city"—which, unbeknownst to him, is only his native soil.

The passage where Lovecraft describes the fate of King Kuranes of Celephais is symbolic of the message of the novel as a whole. Kuranes is a king in the dream-world, but keeps longing to return to the English countryside where he spent his youth. He cannot return, however, to the waking world because his "body was dead"; that is to say, he had died in the real world, and is now confined solely to the dream-world, which thus becomes a type of Hades in the Greek and Roman religious system. Kuranes tells Carter that he doubts

> whether his quest would profit aught by coming to the [sunset] city even were he to gain it. He himself had dreamed and yearned long years for lovely Celephais and the land of Ooth-Nargai, and for the freedom and colour and high experience of life devoid of chains, conventions, and stupidities. But now that he had come into that city and that land, and was king thereof, he found the freedom and the vividness were all too soon worn out, *and monotonous for want of linkage with anything firm in his feelings and memories* [emphasis mine]. He was a king in Ooth-Nargai, but found no meaning therein, and drooped always for the old familiar things of England that had shaped his youth. All his kingdom he would give for the sound of Cornish church bells over the downs, and all the thousand minarets of Celephais for the steep homely roofs of the village near his home. So he told his guest that the unknown sunset city might not hold quite the content he sought, and that perhaps it had better remain a glorious and half-remembered dream. For he had visited Carter often in the old waking days, and knew well the lovely New England slopes that had given him birth.

Here the whole concluding revelation of the novel is openly hinted at, although we do not realize its significance until the end.

But Lovecraft's message clearly transcends a mere autobiographical interpretation. He is saying, in effect, that we should cherish those realities of our individual lives rather than chasing after phantasmal illusions, for only those realities hold any significance for us. Here is the reason for the use of the dream-setting: Carter encounters many charming and picturesque lands in his dreams —and Lovecraft makes a point of describing them vividly and exotically (although it is to be noted that on the whole he describes only their externals)—but in none does Carter find any real "meaning therein": he can only find satisfaction in the "sunset city" which is only the "sum of what [he has] seen and loved in youth." Indeed, Lovecraft even notes that the gods themselves feel a similar longing for the scenes of their youth: Nyarlathotep tells Carter that the "truant" Great Ones have dashed off to dwell in Carter's own "sunset city," and while they find it all very delightful, it is not where they belong. Gods and men alike feel the need for an environment that has some meaning for them.

It is often thought that fantasy is some sort of *escape* from "reality," whatever that may be. But Lovecraft in this dream-novel shows that it is through fantasy itself that we can rediscover reality. Carter did realize that the "sunset city" for which he sought was merely his own native land: he was forced to search all through his dreams (that is to say, through fantasy) to come upon this truth. Fantasy makes us question our own notions of reality by presenting an alternative universe; and the author of fantasy declares: "Why cannot this alternative world that I have made actually exist? Why is it any less real than the world which you believe is real? Lovecraft wrote another story, "The Silver Key," which also concerns Randolph Carter:

> Custom had dinned into his ears a superstitious reverence for that which tangibly and physically exists, and had made him secretly ashamed to dwell in visions. Wise men told him his simple fancies were inane and childish, and he believed it because he could see that they might easily be so. What he failed to recall was that the deeds of reality are just as inane and childish, and even more absurd because their actors persist in fancying them full of meaning and purpose as the blind cosmos grinds aimlessly on from nothing to something and from something back to nothing again, neither heeding nor knowing the wishes or existence of the minds that flicker for a second now and then in the darkness.

The tangible and physical world may not be all there is to reality; and imaginative fiction, by showing us worlds which are imaginary, heighten our perception of reality: we come to see that physical reality need not encompass all reality; that there is such a thing as the life of the mind. I'm not implying that reading fantasy will turn us all into mystics who believe in the existence of all sorts of worlds and entities which don't exist; but what fantasy does is to liberate us from the tyranny of the physical and the present: when Carter finds his "sunset city," it is not his *actual* childhood that he discoverś, but only his *memories* of it. Carter sees that his surroundings—which he at first had thought were quite prosaic—actually hold more meaning to him than he had previously believed. After his vast dream-quest, he is now ready to face the real world again because his perception of that real world has gained depth and significance.

The Sources for "From Beyond"
S. T. Joshi

It is unlikely that "From Beyond" (1920) will ever be regarded as one of Lovecraft's better tales; and such a judgment is perfectly justified, since in its slipshod style, melodramatic excess, and general triteness of plot, the tale compares ill even with some of Lovecraft's other early tales, such as "Dagon" (1917), "The Picture in the House" (1920), and "The Outsider" (1921). But, as with everything Lovecraft wrote, the tale's poor quality does not prevent it from displaying certain features of enormous interest. In the first place, the philosophical sources of the tale can now be traced with some certainty; secondly, the story seems itself to have provided sources for several later tales.

The philosophical interest of the tale is considerable, for it centers upon an issue of fundamental importance in all modern philosophical speculation since Descartes—the problem of knowledge. How do we know what we know? How can we be certain that the sense-impressions we receive are accurate reflections of external reality? Is there an external reality of which they are the reflections? This problem certainly occupied some of the ancient philosophers. Parmenides and Democritus questioned the truth-value of sense-perception, and Gorgias the Sophist wrote a celebrated treatise, *On Not-Being* (c. 440 B. C.), wherein he maintained that (1) nothing exists; (2) even if anything existed, it would be incomprehensible; (3) even if it were comprehensible, it would be incommunicable—and his whole argument was based upon the unreliability of sense-perception.[1] Finally, the ancient Skeptics similarly believed that nothing can be known (and some were as rigorously consistent as to doubt whether even this—that nothing can be known—can be known!), and waged extended polemics against their opponents (especially the Stoics and the Epicureans) who tried to assert both the possibility of knowledge and the reliability of sense-data. After Descartes instituted his system of "Cartesian doubt," the problem of knowledge became a focal point—some would say a bane—of philosophical enquiry. Lovecraft reflects this problem in "From Beyond" by conceiving of a way to "break down the barriers"[2] which our five senses impose and which prevent our catching a glimpse of reality "as it really is."

Part of the philosophical foundation of the tale is indeed derived from Descartes, although in a parodic way. Crawford Tillinghast tells the unnamed narrator how it is that we may glimpse "vistas unknown to man":

> "You have heard of the pineal gland? . . . That gland is the great sense-organ of organs—*I have found out*. It is like sight in the end, and transmits visual pictures to the brain. . . ."

This is actually a joke at Descartes's expense: when Descartes, in the *Meditations on First Philosophy*, established the distinction between a material body and an immaterial and immortal soul (one of the most pernicious ideas in the history of philosophy, rivaled perhaps only by Plato's Forms or Kant's *a priori* knowledge), he found himself in the awkward position of being unable to explain how two such fundamentally different entities could ever interact, as they clearly do in the human being; he then (in *The Passions of the Soul*) seized upon the pineal gland as the mediator between body and soul. Lovecraft was fully aware of this celebrated venture into fatuity,[3] and he is surely having a bit of fun with it in "From Beyond."

But a more immediate and pervasive influence for the genesis of the whole tale can be found—in the form of Hugh Elliot's *Modern Science and Materialism* (1919). Lovecraft mentions this work only in a letter of June 1921 (SL I.134; also SL I.158), but it is almost certain that he had read it before November 1920, the date of writing of "From Beyond" (cf. SL I.121). That Lovecraft found this triumphant exposition of mechanistic materialism stimulating can be seen by a few entries in his Commonplace Book which I have hypothesized were inspired by the volume:[4]

34 Moving away from earth more swiftly than light—past gradually unfolded—horrible revelation.

35 Special beings with special senses from remote universes. Advent of an external universe to view.

36 Disintegration of all matter to electrons and finally empty space assured, just as devolution of energy to radiant heat is known. Case of *acceleration*—man passes into space.

It can be shown that each of these entries has a correlation in various passages in Elliot's book which discuss the points in question. Entry 35 is particularly interesting for our purposes, since it is precisely such an "external universe" that is brought to view in "From Beyond."

A still more concrete case for Elliot's book as inspiration for "From Beyond" can be made by collation of actual passages from the two works. In Lovecraft's tale Tillinghast boldly dilates upon the fallibility of the senses in a striking passage:

"What do we know," he had said, "of the world and the universe about us? Our means of receiving impressions are absurdly few, and our notions of surrounding objects infinitely narrow. We see things only as we are constructed to see them, and can gain no idea of their absolute nature. With five feeble senses we pretend to comprehend the boundlessly complex cosmos, yet other beings with a wider, stronger, or different range of senses might not only see, but might see and study whole worlds of matter, energy, and life which lie close at hand yet can never be detected with the senses we have. . . ."

Note a very similar passage in the introduction to Elliot's book:

Let us first ask why it is that all past efforts to solve ultimate riddles have failed, and why it is that they must continue to fail. It is, in the first place, due to the fact

> that all knowledge is based on sense-impressions, and cannot, therefore, go beyond what the senses can perceive. Men have five or six different senses only, and these are all founded on the one original sense of touch. Of these five or six senses, the three of the most importance for the accumulation of knowledge are those of sight, hearing, and touch. By these senses we are able to detect three separate qualities of the external Universe. Now, supposing that we happened to have a thousand senses instead of five, it is clear that our conception of the Universe would be extremely different from what it now is. We cannot assume that the Universe has only five qualities because we have only five senses. We must assume, on the contrary, that the number of its qualities may be infinite, and that the more senses we had, the more we should discover about it.[5]

Later in the tale the narrator is baffled by a "pale, outre colour or blend of colours which I could neither place nor describe"; Tillinghast replies:

> "Do you know what that is? . . . That is ultra-violet." He chuckled oddly at my surprise. "You thought ultra-violet was invisible, and so it is—but you can see that and many other invisible things *now*."

This has its exact correlate in Elliot:

> Not only are our senses few, but they are extremely limited in their range. The sense of sight can detect nothing but waves of aether; all sensations of light and colour are no more than aethereal waves striking upon the retina with varying strength and frequency. And even then, it is only special aethereal undulations that give rise to the sensation of sight. The majority cannot be perceived by the retina at all; it is only when the waves follow one another within certain limits of rapidity (between four hundred billion and seven hundred billion a second) that sight ensues. If the waves are below the lower limit of rapidity, they do not give rise to the sensation of light at all, though they may give rise to a sensation of heat. If they are more rapid than the higher limit (as in the case of ultra-violet rays) they are not discernible by any sense at all.[6]

Finally, the narrator at one point experiences great alarm when he sees, as a result of Tillinghast's machine, "huge animate things brushing past me and occasionally *walking or drifting through my supposedly solid body.*" Lovecraft is here simply reflecting in a vivid way the simple physical fact that solid matter is largely merely empty space. Elliot writes of it at length:

> Let us now . . . see what matter would look like if magnified to, say, a thousand million diameters, so that the contents of a small thimble appeared to become the size of the earth. Even under this great magnification, the individual electrons would still be too small to be seen by the naked

eye. Small aggregations of these invisible electrons, moving in invisible orbits round a centre, would be aggregated to form atoms, and these again to form molecules, appearing (if they could be seen) to occupy the same volume as a football. The first circumstance that strikes us is that nearly the whole structure of matter consists of the empty spaces between electrons. Matter, which appears to us so continuous in its structure, is really no more than empty space, in which at rare intervals here and there an inconceivably minute electron is traveling at high velocity upon its way. It ceases, therefore, to be remarkable that X-rays can penetrate matter and come out on the other side. How should the tiny electrons obstruct their passage? It ceases to be remarkable that an electron from radium can be shot clean through a plate of aluminium; for, from the electron's point of view, the aluminium plate is very little different from empty space.[7]

Clearly, then, the immediate inspiration for "From Beyond" was Elliot's *Modern Science and Materialism* and the philosophical vistas it opened to Lovecraft's fertile and imaginative mind. But "From Beyond," however imperfect a product in itself, very clearly served as a springboard for certain later stories of Lovecraft's. It is as if Lovecraft, dissatisfied with the treatment of some themes in his early story, decided to give them fuller and better treatment elsewhere.

Firstly, the narrator of "From Beyond" remarks at the outset: "That Crawford Tillinghast should ever have studied science and philosophy was a mistake." We are immediately reminded of "The Dreams in the Witch House," where it is said: "Perhaps Gilman ought not to have studied so hard. Non-Euclidean calculus and quantum physics are enough to stretch any brain. . . ."[8] A later passage in "From Beyond" is also suggestive of Gilman's voyages into hyperspace:

I was now in a vortex of sound and motion, with confused pictures before my eyes. . . . After that the scene was almost wholly kaleidoscopic, and in the jumble of sights, sounds, and unidentified sense-impressions I felt that I was about to dissolve or in some way lose the solid form.

We have already alluded to the "pale, outre colour or blend of colours" which the narrator of "From Beyond" sees—and we can hardly fail to recall "The Colour out of Space": "The colour . . . was almost impossible to describe; and it was only by analogy that they called it a colour at all."[9]

Finally, the central philosophical theme of "From Beyond"— the fallibility of the senses—is emphasized in several later stories. I have studied this concept elsewhere,[10] and the idea of what I have termed "supra-reality"—a reality beyond that revealed to us by the senses, or that which we experience in everyday life (what Onderdonk called the "super-normal")—is central to much of Lovecraft's fiction; finding expression particularly in "Hypnos" (1922), "The

Unnamable" (1923), "The Colour out of Space" (1927), "The Dreams in the Witch House" (1932), "Through the Gates of the Silver Key" (1932-33), and others. Note also the following passage from "The Shunned House" (1924):

> To declare that we were not nervous on that rainy night of watching would be an exaggeration both gross and ridiculous. We were not, as I have said, in any sense childishly superstitious, but scientific study and reflection had taught us that the known universe of three dimensions embraces the merest fraction of the whole cosmos of substance and energy. . . . To say that we actually believed in vampires or werewolves would be a carelessly inclusive statement. Rather must it be said that we were not prepared to deny the possibility of certain unfamiliar and unclassified modifications of vital force and attenuated matter; existing very infrequently in three-dimensional space because of its more intimate connexion with other spatial units, yet close enough to the boundary of our own to furnish us occasional manifestations which we, for the lack of a proper vantage-point, may never hope to understand.[11]

The closeness of wording between this passage and parts of "From Beyond" suggests that the idea was one of recurrent fascination to Lovecraft—and it is an idea derived from his continuing researches into the findings of modern science and philosophy, especially such books as Elliot's *Modern Science and Materialism*, Ernst Haeckel's *The Riddle of the Universe*, and Bertrand Russell's *Our Knowledge of the External World*.

Hence "From Beyond" has in its clumsy way shown once again the unity and integration of Lovecraft's work and thought. Science and philosophy, far from being antagonistic to the creation of literature, were for Lovecraft direct stimuli for it; and his untiring delvings into the strange worlds revealed by astrophysicists, biologists, and philosophers proved to be a central—perhaps even a necessary—inspiration for some of the greatest weird tales of the century.

NOTES

[1] See G. B. Kerferd, *The Sophistic Movement* (Cambridge: Cambridge University Press, 1981), ch.

[2] "From Beyond," in *Dagon and Other Macabre Tales* (1965), p. 61. All citations of the story derive from this edition, although textual errors have been corrected through collation with the A.Ms. (John Hay Library).

[3] See "Some Causes of Self-Immolation" (1931), in *Marginalia* (1944), p. 185 (although "pineal" is mistranscribed as "piveal" and "gratuitous" as "factuitous").

[4] The numbering of entries is that established by me for my forthcoming edition of Lovecraft's Collected Works; it will be used by David E. Schultz in his forthcoming critical edition of the *Commonplace Book*.

[5] Hugh Elliot, *Modern Science and Materialism* (London: Longmans, Green & Co., 1919), pp. 2-3.
[6] Ibid., p. 3.
[7] Ibid., p. 54.
[8] *At the Mountains of Madness and Other Novels* (1964), p. 249.
[9] *The Dunwich Horror and Others* (1963), pp. 65-66.
[10] "'Reality' and Knowledge: Some Notes on the Aesthetic Thought of H. P. Lovecraft," *Lovecraft Studies*, 1, No. 3 (Fall 1980), 18f.
[11] *At the Mountains of Madness*, p. 237.

Lovecraft and the *Regnum Congo*
S. T. Joshi

> The first object of my curiosity was a book of medium size lying upon the table and presenting such an antediluvian aspect that I marvelled at beholding it outside a museum or library. It was bound in leather with metal fittings, and was in an excellent state of preservation; being altogether an unusual sort of volume to encounter in an abode so lowly. When I opened it to the title page my wonder grew even greater, for it proved to be nothing less rare than Pigafetta's account of the Congo region, written in Latin from the notes of the sailor Lopez[1] and printed at Frankfort in 1598. I had often heard of this work, with its curious illustrations by the brothers De Bry, hence for a moment forgot my uneasiness in my desire to turn the pages before me.[2]

This celebrated passage from "The Picture in the House" (1920) has perhaps led many to marvel at Lovecraft's recondite knowledge of Renaissance science and literature. Further descriptions of Pigafetta's *Regnum Congo* later in the story would lead us to believe that Lovecraft had not only consulted the rare volume, but had actually read it in detail. Where, then, could Lovecraft have gained access to the tome? I have ascertained that a copy exists in the John Carter Brown Library of Brown University, and Lovecraft might have seen it here; but what could have led Lovecraft even to suspect the existence of this volume? The answer is now not difficult to find; and it reveals, unfortunately, that Lovecraft did not in fact consult the actual volume and that, in relying on second-hand accounts of the book, he made embarrassing mistakes concerning it.

The source for Lovecraft's knowledge of Pigafetta is nothing less than Thomas Henry Huxley's collection of essays, *Man's Place in Nature and Other Anthropological Essays* (New York: D. Appleton & Co., 1902). Lovecraft certainly knew of and read this volume, since he cites from Huxley's essay "On the Methods and Results of Ethnology" in the early essay "The Crime of the Century" (1915). In that essay Lovecraft makes use of Huxley's coined term "Xanthochroi" in reference to the yellow-haired and pale-complexioned people whom Lovecraft identified with the Aryan race. But an earlier essay in Huxley's volume—"On the Natural History of the Man-like Apes" (pp. 1-75)—provided Lovecraft all his information on the *Regnum Congo*, and he has repeated some errors and omissions which Huxley made in his own essay. The essay deals with the history of scholarship of the simian species in the two hundred years before Huxley's time, and in the very opening Huxley discusses the *Regnum Congo* in some detail.

> I have not met with any notice of one of these *Man-like Apes* of earlier date than that contained in Pigafetta's "Description of the Kingdom of Congo," drawn up from the notes of a

Portuguese sailor, Eduardo Lopez, and published in 1598 (pp.1-2)

In a footnote Huxley gives the Latin title:

REGNUM CONGO: hoc est VERA DESCRIPTIO REGNI AFRICANI QUOD TAM AB INCOLIS QUAM LUSITANIS CONGUS APPELATUR, per Philippum Pigafettam, olim ex Eduardo Lopez acroamatis lingua Italica excerpta, num sermone donata ab August. Cassiod. Reinio. Iconibus et imaginibus rerum memorabilium quasi vivis, opera et industria Joan. Theodori et Joan. Israelis de Bry, fratrum exornata. Francofurti, MCXCVIII (p. 2 note).

(A translation of the above is as follows: REGNUM CONGO, i.e., a true description of the African kingdom which is called "Congo" both by its inhabitants and by Spaniards, previously rendered into Italian by Filippo Pigafetta from the verbal accounts of Eduardo Lopez, now translated into Latin by A. C. Reinius. Decorated with maps and virtually live illustrations of memorable phenomena by the toil and diligence of the brothers J. T. and J. I. De Bry. Frankfurt, 1598.)

Unfortunately, neither Huxley nor Lovecraft seemed to know that this is not the first printing of Pigafetta's account. Rather, it was first published in Italian (hence the *lingua Italica* above) in 1591. The title of this edition is as follows: *Relatione reame di Congo et della cironvicine contrade, tratta dalli scritti & ragionamenti di Odoardo [sic] Lopez, Portoghese, per Filippo Pigafetta* (Roma: Appresso B. Grassi, 1591). What is more, there was a Dutch translation of this in 1596 (Amsterdam: Cornelis Claesz), an English translation in 1597 (London: John Wolfe), and a German translation in 1597 (Frankfurt am Mayn: Johan Saur). It was in this German edition that the De Bry plates first appeared, whence they were transferred to the Latin edition of the following year.[3] And the Latin translation is not the work of Pigafetta, as Lovecraft seems to have believed, but is by A. C. Reinius (*Latio sermone donata ab . . . .*). In addition, the real name of the "sailor Lopez" seems to have been Duarte Lopes.[4]

But what of Lovecraft's detailed descriptions of the plates by the brothers De Bry which he provides in the story? It happens that Huxley actually reprints (or, rather, has had redrawn) two plates from the *Regnum Congo*, including the important plate xii representing the butcher shop of the cannibal Anxiques. Before discussing that plate, let us consider the other details in Lovecraft's account. Lovecraft's indication that the book "was bound in leather with metal fittings" is apparently derived from his imagination; and in any case such clasps need not have been affixed at the time of publication. (It may be worth noting that, although Lovecraft seems to imply that the book is rather large, it is in fact quite small; the Latin version is only 60 pages,[5] while a modern English translation[6] is 137 pages, and a modern French translation[7] is 147 pages.)

Later in the story Lovecraft records some remarks by the

preternaturally aged owner of the volume:

> "Queer haow picters kin set a body thinkin'. Take this un here near the front. Hev yew ever seed trees like thet, with big leaves a floppin' over an' daown? And them men—them can't be niggers—they dew beat all. Kinder like Injuns, I guess, even ef they be in Afriky. Some o' these critters looks like monkeys, or half monkeys an' half men. . . ."

Now this is an exact description of a plate reproduced or redrawn in Huxley's volume. Huxley describes the plate as follows:

> So much of the plate as contains these apes is faithfully copied in the woodcut (Fig. 1), and it will be observed that they are tailless, long-armed, and large-eared; and about the size of Chimpanzees. (p. 3)

FIG. 1.—Simiæ magnatum deliciæ.—De Bry, 1598.

Lovecraft's character then continues:

> ". . . but I never heerd o' nothin' like this un." Here he pointed to a fabulous creature of the artist, which one might describe as a sort of dragon with the head of an alligator.

This too derives directly from Huxley, who writes:

> It may be that these apes are as much figments of the imagination of the ingenious brothers [i.e., De Bry] as the winged, two-legged, crocodile-headed dragon which adorns the same plate. . . . (p. 3)

This dragon figure is not reproduced in Huxley's plate, and Lovecraft had to work merely from Huxley's verbal description.

Let us now return to Lovecraft's description of the twelfth De Bry plate:

> The engravings were indeed interesting, drawn wholly from imagination and careless descriptions, and represented negros with white skins and Caucasian features; now would I soon have closed the book had not an exceedingly trivial circumstance upset my tired nerves and revived my sensation of disquiet. What annoyed me was merely the persistent way in which the volume tended to fall open of itself at Plate xii, which represented in gruesome detail a butcher's shop of the cannibal Anziques. I experienced some shame at my susceptibility to so slight a thing, but the drawing nevertheless disturbed me, especially in connexion with some adjacent passages descriptive of Anzique gastronomy.

This entire description is drawn from an appendix to Huxley's essay (pp. 73-75), "African Cannibalism in the Sixteenth Century," where he recounts what Pigafetta says in chapter 5 of Book I of the *Regnum Congo*. It is here that the brothers De Bry's plate xii is reprinted—redrawn, apparently, as a woodcut by W. H. Wesley, who was presumably responsible for the redrawing of the earlier plate. Of the plate Huxley remarks:

> The careful illustrators of Pigafetta have done their best to enable the reader to realize this account of the "Anziques," and the unexampled butcher's shop represented in Fig. 12 [i.e., of Huxley's book], is a facsimile of part of their Plate xii. (p. 75)

Lovecraft's aged character now describes the plate:

> "That fellow bein' chopped up gives me a tickle every time I look at 'im—I hev ta keep lookin' at him—see whar the butcher cut off his feet? Thar's his head on thet bench, with one arm side of it, an' t' other arm's on the graound side o' the meat block."[8]

All this again tallies with the illustration in Huxley's book. Now comparison of this illustration with the actual De Bry plate from the German or Latin edition of *Regnum Congo* (reprinted by W. S. Home in *The Dark Brotherhood*) brings to light some interesting facts. Wesley has chosen only to redraw the butcher shop at the far right of the original De Bry plate, and it seems to be he—and not the brothers De Bry—who has endowed the negroes "with white skins and Caucasian features"; the figures on the left side of the De Bry plate—left out by Wesley—are actually much more negroid in appearance.

The secondhand nature of Lovecraft's erudition in this case would be rather less culpable had he not himself accused Poe of doing similar things. In remarking on Poe's borrowing of the term "Afrasiab" in "The Premature Burial" Lovecraft notes: "He [Poe]

FIG. 12.—Butcher's Shop of the Anziques Anno 1598.

was a great boy for second-hand erudition" (SL IV.162); while in *Supernatural Horror in Literature* he notes that among Poe's "defects and mannerisms" was "his pretence to profound and obscure scholarship." I am not about to assert that most of Lovecraft's knowledge was secondhand—indeed, he had a far greater and more authentic grasp of classical literature and philosophy, modern science, and many other subjects than Poe, and he integrated this knowledge into a philosophy far more profound and coherent than Poe could ever have managed—but Lovecraft's secondhand borrowings and attempts to assert knowledge in subjects on which he was ignorant landed him on occasion in trouble; as witness his bumbling derivation of the Greek word *Necronomicon* (although later scholars such as George Wetzel, William Scott Home, E. F. Bleiler, and others, all blithely ignorant of Greek, have been no less incompetent at the task), or the embarrassing errors of detail he made when he tried to explain the Greek-Hebrew incantation he had cribbed from the *Encyclopaedia Britannica* for "The Horror at Red Hook." Other secondhand borrowings have come to light which, while not erroneous, perhaps ought to make us cautious of attributing all-encompassing knowledge to Lovecraft: the books on cryptography, for example, cited so impressively in "The Dunwich Horror" are all derived from the article on "Cryptography" (by John Eglinton Bailey) in the 9th edition of the *Britannica*.

But it can be noted that these borrowings are always minor and rarely affect the success of the story in which they appear; and Lovecraft's letters testify abundantly to the real knowledge he had acquired over a lifetime's scholarship in a bewildering number of diverse fields. We all take short-cuts when it is convenient to do so, and to believe that Lovecraft was exempt from the habit is only to indulge in blind idolatry or special pleading.

NOTES

[1] The printed texts read "Lopex," an obvious error.
[2] *The Dunwich Horror and Others* (1963), pp. 123-24.
[3] William Scott Home is therefore incorrect when he remarks ("The Lovecraft 'Books': Some Addenda and Corrigenda," *The Dark Brotherhood and Other Pieces* [1966], p. 143) that "it was very likely the 1598 Frankfort edition in which the De Bry illustrations first appeared." Indeed, Home ought to have known that this was not the case, since he reprints the plate (facing p. 134) which obviously derives from the German, and not Latin, edition, since all the accompanying print on the page is in German black-letter! It ought to be remarked that Home's essay is riddled with errors of detail and had best be used, if at all, with caution.
[4] See the modern French translation of the *Regnum Congo* (*Description du Royaume de Congo et des Contrees Environnantes*) by Willy Bal (Louvain/Paris, 1965), whose introduction (esp. pp. xxif.) gives much information on early editions.
[5] Cf. *Catalogue of Books Printed on the Continent of Europe 1501-1600 in Cambridge Libraries*, comp. H. M. Adams (Cambridge: Cambridge University Press, 1967), II.79. I have not actually consulted the Latin edition.
[6] *A Report of the Kingdom of Congo, and of the Surrounding Countries*, tr. Margarite Hutchinson (1881; rpt. New York: Negro Universities Press/Greenwood Press, 1969).
[7] See note 4.
[8] Rendered as "other" in the Arkham House text.

Tentacles in Dreamland:
Cthulhu Mythos Elements in the Dunsanian Stories
Will Murray

Disciples of H. P. Lovecraft have tended to divide his fiction into three distinct categories—his Dunsanian dreamworld fantasies, straight horror stories, and Cthulhu Mythos tales. While these are useful labels, their validity may be questioned in the light of HPL's penchant of allowing a free cross-pollenization of concepts between what were originally separate kinds of stories as his writing progressed. While his critics are comfortable, for example, calling "The Dunwich Horror" a Cthulhu Mythos story (which it is), to Lovecraft it was part of what he called "the Arkham cycle," which obviously included such non-Mythos ventures as "The Colour out of Space" and "Herbert West—Reanimator."

If Lovecraft's Mythos and non-Mythos fiction should be so difficult to separate, what about the relationship between them and the distinctly different Dunsanian tales?

The earliest Dunsanian story Lovecraft produced was "Polaris," which was actually written about a year before HPL discovered Lord Dunsany's work in 1919. From then until 1922, he wrote about ten stories in the Dunsanian vein. This was early in his career and well before the commission of Lovecraft's major horror or Cthulhu Mythos stories. These early Dunsanian pieces were short, ethereal excursions into fantasy, largely devoid of horror. They have their own characters, place-names, deities, and in short, their own reality. There is little in them which foreshadows the Cthulhu Mythos and its terrors until "The Other Gods," the last of HPL's early experiments in Dunsanian prose.

In "The Other Gods," which is set in Ulthar, a dream-city Lovecraft had used before, an audacious dreamer named Barzai the Wise climbs the mountain Hatheg-Kla, in search of earth's gods, but finds instead, to his horror and doom, "the other gods! The gods of the outer hells that guard the feeble gods of earth." "The Other Gods," with its veiled horrors, is unique compared to Lovecraft's early dream fantasies, and its surprise ending seems to indicate that Lovecraft's imagination was no longer satisfied with Dunsanian imitation and was instead drawing him toward the cosmic concepts at which these "other gods" hint.

Up to this point, these pastiches—for such they are—contain only a handful of concepts which found their way outside of this essentially self-contained dream reality. The *Pnakotic Manuscripts* are mentioned in "Polaris" and "The Other Gods." The latter story contains the first reference to "unknown Kadath in the cold waste." "Celephais" mentions Innsmouth—but it is a city in England, not New England, which is referred to. "Celephais" also makes mention of "the high-priest not to be described, which wears a yellow mask over his face and dwells all alone in a prehistoric stone monastery in the cold desert plateau of Leng."

There are gods mentioned in these stories, but they are

barely named in passing. The gods of Sarnath, according to "The Doom That Came to Sarnath," are Zo-Kalar, Tamash, and Lobon, while in Ib, the water-lizard, Bokrug, is worshipped.

Lovecraft did not return to his dream-world stories until late 1926, shortly after writing "The Call of Cthulhu," and perhaps significantly, after he separated from his wife, Sonia, and returned to Providence. The first of these new ventures was "The Silver Key," which concerned itself with Randolph Carter, the protagonist of HPL's earlier story, "The Statement of Randolph Carter." This is the first Dunsanian story which linked itself with a non-Dunsanian tale—unless we count "The Nameless City," a horror story with brief mentions of Sarnath the Doomed and Ib. Although not a horror story by any means, "The Silver Key" does mention the haunted New England towns of Arkham and Kingsport as well as the Miskatonic River.

Shortly afterward, Lovecraft penned "The Strange High House in the Mist," in which dream-fantasy elements mix freely with more horrific concepts. Kingsport and Arkham are mentioned, as is the Terrible Old Man of the otherwise unrelated story by the same name. Even the "other gods" and the "Elder Ones" are discussed suggestively. Unknown Kadath is alluded to as well.

This transfusion—even confusion—of ideas reaches a crescendo in Lovecraft's novel, *The Dream-Quest of Unknown Kadath*, in which Randolph Carter returns to venture into the dreamworld to seek out earth's gods atop Unknown Kadath, just as Barzai the Wise had done. This episodic story is vaguely disquieting even in its more picturesque moments, unlike the earliest Dunsanian efforts. It never breaks out into sheer horror, but *Dream-Quest* is distinctly suggestive of evil and malignant forces. References and allusions to other stories abound. Carter encounters Richard Upton Pickman from "Pickman's Model," the green flame from "The Festival," the high priest with the yellow mask (whose identity is finally revealed) and Nodens, Lord of the Great Abyss, a Roman sea-deity who appeared in "The Strange High House in the Mist." Again, HPL makes mention of the Elder Ones, without any specificity, and first refers to the Elder Sign. And again, much is made of the "mild gods of earth" as opposed to the "Other Gods from Outside." The *Pnakotic Manuscripts* are listed with the *Seven Cryptical Books of Hsan*, first mentioned in "The Other Gods." Virtually all the ideas from earlier dream-fantasies are reused, and the events of those tales are even recapitulated for the reader. If there were any lost Dunsanian stories written by Lovecraft, they are probably summarized in *The Dream-Quest of Unknown Kadath*.

Most significantly, two major Cthulhu Mythos entities are important parts of this novel. They are Azathoth, the "boundless daemon sultan," one of the Other Gods, and Nyarlathotep, "the crawling chaos." *Azathoth* was the title of an abortive novel Lovecraft abandoned in 1922, after writing "The Other Gods." The fragment which survives is vaguely Dunsanian and, like *Dream-Quest*, is about a dreamer's quest. In his Commonplace Book, Lovecraft described *Azathoth* as "A terrible pilgrimage to seek the nighted throne of the far daemon-sultan Azathoth." Nyarlathotep originated in another fragment written in 1920, and appeared again in "The Rats in the Walls." Later to become two of the most important presences in the Cthulhu Mythos, both Azathoth and Nyarlathotep actually gravitated into the Mythos after having been developed elsewhere first.

The *Dream-Quest* is a sort of lodestone attracting many of Lovecraft's previous concepts, just as "The Whisperer in Darkness" incorporated Mythos ideas belonging to HPL and other writers. With the exception of Cthulhu, virtually all of Lovecraft's concepts to date found their way into *Dream-Quest*. Had the Cthulhu Mythos been developed at all by this time, certainly more elements would be present in what Lovecraft evidently intended to be a final Dunsanian experiment, as well as a summary of his previous ones.

This is proven in "Through the Gates of the Silver Key," a story Lovecraft wrote from E. Hoffmann Price's draft, "Lord of Illusion," in 1932-3. The Price story is a sequel to "The Silver Key," and concerns the further adventures of Randolph Carter. Written as a dream fantasy, Lovecraft recast it into a hybrid, as much a sequel to *Dream-Quest* as to "The Silver Key." While retaining many dream fantasy touches, it is also a cosmic horror story, and it is riddled with Cthulhu Mythos elements, including some not of Lovecraft's invention. A simple listing of Mythos concepts will give a sense of the texture of the story. Mentioned are Cthulhu, R'lyeh, Tsathoggua, the *Necronomicon*, Yuggoth, Arkham, Kingsport, Hyperborea and a curiously friendly Yog-Sothoth. As a Dunsanian fantasy, the Price/Lovecraft collaboration is a failure; as a Mythos story, it is rich with ideas, but curiously diluted. In truth, Lovecraft would never have written "Through the Gates of the Silver Key" had Price not written his draft and essentially compelled him to rework it into something he felt comfortable with. As Lovecraft expressed it in a letter to J. Vernon Shea in June 1931, about a year before rewriting this story, "I don't care much for the ultra-fantastic tales I wrote under extreme Dunsanian influence."

This is clear from the later Dunsanian stories. Before HPL imbued them with their own wondrous reality because then he believed in those dreams. But later in life, after many personal disappointments, he ceased to believe and turned to cosmic horror for his expression, and the tentacles of Cthulhu and others gradually crept into those later Dunsanian stories, in essence darkening their beauty, even as those stories drained some of the power from those Cthulhuoid concepts which found their way into dreamland.

Ultimately, the line between H. P. Lovecraft's various kinds of fiction is blurred. Even as Mythos ideas slipped into the waning Dunsanian pieces, Dunsanian ideas seeped into the rapidly developing stories of the Cthulhu Mythos. The *Pnakotic Manuscripts* is often brought up in the same breath as the *Necronomicon*. Unknown Kadath is mentioned in "The Dunwich Horror," and then again in *At the Mountains of Madness*, although its location and relationship to the Plateau of Leng as described here appears to conflict with *Dream-Quest*. Other Dunsanian place-names such as Mnar, Ib, Lomar, and Thok recur in *At the Mountains of Madness, Fungi from Yuggoth* and other works, comfortably alongside strictly Cthulhu

Mythos ideas. Because Lovecraft allowed such a free and undisciplined cross-pollenization of ideas to take place between his various fictional undertakings, it is nearly impossible to separate his stories from one another in any meaningful manner--just as it is difficult to understand what relationships--if any--exist between the Dunsanian Other Gods and the various Old Ones, Great Old Ones, Elder Ones, and similar groups of the Cthulhu Mythos.

Self Parody in Lovecraft's Revisions
Will Murray

In the fiction H. P. Lovecraft "revised" (read: ghost-wrote) for his various clients, he not only frequently discarded the original drafts submitted to him, but also ransacked his own fiction for ideas. Much in the way Raymond Chandler incorporated parts of *his* pulp stories into his later mystery novels, so did Lovecraft "cannibalize" (to use Chandler's own term for the practice) his own work when rewriting fiction for clients—although HPL did this in a less flagrant manner. Chandler often reused characters, scenes, and whole passages with little or no change. Lovecraft never went that far, but aside from sticking Yog-Sothoth and his train into revision efforts, he sometimes approached these secondary endeavors as exercises in alternate treatments of his famous fiction.

This may have been conscious, and it may not. But it's obvious from the revision work we know about that HPL seldom if ever put as much effort into these horror stories as he did in his own work. Taking a less craftsmanlike approach seems to have produced a body of Lovecraft fiction which is not merely uneven, but often descends into the dangers of self-parody.

One of the most famous of Lovecraft's revisions is "The Horror in the Museum," written for Hazel Heald. Praised upon its initial *Weird Tales* publication in 1933, today it seems to be the most flagrant of Lovecraftian parodies. Stripped to its bare bones, this story concerns the bloodsucking entity with the un-Lovecraftian name of Rhan-Tegoth (supplied by Heald?) who allegedly came from Yuggoth. Rhan-Tegoth (better known as "IT") now haunts a rather unusual wax museum. Its "Adults Only" section contains some unique exhibits:

> Some were the figures of well-known myth—gorgons, chimeras, dragons, cyclops, and all their shuddersome congeners. Others were drawn from darker and more furtively whispered cycles of subterranean legend—black, formless Tsathoggua, many tentacled Cthulhu, proboscidian Chaugnar Faugn, and other rumored blasphemies from forbidden books like the *Necronomicon*, the *Book of Eibon*, or the *Unaussprechlichen Kulten* of Von Junzt.

For my part, I find it hilarious to consider wax images of the entities Lovecraft always described obliquely to be on display to the public. After all, isn't their very existence a secret? The first line of the above quote is cannibalized from the Charles Lamb extract which heads "The Dunwich Horror."

There's nothing oblique or evocative about Rhan-Tegoth, however. Lovecraft lets it all hang out. The creature is a big globe furred with small tentacles, sports six crablike appendages, has a bubble of a head with three fishlike eyes, an elephantine trunk and gills. "To say that such a thing could have an *expression* seems paradoxical; yet Jones felt that that triangle of bulging fisheyes and that obliquely poised proboscis all bespoke of a blend of hate, greed, and sheer cruelty. . . ." Greed? That isn't paradoxical; it's ludicruous! When HPL described the star-headed Old Ones of *At the Mountains of Madness* or the Great Race in "The Shadow out of Time," he did so with a leisurely suggestiveness which made them seem plausible. But he tosses off Rhan-Tegoth's description in a curt, unconvincing paragraph.

The wax museum plot is hackneyed, and for good measure an obvious device concerning a photograph of the final horror right out of "Pickman's Model" is thrown into this potboiler. Another aspect of this plot, the all-revealing painting, is reused in "Medusa's Coil."

"Out of the Eons," also written for Heald, is no less than a retelling of "The Call of Cthulhu," substituting another Yuggothian entity, Ghatanothoa, who now rests in a Cyclopean fortress in the Pacific which no doubt lies near to R'lyeh; he is "gigantic—tentacled —proboscidian—octopus-eyed—semi-amorphous—plastic—partly squamous and partly rugose—ugh!" Ugh, indeed. This reads as if Lovecraft had picked the dominant adjective from each of his Great Old Ones and set them down in random order. If anything tells me HPL didn't exactly take this story seriously, it's his mention of Shub-Niggurath, Nug, Yeb and Yig as "gods friendly to man." The wife of Yog-Sothoth and her spawn on the side of the angels? (See the collaboration "Through the Gates of the Silver Key" for a disturbingly benign portrayal of Yog-Sothoth.)

My favorite descent into parody in a revision story is the character who launches into disconnected chanting in "The Electric Executioner." First, he's muttering about Aztec gods, which makes sense given the Mexican story-setting: "Ia! Huitzilopotchitli! . . . Nahuatlcatl! Seven, seven, seven . . . Xochimilca, Chalca, Tepaneca, Acolhua, Tlahuica, Tlascalteca, Azteca! . . . I have been to the Seven Caves of Chicomoztoc, but no one shall ever know!" But next he's babbling on in Grecian ecstasy: "Here, O youth—a libation! Wine of the cosmos—nectar of the starry spaces—Linos—Iacchus—Ialemus—Zagreus—Dionysos—Atys—Hylas—sprung from Apollo and slain by the hounds of Argos—seed of Psamthe—child of the sun —Evoe! Evoe!" Finally, he really flips out and starts mixing up his Nahuatl and his R'lyehian: "Ia! Tonatiuh-Metztli! Cthulhu! Command, and I serve!" To which his frightened fellow traveler responds with what he calls "gibberish" in an attempt to placate him: "Ya-R'lyeh! Ya-R'lyeh! . . . Cthulhu fhtaghn! Niguratl-Yig! Yog-Sototl—" It's a silly scene in a silly story, and I can only assume the silliness is deliberate.

Some detractors have criticized Lovecraft for his reliance upon adjectives, and especially adjectives like "eldritch," "horrible" and "hellish," which some say don't belong in horror fiction, but I notice this habit of Lovecraft's is pointedly absent in his revision work. The result is substantially less effective than the Master in full cry. Stripped of Lovecraftian language, many of these stories lack the atmosphere which would otherwise make them raise the hackles.

One exception to this is the C. M. Eddy revision, "The Loved Dead," whose necrophiliac theme was certainly taken seriously by *Weird Tales* readers back in 1924. It's a well-wrought little tale, but at least one critic has suggested it's a deliberate parody of the worst of *Weird Tales'* fiction and that when the narrator finished the story with a disjointed "I can--write-no-more. . . ." he's speaking for HPL, who is convulsed with laughter at his own efforts.

There are many bits of Lovecraftian prose which are echoed in the revisions. The ending of "The Green Meadow," for instance, ("The Green Meadow. . . . I will send a message across the horrible immeasurable abyss") echoes the opening of "Nyarlathotep": ("Nyarlathotep . . . the crawling chaos . . . I am the last . . . I will tell the audient void. . . ."). The recently rediscovered "The Tree on the Hill" opens just like "The Colour out of Space" and ends in a manner evoking Lovecraft's "The Tree." These are not parody, but cannibalization. Lovecraft seems to have taken some revisions more seriously than others. But it's interesting to note that HPL loved to reuse his openings a lot. The first sentence of "The Horror in the Burying Ground"—a revision—is distinctly modeled after the opening of "The Dunwich Horror."

Of course Lovecraft cannibalized some of his own work in later nonrevisions--even to a point close to self-parody. "The Temple" reworked "Dagon." *The Dream-Quest of Unknown Kadath* incorporates many elements of HPL's Dunsanian tales. The ending of the Lovecraft/E. Hoffmann Price revision "Through the Gates of the Silver Key" apes the terminal shock of "The Whisperer in Darkness." This last story, in which Lovecraft drops names out of his past stories (and those of others) is one where he comes closest to self-parody, although the story, like others listed above, is quite serious and effective.

This list of cannibalizations and correspondences could go on and on to a point where drawing a line between deliberate fun and accidental self-plagiarism would be lost. That would be unfair to all concerned, who can no longer speak for themselves.

But be honest . . . who can read the ending of the Lovecraft/Hazel Heald story "Winged Death" in which the protagonist, after being turned into a tsetse fly, dips its legs in ink and writes a dying message on the ceiling of his lab, and not break out laughing?

The First Cthulhu Mythos Poem
Will Murray

For all the attention given to H. P. Lovecraft's sonnet sequence *Fungi from Yuggoth*, his short poem "The Outpost," written in November 1929—just a scant month before *Fungi*—is the first of Lovecraft's poems to reflect the cosmic horror of his then-nascent Cthulhu Mythos.

Certainly, HPL had penned horrific verse in the Poe tradition before this. There was "The Nightmare Lake" in 1919, and the lengthy "Psychopompos" composed the year before. Their moody horror remains memorable, but their themes are not beyond the pale of Poe, who knew nothing of the cosmic. Even "Recapture," penned just before "The Outpost," and subsequently incorporated into *Fungi from Yuggoth*, only suggests these cosmic concerns, and then only ambiguously and without reference to the Mythos.

"The Outpost" is another matter. It concerns the terrible dream-experience of King K'nath-Hothar of ancient Zimbabwe who, "alone of all mankind" ventures beyond "the swamp that serpents shun" to "the veldt that lies behind" where he discovers "the Elder Secret's lair."

This lair is a deserted city whose "strange turrets rose beyond the plain" and "distant domes . . . fouled the ground." The King recognizes the ruins for what they really are—the handiwork of ancient beings whose:

> Inhuman shapes, half-seen, half-guessed,
>   Half solid and half ether-spawned,
>   Seethed down from starless voids that yawned
> In heav'n, to these blank walls of pest.
>
> And voidward from that pest-mad zone
>   Amorphous hordes seethed darkly back,
>   Their dim claws laden with the wrack
> Of things that men have dreamed and known.
>
> The ancient Fishers from Outside—
>   Were there not tales the high-priest told,
>   Of how they found the worlds of old,
> And took what pelf their fancy spied?
>
> Their hidden, dread-ringed outposts brood
>   Upon a million worlds of space;
>   Abhorred by every living race,
> Yet scatheless in their solitude.

At sight of these haunted ruins, the King, "sweating with fright," makes his way back until he is "safe in the palace where he slept." But Lovecraft adds a further odd note to the King's visit to the outpost. For one, "none saw him leave, or come at dawn," and he bears no marks of his journey through jungle and swamp. Furthermore, Lovecraft repeats the first stanza of the poem as its last, and the poem ends where it began, with "Zimbabwe's palace fires ablaze / For a great King who fears to dream."

That "The Outpost" is a Cthulhu Mythos poem is self-evident. Its mention of "inhuman shapes" who "seethed down from the starless voids" intentionally echoes mentions of "the great 'Old Ones' that had filtered down from the stars when the earth was young—the beings whose substance an alien evolution had shaped" as described in *At the Mountains of Madness*. According to that story, these Old Ones warred with "a land race of beings shaped like octopi and probably corresponding to the fabulous prehuman spawn of Cthulhu" who "began filtering down from cosmic infinity and precipitated a monstrous war which for a time drove the Old Ones back to the sea." Later, the Cthulhu spawn built cities all over the earth. More than likely, the ruins described in "The Outpost" are a remnant of one of their cities.

The intimation that the King did not visit the outpost in body, but in spirit or through his dreams, evokes the tactic used by Cthulhu himself in "The Call of Cthulhu." In order to sway humans to do his bidding, Cthulhu influences them through their dreams. Who influences the King in this poem is not made explicit, but the supposition that these ruins are connected with Cthulhu is supported by a reference in the 1934 story HPL revised for Hazel Heald, "Winged Death."

In "Winged Death," which takes place in Uganda, the narrator clearly stumbles across the selfsame ruins King K'nath-Hothar did generations before and describes the outpost in his journal:

> In one spot we came upon a trace of Cyclopean ruins which made even the Gallas run past in a wide circle. They say these megaliths are older than man, and that they used to be a haunt or outpost of "The Fishers from Outside"—whatever that means—and of the evil gods Tsadogwa and Clulu.

Tsadogwa and Clulu are obviously variant spellings of Tsathoggua and Cthulhu respectively. The term "Fishers from Outside," which occurs in "The Outpost," is, as has been noted elsewhere, an oblique reference to one of Charles Fort's conceits—namely, that there are beings outside of our knowledge and planet who look upon us as unintelligent animals and sometimes "fish" for us. Fort used the notion to explain away mysterious disappearances throughout history. The activities of the inhabitants of the outpost, who came down from the stars and returned with unnamed "pelf," is certainly a kind of cosmic fishing. As a matter of fact, they bear a resemblance to the activities of "those birds of space" who "had been *Outside*" and brought unknown things to earth from other worlds, as described in Sonnet X of *Fungi from Yuggoth*, "The Pigeon-Flyers."

Several of Lovecraft's revision stories allude to dark areas of Africa where the Old Ones are worshiped. "The Last Test" mentions the "Hoggar region" without going into any detail, but in "Medusa's Coil," ghosted for Zealia Bishop in 1930, Lovecraft hints darkly of "forgotten sources of hidden truth in lost African civilizations—the great Zimbabwe, and dead Atlantean cities in the Hoggar

from the *Crypt of Cthulhu*

region of the Sahara" and about calling up "what lies hidden in Yuggoth, Zimbabwe, and R'lyeh." Plainly, Cthulhu-worship is deeply entrenched in that region even if HPL never detailed it in his fiction.

Sonnet XXXII of *Fungi*, "Alienation," contains several strong correspondences to the theme of "The Outpost" in abbreviated form, although it is impossible to tell from internal evidence whether or not the sleeper whose "spirit loved to race / Through gulfs and worlds remote from common day" is identical with the subject of "The Outpost." Of the former, however, Lovecraft wrote:

> He had seen Yaddith, yet retained his mind,
> And come back safely from the Ghooric zone,

This is the only reference to the "Ghooric zone" in Lovecraft; it very probably is the term coined for "that pest-mad zone" of ruins which Lovecraft described in "The Outpost." It makes sense within this context.

It's interesting that a complete appreciation of "The Outpost" cannot be gained from the text alone. What Lovecraft suggests in this work, he explicates elsewhere. For instance, the King whose experience forms the heart of "The Outpost" is nowhere named in the work itself. Yet in a letter to James Ferdinand Morton dated October 30, 1929, HPL not only gives his name as K'nath-Hothar, but names his father, King Zothar-Nin. Of the poem, Lovecraft wrote:

> The title of this beautiful lil' bullet is *The Outpost*, and the scene is the celebrated continent of Africa—in the days when great cities dotted the eastern coast, and swart Arab and Phoenician Kings reign'd within the walls of the great Zimbabwe—now a mass of cryptic ruins overrun by apes and blacks and antelope—and work'd the illimitable mines of Ophir. But far, far in the interior . . . on the never-glimps'd plain beyond the serpent-shunn'd swamp . . . rumour hinted that a frightful and unmentionable outpost of THEM brooded blasphemously—and so K'nath-Hothar the Great King, who fear'd nothing, stole thither in secret one night . . . though whether he did so in body or in his dreams, not even he can certainly tell. N. B.—Knath-Hothar was *not* oulothrix—and he had *thin lips*, a *very large* aquiline nose, and a *light* complexion inherited from his *Nordick* stream. And P. S.—his father's hair was *straight*, and the paternal nose *long* and the paternal lips *thin*. This father, the late great King Zothar-Nin, was born in Sidon of pure Phoenician stock. . . .

Someone—I think it was Ernest Hemingway—once observed that a piece of writing is like an iceberg. The reader reads what is only the tip of the iceberg, and it is good only because of the portions he doesn't see—the early drafts and notes and unspoken ideas—which are likened to the larger, submerged portion of the iceberg. This analogy certainly applies to the works of H. P. Lovecraft, himself a meticulous rewriter, and nowhere is this more evident than in "The Outpost." The poem itself communicates its mood and certain ideas very effectively, and Lovecraft wasn't afraid to leave out certain particulars, such as the King's name and the exact identity of the outpost's builders, which he clearly gave considerable thought, but refrained in the interest of his art from using in the work itself. It might very well be that King K'nath-Hothar's name and background—so stressed in Lovecraft's letter—were included in an early draft of "The Outpost," and deleted in subsequent revisions for aesthetic reasons.

"The Outpost" may not be Lovecraft's most famous poem. Nor is it his most ambitious. But it is significant in that it was the first, as well as one of the few poems, which took as its subject a manifestation of the Cthulhu Mythos. It is as much a part of the Mythos as *Fungi from Yuggoth*, and, like that sonnet sequence, can only be fully appreciated when its concepts are collated with those of Lovecraft's fiction.

Prehuman Language in Lovecraft
Will Murray

In addition to being treasure-troves of elder lore, the dark books cited in H. P. Lovecraft's many stories are rich in linguistic arcana. Specifically, they contain multitudinous examples of what Lovecraft liked to call "prehuman language," the speech of the Great Old Ones who inhabited the earth before the advent of man. Lovecraft dished out examples of this tongue sparingly, but he seems to have done so with great care, as if these transcribed approximations carried real meaning and were not merely a function of atmospheric verisimilitude.

Perhaps for Lovecraft, they did possess meaning, for certain words and phrases—or their phonetic equivalents—recur again and again in HPL's stories and letters. Some are obviously names; others convey less clear resonances. All defy ready understanding while seeming to be almost accessible in a maddeningly tantalizing way.

Early instances of prehuman language in Lovecraft's fiction occur in *The Case of Charles Dexter Ward* and amply illustrate a basic reality of this language—that written-down versions of what may originally have been spoken words are always approximate and subject to aural interpretation. These are the twin formulae for raising the dead from their "essential salts" and returning them to granular form later:

Y'AI'NG'NGAH	OGTHROD AI'F
YOG-SOTHOTH	GEB'L—EE'H
H'EE—L'GEB	YOG-SOTHOTH
F'AI THRODOG	'NGAH'NG AI'Y
UAAAH	ZHRO

According to the story, the second formula is "no more than the first written syllabically backward with the exception of the final monosyllables and of the odd name *Yog-Sothoth*." This is an oversimplification in that it ignores the fact that the line-ranking is inverted as well, but this doesn't affect the words involved.

It's interesting to note that the many apostrophes invariably mark syllable breaks in these incantations. But more than that, some seem to act as word separators as well. Although they were new when originally presented in this novel, certain words imbedded in these formulae appear by themselves in many later stories.

Yog-Sothoth is one, of course. But so is the curious coinage *'Ngah*, in one form or another. More on it later. A phonetic equivalent to *Uaaah—Ya*—also reappears in subsequent stories. *Geb* does not, but it should be pointed out that it is the name of a minor Egyptian deity. *Ai*, on the other hand, is the Greek cry meaning "woe!" Reversed, it becomes that oft-heard prehuman cry *Ia*! Make of this what you will.[1]

These two formulae contain both primary characteristics of Lovecraftian prehuman language: the hyphenated proper names and the high incidence of apostrophes, which also serve to mark missing or doubtful letters. Various keys are given in this novel to suggest phonetic interpretations of the first formula. On page 161, it is overheard as "Yi-nash-Yog-Sothoth-he-lglb-fi-thro-dag" with the terminal shout given as "Yah!" An older text than the one giving the formulae as rendered above spells the first line of the initial formula as "Aye, cngengah, Yogge-Sothotha," providing an unexpected "c" and "e" in place of the apostrophes in the second word, which was elsewhere pronounced as "nash."

Obviously the rules of spelling and pronunciation in prehuman speech are not easily deciphered. This is also true of syntax, as is clear from the first and most famous example of the tongue given in "The Call of Cthulhu." This is the line which reads:

"*Ph'nglui mglw'nath Cthulhu R'lyeh wgah'nagl fhtagn.*"

and translates as:

"In his house at R'lyeh dead Cthulhu waits dreaming."

Lovecraft informs us that R'lyeh is the undersea palace of the entity Cthulhu. It would seem that "fhtagn" probably means "waits" because the line is compressed to "Cthulhu fhtagn" later in the story.[2] It might possibly mean "Cthulhu dreams" instead, but "fhtagn" is unlikely to mean both "dreams" and "dreaming." We would expect some change in verb-form. In any event, there are nine English words to the phrase, and if we count the apostrophes as word breaks (disregarding the one in R'lyeh, of course) there are nine prehuman words in the original, too. But the arrangement of those words makes generating a grammatical structure—and thus translating the rest of the words—virtually impossible. No syntactical arrangement, in which *R'lyeh wgah'nagi* separates the subject-verb combination "Cthulhu waits," works.

Linguists know that grammar is a function of the mind and that while several combinations of words can convey the same meaning ("Dead Cthulhu waits dreaming in his house at R'lyeh") is just as sound as Lovecraft's translation), the arrangement must conform to instinctive language patterns. Thus, "In his house at Cthulhu R'lyeh dead dreaming waits," among others, is an unworkable grammatical transformation, and one which the mind quickly perceives as false.

The *human* mind, that is. Perhaps in the minds of the Great Old Ones, that or some other arrangement is perfectly intelligible. But the fact remains that for us, prehuman syntax appears inaccessible. This is probably a deliberate act on Lovecraft's part, although the principles of Transformational Grammar alluded to here were unknown in Lovecraft's time.

While this may be so, there are indications that individual words carry definite meaning. Not content to lace his stories with prehuman language extracts, HPL rattled them off in his letters as well. One is a variant on the "Call of Cthulhu" extract, and is from a letter to Clark Ashton Smith dated December 3, 1929. It reads: "Yug! n'gha k'yun bth'gth R'lyeh gllur ph'ngui Cthulhu Yzkaa . . ."

Several of these words are familiar. There is a *Y'kaa* in "The Horror in the Museum." "Ph'ngui" is only one letter different from "ph'n-glui," and "n'gha" is very close to "'Ngah" from the

Charles Dexter Ward formulae. Various forms of 'Ngah appear throughout Lovecraft's stories and letters. Two separate letters to Smith, one dated October 17, 1930, and the other dated November 7, 1930, make references to "the year of N'GaH" and "the Seal of N'GaH" respectively. Other forms include "n'ggah" (Lovecraft to Long, November 22, 1930) and "n'gha'ghaa" ("The Dunwich Horror").

More interesting is the frequency of incidence where a variation of this word appears with a variation of "*k'yun*," as in the phrase "*n'gha k'yun*" cited above in the December 3, 1928, letter. Other variations include "*N'ggah-kthn-y'hhu!*" (Lovecraft to Smith, October 7, 1930) and, just possibly, the mention of "The Worm Bgn-gghaa-Ythu-Yaddith" in a January 1931 letter to Smith. All of these fall under the heading of whimsical scribblings, perhaps, but it's interesting that in "The Whisperer in Darkness," which was being penned during the same months these letters were composed, reference is made to an ". . . unpronounceable word or name, possibly *N'gah-Kthun*." This name (even in the letters it is most often hyphenated, a sure indication that it is a name) appears in a different form in the 1933 revision, "The Horror in the Museum" thusly: "Spawn of Noth-Yidik and effluvium of K'thun." See also "the Black Sun Gnarr-Kthun" (HPL to CAS September 11, 1931).

We don't know what *N'gah* means. *Kthun* vaguely echoes Cthulhu, but this needn't be meaningful. It might just be that these were sounds that Lovecraft found especially alien. Certainly *N'gah* is a special favorite of his.

N'gah is done to death in an untranslated line from the *Necronomicon* (from "The Dunwich Horror") which reads: "*N'gai, n'gha'ghaa, bugg-shoggog, y'hah; Yog-Sothoth, Yog-Sothoth.*" As with the formulae from *Charles Dexter Ward*, spoken versions are given later in the story. Here, they are spoken by Wilbur Whateley's inhuman brother, who has difficulty with the words and throws in some improvisations of his own. The first begins thusly: "*Ygnaiih . . . ygnaiih . . . thflthkh'ngha . . . Yog-Sothoth . . .*" To this is added: "*Y'bthnk . . . h'ehye—n'grkdl'lh. . . .*" A second attempt starts off ín prehuman, but ends up in English crying: "*Bh-ya-ya-ya-yahaah—e'yayayayaaaa . . . ngh'aaaa . . . ngh'aaa . . . h'yuh . . .* HELP! HELP! . . . *ff—ff—ff—*FATHER! FATHER! YOG-SOTHOTH!"

It's odd that the word *N'gai* (which also appears at the end of "The Haunter of the Dark" in the disjointed muttering "Ia . . . ngai . . . ygg . . .") comes out as "Yngaiih" verbally. It's also odd that the compound word *bugg-shoggog* is left out of the spoken version of the quote. Except for the lack of capitalization, this word seems to be a name, yet Wilbur's brother leaves it out of the incantation. Perhaps *bugg-shoggog* is not a proper name, but a general term, like horse or cat. This is pure speculation, of course, but it could be that *bugg-shoggog* is a term meaning one of the offspring of Yog-Sothoth. While the word is not repeated within the story, it crops up quite mysteriously two years later in a letter to Frank Belknap Long dated March 14, 1930. HPL mentions in passing that Clark Ashton Smith is sending him pieces of dinosaur bone, whereupon he lapses into prehuman, saying "YSSShh . . .

Later, he adds a solitary "*W'ygh*."

The monosyllabic "*ya*," probably a variant of *Ia*, also survives into other writings, for some reason as "Ya-R'lyeh" ("The Electric Executioner," cf. "Iä R'lyeh!" in "The Man of Stone"), a cry that seems to appear only in HPL's letters and revisions. A variant, "Y'aaah!" is found in "The Curse of Yig," and "The Shadow out of Time" mentions a Cimmerian chieftain of 15,000 BC named Crom-Ya. Again, there is an inner logic in which a word is attached to a known name.[3] Another possible variant may be Y'ha-nthlei, the sunken city of "The Shadow over Innsmouth."

While Lovecraft's letters and stories are rife with other examples of prehuman language, it would serve no clear purpose to cite them all. Instead, certain general observations can be made about this tongue.

First, the language is absolutely riddled with apostrophe marks, which seem to stand for missing letters and also serve as word divisions. Where we know the exact missing letters, there seems to be no discernible pattern: the marks can stand for consonants as well as vowels. Probably these marks are a carryover from the Arabic text of the *Necronomicon*, inasmuch as that language is also heavily festooned with apostrophes.

Secondly, pronunciation of these words is itself problematical, as Lovecraft reports many variant pronunciations of a single name. For example: Relex for R'lyeh; Clooloo and Tulu for Cthulhu; Xinian for K'n-yan; Iog-Sotot for Yog-Sothoth, and others. In some cases, letters do not even remotely correspond to actual sounds those letters are supposed to represent. When this happens we may be dealing with written variants produced by adaptation to the speakers' native languages, as in the case of John=Johann=Juan=Jon=Yahya=Yokhannon, etc.

Thirdly, there is evidence to suggest some prehuman words have survived into human languages. For example, the name of the living dead men in "The Mound" is *y'm-bhi*, which approximates the West Indian term, *jumbee*, also spelled zombie. The reverse is also true, it would seem. When, near the end of *The Dream-Quest of Unknown Kadath*, Randolph Carter mounts a Shantak bird, Nyarlathotep exclaims, "Hei! Aa-shanta 'nygh! You are off!" *Ashanta* would seem to be the prehuman original of what HPL anglicized as "Shantak."

Fourth, there's a tendency to collapse prehuman words when rendering them in English. One letter extract (HPL to CAS, October 7, 1930) includes the name *Cthua*, possibly an elided version of Cthulhu. This kind of word compression could explain the odd "*Ia . . . ngai . . . ygg*" fragment scribbled by Robert Blake as doom descends upon him at the climax of "The Haunter of the Dark." Earlier in his terminal writings, he began free-associating names from the Cthulhu Mythos, but they are the standard English spellings. Among them are Shaggai and Yuggoth, which might be represented as *Ngai* and *Ygg*, respectively, in prehuman.

Lastly, while there are recognizable patterns to Lovecraft's construction and use of prehuman words and phrases, there may not be a systematic logic to the language as a whole. But neither is

Lovecraft guilty of free-associating sounds in the manner of Robert Blake. As always, he seems to have given as much thought to his linguistic extracts--the total sum of which probably wouldn't fill a single printed page—as he did to his carefully worked-out plots. If there's a key to translating the tongue of the Old Ones, it has so far not been rediscovered. But the haunting possibility remains that the writer who translated his own initials into the prehuman Eic'h-Pi-El may have left a Rosetta Stone of sorts buried in one of his stories or letters . . . if only we knew enough to recognize it.

NOTES

[1] Iä seems to equate to the variants *hei*, *ei*, and *ii*. There is also a River Ai mentioned in several dreamworld stories, though this may have simply been borrowed from the city Ai in Joshua 7:2ff.

[2] Fhtagn is elsewhere rendered as *fthagn* ("Out of the Eons"), *fhtaghn* ("The Electric Executioner"), and *fhgthagn* (HPL to Frank Belknap Long, November 22, 1930.

[3] Speculation: Lovecraft often spoke of "Great Cthulhu." Let's suppose *ya* means great. Thus, we have Great R'lyeh, Crom the Great, Great Nthlei, and even "Great Shub-Niggurath"! if we include the variant "Iä." Or substitute some other like adjective; they all work. Another word that works this way is *ho*. See *Yian-Ho* ("The Diary of Alonzo Typer" and "Through the Gates of the Silver Key"), *Shaurash-ho* (HPL to CAS, August 1932), all proper names.

H.P. Lovecraft's *Fungi from Yuggoth*
David E. Schultz

I.

In November 1928, Lovecraft informed a fellow poet that "a friend of mine in Wisconsin has written a book which I would like to recommend . . . but alas! it is not quite finished, although accepted (from a survey of the unpublished ms.) by Macmillan Co. This will be *The Gateway to Poetry* by Maurice Winter Moe."[1] Maurice Moe (1882-1940), one of Lovecraft's earliest friends in amateur journalism and a long-standing correspondent, was a high school teacher in Milwaukee, Wisconsin. Lovecraft described Moe's book, later entitled *Doorways to Poetry*, as "a treatise on the appreciation of poetry."[2] Moe had invited Lovecraft to examine the manuscript with an eye toward possible revision. Lovecraft accepted the task, but declined to accept payment for what he called "giving it a once-over."[3]

Lovecraft thought highly of the book and claimed it needed little editing, but he confessed to a correspondent that, "The job does take time, confound it!"[4] His work on the book was completed by the fall of 1929.[5] Despite the initial acceptance of the book by Macmillan and the later interest shown by both Holt and the Kenyon Press, the book was never published. However, Lovecraft's investment of time and effort in Moe's book was not without benefit.

While Lovecraft was working on Moe's book, he wrote a letter to Moe in heroic couplets[6] that began prophetically, "Thanks for the gift, nor blame me if I teter / And slip into my antient vice of meter." In October, Lovecraft slipped further into his "antient vice": "Some malign influence—prob'ly revising that Moe text book on poetick appreciation—has got me invadin' one of Klarkash-Ton's provinces—and relapsin' back into my antient weakness of attempted prosody."[7] The first product of Lovecraft's "relapse" was a 52-line poem entitled "The Outpost" which was sent promptly to *Weird Tales* for publication. In mid-November Lovecraft tried to express "a recent dream tableau" in a sonnet that he called "Recapture."[8] "Recapture" was quickly followed by "The Ancient Track," a fairly long poem written in tetrameter couplets. Both poems were likewise submitted to *Weird Tales*. Farnsworth Wright rejected "The Outpost," claiming it was too long, but bought "Recapture" and "The Ancient Track" for $14.50.[9]

In late November, Lovecraft became engaged in a written discussion of weird fiction with the literary editor of *The Providence Journal*, Bertrand K. Hart (1892-1941). Hart's column, "The Sideshow," had begun to appear earlier that year and had become a favorite of Lovecraft's. When Hart wrote in his column about the mysterious disappearances of several trains, Lovecraft wrote Hart on the subject and the subsequent exchange of letters eventually turned to "the most eery story ever written."[10] Lovecraft's observations on weird fiction and his famous list of favorite stories appeared in "The Sideshow." As that exchange occurred, Hart ironically stumbled upon a recent collection of weird stories called *Beware after Dark!*[11]

He was startled to find that his former residence at 7 Thomas Street in Providence had, by coincidence, served as the setting of a scene in a story entitled "The Call of Cthulhu," and that the author of that story was none other than Lovecraft. "The Sideshow" for Friday, 29 November 1929, carried the following comment from Hart:

> Personally I congratulate him upon the dark spirits he has evoked in Thomas Street, but I shall not be happy until, joining league with wraiths and ghouls, I have plumped down at least one large and abiding ghost by way of reprisal upon his own doorstep in Barnes Street. I think I shall teach it to moan in a minor dissonance every morning at three o'clock sharp with a clanking of chains.[12]

In response to Hart's mock threat, Lovecraft wrote a sonnet describing a call from the ghost and dedicated it to Hart. "The Messenger" appeared in "The Sideshow" the following Tuesday.

On 7 December Lovecraft wrote "The East India Brick Row," a 48-line poem lamenting the demolition of the old brick warehouses on South Water Street in Providence. It appeared on the literary page of the *Journal* for 8 January 1930. Lovecraft was finding poetry to be a suitable medium for expression of his thoughts, and professional publications were printing his poetry.

Then in late December, Lovecraft commenced his long poem *Fungi from Yuggoth*, a culmination of recent philosophical musings and personal experiences. When Lovecraft drafted the poem, he composed only thirty-five stanzas.[13] He mockingly complained, "I had sworn to cut out rhyming—but that bird [Moe] got me doing jingles for metrically illustrative purposes, and now—confound it—I can't stop!"[14] Except for "Recapture," the poems were written in the order in which they now appear; "Recapture" was inserted into the sequence approximately five years later.

The autograph manuscript of the poem consists of twenty pages. R. H. Barlow wrote of the manuscript, "The *Fungi from Yuggoth* . . . consists of an interesting set of draughts which would lend themselves to facsimile reproduction some day."[15] Indeed they would, for they illustrate the labor that went into their composition. Each page is covered with Lovecraft's cross-outs, additions, and interlinings. Individual lines, unfinished stanzas, and even a draft of one of the poems were all deleted and replaced.

On the first page, Lovecraft wrote "Dec. 27, 1929" and "14 sonnets 196 lines." The date is often given as the date Lovecraft began to write *Fungi from Yuggoth*, but it is unlikely that he wrote so much on one day, as evidenced by the rewriting of each stanza and the time devoted to the later stanzas. Comments on page 8 of the manuscript state, "16 additional sonnets—Dec. 28, 1929 - Jany 2, 1930" and "Total to Jany 2—30 sonnets = 420 lines $105.00 at W.T. rates." It is obvious that Lovecraft was contemplating selling the entire sequence to *Weird Tales*. The date "Jany 3, 1930" appears on the draft of "Harbour Whistles." The final poems were dated "Jany 4, 1930." The original draft, then, consisted of 490 lines that would have earned Lovecraft $122.50 had he sold the entire poem to *Weird Tales*. In a 40-day period, Lovecraft had completed 40 poems; he probably wrote no more than ten more poems before his death in 1937.

II.

Fungi from Yuggoth was never published in its entirety in Lovecraft's lifetime. Although Lovecraft would have been pleased to see the poem published in its entirety, he was content to have the stanzas published individually. He had written to a correspondent that:

> Aside from the introductory three they are meant for independent publication. I am letting the *Prov. Journal* have a first chance at them, & what they return I shall send to *Weird Tales*. The residue after this will go to *Driftwind* (a Vermont magazine which comes close to the domain of the *Circle & Carillon* class, & which uses the work of many of these groups) & what they don't want I shall dump on the amateur press.[16]

An informal log kept on the first page of the autograph manuscript of the poem shows that Lovecraft followed that plan. Although Lovecraft had apparently intended to send the entire poem to *Weird Tales*, he did indeed send it first to *The Providence Journal*. He was paid $17.50 for five poems that were published in the literary section of the Wednesday edition.[17]

Weird Tales took only ten of the poems, which appeared in seven consecutive issues between September 1930 and April 1931.[18] They were numbered 1 through 10 to show that they were somehow unified, as Donald Wandrei's *Sonnets of the Midnight Hours* had been.[19] Lovecraft's ordering and numbering of the stanzas were not followed. In each issue, the poems appeared under the title *Fungi from Yuggoth* and an illustration by Hugh Rankin that depicted scenes from "The Courtyard," "Hesperia" and "Star-Winds." Lovecraft never resubmitted the rejected poems to *Weird Tales*, but *Weird Tales* published most of them after Lovecraft's death.

Walter J. Coates of *The Driftwind* then accepted four of the poems. "Harbour Whistles" was taken by both *The Silver Fern*, an amateur publication from New Zealand, and *L'Alouette*, edited by Charles A. A. Parker. W. Paul Cook accepted six poems for the second issue of his now legendary publication *The Recluse*. Cook had gotten as far as setting about 100 pages, or half the issue, in type and printing about 40 pages. Lovecraft had even seen page proofs of "The Strange High House in the Mist," which was to appear in the same issue. However the death of Cook's wife at that time was a terrible strain on Cook, and he eventually abandoned *The Recluse* as well as the binding of Lovecraft's *The Shunned House*.[20]

Lovecraft transferred most of his log of submittals onto a typescript of the poem. The typescript was circulated to interested parties who could then select stanzas to publish from the unpublished ones. The sonnets that had been submitted to *The Recluse* were not so identified on the typescript, indicating that they were free for publication. In 1931, Lovecraft resubmitted *Fungi from Yuggoth* to *Driftwind*, which accepted five more poems.[21] Of those poems,

"The Canal" was later published in an anthology edited by Coates entitled *Harvest: A Sheaf of Poems from Driftwind*.[22] "The Pigeon-Flyers" and "A Memory" had been selected by Earl Clifford Kelley for *Ripples from Lake Champlain*, but they were not published because Kelley committed suicide in July 1932. In mid-1932, "Evening Star" and "Continuity" appeared in an amateur journal called *The Pioneer*, edited by Walter M. Stevenson.

In 1932, Harold S. Farnese, dean of the Institute of Musical Education, Ltd., in Los Angeles, asked Lovecraft for permission to set two of the *Fungi from Yuggoth* to music.[23] Lovecraft granted his permission, and by September Farnese had written music for "Mirage" and "The Elder Pharos" from the February-March 1931 *Weird Tales*.

In 1934, Lovecraft began to receive requests from young publishers for material for their fan publications. Lovecraft complied by submitting stories that had not been reprinted since their initial appearances in early amateur journals or items that had been rejected and never published. *The Fantasy Fan*, edited by Charles D. Hornig, was the first of the fan publications to print selections from *Fungi from Yuggoth*. "The Book" and "Pursuit" appeared in the October 1934 issue, which was dedicated to Lovecraft. Lovecraft neglected to note that he had sent "Homecoming" to Hornig and inadvertently sent it to Willis Conover c. July 1935 for the *Science-Fantasy Correspondent*.[24] Donald Wollheim and Wilson Shepherd took five poems for *The Phantagraph*, Lloyd Arthur Eachbach took "Background" for *The Galleon*, and Ernest A. Edkins took "Continuity" for *Causerie*. Wollheim and Shepherd also prepared a special publication that consisted of a single stanza from *Fungi from Yuggoth*. "Background" was published as "A Sonnet" in what was called the "Fourty-Sixth [sic] Anniversary Issue" of *The Lovecrafter*.[25]

Lovecraft also submitted three of the poems and various other items to Conrad Ruppert and Julius Schwartz for their *Fantasy Magazine*, but the poems were not published. Lovecraft's submittals were turned over to Conover in January 1937 for use in *Science-Fantasy Correspondent*, which also ceased publication before the poems could appear. The three *Fungi from Yuggoth* originally submitted to *Fantasy Magazine* and "Homecoming" were published shortly after Lovecraft's death in *The Democrat & News*, the newspaper in Conover's hometown of Cambridge, Maryland.[26] All but four stanzas of *Fungi from Yuggoth* appeared in print before Lovecraft's death; only "Expectancy" never saw publication in a periodical.

FOOTNOTES

[1] Lovecraft to E. Toldridge, 20 November 1928, *Selected Letters* II (Sauk City, WI: Arkham House, 1968), p. 253.
[2] Lovecraft to E. Toldridge, 14 August 1929, *Selected Letters* III (Arkham House, 1971), p. 13.
[3] Lovecraft to M. W. Moe, January 1929, *Letters* II.255.
[4] Lovecraft to J. F. Morton, 30 July 1929, *Letters* III.10.
[5] Lovecraft to J. F. Morton, 15 March 1930, *Letters* III.129.
[6] "An Epistle to the Rt. Hon'ble Maurice Winter Moe, Esq., of

Zythopolis, in the Northwest Territory of His Majesty's American Dominions" as by "L. Theobald, Jun." 212 lines; unpublished. Cf. *Letters* III.11.

[7] Lovecraft to J. F. Morton, 30 October 1929, *Letters* III.55.

[8] Lovecraft to C. A. Smith, 19 November 1929, *Dreams and Fancies* (Arkham House, 1962), p. 28

[9] Lovecraft to J. F. Morton, 6 December 1929, *Letters* III.90. "The Ancient Track" is only eight lines shorter than "The Outpost." "The Outpost" was probably rejected because it was only slightly too long to fit on a single printed page.

[10] "The Sideshow" in *The Providence Journal*, 23 November 1929. The exchange between Lovecraft and Hart is described by Kenneth W. Faig, Jr., in "Lovecraft's Own Book of Weird Fiction," in *The HPL Supplement No. 2*, July 1973, pp. 4-15.

[11] *Beware after Dark! The World's Most Stupendous Tales of Mystery, Thrills and Terror*, selected, and an introduction, by T. Everett Harre (New York: Macaulay, 1929).

[12] *The Sideshow of B. K. Hart: A Selection of Columns Written for The Providence Journal 1929-1941*, ed. Philomena Hart (Providence: The Roger Williams Press, 1941), p. 48.

[13] It should be noted that Lovecraft had written to Elizabeth Toldridge and August Derleth that the sequence consisted of only thirty-three stanzas, though the dates of those letters are inexact and Lovecraft's manuscript suggests that he completed "Continuity" by very early January.

[14] Lovecraft to J. F. Morton, 15 March 1930, *Letters* III.129.

[15] "The Wind That is in the Grass" by R. H. Barlow, in *Marginalia* (Arkham House, 1944), p. 317.

[16] Lovecraft to E. Toldridge, 11 February 1930, *Letters* III. 117.

[17] Lovecraft to J. F. Morton, 15 March 1930, *Letters* III.129.

[18] Two poems appeared in the September 1930, January 1931 and February-March 1931 issues. As noted above, the entire sequence would have earned Lovecraft $122.50 had it been accepted by *Weird Tales*. Perhaps *Weird Tales* did not accept all of the poems because they felt the price would have been inordinately high for the amount of space the poems would have taken. Lovecraft was paid $165.00 for "The Call of Cthulhu" (*Weird Tales*, February 1928); $122.50 would have been a rather high price to pay for what was essentially filler material.

[19] Twelve of Wandrei's *Sonnets* appeared in eleven consecutive issues of *Weird Tales* between May 1928 and March 1929 (two appeared in May 1928).

[20] "An Appreciation of H. P. Lovecraft" by W. Paul Cook, in *Beyond the Wall of Sleep* (Arkham House, 1943), p. 454.

[21] "The Book," which appeared in the April 1937 *Driftwind*, was the tenth sonnet to appear in that magazine. However, it was probably not submitted by Lovecraft. Its previous appearance in *The Fantasy Fan* was acknowledged by *Driftwind*.

[22] *Harvest* was printed in an edition of two hundred twenty-five copies, of which seventy-five were bound in boards. Lovecraft had claimed that this was the only appearance of his poetry between

hard covers, although *The Poetical Works of Jonathan E. Hoag* (1923) contains seven poems by Lovecraft. He may have dismissed this publication for he edited the book along with James F. Morton and Samuel Loveman. The biographical description of Lovecraft in *Harvest* stated that "His sequence of sonnets, *Fungi from Yuggoth*, have [sic] not yet seen book publication" (p. 55).

[23] Lovecraft to E. Toldridge, 12 August 1932, *Selected Letters* IV (Arkham House, 1976), p. 54.

[24] *Lovecraft at Last* by H. P. Lovecraft and Willis Conover (Arlington, VA: Carrolton Clark, 1975), p. 127.

[25] *The Lovecrafter* was "printed with the deep gratitude and best wishes of Wilson Shepherd and Donald A. Wollheim" in the 20 August 1936 issue (Vol. 47, No. 1). The date is, of course, that of Lovecraft's forty-sixth birthday; the volume number is equivalent to the start of Lovecraft's forty-seventh year. Despite the numbering, it was actually the only issue (although Dirk Mosig issued an "Eighty-Fifth Anniversary Issue" of *The Lovecrafter* in 1975).

[26] "Observations and Otherwise" by Willis Conover appeared in the Thursday, 8 July 1937 paper. This constituted the first appearance in print of "The Pigeon-Flyers" and "A Memory."

Lovecraft's New York Exile
David E. Schultz

    H. P. Lovecraft's short residence in New York probably affected him as profoundly as any other experience of his life. W. Paul Cook has said that, following Lovecraft's so-called "exile" in New York, Lovecraft "came back to Providence a human being--and *what* a human being! He had been tried in the fire and came out pure gold."[1] Cook himself had a significant role in helping Lovecraft survive his trial, a role that Cook surely realized but never acknowledged. Lovecraft scholars already recognize one great debt they owe Cook: If not for Cook's persistent urgings in 1917 that Lovecraft once again try his hand at fiction, Lovecraft may never have returned to story writing. As we shall see, we are indebted to Cook for another important nudge he gave Lovecraft in 1925.
    Lovecraft's move to New York was necessitated by his marriage on 3 March 1924 to Sonia Greene, a fellow amateur journalist. Following their honeymoon in Philadelphia, the Lovecrafts settled down at Sonia's apartment at 259 Parkside in Brooklyn, where they remained until they were forced to take up less expensive quarters at 169 Clinton Street, also in Brooklyn. Sonia left for Cincinnati on 31 December to take a position with a department store, and Lovecraft remained in New York until April 1926 when he left to live with his aunts in Providence.
    In New York Lovecraft wrote relatively little because his wife and cronies in the Kalem Club occupied much of his time. He became increasingly despondent with his inability to find a job to his liking. He also complained that he "couldn't form a single well-defined thought in that damnable Clinton Street pigsty."[2] With each passing day, he became more acutely aware that what he called "background," the most essential ingredient of his life (so eloquently described in his sonnet of the same name), was painfully absent. Lovecraft's first letter to James F. Morton following his marriage to Sonia shows that he recognized very early that his "Novanglian background [had been] but imperfectly shed"[3] following his departure from Providence. The sense of being uprooted from his background became more painful as time went on.
    The last story Lovecraft wrote before his move was "Under the Pyramids," a story ghost-written for Harry Houdini. It formed a hectic, if not humorous, part of his arrival in New York, for he lost the manuscript and spent his wedding day retyping the story with assistance from his bride. The story earned Lovecraft $100, and his new life seemed to be off to a promising start. But it was eight months before Lovecraft composed a new story—even longer if "Under the Pyramids" is dismissed as not a true Lovecraft story. The last story that sprang from his own thoughts was "The Festival" from late 1923. The composition of "The Shunned House" in October 1924 was a particularly remarkable feat for its setting was Providence and it described a real house, at 135 Benefit Street, which

Lovecraft knew well—indeed, one of his aunts had resided there. The story was prompted by a note in his commonplace book and the recollection of a recent visit to Elizabeth, New Jersey:

> On the northeast corner of Bridge Street and Elizabeth Avenue is a terrible old house—a hellish place where night-black deeds must have been done in the early seventeen-hundreds —with a blackish unpainted surface, unnaturally steep roof, and an outside flight of steps leading to the second story, suffocatingly embowered in a tangle of ivy so dense that one cannot but imagine it accursed or corpse-fed. It reminded me of the Babbit House in Benefit Street. . . . Later its image came up again with renewed vividness, finally causing me to write a new horror story with its scene in Providence and with the Babbit House as its basis.[4]

Although Lovecraft could not observe the real "shunned house" firsthand, he described it vividly and accurately.

Why did Lovecraft write "The Shunned House" so far from its setting? Quite simply, he was homesick. At around the time he wrote that story, he wrote a poem entitled "Providence," a nostalgic paean to the city for which he so deeply yearned, as evidenced by the following lines:

> Thou dream'st beside the waters there,
>   Unchang'd by cruel years;
> A spirit from an age more fair
>   That shines behind our tears.
>
> Thy twinkling lights each night I see
>   Tho' time and space divide;
> For thou art of the soul of me,
>   And always at my side![5]

In the letters of his New York period, Lovecraft wrote repeatedly of the importance of background. To maintain his sense of background, Lovecraft exchanged a voluminous and regular correspondence with his aunts living in Providence.

Lovecraft's spirit was increasingly sapped by the oppressive atmosphere of New York. It was not fully ten months after writing "The Shunned House" that he produced a new story, "The Horror at Red Hook," set in the Red Hook section of Brooklyn where he lived, was written on 1-2 August. Within a fortnight, he wrote the autobiographical "He," also set in New York. "He" was begun on 11 August in Scott Park in Elizabeth, New Jersey, the city that inspired Lovecraft to write "The Shunned House" the previous year and which Lovecraft "haunt[ed] continually" for respite from New York. It was completed the same day on the return trip to New York.

"The Horror at Red Hook," "He" and "Cool Air" are the only fictional impressions of Lovecraft's stay in New York, but "He" is the most revealing:

> My coming to New York had been a mistake; for whereas I had looked for poignant wonder and inspiration in the

teeming labyrinths of ancient streets that twist endlessly
from forgotten courts and squares and waterfronts to courts
and squares and waterfronts equally forgotten, and in the
Cyclopean modern towers and pinnacles that rise blackly
Babylonian under waning moons, I had found instead only a
sense of horror and oppression which threatened to master,
paralyse, and annihilate me. . . . Instead of the poems I
had hoped for, there came only a shuddering blankness and
ineffable loneliness. . . . I . . . refrained from going home
to my people lest I seem to crawl back ignobly in defeat.[6]

The city, whose skyline Lovecraft had rapturously described as "almost dreamlike and Dunsanian" in 1922, had become for him "a dead city." In "He," Lovecraft called it a "corpse-city," a term he used to describe R'lyeh in "The Call of Cthulhu." In fact, within two days of writing "He," Lovecraft wrote out the "story plot" for "The Call of Cthulhu," though he did not write that story for another year. On 18 September he wrote "In the Vault," a weak story based on a suggestion made by a friend.

It was into this lonely, depressing and unproductive period of Lovecraft's life that W. Paul Cook entered in November 1925 with a request that Lovecraft write "an article . . . on the element of terror & weirdness in literature"[7] for a new magazine Cook was preparing called *The Recluse*. L. Sprague de Camp has dismissed that article, *Supernatural Horror in Literature*, as a monumental waste of Lovecraft's time—a "piece of frivolous self-indulgence"—because Lovecraft wrote the lengthy piece for no payment and because it was the sort of thing "that any professor of English literature could do. Many scholars could have written [it]."[8]

The writing of *Supernatural Horror in Literature* was hardly as "frivolous" as de Camp suggests. Work on the essay improved Lovecraft's spirits. He wrote to James F. Morton that "My own favorite pastime lately has been writing that weird-tale article for Cook, and doing the incidental reading essential thereto."[9] He wrote to his aunt Lillian that he found the reading and writing

excellent mental discipline, & a fine gesture of demarcation
betwixt my aimless, lost existence of the past year or two
& the resumed Providence-like hermitage amidst which I hope
to grind out some tales worth writing. . . . it exercises my
literary inventiveness & prose style. And . . . it restores
my mind to its natural field of bookish seclusion & accelerates my speed & retentiveness in reading to something like
their old Providence standard. The article done . . . I
shall devote myself to the composition of more stories to
submit to *Weird Tales*.[10]

He had hoped to finish the article within a few weeks, but it did not achieve final form until May of the following year. Nevertheless Lovecraft began to regain his self-confidence as a writer, and he eventually did follow his plan to compose new stories, although that did not effectively occur until he left New York.

By March 1926, Lovecraft had completed work on Chapter

VII, the chapter on Poe. Within the month he completed "Cool Air," the first story to be produced following the reading needed to write *Supernatural Horror in Literature*. "Cool Air" was obviously influenced by Poe's writing, especially "The Facts in the Case of M. Valdemar" which Lovecraft considered second only to "The Fall of the House of Usher." It was the first of a large group of stories to focus on what Lovecraft called "Tales of dream-life, strange shadow and cosmic 'outsideness,' notwithstanding sceptical rationalism of outlook and keen regard for the sciences."[11] The scope of Lovecraft's work, defined formally in 1928, was a direct outgrowth of his work on *Supernatural Horror in Literature*, for that essay was not merely an "article of the element of terror and weirdness in literature." While it was being researched and drafted, it was a welcome diversion—a kind of therapy—that helped Lovecraft forget his surroundings. It became a codification of what Lovecraft thought to be essential to a good weird story as observed in the writings of the masters in the genre and a collection of standards that he himself then sought to match.

"Cool Air," the last story Lovecraft wrote in New York, was written about one month before he left for Providence. It was partially inspired by the brownstone apartment in which Lovecraft lived on Clinton Street. "Cool Air" is about the unsettling juxtaposition of opposites—coolness amidst sweltering heat, refinement amidst squalor, death amidst life, and horror amidst the commonplace—and about emotions more likely to be experienced at night experienced in the middle of a sunlit day. The story is chillingly convincing, not only because it reflects Lovecraft's aversion to cold temperatures, but also because it described Lovecraft's situation. The contrast between the "rich and tasteful decoration" of Dr. Muñoz's apartment and the "nest of squalor and seediness" without could be seen in Lovecraft's own apartment. He had brought so many of his personal belongings with him to New York that "visitors not infrequently commented on the virtual transition from one world to another implied in the simple act of stepping within my door. Outside—Red Hook. Inside—Providence, R. I.!"[12] Like Dr. Muñoz, Lovecraft was merely an animated body: essentially a dead man who merely appeared to be alive.

Lovecraft's aunts eventually asked him to come back to Providence. When he received their initial request for a mere visit he was ecstatic:

> And now for your invitation. Hooray!! Long live the State of Rhode-Island & Providence-Plantations!!! But I'm past the visiting-point. Even if my physique is flourishing, my nerves are a mess—& I *could never board a train away from Providence toward New York again.* . . . I'm not eager for ignominious returns via the smaller orifice of the trumpet; but if you & AEPG think it's perfectly dignified for me to slip back toward civilisation & Waterman St., I'm sure I couldn't think of anything else for me who is an integral part of Rhode Island earth.[13]

On 17 April 1926, Lovecraft boarded the train and returned home.

He reveled in his homecoming. Cook did not exaggerate when he said Lovecraft "was so happy he hummed—if he had possessed the necessary apparatus he would have purred."[14] Consider Lovecraft's letter to Frank Belknap Long:

> And now Grandpa will tell you—all of you boys--about his return to normalcy and his awakening from the queer dream about being away from home. . . .
> Well--to begin with--back in the dream period Grandpa has some notion of having boarded a train somewhere. A blur of stations follow'd, and all at once there came a sight which presaged a return to the world of reality—an old-fashion'd wall of tumbled stone betwixt rolling meadows! Memory! Broken threads! . . . Who am I? What am I! Where am I? I—a corpse—once lived, and here are the signs of resurrection! The year? It must be 1923-24 . . . and the place. . . . look! . . . His Majesty's Province of Connecticut. . . . A sense of rushing through chartless corridors seized me, and I saw dates dancing in aether 1923—1924—1925—1926—1925—1924—1923—crash! Two years to the bad, but who the hell gives a damn? 1923 ends 1926 begins! . . . something snapped--and everything unreal fell away. There was no more excitement; no sense of strangeness, and no perception of the lapse of time since last I stood on that holy ground. . . . What I had seen in sleep every night since I left it, now stood before me in prosaic reality. . . .
> Contented? Why, gentlemen, I am *home*![15]

The impression of not having really been away became, about nine years later, the cornerstone upon which Lovecraft built his masterpiece, "The Shadow out of Time." But his glorious homecoming found its way into a story much sooner. *The Case of Charles Dexter Ward* describes a homecoming to a sorely missed Providence which Lovecraft knew only too well:

> The young wanderer quietly . . . traversed the long miles to Providence by motor coach, eagerly drinking in the green rolling hills, the fragrant, blossoming orchards, and the white steepled towns of vernal Connecticut. . . . His heart beat with quickened force, and the entry to Providence along Reservoir and Elmwood Avenues was a breathless and wonderful thing despite the depths of forbidden lore into which he had delved. . . . His head swam curiously as the vehicle rolled down to the terminal behind the Biltmore, bringing into view the great dome and soft, roof-pierced greenery of the ancient hill across the river, and the tall colonial spire of the First Baptist Church limned pink in the magic evening light against the fresh springtime verdure of its precipitous background.
> Old Providence! . . . It was twilight, and Charles Dexter Ward had come home.[16]

Lovecraft's hatred of New York remained undiminished. On

hearing of the death of his elderly friend, Everett McNeil in December 1929, Lovecraft recounted in letters to friends his first visit to New York, and how McNeil had shown him Hell's Kitchen.[17] Within two weeks of sharing this recollection, Lovecraft wrote "The Pigeon-Flyers," originally entitled "Hells Kitchen," as part of *Fungi from Yuggoth*:

> They took me slumming where gaunt walls of brick
> Bulge outward with a viscous stored-up evil,
> And twisted faces, thronging foul and thick,
> Wink messages to alien god and devil.
> A million fires were blazing in the streets,
> And from flat roofs a furtive few would fly
> Bedraggled birds into the yawning sky
> While hidden drums droned on with measured beats.[18]

In the first year following Lovecraft's return, he wrote his largest output of fiction, including several major works. The stories of that period include "The Call of Cthulhu," "Pickman's Model," "The Silver Key," "The Strange High House in the Mist," *The Dream-Quest of Unknown Kadath*, *The Case of Charles Dexter Ward*, and his finest story, "The Colour out of Space." The last six of these were written in a six-month period, and it must be remembered that during that time Lovecraft was still working on *Supernatural Horror in Literature*!

The work on the article and the escape from New York had a remarkable effect on Lovecraft. With the restoration of his background, he was inspired to write again. The stories that poured forth from his pen are among the most personal that he produced. The main characters of Lovecraft's homecoming tales—Anthony Wilcox, Richard Pickman, Randolph Carter, Charles Dexter Ward—are all autobiographical characters. The familiar surroundings of Providence and the recent exposure to and study of the great writers of weird literature had opened the gateway to Lovecraft's imagination. Ideas that had been pent up or lain dormant in his commonplace book (some for as long as six years) now sought expression. Virtually every story from the one-year period following his homecoming contained at least one element derived from his commonplace book; most contain several such elements.

Unfortunately, few of those stories brought Lovecraft any satisfaction beyond the enjoyment of writing them. "The Call of Cthulhu" was rejected upon its first submission to *Weird Tales*. The two novels were never published in his lifetime—indeed, he never retyped them or even considered submitting them for publication. His personal favorite, "The Colour out of Space," earned him the insultingly small and belated payment of $25 for its appearance in *Amazing Stories*, and even though it was recognized in a best-of-the-year collection of stories, the story itself was not reprinted there.

In 1927, Lovecraft became inundated with revision work and as a result he wrote no major works until more than a year later when he wrote "The Dunwich Horror"; his fiction output declined thereafter. Excluding collaborations and ghost-writing, he wrote only seven stories in the next eight years. There were years when he wrote no stories at all. He was disappointed by the rejection of his most ambitious effort, *At the Mountains of Madness* (1931) and became dissatisfied with the stories he was producing.

Around 1933, Lovecraft seems to have embarked on a reading program not unlike the one he engaged in for the writing of *Supernatural Horror in Literature*. Among his surviving papers we find pieces entitled: "Suggestions for Writing Story," "Elements of a Weird Story," "Types of Weird Story," "A List of Certain Basic Underlying Horrors Effectively Used in Weird Fiction," "List of Primary Ideas Motivating Possible Weird Tales," and "Weird Story Plots" (the last of which remains unpublished). These items consist of brief summaries of plots and ideas used by other writers in their great works of weird fiction and the method by which Lovecraft wrote his own stories. Lovecraft seems to have prepared these items as aids in improving his writing.

Lovecraft longed to return to the kind of writing he produced very early in his career:

> The more I look over my old stuff the more disgusted I get with it—and with my efforts as a writer. Only once in a while do I approach what I am really trying to do. I need to make a clean break with whatever I have been doing, and start afresh after a rest. . . . I shall try to do with greater skill what I did crudely and half-accidentally around 1920 and 1921. My work of that period was . . . especially my own, because I had no idea of publication. . . . I am going to take my added technical knowledge and go back to 1921, emotionally speaking. It may be that I cannot regain the lost ground—that I am definitely written out—but the only way to find out is to try.[19]

After a couple of false starts, Lovecraft produced "The Shadow out of Time" in March 1935. The story exhibits the very return to his own ideas that he wished to achieve. Later that year he wrote "The Haunter of the Dark," a story that is on the surface about his young protege Robert Bloch, but which is actually more autobiographical. Robert Blake's return to Providence is described with the same fervor found in *The Case of Charles Dexter Ward*, particularly since the view from Blake's window is exactly the view seen from Lovecraft's room at his last residence. The two stories from 1935 indicate that Lovecraft was making the comeback that he sought. Unfortunately his health failed, and he died in 1937 without completing another story.

The eleven years that followed Lovecraft's brief residence in New York saw the creation of most of his major stories. It is difficult to say which were influenced by that period of time, for Lovecraft always drew upon his entire past as a source for his writings. But we can be certain that W. Paul Cook's suggestion that Lovecraft write a history of weird fiction helped Lovecraft weather his exile in New York and achieve a dramatic change in his writing, not only in style but also in the trend toward certain personal themes and attitudes that may not have come about had he not studied the major writers of weird fiction.

NOTES

[1] W. Paul Cook, "An Appreciation of H. P. Lovecraft," *Beyond the Wall of Sleep* (Sauk City, WI: Arkham House, 1943), p. 430.
[2] *Selected Letters* II (Arkham House, 1968), p. 80.
[3] *Selected Letters* I (Arkham House, 1965), p. 325.
[4] Ibid., p. 357.
[5] These final two stanzas do not appear in "Providence" as it appears in Lovecraft's *Collected Poems* (Arkham House, 1963).
[6] *Dagon and Other Macabre Tales* (Arkham House, 1965), pp. 230-31.
[7] Lovecraft to Lillian D. Clark, 11-14 November 1925, MS. John Hay Library.
[8] L. Sprague de Camp, *Lovecraft: A Biography* (Garden City, NY: Doubleday, 1975), pp. 245, 247.
[9] *Letters* II.36.
[10] Ibid., p. 37.
[11] *Uncollected Prose and Poetry*, edited by S. T. Joshi and Marc A. Michaud (West Warwick, RI: Necronomicon Press, 1978), p. 44.
[12] *Letters* II.115-16.
[13] Lovecraft to Lillian D. Clark, 29 March 1926, in *Lovecraft: A Biography*, p. 258.
[14] Cook, p. 431.
[15] *Letters* II.45-48.
[16] *At the Mountains of Madness and Other Novels* (Arkham House, 1964), pp. 155-56.
[17] See *Selected Letters* III (Arkham House, 1971), pp. 93-94 and 112-13.
[18] *Collected Poems* (Arkham House, 1963), pp. 115, 117.
[19] *Selected Letters* V (Arkham House, 1976), pp. 45-46.

E.R.B. and H.P.L.
William Fulwiler

For the most part, H. P. Lovecraft's literary influences have been easily identified. It is generally known that Lovecraft's fiction was influenced by the works of Edgar Allan Poe, Lord Dunsany, and Arthur Machen. However, one of Lovecraft's important literary influences has remained completely unrecognized: the works of Edgar Rice Burroughs.

That Lovecraft was familiar with the works of Edgar Rice Burroughs, there is no doubt. Almost all of Burroughs's fiction for the period 1912-1920 was published in *All-Story*. In a letter published in the March 7, 1914, issue of *All-Story*, Lovecraft stated that he had read every number of the magazine since its initial issue dated January 1905. There is every reason to believe he continued his interest into the 1920s.

In this same letter, Lovecraft contributed this evaluation of the recently discovered author: "At or near the head of your list of writers, Edgar Rice Burroughs undoubtedly stands. I have read very few recent novels wherein is displayed an equal ingenuity in plot, and verisimilitude in treatment."

Despite the fantastic nature of their themes--the creation of men from inorganic matter, the raising of a superman by apes, travel to Mars—Burroughs's novels are realistic in treatment. Lovecraft admired Burroughs's method, and in his own work showed a similar concern for the creation of a realistic atmosphere.

The Burroughs novels which had the most influence on Lovecraft's fiction are *At the Earth's Core* (1914) and *Pellucidar* (1915), both published in *All-Story*. These novels detail the adventures of David Innes and Abner Perry, who travel in the earth's interior in a mechanical mole and discover an inner world of eternal day, lighted by a sun at the center of the earth.

This inner world, Pellucidar, is populated by prehistoric creatures and Stone Age men. The dominant race of Pellucidar are the Mahar, winged web-footed reptiles, six to eight feet in height, descended from the rhamphorhynchus of the Mesozoic Era ("rham" spelled backwards is Mahr . . . add an "a" to spell Mahar.)

The Mahar, who live in great underground cities hewn from limestone, are an intelligent scholarly race, well advanced in "genetics and metaphysics, engineering and architecture."

They have made their lives more comfortable by making good use of the lower orders of life. They employ Sagoths, a race of gorilla-like men, as soldiers, to supply them with captives from among the human races of Pellucidar. These captives become servants and slaves, doing all of the manual labor. Escaped captives are tracked down by the "thipdar," giant pterodactyls, who serve as the "bloodhounds" of the Mahar.

Having neither voices nor ears, the Mahar do not communicate through speech. They "project their thoughts into the fourth dimension, where they become appreciable to the sixth sense of the listener." Since man cannot communicate in this manner, the Mahar have no way of knowing that men reason or communicate among themselves.

The Mahar regard man as man regards the lower orders, and they keep humans like cattle. They breed them carefully, fatten them, and eat them. Sometimes, in the course of their scientific researches, they vivisect them without the use of an anesthetic.

However, despite their ill treatment of man, the Mahar are not a villainous race. Abner Perry translates and studies Maharian writings during his captivity and concludes that they are a just race, and that their attitude toward man is understandable under the circumstances.

Later, David Innes is spared by the Mahar because of his kind treatment of a Mahar he once had in his power. Although he is repulsed by their appearance and their treatment of humans, Innes is forced to admit that "gratitude was a characteristic of the dominant race of Pellucidar."

H. P. Lovecraft was undoubtedly greatly impressed with Burroughs's depiction of the Mahar. The Pellucidar novels seem a likely source of inspiration of one of Lovecraft's favorite themes: that man was not the first intelligent ruler of this planet, and is not likely to retain his position of dominance in the future.

Lovecraft was a devotee of the horror tale, and he perceived that the idea most horrifying and unacceptable to man is the concept of his own insignificance. Thus, again and again in his tales, Lovecraft confronts his human characters with alien races more powerful and more intelligent than man, emphasizing the inferiority of the human race.

Lovecraft used the theme of an ancient prehuman race which will someday rise to conquer humanity in his first professional tale, "Dagon" (1917), written only three years after the publication of *At the Earth's Core*.

In this tale a sailor adrift in a lifeboat discovers a portion of ocean floor that has been recently raised to the surface through a volcanic upheaval. Exploring this newborn island, he discovers a body of water, on the opposite shore of which is an incredibly ancient carven obelisk. As he watches, a gigantic fishlike monster arises from the water, flings its scaly arms around the monolith, and gives vent to "certain measured sounds." The sailor escapes and the island sinks, but he dreams of the day when the fishlike monsters will rise to conquer mankind.

Lovecraft returned to the theme of an ancient prehuman race in "The Nameless City" (1921), a tale which seems to have been directly inspired by *At the Earth's Core*.

In the Arabian desert a student of the occult seeks and discovers an ancient city. He enters a temple and descends a steep passage into the earth for miles. Finally, he reaches a level passage lined with rows of mummified corpses of a strange prehuman reptile race.

From the frescos on the walls and ceilings he is able to reconstruct the history of the city. It was once a seacoast metropolis "that ruled the world before Africa rose out of the waves," but the sea receded, and the desert encroached on its fertile valley. Its inhabitants, the reptile race, were forced to chisel "through the rocks in some marvelous manner to another world whereof their prophets had told them."

Near the end of the passage are painted scenes of the world under the earth, paradisiacal scenes "almost too extravagant to be believed, portraying a hidden world of eternal day filled with glorious cities and ethereal hills and valleys."

At the end of the passage is a door opening into a great abyss, "an illimitable void of uniform radiance, such as one might fancy when gazing down from the peak of Mount Everest upon a sea of sunlit mist." From the passage into the abyss a steep flight of steps leads downwards.

As he ponders whether or not to descend into the abyss, he hears a sound behind him, a deep, low moaning, and is struck by the night-wind gushing from the city above. He tries to retreat up the tunnel, but the howling wind strikes with terrible force, pushing him toward the abyss. Turning, he sees outlined against the light of the abyss the half-transparent wind-wraiths of "the crawling reptiles of the nameless city."

There is a striking similarity of several elements of this tale to several elements in *At the Earth's Core*: the reptile race, the tunnel to the interior of the earth, and the "hidden world of eternal day" at the earth's core.

In 1926, with "The Call of Cthulhu," Lovecraft introduced a modification of this theme of ancient prehuman races by revealing that these races were of extraterrestrial origin. According to the mythology Lovecraft presented in this tale and in tales that followed, the earth was colonized in ancient times by several different extraterrestrial races, known generically as the "Old Ones." The Old Ones lie dreaming in their buried cities beneath the earth and under the sea, but one day, when the stars are right, they will rise to claim the earth.

"The Call of Cthulhu" was followed by five other tales of the Old Ones: "The Colour out of Space" (1927), "The Whisperer in Darkness" (1930), "The Shadow over Innsmouth" (1931), *At the Mountains of Madness* (1931), and "The Shadow out of Time" (1934). Only one of these tales, *At the Mountains of Madness*, shows definite traces of Burroughs's influence.

At the Mountains of Madness was inspired by the Byrd expedition's recent discovery of fossils in Antarctica which indicated a tropical past. Modeled after "The Nameless City," it is the tale of the discovery of an ancient city in the Antarctic wasteland.

Using a radically new drilling apparatus, an Antarctic expedition uncovers a limestone cavern filled with plant and animal fossils from several geologic eras. Among their finds are the bodies of fourteen star-headed, web-footed, barrel-shaped creatures, not fossilized, yet somehow preserved.

Six of the bodies are badly damaged but eight are in perfect condition. They are taken to one of the expedition's encampments, where a biologist proceeds to vivisect one of the damaged creatures. Meanwhile, the heat of the sun revives the eight undamaged creatures, who come upon the biologist and, scientific race that they are, having never encountered such a creature before, they proceed to vivisect him!

The next day members of a neighboring camp try to contact the biologist's camp by radio, and failing to establish contact they investigate in person. They find the camp in shambles, and all of the men and sled dogs horribly butchered. A sprinkling of salt in the neighborhood of the corpses suggests the provisionment of a supply of salted meat.

Six of the star-headed creatures have been curiously buried. The other eight are missing, as are a number of sledges.

The following morning two members of the expedition explore a mountain range by air and discover a gigantic hidden city on a plateau twenty thousand feet high. The scientists land and enter the city. Mural carvings cover the inner walls of every dwelling, and by studying them the two explorers are able to reconstruct the history of the incredibly ancient race of star-headed Old Ones.

The star-headed Old Ones used their ether-resistant wings to fly through the interstellar void to our lifeless planet, where they built many cities, both on land and under the sea. They created earth life under the sea, for food for the production of shoggoths.

The shoggoths, mindless blobs of protoplasm, were the slaves of the Old Ones. At times they were difficult to control, and on one occasion they revolted against their masters, killing many of the Old Ones by decapitation before order was restored.

In addition to the shoggoths, the Old Ones made good use of other lifeforms. These lifeforms developed through the unguided evolution of the life cells the Old Ones had introduced under the sea. One of these accidental creatures of the Old Ones, depicted in some of the more recent mural carvings, was "a shambling primitive animal, used sometimes for food and sometimes as an amusing buffoon . . . whose vaguely simian and human foreshadowings were unmistakable." The Old Ones also employed the services of gigantic pterodactyls, who lifted huge stone blocks for the building of high towers.

With the coming of the Ice Age, the Old Ones deserted their land cities and retreated to their cities beneath the sea. The Old Ones of this Antarctic city built a city in a hidden subterranean sea, a sea accessible to the surface city by a network of limestone caverns. The Old Ones improved on these natural tunnels, and for a time they continued to use the surface city for summer residence. Finally the advancing ice forced them to totally abandon the surface city.

While exploring the underground tunnels of the city, the two scientists come upon the decapitated remains of four of the eight revived Old Ones, murdered by a shoggoth. The men react sympathetically:

> Scientists to the last—what had they done that we would not have done in their place? God, what intelligence and persistence! What a facing of the incredible, just as those carven kinsmen and forbears had faced things only a little

less incredible! Radiates, vegetables, monstrosities, star-spawn--whatever they had been, they were men!

The similarity of *At the Mountains of Madness* to *At the Earth's Core* is obvious.

Consider the similarity of Burroughs's Mahar to Lovecraft's Old Ones, both of whom are presented sympathetically despite their ill-treatment of man: both are winged, web-footed, dominant races; both are scientific scholarly races with a talent for genetics, engineering, and architecture; and both races use men as cattle.

In addition, there are several other elements common to both novels which seem too numerous to be attributed to coincidence: the radically new drilling apparatus, the vivisection of humans, the Sagoths/shoggoths, the pterodactyls, and the limestone caverns.

Some may disagree, but the evidence convinces me that in writing "The Nameless City" and *At the Mountains of Madness* Lovecraft was directly influenced by Burroughs's Pellucidar novels. Moreover, I suspect that the Pellucidar novels inspired not only these tales but *all* of Lovecraft's tales which share the theme that man was not the first intelligent ruler of this planet and won't be the last.

The Pellucidar novels are not the only possible source of Burroughs's influence on Lovecraft. One must also consider the Mars novels.

In 1919 Lovecraft created a fictional alter ego, Randolph Carter, to represent himself in "The Statement of Randolph Carter," a tale based on one of his dreams. The fact that Lovecraft had read Burroughs's first three Mars novels may have influenced his choice of "Carter" as his character's surname.

In the novel *The Dream-Quest of Unknown Kadath* (1926), Randolph Carter has a number of strange and terrifying adventures in the dreamland of earth, a land reached through slumber. This is not a science fiction tale, but a fantasy tale in the tradition of Lord Dunsany.

In "The Silver Key" (1926), Randolph Carter finds that at the age of thirty he has gained an unhealthy respect for reality, such as is shared by most people, and thus he can no longer enter earth's dreamland. Finally, after years of searching, he finds the silver key, the key to the gate of dreams left to him by his ancestors. He uses it to double back in time, entering the mind of himself at age nine.

The younger Randolph Carter then enters the "snake-den," a strange cave used by his ancestors for sorcerous purposes. He approaches the farther wall of the cave holding the key before him. When the boy returns home that night, the soul of the older Randolph Carter has left him, seeking other realms.

One wonders if in writing this tale Lovecraft was thinking of John Carter and the strange transformation he underwent in a cave prior to his transportation to Mars.

Even the Tarzan novels must be considered as a possible source of Burroughs's influence on Lovecraft. In Lovecraft's "Arthur Jermyn" (1920), a young English nobleman discovers that his great-great-great-grandmother was part ape. She was one of a hybrid race resulting from the matings of apes with the inhabitants of an ancient African city, the last surviving city of a prehistoric white civilization. This tale may have been inspired by *The Return of Tarzan* (1913) or *Tarzan and the Jewels of Opar* (1917), in which Tarzan visits the city of Opar. Opar is the last surviving outpost of lost Atlantis, peopled by a hybrid race resulting from the matings of men with apes.

In conclusion, it seems to me that the clues suggesting Burroughs's influence on Lovecraft are many and varied. Perhaps the reason they have never, to my knowledge, been noticed before is that Burroughs wrote science fiction *adventure* tales, whereas Lovecraft wrote science fiction *horror* tales. It would not occur to most people, I think, to associate one genre with the other.

Randolph Carter, Warlord of Mars
Robert M. Price

In his ground-breaking essay "E. R. B. and H. P. L.," William Fulwiler demonstrated beyond reasonable doubt that H. P. Lovecraft had been significantly influenced by his early reading of the novels of Edgar Rice Burroughs in their initial appearance in *All-Story* magazine. Indeed, at the time, HPL had written to the magazine praising the fiction of Burroughs: "At or near the head of your list of writers, Edgar Rice Burroughs undoubtedly stands. I have read very few recent novels wherein is displayed an equal ingenuity in plot, and verisimilitude in treatment" [quoted in Fulwiler, "E. R. B. and H. P. L.," *Crypt of Cthulhu*, Vol. 8, No. 7, Lammas 1989, page 28]. Specifically, Fulwiler suggests connections between Burroughs's first two Pellucidar novels and Lovecraft's *At the Mountains of Madness* and "The Nameless City." In fact the similarity of conception in detail between the latter and its Burroughsian prototype leads one almost to consider "The Nameless City" a Lovecraftian adjunct to the Pellucidar canon. Fulwiler also notes intriguing similarities between *Tarzan and the Jewels of Opar* and "Arthur Jermyn." He notes that there may even be a minor link between Lovecraft's dreamer Randolph Carter and Burroughs's interplanetary adventurer John Carter. When Randolph (in "The Silver Key") enters the "snake den," a cave containing a mystic portal to the past, do we find an echo of John's departure for Barsoom from a desert cave in Arizona? More than likely we do. In the present article, I mean merely to append a few notes to Fulwiler's illuminating investigation. I believe we can find yet a few more instances of Burroughsian influence on Lovecraft, specifically, between the Mars books and four quite varied Lovecraft works.

To begin where Fulwiler left off, I believe that we can spot an even more important influence of the Mars novels on Lovecraft's adventures of Randolph Carter. Ever since reading *The Dream-Quest of Unknown Kadath*, I have been struck by the Burroughsian nature of the whole thing in broad outline. In fact, reading Fulwiler's article some seven years later served as a kind of corroboration of my early suspicions. In Lovecraft's novella, the traditional Dunsanianism of his Dreamlands fantasies serves only as background, mere landscape. The action and plot are essentially Burroughs. In this book, what is Randolph Carter but an otherworldly interloper who arrives on the scene in an extramundane world not as a cowed outsider, but rather as a bold adventurer who loses no time in establishing himself at the head of a force of strange alien races whom he enlists in a crusade against evil forces threatening his own happiness. Of course, Lovecraft's bachelor protagonist has no interest in any Dreamland Dejah Thoris, being enamored instead, as we might suspect, with a scene of a sunset terrace city aglow with antiquarian wonder.

Do not Lovecraft's fighting ghouls correspond quite nicely to the Tharks of Barsoom, the canine Richard Pickman to Tars Tarkas? *Dream-Quest*'s Pickman surely bears little resemblance to the character of the same name we met in "Pickman's Model," though he is ostensibly the same person. The ghouls fight shoulder to shoulder with their earthly warlord against a villainous race of pirates who fly between the Dream-earth and the moon in aerial ships. Here are Lovecraft's analogues to Burroughs's race of airborne pirates, the Firstborn. We find that the Firstborn are only reputed to live on the moon, whereas Lovecraft's Moonbeasts actually do, but this variation only strengthens the connection! Lovecraft simply decided to go Burroughs one better. Burroughs's Firstborn actually lived in an underground world, sort of a Martian Pellucidar, called Omean. (That this feature of *The Gods of Mars* fired Lovecraft's imagination we will shortly see.)

Burroughs describes the Firstborn as having jet-black skin, yet with Caucasian features. Is not Nyarlathotep described in the *Dream-Quest* in precisely the same terms?

Some have criticized Burroughs for never precisely explaining (because he had presumably never figured it out himself!) how John Carter could leave his physical body inert upon earth and appear on Mars not as a drifting spectre, but rather as a flesh and blood man. Whence the new body? I wonder if HPL made explicit in the case of his Carter what he inferred was the case with ERB's Carter: he had left his fleshly form inert *in sleep* and reached another world *in his dreams*, in which his good right arm seemed solid enough!

The underground world of Omean is entered through a hollow mountain at the Martian South Pole. John Carter describes his first sight of this mountain: "I discerned over our starboard bow what appeared to be a black mountain rising from the desolate waste of ice. It was not high and seemed to have a flat top" (*The Gods of Mars*, Ballantine edition, page 76). Later he describes "its conelike summit" (page 168). It is not hard to see, or rather I think it hard *not* to see, some echoes of these scenes from Burroughs in Lovecraft's sonnet "Antarktos" (XV of *Fungi from Yuggoth*):

> Deep in my dream the great bird whispered queerly
> Of the black cone amid the polar waste;
> Pushing above the ice-sheet lone and drearly,
> By storm-crazed aeons battered and defaced.
> . . .
> If men should glimpse it, they would merely wonder
> What tricky mound of Nature's build they spied;
> But the bird told of vaster parts, that under
> The mile-deep ice-shroud crouch and brood and hide.
> God help the dreamer whose mad visions show
> Those dead eyes set in crystal gulfs below!

Here not only are the South Polar "waste" and the "black" "cone" mountain, but the cone turns out to be a secret gateway to a subterranean realm!

Omean is lit by phosphorescence, not by an inner sun like Pellucidar. Cavern worlds were beloved by HPL, and in "The Mound" he supplies no less than three of them. They are lit by eerily colored phosphorescence as well. I have to wonder if N'kai, Yoth, etc., were not suggested to HPL by Burroughs's Omean.

Speaking of strange colors, we read in *The Gods of Mars* of the ultratelluric hues of Barsoomian gems: "where are the words to describe the glorious colours that are unknown to earthly eyes? where the mind or the imagination that can grasp the gorgeous scintillations of unheard-of rays as they emanate from the thousand nameless jewels of Barsoom?" (page 82). Do we meet here the first inspiration of that "colour" that "was almost impossible to describe," that might "only by analogy" be called a colour at all ("The Colour out of Space")?

Admittedly, some of these Burroughs/Lovecraft parallels are fairly minor, perhaps others not so minor, but when added to those more significant instances adduced by Fulwiler, they must raise the question as to why Lovecraft scholars have been slow to recognize Burroughs's influence on Lovecraft. I think the answer is readily apparent. As is well known, in his "Notes on Writing Interplanetary Fiction" Lovecraft later poured scorn on the sort of space-opera science fiction that centered on human heroes and described alien worlds as closely analogous to our own. Earthmen with green skin are still earthmen. To make an unearthly setting worth using, HPL said, one should create a sense of utter alienage, something wholly other, absolutely strange to human experience. The sheer atmosphere of strangeness should be so overwhelmingly potent that no character-centered plot need come into it. Most likely in all this HPL was aiming his ray-guns at Edmond Hamilton, whose work he considered puerile trash. But implicit in his discussion is a repudiation of his earlier praise of Burroughs. Indeed, one cannot help but notice that there is almost a smooth and seamless transition between John Carter's battles with American Indians at the beginning of *A Princess of Mars* and his battles with the Tharks on Barsoom a little later. It almost seems as if John Carter simply fell asleep in that cave, and in his dream the Indians were transmogrified into both the sadistic Tharks on the one hand (both Apache and Thark sadism are described) and the comely red Martians of Helium on the other, much as the three farmhands and Professor Marvel are transformed in Dorothy's dream into the Lion, the Scarecrow, the Tin Man, and the Wizard in *The Wizard of Oz*! All that is really involved is a change of names and locales, and HPL considered this a cheat.

I think that recent Lovecraft scholars, so devoted to the aesthetic canons of HPL, and thus sharing his later antipathy for Burroughs-type science fiction, simply would have been too embarrassed to admit that not only had Lovecraft once enjoyed Burroughs (i.e., before he was old enough to know any better), but that Burroughs remained an important influence on his fiction. Such scholars found it more comfortable to trace the undeniable influence on HPL of Blackwood, Poe, Machen and Dunsany, writers he continued to admire. These writers fit into the mature Lovecraft's aesthetic orthodoxy, whereas Burroughs no longer did. But ERB deserves due recognition. It is to William Fulwiler's credit that he brought the fact to our attention.

The Pseudo-Intellectual in Weird Fiction
Robert M. Price

In his *Supernatural Horror in Literature*, Lovecraft gave a thumbnail sketch of the "typical protagonist" in the tales of Edgar Allan Poe. Poe's hero "is generally a dark, handsome, proud, melancholy, intellectual, highly sensitive, capricious, introspective, isolated, and sometimes slightly mad gentleman of ancient family and opulent circumstances; usually deeply learned in strange lore, darkly ambitious of penetrating to forbidden secrets of the universe" (page 59). Needless to say, Lovecraft appropriated the same model for many of his own doomed heroes. Some have suggested, with apparent justification, that HPL even adopted this persona as his own personal role model. In any case, we would like to develop the possibility that the qualities listed by Lovecraft have often combined in weird fiction, his own and others', to form the picture of what we would nowadays call the "pseudo-intellectual."

The general outlines of the pseudo-intellectual are supplied by L. Sprague de Camp in his controversial biography of Lovecraft. Without venturing to comment upon the applicability of this portrait to Lovecraft himself, we reproduce de Camp's description as our working paradigm.

> Although erudite, [the pseudo-intellectual is] wont to pontificate on subjects of which he ha[s] the merest literary smattering, without the correctives of firsthand knowledge or worldly experience. [There is] instilled in him "that haste to form judgments and that lack of critical sense in testing them, which are often the result of self-education conducted by immense and unsystematic reading" (page 103).

If weird fiction makes extensive use of characters matching this description, we may suggest three principal reasons for it.

First, weird fiction may feature pseudo-intellectuals prominently though unwittingly, because it is written by them. Let us recall de Camp's mention of a broad but shallow and lopsided program of self-education. We may think of the limited educational opportunities available to Robert E. Howard. His minor tale "The Children of the Night" is memorable, if at all, for its repulsive racist fanaticism. (Get a load of this: "And my ancestors . . . destroyed the scum that writhed beneath our heels, so shall I . . . exterminate the reptilian thing, the monster bred of the snaky taint that slumbered so long unguessed in clean Saxon veins.") This story opens amid a stifling exchange of pontifications among a clique of stuffed-shirts and dilettantes. Wearying speeches about the skull-types of Aryan and other races are fired back and forth. There is little doubt that Howard, like Lovecraft, personally embraced such propaganda-masquerading-as-anthropology (for the roots of which, see Poliakov, *The Aryan Myth*).

Or take Colin Wilson's *The Philosopher's Stone*, where the main character champions such offbeat hobbyhorses as "vitalist" (or "teleological") evolutionism and the Baconian authorship of Shakepeare's plays. Wilson has often been vilified up and down for his wide-but-weird self-education and the skewed perspectives issuing from it. As Clifford Bendeau (*Colin Wilson: The Outsider and Beyond*) has contended, most of this criticism stems merely from critics' irritability and ruffled sensibilities, but such criticisms are at least occasioned by these eccentric pet-theories.

Second, we must ask if pseudo-intellectuals do not infest the pages of weird fiction so as to cater to its "fans," many of whom may never have passed intellectual adolescence. ("Physician heal thyself," you say? *Touche*.) On a fairly superficial level, this is almost certainly true. For example, returning to Howard's "The Children of the Night," the narrator describes the setting as a "bizarrely fashioned study, with its queer relics from all over the world and its long rows of books. . . ." These "shelves throng with delightful nightmares of every variety." Specifically, "you'll find there a number of delectable dishes—Machen, Poe, Blackwood, Maturin—look, there's a rare feast—*Horrid Mysteries*, by the Marquis of Grosse—the real Eighteenth Century edition." This kind of literary name-dropping and collecting-mania is of course a hobby passionately enjoyed by most of our readers, as well as the present writer. And whether we have derived this predilection from weird fiction, or whether the influence runs the other way, is a moot point. It is, safe to say, one of those famous chicken-and-egg problems.

But on a more serious level, we may suspect that writers in the macabre tradition are playing up to the delusions of certain immature cranks among their audience. For instance, in Frank Belknap Long's story "The Hounds of Tindalos," the main character Chalmers facilely dismisses Darwin and Bertrand Russell in favor of medieval alchemy. The narrator chides him: "'You have always scoffed at modern science,' I said, a little impatiently." No doubt the eccentric Chalmers has felt the sting of such skepticism before, but this time he will be vindicated. And of course, by the end of the story, he wishes he *hadn't* been! At any rate, we hear here the chorus of celluloid mad-scientists intoning, "The blind fools! I'll show them *all!*" No doubt many readers vicariously relish the same vindication in the face of parents and junior-high teachers who are blind to their tightly-clutched truths of UFOs and lost continents.

Our third reason is by no means exclusive of the second, though it probably does exclude the first. Pseudo-intellectuals loom large in weird fiction because their beliefs are often presupposed in the structure of the stories. We refer to what might be called the "crackpot cosmology," including magic, miracles, and sunken continents like Atlantis, Lemuria, Mu, Hyperborea (and New Jersey? Well, one can only wish. . . .). For instance, in August Derleth's *The Lurker at the Threshold*, Dr. Seneca Lapham expresses his credence in "a very large, though usually suppressed, body of occurrences antipodally contradictory to the total scientific knowledge of mankind . . . some of which have been collected and chronicled in two remarkable books by . . . Charles Fort—*The Book of the Damned* and *New Lands*—I commend them to your attention."

While the use of racist anthropology by Howard and Lovecraft reflected their own erroneous beliefs, the presence of these other, equally baseless, notions serves quite a different function. Quack beliefs are handy symbols for that awful cosmic otherness and threatening meaninglessness that Lovecraft deemed the true horror. He himself scorned supernaturalism and occultism and wisely noted that of all people, materialists and skeptics were best suited to write weird fiction. Who would feel more horror if the trusted laws of nature were suddenly to bend and break? Not the believer in the occult! If Nyarlathotep should peer into his window, so what? Last week it was Godzilla.

So the chill of supernatural horror written by naturalists lies in how chagrined, nay terrified, they would be if the cranks and pseudo-intellectuals turned out to be right after all! A good example of this concerns a classic pseudo-intellectual jerk to whom deceptively sidelong reference is made in "Pickman's Model": "Reid, you know, had just taken up comparative pathology, and was full of pompous 'inside stuff' about the biological or evolutionary significance of this or that mental or physical symptom. He said Pickman repelled him more and more every day, and almost frightened him toward the last—that the fellow's features and expression were slowly developing in a way . . . that wasn't human." But it is this smartass dilettante who turns out to have been closest to the devolutionary truth—Pickman was in fact a "ghoul-changeling" who had begun to revert to type.

In conclusion, we have considered the possibility that weird fiction often features pseudo-intellectual characters because the writers themselves sometimes fall into this category (at least relative to this or that given issue). We also suggested that the goal might be to cater to the adolescent cranks in the reading audience. Such readers could hold Lovecraft in one hand and Colonel Churchward in the other, imagining that the former vindicated a belief in the latter. But the last laugh is on such a reader; the apparent championing of eccentric beliefs in weird stories tends in exactly the opposite direction. The greatest astonishment, the wildest *fantasy* imaginable would be for such pseudo-intellectual clap-trap to be true!

August Derleth: Myth-Maker
Robert M. Price

Among the crimes with which Dirk W. Mosig has charged August Derleth, two stand out as of key importance. First, Derleth remolded Lovecraft's Mythos along the lines of the Judaeo-Christian story of Lucifer's rebellion against God. Only in Derleth's version, it has become Cthulhu and the Ancient Ones versus Nodens and the Elder Gods. The latter are even pictured, like God in Exodus, as pillars of fire. All this is not mere surmise on Mosig's part. Derleth himself spells it out,

> The Great Old ones . . . rebelled against the Elder Gods, and were thrust—like Satan—into outer darkness. . . . Its similarity to the Christian mythos . . . will be immediately apparent to the literate reader ("A Note on the Cthulhu Mythos"). I was indeed familiar with the Cthulhu Mythos, with its remarkable lore in essence so similar to the Christian Mythos of the expulsion of Sathanus and his followers and their ever-ceaseless attempts to reconquer heaven ("The Black Island"). This lore . . . was in fact, a distortion of ancient Christian legend ("The House in the Valley").

The second offense with which Derleth is charged is that of domesticating HPL's transcendent Old Ones as mere "elemental forces." And, no question about it, Derleth is guilty of this one, too. He speaks of "Great Old Ones akin to the elemental forces" ("The Watcher from the Sky"), of "certain elemental Ancient Ones" ("The House in the Valley"), and "representations of elemental forces" ("The Seal of R'lyeh"). Derleth generally parceled the Old Ones out among the traditional categories of earth, air, fire, and water. Earth spirits included Yog-Sothoth, Nyarlathotep, Shub-Niggurath, and Tsathoggua. The water elemental was, of course, tentacled Cthulhu. The fire-spirit was Cthugha, Derleth's own invention. The "Lords of the Air" were Lloigor, Zhar, Hastur, and Ithaqua (this last sometimes identified with the legendary Wendigo, as in "The Thing That Walked on the Wind," but sometimes not, as in "The Seal of R'lyeh" and "Witches' Hollow"). Yet sometimes Derleth made Ithaqua alone the air-elemental, designating Hastur the scion of "interplanetary spaces," Shub-Niggurath of fertility, and Yog-Sothoth of "the time-space continuum." Derleth's own difficulties, let alone those pointed out by hostile critics, demonstrate the complete arbitrariness of the system thus imposed on Lovecraft's entities.

Most of Derleth's detractors, having reached this point, are content to dismiss both of Derleth's developments as sad corruptions, and then move on. And insofar as *Lovecraft's* Mythos is one's concern, this is entirely proper. But we are also curious about the meaning of *Derleth's* Mythos as he saw it. If we had to strip away Derleth's accretions to appreciate Lovecraft as a "myth-maker" (Dirk W. Mosig), perhaps we can now take a second look at the "Derleth Mythos" (Richard L. Tierney).

The key to Derleth's system is that the two aspects noted above (the biblicizing and the transformation into "elementals") are really one. The accurate understanding of the Derleth Mythos has been waylaid by Derleth's own partly misleading statement that the principal biblical parallel is to Satan's revolt. For Satan has little to do with elemental spirits. Another Old Testament demon, Baal, however, does. The mythic struggle reflected in Derleth's saga is not only that of Satan's storming heaven, but also the contest between Baal (or the Baals) and Yahweh (God). This was a battle fought through the agency of very real combatants over generations, as the Yahwists Jehu, Elijah, and Elisha contended with the prophets and patrons of Baal, e.g., Queen Jezebel. As described by G. Ernest Wright and other biblical scholars, the nature of the conflict was this: Canaanite polytheism centered about the worship of the seasonal fertility deities Baal, Astarte, etc., who embodied the forces of nature and agriculture. One must supplicate them with orgies and human sacrifices in hopes of having good crops this year. The view of life and history thus promoted was cyclical and static. On the one hand, Baal-worship produced immorality, and on the other an oppressive social status quo. The prophets of Yahweh, by contrast, preached a deity not of static nature, but of dynamic history, who demanded righteousness and promised liberation from oppression (e.g., in Egypt). The triumph of Yahweh-worship meant a new understanding whereby human beings must not worship nature, but rather, as God's servants, are responsible for "tending the garden." Under Yahweh-worship, humanity is served by nature, whereas under Baal-worship, it is the other way around. (See Wright, *The Old Testament Against Its Environment*; William Foxwell Albright, *Yahweh and the Gods of Canaan*.)

Derleth's identification of the Old Ones with the elements of nature implies that they are like Baal and Astarte, and that the struggle of humanity against them is like that of Elijah against the prophets of Baal. Humanity's task is to "fill the earth and subdue it" (Genesis 1:28) rather than worship it in fearful bondage. Even so, protagonists, like Dr. Laban Shrewsbury must fight to check Ithaqua and Cthulhu, to keep them in their place.

When he outlined the parallel he saw between the Cthulhu Mythos and the biblical one, Derleth usually discussed Satan's fall from heaven, but he does mention "Beelzebub" in the same breath with Cthulhu and company in "The Horror from the Middle Span." "Beelzebub" (= "Lord of the Flies") is a corruption of "Beelzebul" (= "Lord of the House"), but either would be a member of the Canaanite pantheon of "Baals" (= "Lords"). Seen in these terms, Derleth's alteration of Lovecraft's Mythos has its own unique logic. Whereas Lovecraft's picture was of the crushing threat of cosmic Powers indifferent to humanity, Derleth is depicting an intra-worldly struggle of humanity against the forces of nature. Derleth's is an ecological battle that humanity stands a chance of winning. The goal, of course, is not to vanquish nature with pollution, but rather to survive nature's onslaughts. As a naturalist himself, Derleth would have felt this struggle keenly, and he has mythologized it in his additions to the Cthulhu Mythos.

"Lovecraftianity" and the Pagan Revival
Robert M. Price

Today we are witnessing revivals of interest in both the fiction of H. P. Lovecraft and the pre-Christian "Pagan" nature religion. And quite often the same individuals are interested in both. Now well-balanced people are traditionally supposed to be able to juggle several disparate interests simultaneously. Yet perhaps there is some more-than-coincidental link between Lovecraft fandom and Neo-Paganism. Both certainly have in common a certain sense of the *outre* and the unconventional, but there may turn out to be a few even more specific points of contact that bear closer examination.

Lovecraft the Pagan

Margot Adler, author of *Drawing Down the Moon*, recounts a childhood experience which would one day come to fruition in her admission to a Pagan coven.

> At the age of twelve, a traditional time for rites of passage. . . . I remember entering into the Greek myths as if I had returned to my true homeland. . . . I wrote hymns to gods and goddesses and poured libations (of water) onto the grass of neighboring parks. In my deepest and most secret moments I daydreamed that I had become these beings, feeling what it would be like to be Artemis or Athena. I acted out the old myths and created new ones in fantasy and private play. . . . But like many other things it was not unique to me. I have since discovered that these experiences are common. (*Drawing Down the Moon*, pages 15-16.)

Adler was pleasantly surprised to find that others with such experiences had gotten together to revive the worship of the ancient and classical divinities. And readers of H. P. Lovecraft may be just as surprised to learn that as a boy Lovecraft had an experience strikingly parallel to Adler's. He described it in a letter to J. F. Morton in 1923:

> When about seven or eight I was a genuine pagan, so intoxicated with the beauty of Greece that I acquired a half-sincere belief in the old gods and nature spirits. I have in literal truth built altars to Pan, Apollo, and Athena, and have watched for dryads and satyrs in the woods and fields at dusk. Once I firmly thought I beheld some kind of sylvan creatures dancing under autumnal oaks; a kind of "religious experience" as true in its way as the subjective ecstasies of a Christian. If a Christian tells me he has *felt* the reality of his Jesus or Jahweh, I can reply that I have *seen* hoofed Pan and the sisters of the Hesperian Phaethusa. (Quoted in L. Sprague de Camp, *Lovecraft: A Biography*, page 19.)

Note that both Lovecraft and Adler had their experiences at a tender age, and that both even performed acts of worship to the

Greek gods. And Lovecraft even characterizes his youthful self by the same term used in the current "Pagan" revival.

HPL often used his own dreams in writing his weird fiction, and he could not resist using the visionary experience just described in the same way. The young dreamer and decadent Jervas Dudley, hero of "The Tomb," recounts an experience that is obviously modeled on that of his creator. "Well did I come to know the presiding dryads of those trees, and often have I watched their wild dances in the struggling beams of a waning moon." This quote, appearing as it does in Lovecraft's fiction, provides a clue as to the importance his pagan vision would have in his adult life.

As he matured, Lovecraft did not follow through on his pagan religiosity, though his love of classical literature and culture never left him. In fact, HPL repudiated all forms of religious belief. "I am an absolute materialist." He had been influenced much by the writings of atheists and skeptics including Thomas Henry Huxley and Bertrand Russell. But this did not mean Lovecraft's love of myth disappeared. The influence of classical mythology is clearly evident in stories like "Hypnos," "The Tree," and "The Temple." But Lovecraft is best known for creating his own distinctive body of mythology, the now famous "Cthulhu Mythos." George Wetzel (in his "Some Notes on the Cthulhu Mythos") has traced classical influence even here, though his argument is sometimes less than convincing. At any rate, we want to note at this point simply that, despite Lovecraft's rejection of religious faith, myth played if anything a larger role in his life than before, since his literary work was preoccupied with it.

Lovecraft and Witchcraft

So HPL did not embrace Paganism as many who have shared his childhood visions have done since. Of course, the organizations were harder to find, though he could have followed his literary hero Arthur Machen into the Order of the Golden Dawn. The Wicca movement was neither so widespread nor so visible as it has recently become. Yet, again, we find an odd sort of connection between Lovecraft and the sources of Neo-Pagan inspiration. Lovecraft read, used, and recommended Margaret A. Murray's volume *The Witch Cult in Western Europe*. Adler has made clear just how formative Murray's reconstruction of witch-history has been on the Neo-Pagan self-conception. While not denying the tenuousness of Murray's theories of a pre-Christian religion of the Goddess and the Horned God, today's Pagans have made Murray's theoretical witch-cult their own living faith. What did Lovecraft think of the book?

He had been intrigued by Arthur Machen's stories of "the Little People," a dwarflike aboriginal race that dwell in (or under) the Welsh hills, hiding from the Celtic inhabitants. Machen describes these natives as being possessed of eldritch lore and powers. Robert E. Howard, creator of the popular character Conan the Cimmerian, appropriated Machen's little people lock, stock, and barrel for such stories as "The Children of the Night" and "The People of the Dark." Lovecraft was a bit more imaginative in adapting them, but before his imagination went to work, he wanted to make sure of his facts. He did so in the pages of Murray's *Witch Cult*. In a letter to Howard in 1933, Lovecraft discussed "the survival of some pre-Aryan sorcerers who preserved primitive rites like those of the witch-cult—I had just been reading Miss Murray's *Witch-Cult in Western Europe*" (SL IV.297).

In "The Festival," we find a Yuletide celebration conducted in awesome silence by a hooded company, an ancestral cult sharing "rituals of mysteries that none living could understand." In fact, the celebrants turn out to be awful creatures evolved from the charnel worms that had devoured sorcerers long dead. Lovecraft acknowledged the influence of Murray's book, albeit indirectly, on the events of this tale. "The Horror at Red Hook" sticks a bit closer to Murray's theories, however. In the latter story, a police detective discovers an inner-city coven engaged in child sacrifice and other abominations. The story's hero is aghast at the blasphemous goings-on, but not exactly surprised.

> He had not read in vain such treatises as Miss Murray's *Witch Cult in Western Europe*; and knew that up to recent years there had certainly survived among peasants and furtive folk a frightful and clandestine system of assemblies and orgies descended from dark religions antedating the Aryan world, and appearing in popular legends as Black Masses and Witches' Sabbaths.

Obviously, Lovecraft has added to Murray's portrayal stories of atrocities derived from medieval inquisitors' manuals like the *Malleus Maleficarum* and Remy's *Daemonolatria*. But keep in mind, Lovecraft is writing horror fiction, and is not trying to promote or even describe real Paganism. All in all what seems to have fascinated him most was the idea that there might survive an ancient race with ancient rites and magic.

Lovecraftianity

Lovecraft was an atheist and took genuine religions about as seriously as his own fictional Cthulhu Mythos. This was a rudimentary system of lore concerning the "Great Old Ones," an ancient race of interdimensional aliens who had once ruled our earth, but who for some reason no longer do. Chief among these are Cthulhu, Nyarlathotep, and Yog-Sothoth. They strive ever to regain their dominion and to wipe the planet clean of human life. Certain perverted cultists (again derived, however obliquely, from Murray) seek to aid them in their bloodcurdling designs. Sometimes they nearly succeed, with the aid of a fabled grimoire called the *Necronomicon*.

HPL himself did *not* by any means believe in his fiendish creations. Yet even in his own day, he was beginning to see that other people very nearly *did*! He was amused that his eccentric acquaintance William Lumley believed Lovecraft to be the unwitting oracle of Cthulhu himself! And several readers wrote him asking if the (actually fictitious) *Necronomicon* might be reprinted. He assured them all it was only fiction.

Today's renewal of interest in Lovecraft attests to the continuing evocative power of HPL's mythic conceptions, though few if any fans mistake those myths for literal truth. No one is reading Lovecraft and becoming a real live Cthulhu cultist. But we do find a good deal of playful mock-religiosity among HPL's fans. They are not taken in by the claims of two or three books purporting actually to be the *Necronomicon*, but they cannot resist buying a copy to display on the shelf. They may spoof fundamentalist "I found it" campaigns by sporting buttons reading "Campus Crusade for Cthulhu --It Found Me" or "Yog-Sothoth Saves." A Lovecraft fan organization calls itself "The Esoteric Order of Dagon" after a secret cult in Lovecraft's "The Shadow over Innsmouth." The Necronomicon Press in Rhode Island has even published a leaflet entitled *An Introduction to Lovecraftianity*, satirizing evangelistic tracts. It encourages the reader to accept Lovecraft as his or her personal savior. "Thank you, Howard!" Hallelujah!

Now none of this is seriously meant, except in the sense that these Lovecraftians are serious about having fun. And they have it by embracing the symbols provided by Lovecraft. Readers of Adler's book may recall that something similar lies at the root of groups like the Discordians and the Church of All Worlds. The former is connected with Robert Anton Wilson's "Illuminati" books, while the latter stems from the fiction of Robert A. Heinlein. And in both cases, as Adler points out, it is difficult to draw any line between fun and faith. As is often the case in the Pagan movement, it would be hard to pin down anybody's actual *beliefs*. Members of these movements may well be agnostics intellectually, even atheists as Lovecraft was. Their deities and rituals are important for their archetypal, symbolic value.

It is tempting to wonder if in Lovecraft fandom we are not witnessing the formation of yet another playful religion, "Lovecraftianity," which may take its place alongside the rest of the larger Pagan Revival. What would Lovecraft have thought of the prospect? One suspects that, deep down, a youthful part of him wouldn't have minded.

[Since the original appearance of this essay, things seem to have evolved farther in a direction that HPL certainly *would* have minded. There is now apparently more than one Mythos cult in which the *Necronomicon*, perhaps one of its tentacle-in-cheek avatars, is solemnly cited as sacred writ, the Old Ones invoked as real deities. Lovecraft maintained that, to gain the proper verisimilitude, an author must lend his fiction all the energy one might expend upon an actual hoax. It appears that in this case he may have done his work a bit *too* well.]

Cosmic Fear and the Fear of the Lord: Lovecraft's Religious Vision
Robert M. Price

In my opinion the greatest and most penetrating exposition of Lovecraft's work is that of Fritz Leiber in a small series of essays including "A Literary Copernicus" and "Through Hyperspace with Brown Jenkin." Among the many excellent thoughts to be found in these essays is the pivotal insight that Lovecraft had furnished a new fulcrum on which to hoist the weight of literary horror. Though perhaps not quite the first to employ it, he was certainly the one to perfect the aesthetic of "cosmic horror" or "cosmic fear." That is, it was the universe and its vastness, indifferent and unfriendly toward man, that Lovecraft made into the chief horror. It was no longer the threat of an untimely death, not the possible visitation of vampires and spectres, nor even the destruction of the world, that was to provide the chillest shudders, but the destruction of the comfortably human-centered world*view* that had prevailed until the discoveries of Copernicus, Darwin and Freud. These thinkers had effectively dethroned *homo sapiens* from his imagined lordship over space and time. And this was a revelation *homo sapiens* by no means welcomed!

The now-famous epigram to "The Call of Cthulhu" predicted that if the revelations of modern science continued unabated in their tendency to minimize and marginalize human significance, reducing us to mere flotsam and jetsam in the vast scheme of things, then sooner or later, insecure humanity, its delusions of self-importance forever threatened, would surely take up again the self-blinded perspective of primitivism and superstition.

That the prospect of science's impact on the human self-estimate was a real and terrible threat, and no mere fancy of Lovecraft's, is clearly evident from the history of ecclesiastical opposition to science. What discoverer did the Church not attempt to silence at the stake or in the dungeon in order to preserve the illusion that God had created the tidy little universe as an ideal habitat for humanity, indeed that God spent his time occupied with little else than the bliss and advantage of humanity? The quixotic crusades of today's "scientific creationists" demonstrate that the "new dark age" is already well-advanced.

So for Lovecraft the element of cosmic fear was the distaste of facing the truth of a boundless universe in which humanity has but a minimal and insignificant temporary role. The universe itself becomes, as Maurice Levy correctly sees, a terrible abyss of potential horrors "too deep for any line to sound." The starry heaven has become hell, for its stars have turned out to be, not angels watching over man, but rather immense fire-balls burning for no one in particular to see, and ever threatening to extinguish us in an unfelt ecstasy of supernova.

Yet I am convinced that in this scenario we have but half the story. And the remainder of the tale is surprising indeed. As implied above, the cosmic vision Lovecraft espoused was perceived as a threat to conventional religion (though the degree to which even Victorian Evangelicalism rejected Darwinism has been much overestimated). It was certainly the anti-science obscurantism of many in the religious establishment that fueled the fires of Lovecraft's contempt for religion. Yet I am going to argue that Lovecraft's own experience of "cosmic fear" produced in him what we would readily recognize as an essentially religious and mystical worldview if we were not led off track by his various fulminations against traditional theism.

We must begin with a second look at his "cosmicism." Here is a typical statement on the matter.

> The true function of phantasy is to give the imagination a ground for limitless expansion, and to satisfy aesthetically the sincere and burning curiosity and sense of awe which a sensitive minority of mankind feel toward the alluring and provocative abysses of unplumbed space and unguessed entity which press in upon the known world from unknown infinities and in unknown relationships of time, space, matter, force, dimensionality, and consciousness. I *know* that my most poignant emotional experiences are those which concern the lure of unplumbed space, the terror of the encroaching outer void, and the struggle to transcend the known and established order" (from a letter to Clark Ashton Smith, October 17, 1930).

Anyone familiar with Rudolf Otto's classic treatment of religious phenomenology, *The Idea of the Holy*, will recognize in this passage a perfect example of the core religious experience, the numinous experience, the encounter with the Holy. Otto scrutinized the archives of visionary and worship experiences through history and across cultures and found that when one penetrated beneath differing dogmatic formulae and varying names for the Divine, one found a broad commonality of underlying pre-rational, pre-conceptual religious experience. It all proceeds from the encounter with the Wholly Other, the Infinite, the Eternal, the Absolute, and that encounter calls forth a double-edged reaction, both of holy terror and of enthralling fascination.

Otto spoke first of the encounter with the Holy perceived as the *Mysterium Tremendum*, the great Mystery at which we tremble. We shudder with consuming fear at that which is utterly alien, weird and uncanny, defying all worldly categories and inexpressible in worldly terms. The *Mysterium* is, as Otto put it, overpowering, full of awe, and full of being. Before it we feel we are the merest shadows. The fear we experience is not that of a concrete threat to life and safety, but rather that "oldest emotion of mankind," by Lovecraft's reckoning, spectral fear, fear of the great Unknown, now about to be terribly unveiled. We shrink before it in a kind of shame, yet it is not so much moral guilt we feel as *ontological* deficiency. We are nothing. Otto called it "creature feeling."

What Lovecraft derided and rejected religion for, ironically, was its humanistic hubris. A self-arrogating Church had set mankind in the center of the cosmic scheme, but if Otto is correct, as I believe he is, the essential religious experience is precisely that of the great ontological shock of apprehending the insignificance of man in the face of the infinity of "elder, outer entity." As the Psalmist put it, "When I consider the heavens, the work of thy hands, the moon and the stars which thou hast ordained, what is man that thou art mindful of him?" (Psalm 8:3-4). It is not ageless, dreaming Cthulhu, but Yahweh who is addressed this way: "A thousand years in thy sight are but as yesterday when it is past, or as a watch in the night. Thou dost sweep men away; they are like a dream" (Psalm 90:4-5). When still another Psalmist laments, "How they are destroyed in a moment, swept away utterly by terrors! They are like a dream when one awakes; on awaking, you despise their phantoms" (Psalm 73:19-20), we might first think we are hearing a Lovecraft protagonist bemoaning humanity's eventual fate at the hands of the blind forces of cosmic indifferentism! But it is the infinitude of God which serves nicely to annihilate man's smug pretensions.

At the same time man experiences the siren-call of the Holy perceived as the *Mysterium Fascinans*, that Mystery which enthralls even as it repels. How can it do both? Simply because what we cringe from is exactly what promises us fulfillment: we are pathetically finite. The Holy is gloriously and bogglingly infinite. Its uncanny Otherness frightens, yet its Otherness is what we know we require, what would fill up that ontological deficiency which makes us cringe!

And Lovecraft's words ring loudly with the magnetic fascination exerted by that very same universe which, as an immeasurable abyss, thwarts and dwarfs us! It is equally clear that the cosmic revelation so unwelcome to "self-blinded earth-gazers" is the very fulfillment (albeit imaginary for the purposes of fiction) that would satisfy that burning curiosity of the "sensitive minority." Lovecraft's fascination with cosmic fear was an experience of the central religious awareness.

But, the reader may object, the fact remains that Lovecraft, consistently or inconsistently, did not go on to conclude that God exists. But this objection misses the point. As Otto indicates, the parallels between various Eastern and Western religions make clear that personalistic theism is but one possible theoretical model with which some traditions have thought to articulate the experience of the Holy. It is by no means a necessary one, or one demanded by the numinous experience itself. The Buddhist *Sunyata*, the Vedanta Hindu *Nirguna Brahman*, are by no means personal Gods, but they articulate the same set of experiences. It is a commonplace among scholars of comparative religion that religion need not imply theism. I am arguing not that Lovecraft was a theist (of course he was not), but rather that he was religious in vision and outlook, even though his own tendency to equate (to confuse?) religion with theism prevented him from using the term "religious" to describe himself.

But to recognize this is but the beginning. Another aspect of HPL's unnamed religiosity becomes manifest once we consider the work of another great comparative religions scholar, Mircea Eliade, the author of many fine works of which *The Sacred and the Profane* is exemplary. In this volume Eliade develops and documents the universal religio-cultural apprehension of "sacred time" and "sacred space." Eliade explained that, as perceived by universal religious instinct (and most clearly visible to us in primitive societies and archaic religious practices), there are two kinds of time. Profane, or ordinary, time runs on drearily like Old Man River, with neither end nor goal in view. In the stream of profane time one can do naught but mark time. But profane time is given meaning by the periodic inbreaking of sacred time. This latter is not linear but cyclical. It is the primordial time of creation, when all things received their due allotment of reality. But as the year goes on, all things grow old and wear down. Thus there is a need for rejuvenation. Every new year, it was believed, the sacred time of origins spirals back and intersects the line of profane time, imparting a new dose of reality to the world.

Of course the origin of this whole schema is the cycle of the seasons, but it came to color all aspects of ancient life. Whenever one sought medical care, the shaman would chant of the sacred time of creation, so as to invoke it anew in a special case. If you sewed up the holes in your fish net or mended your axe, you hummed the song about when the ancestors or culture heroes taught these arts, so as to reinvoke their creative power and make the repair successful. Sacred time, then, is an imagined ancient time of greater reality and can intrude into our own profane time to lend it a greater semblance of eternal reality.

Similarly, says Eliade, human beings experience both sacred space and profane space. Sacred space is a higher, primordial, and invisible realm. It is the source of reality, itself realer than the shadowy world of mundane, ordinary, profane space in which we live. Profane space would be utterly undistinguished but for its sporadic penetration by sacred space. Where such epiphanies of the sacred have occurred the mythical imagination has erected "*axes mundi*," vertical links connecting heaven and earth (Mount Olympus, Jacob's Ladder, Yggdrasil, Sentinel Hill). These are places where some of the holiness/reality of sacred space has blazed forth to suffuse just a bit of profane space, lending it a derived holiness, as when Moses is told he has chanced upon holy ground, hence he must take off his sandals and leave them; having touched sacred space they have themselves become holy relics.

These are the places where temples are sooner or later built, where oracles set up shop, where one can catch a glimpse of the Other Reality already here on the hither shore. Their presence lends meaning to the surrounding waste of profane space. The holy sites become the coordinates of the culture's map of reality, centers of government and pilgrimage.

Though one can find traces of it elsewhere, e.g., the final revelatory speech of Nyarlathotep in *The Dream-Quest of Unknown Kadath*, I believe it is in the sonnet-cycle *Fungi from Yuggoth* that we find a rich deposit of what I would call Lovecraft's mysticism of place and past.

The winter sunset, flaming beyond spires
And chimneys half-detached from this dull sphere,
Open great gates to some forgotten year
Of elder splendours and divine desires.
Expectant wonders burn in those rich fires,
Adventure-fraught, and not untinged with fear;
A row of sphinxes where the way leads clear
Toward walls and turrets quivering to far lyres.

It is the land where beauty's meaning flowers;
Where every unplaced memory has a source;
Where the great river Time begins its course
Down the vast void in starlit streams of hours.
Dreams bring us close—but ancient lore repeats
That human tread has never soiled these streets.

              (XIII. "Hesperia")

It is a certain hour of twilight glooms,
Mostly in autumn, when the star-wind pours
Down hill-top streets, deserted out of doors,
But showing early lamplight from snug rooms.
The dead leaves rush in strange, fantastic twists,
And chimney-smoke whirls round with alien grace
Heeding geometries of outer space,
While Fomalhaut peers in through southward mists.

This is the hour when moonstruck poets know
What fungi sprout on Yuggoth, and what scents
And tints fill Nithon's continents,
Such as in no poor earthly garden blow.
Yet for each dream these winds to us convey,
A dozen more of ours they sweep away!

              (XIV. "Star-Winds")

I cannot tell why some things hold for me
A sense of unplumbed marvels to befall,
Or of a rift in the horizon's wall
Opening to worlds where only gods can be.
There is a breathless, vague expectancy,
As of vast, ancient pomps I half recall,
Or wild adventures, uncorporeal,
Ecstasy-fraught, and as a daydream free.

It is in sunsets and strange city spires,
Old villages and woods and misty downs,
South winds, the sea, low hills, and lighted towns,
Old gardens, half-heard songs, and the moon's fires.
But though its lure alone makes life worth living,
None gains or guesses what it hints at giving.

              (XXVIII, "Expectancy")

> I never can be tied to raw, new things,
> For I first saw the light in an old town,
> Where from my window huddled roofs sloped down
> To a quaint harbour rich with visionings.
> Streets with carved doorways where the sunset beams
> Flooded old fanlights and small window-panes,
> And Georgian Steeples topped with gilded vanes—
> These were the sights that shaped my childhood dreams.
>
> Such treasures, left from times of cautious leaven,
> Cannot but loose the hold of flimsier wraiths
> That flit with shifting ways and muddled faiths
> Across the changeless walls of earth and heaven.
> They cut the moment's thongs and leave me free
> To stand alone before eternity.
>
> (XXX. "Background")

> There is in certain ancient things a trace
> Of some dim essence—more than form or weight;
> A tenuous aether, indeterminate,
> Yet linked with all the laws of time and space.
> A faint, veiled sign of continuities
> That outward eyes can never quite descry;
> Of locked dimensions harbouring years gone by,
> And out of reach except for hidden keys.
>
> It moves me most when slanting sunbeams glow
> On old farm buildings set against a hill,
> And paint with life the shapes which linger still
> From centuries less a dream than this we know.
> In that strange light I feel I am not far
> From that fixt mass whose sides the ages are.
>
> (XXXVI. "Continuity")

Can any reader miss here the aching of the mystic for the Eternal, the Real, hidden in the twin realms of sacred space and primordial past, made known in will-o-the-wisp epiphanies in certain evocative seasons and surroundings? I say this is a religious mysticism, even if the word "religion" was rejected by Lovecraft because of past associations or too-narrow definitions. The mysticism of place and past we see in these poems certainly has little in common with "the correct doctrines of theology—preferably those of the Congregationalists" ("The Unnamable").

But Lovecraft's religious vision does indeed have more than a little in common with an entirely different religious tradition: that of Mahayana Buddhism. Here I am thinking primarily of his approach to ethics in a morally neutral universe. As is well known to Lovecraft scholars, HPL rejected the classical attempt to derive ethics from ontology or metaphysics. That is, he thought Plato and his followers in error when they argued that the very nature of reality implied a "right" way to behave, that in being a "good" person, one was acting in accord with the pattern of Being itself. Implicitly, Lovecraft also rejected any connection between aesthetics and ontology, since he chose to make ethics simply a branch of aesthetics, whereas classically philosophers had made both ethics and aesthetics twin branches of axiology (the question of value-judgments), itself derived from the ultimate order of Being. In short, as with modern Existentialists, Lovecraft believed that morality was a human projection onto a neutral universe, not a human discernment of a preexistent moral order inherent in the universe. Perhaps he derived this doctrine from the ancient Sophists contemporary with Socrates and Plato, for like the Sophists, Lovecraft believed that even though one had undermined moral norms by showing their relativity, one ought to abide by them nonetheless. The alternative is distasteful chaos. One ought to act the role of the Gentleman because things were more pleasant that way.

Though of course he derived none of this from Buddhism, the system of Lovecraft has a parallel in Buddhism. Nagarjuna, one of the greatest Mahayana mystics in the Madhyamika tradition, formulated a dialectic by which one might transcend the sterile alternatives of seeing the phenomenal world as truly real, and of seeing it as nothing but illusion (*maya*). Nagarjuna reasoned that if the phenomenal world were not ultimately real, one need not deny its penultimate reality. It might be naught but a thin film on top of a stream of water, but once one admitted how low a grade of reality it possessed, it was by no means to be despised. Thus a "healthy" view of everyday reality became possible for the world-denying mystic. His denial need not be absolute.

Ethics would fit in right at this point: ultimately the One is Void (*Sunyata*) of good/evil distinctions, but insofar as we are involved with the *pen*ultimate realm, the not-quite-real science of morality has its proper place. And ethics seem to occupy the same relative place in Lovecraft's ontology. There is no moral structure inherent in the nature of things. Morality has but the tenuous existence of a shared convention. It is a human projection onto life. Yet knowing that it is merely that does not invalidate it. I am not trying to paint HPL as a Buddhist, but rather to show that a moral outlook such as his is by no means incompatible with a religious sensitivity.

In the parlance of the Yogacara school of the Mahayana, all objects in the phenomenal world are *maya* in the sense that none has any true *dharma*, or nature. All is Emptiness. The proper attitude of the *bodhisattva* (one striving for Buddhahood) toward this realm is not one of loathing, but rather of indifference, detachment. He is quite happy to exist in this world so as to assist all beings toward enlightenment. But nothing in it any longer tempts him. And since he has no axe to grind, nothing to prove, no one to impress, the enlightened one comes to view all beings equally with an eye of compassion (*karuna*). He can do so since he has no reason to prefer one to another. No selfish striving or self-defensiveness enters into it.

I would like to suggest that though Lovecraft certainly did have likes and dislikes (his racism, for example, is notorious), insofar as he did have marked compassion on others it was based neither on self-interest nor on Western religious moralism, but rather on a Buddhist-style compassion of disinterest based on an understanding of Emptiness or no-dharmas. My evidence here is anecdotal.

Samuel Loveman, in one of his valuable reminiscences of his friend Lovecraft, recalls that

> His pity for the peccadillos of his friends or acquaintances was unswerving. I remember a particular instance where one of our friends whose predominating characteristic was that of insincerity, became involved in an incriminating, ghastly episode. Lovecraft's remark, made with a negative gesture of both hands: "Well, only another collection of molecules!" Adding: "I pass no judgements on anyone. I take no one too seriously. Disillusion has its disadvantages, but therein lies safety" ("Lovecraft As a Conversationalist," *Fresco*, Spring 1958, Vol. 8, No. 3, page 35).

How ironic that a radically dim view of human nature, namely that there is no such thing, can produce greater rather than less compassion for one's fellows—just as it does in Buddhism! (And for that matter, remember the words of Psalm 103:13-14: "As a father pities his children, so Yahweh pities those who fear him. For he knows our frame; he remembers that we are dust"—i.e., just another collection of molecules!)

Would Lovecraft have considered himself a religious man? Of course not. His many published remarks make it clear he would have laughed at the thought. But I believe we may press his disavowal no farther than denoting his repudiation of obscurantist creeds and denominations. I suggest that his letters, fiction, and poetry all reveal a strong religious sense, a mysticism of Eternity and its epiphanies in sacred time ("centuries less a dream than this we know") and sacred space ("worlds where only gods can be"), clothed by his imagination in literary symbolism fully as evocative as the mythic symbols of any known religion.

Chariots of the Old Ones
Robert M. Price & Charles Garofalo

Erich von Däniken, author of *Chariots of the Gods?*, *Miracles of the Gods*, and several other books of like nature, may be guilty of the worst case of pseudoscientific overkill in the twentieth century. To him, virtually any ancient relic is proof that beings from outer space once visited the Earth and inspired all the myths of gods and heroes. Any well-made bits of architecture, from the Egyptian and Aztec pyramids, to the Inca walls, to the buildings in Machu Picchu, were built with the help of benevolent men from Mars. Any old sculptures, from the winged men of Assyria and Babylonia, to the ancient stone heads in Mexico, to the Easter Island statues, were inspired by some odd looking alien. Von Däniken refuses to acknowledge *human* ingenuity or imagination, or even local artistic styles, in his crusade to prove man a mental quadriplegic who rode to civilization on the backs of more advanced races. The ironic thing is that H. P. Lovecraft expounded the same theories in his Cthulhu Mythos stories back in the nineteen thirties.

Cthulhu Drives a Flying Saucer

There are some remarkable parallels in Von Däniken's and Lovecraft's work. In Lovecraft's first *major* Cthulhu Mythos story "The Call of Cthulhu," a researcher discovers the cult of the Old Ones, a star-spanning race that once ruled the world, and now sleeps in sunken cities and underground caverns. They will recover "When the stars are right," according to their worshippers, a cult which has existed since prehistory and is now scattered about the world. These groups are found as far apart as China, Arabia, Siberia, and the South Seas. Later Mythos tales ("The Dunwich Horror," "The Whisperer in Darkness," "The Curse of Yig," "The Mound," "Medusa's Coil," and "Out of the Eons") spread the cult all over America, particularly New England, the Southwest, and the Deep South. Cthulhu and similar Old Ones are supposed to have influenced other religions, coming to be mentioned in Hindu myths under different names, and becoming the devils in various books of magic like the *Necronomicon*. Also widespread are idols and bas-reliefs of Cthulhu, portrayed as a giant man with an octopus for a head, scales like a dragon, huge claws, and vestigal wings.

According to Von Däniken, similar figures of a great bulky faceless man (= a person in a space suit) and a being with his or her head enclosed in a globe or halo of some sort are also to be found around the world. Von Däniken provides many pictures to prove it. The similarity between some is striking; in others it is slight, but it's usually there.

Von Däniken makes much of the recurrent theme of a powerful god who uses a lightning bolt as a weapon and begets demi-gods on mortal women. He believes the being was a more human-looking spaceman who somehow reproductively compatible (perhaps because of some artifice) with Earth women. He must have been trying to improve the human race by begetting superior hybrids, as mythical demi-gods are usually depicted as incredibly strong, smart, magical, and given to discovering fire, founding cities, developing the art of weaving and similar useful things. (Personally, considering the behavior of Zeus and the rest, we'd be more inclined to suspect a spaceman on shore leave after being cooped up in that flying saucer for two or three years. The demi-gods were just a side effect. The lightning bolt would have been the ray gun he used to fight off enraged fathers and jealous husbands.)

Lovecraft also believed the alien races could be reproductively compatible with humanity. Hybrid offspring of this nature appear in "The Shadow over Innsmouth," "The Dunwich Horror," and "Medusa's Coil." The creatures in the first story are the spawn of Dagon and the Deep Ones, semihuman fishmen who worship Cthulhu. The second and third tales present the children of the Old Ones Yog-Sothoth and Cthulhu. They are always portrayed as beings of either ugly or odd appearance, with some supernatural ability, both of which are inherited from the inhuman branch of the family.

Admittedly, in his earlier stories, HPL treated the Old Ones as demons or evil gods. "The Call of Cthulhu" and "The Dunwich Horror" are both more supernatural than scientific. In the later tales ("The Horror in the Museum," "The Whisperer in Darkness," "The Shadow out of Time," and *At the Mountains of Madness*) Lovecraft reveals more about the Old Ones. Cthulhu and his kin are one of many races from many planets. *At the Mountains of Madness* mentions the wars between the Cthulhu-spawn and the Mi-Go (winged lobsterlike critters who appeared first in "The Whisperer in Darkness") plus yet a third race of aliens, the star-headed Old Ones. Von Däniken also allows for different species of extraterrestrials, who fought over exactly how much control and what sort to exert over the humans. This was the inspiration of the legends of battling gods: Olympians vs. Titans, the Aesir fighting the Giants, etc. It also explains such characters as Satan and Prometheus, passing on knowledge the other gods don't want passed on.

The Necronomicon: The Origin of a Spoof
Colin Wilson

Ever since the publication of *The Necronomicon* in 1978, I have been receiving letters from readers who take it perfectly seriously, and who want further details about its magical procedures. I suppose that is a kind of compliment to its spurious air of authenticity. An even greater compliment was an indignant article by Gerald Suster, himself a serious student of magic, in a London "underground" newspaper, denouncing the book as a cynical piece of commercial opportunism. The fact that he found it necessary to denounce such an obvious spoof indicates that we succeeded beyond my original expectations.

In fact, anyone with the slightest knowledge of Latin will instantly recognise it for a fake—it is subtitled "The book of dead names"—when the word "necronomicon" actually means the book of dead laws.

The editor of *Crypt of Cthulhu*, Robert Price, has asked me to explain how the book came about, and I do so willingly.

In 1976, I was approached by an old friend from my Soho days, George Hay, who was at one time a leading disciple of L. Ron Hubbard. He had been asked by the publisher Neville Armstrong—who runs Neville Spearman Limited—to edit a spoof volume about the *Necronomicon*. He asked me if I would be willing to contribute an introduction. My first response was one of suspicion. No writer wants to have his name associated with a bad joke. So I asked to see the material he had collected.

It was awful. The writers all seemed to have the idea that all they had to do was to imitate the basic Lovecraft formula. And this formula, as we all know, is deceptively straightforward. The writer explains that he is cringing in a garret in Arkham—or Innsmouth—committing his awful story to paper by the light of a guttering candle. Six months ago, in the library of Miskatonic University, he came across an ancient manuscript written in mediæval German. . . . He ignored the advice of the doddery old librarian, and proceeded to practise its magic spells in the hills behind Arkham. Even the violent death of the old librarian failed to deflect him from his foolishness. And now, too late, he realises that he has unleashed the Thing on the inhabitants of Massachusetts. . . . Even as he writes, he can hear an ominous creaking on the stairs, as if an oversized elephant is trying to tiptoe on its hind feet. . . . But even as the door creaks open, he continues to write: "I can hear its hoarse breathing, and smell its loathsome graveyard stench. . . . Aaaargh!. . . ."

One of the chief contributors was a brilliant young computer expert, David Langford, who worked at an atomic energy establishment (and who has since written some excellent science fiction). He had the amusing idea of producing a lengthy computer analysis that was supposed to prove the real existence of the *Necronomicon*. And, in the usual way, the experts who worked on it were found slumped over their computers, their heads crushed to a horrible pulp, while strange reptilian footprints walked across the room, and vanished out of the open window. Most of the other stories followed roughly the same line.

Now I had myself been responsible for a certain amount of Lovecraftian fiction—I will not go so far as to call it parody—and could see instantly what was wrong. Lovecraft himself enjoyed playing the scholarly game, dragging in his references to the mad Arab Abdul El Hazzred or the insane German scholar Von Junzt. In my few ventures into the genre (*The Mind Parasites*, *The Philosopher's Stone*, "The Return of the Lloigor"), I had attempted to go one stage further, and make the various references sound still more authentic, dragging in chunks of archaeology, anthropology, and demonological magical lore. It is a very easy game to play if you happen to have a turn in that direction.

So obviously, the first thing to do was to find someone who really knew something about magic, and persuade him to concoct a book that could have been a perfectly genuine magical manuscript. I turned to my friend Robert Turner, a one-time member of a Gerald Gardner witchcraft coven and the head of a contemporary magical order.

Before I go any further, let me explain that, unlike Lovecraft, I am by no means a sceptic about "the supernatural." I was always convinced, for example, that poltergeist phenomena really occur, although I was inclined to believe that these are due to some unknown power of the unconscious mind. When in the mid-1960s, I was commissioned by Random House to write a book about "the occult," I decided to accept because the idea sounded amusing, and because I had always been interested in the lunatic fringe of cosmology—from Hoerbiger and Velikovsky to Madame Blavatsky and Rudolf Steiner. But as I wrote *The Occult*, it slowly became clear to me that traditions about magic and "the spirit world" have an extraordinary similarity in all ages and all continents. It was astonishing to discover, for example, that Eskimo *shamans* held almost precisely the same belief as the shamans of Siberia, those of Northern Japan, and of African witch doctors and Red Indian medicine men. Even so, *The Occult* was basically "sceptical" in outlook—for example, I took it for granted that the kind of powers possessed by witches are basically nonharmful, and that the mediæval witch persecutions were based upon the hysteria of the inquisitors. It was some years later that it struck me that I had accepted without question certain accounts of the magical power of African witch doctors (for example, to cause rain), yet had rejected completely the notion that the North Berwick witches could have caused the storm which almost drowned James VI of Scotland—and I held to this belief in spite of the fact that the witches had confessed to the attempt to sink the ship without being tortured.

Later still, when writing a history of poltergeist phenomena, I slowly came to accept the view of Guy Playfair, that poltergeists are, in fact, "spirits" and not some unconscious power of the human mind—even though, by that time, I had discovered in the new science of split-brain physiology a possible explanation of the origin of the forces that can cause objects to fly around the room without anyone touching them.

Now the problem of concocting a spoof *Necronomicon* was simply that Lovecraft himself remained a sceptic to the end of his life. If he had been a genuine student of magic—or even of spiritualism—it might have been possible to concoct a story about a genuine magical work which he used as a basis of his fiction. The real problem, therefore, was to explain how a man who was known to be a sceptic could possibly have made use of a genuine magical grimoire. Still, the problem presented no real difficulty to the author of a dozen or so novels—since a novelist is, by profession, an ingenious liar. The answer, I decided, lay in Lovecraft's father, Winfield Lovecraft, who died of syphilis when Howard was a child, and about whom very little is known. I claimed to have come upon evidence that Winfield Lovecraft was a Freemason—which, in America towards the end of the 19th century, was commonplace enough. But I went on to claim that Winfield Lovecraft had drifted into Egyptian Freemasonry, founded by the "magician" Cagliostro and that the Egyptian Freemasons studied various ancient volumes on transcendental magic, such as the *Key of Solomon* and the *Sacred Magic of Abra-Melin the Mage*. Next, I invented a German scholar named Stanislaus Hinterstoisser, the founder of the Salzburg Institute for the Study of Magic and Occult Phenomena. It was Hinterstoisser who had insisted that *The Necronomicon* was a real book and that it had been bequeathed by Cagliostro to his followers.

Now it was a fairly straightforward matter of persuading some scholar to impersonate Hinterstoisser, and to write me a letter explaining how he had succeeded in tracking down the original *Necronomicon* which was translated in 1571 by Dr. John Dee, the English magician. It required a scholar who spoke fluent German, and I approached my friend Ellic Howe, the author of a classic study of the Order of the Golden Dawn. But Ellic felt that he had not enough material to go on. I turned to another friend, Dominic Purcell, a professor of economics at the University of Vienna. Dominic wrote the "Hinterstoisser letter." From then on, it was plain sailing. *The Necronomicon* was actually identified as a magical compilation by a number of Arabs, including the celebrated alchemist Alkindi. The manuscript was tracked down in the British Museum, and the magical code was solved with the aid of a computer (this is where David Langford came in—and it was necessary for him to scrap his original essay and write a new one based on material provided by Robert Turner). My friend L. Sprage de Camp—the author of the standard biography of Lovecraft—was persuaded to write a short essay about the young Lovecraft—making no mention of the Hinterstoisser theory, but giving the volume that additional touch of authenticity. A couple of the original essays on Lovecraft were thrown in for good measure, and the thing was finally completed.

I should mention that Gerald Suster's accusations about commercial opportunism were wide of the mark—I doubt whether the book has made most of its contributors more than about ₤100 each. But it gave its compilers a great deal of harmless pleasure. And I am fairly sure that Lovecraft would have accepted it as a compliment.

The Diary of Alonzo Typer
Found after his mysterious disappearance.
William Lumley

Arrived here yesterday at 6 p.m. There was a dreadful storm coming on, [and I] was unable to get any conveyance to take me to my destination. The place is no better than an old backwater and its few inhabitants little better than idiotic. May 1 after Walpurgis Night, witches sabbaths, and all that, yet I have always been fascinated by unholy mysteries, for what else has brought me to this shunned old house? Well the coming storm so darkened everything, I got but a glimpse of my surroundings as I hurried on to reach my destination before it broke. I could only see by the lightning flashes—it sets in a small swampy valley of strange weeds and fungus surrounded by scraggy ill-looking trees while at its back just beyond this [sits] a dismal looking hill upon whose top stand several great stones seemingly within a circle. The house has a decidedly forbidding aspect, which does not belie the rumors I have heard about it. This was all I could see. I managed to reach the porch just as a terrific downpour of rain fell, accompanied by a bolt of thunder that might well have announced the day of general dissolution to be at hand.

- - - - -

I am conscious of several evil presences in this house, one in particular that is decidedly hostile towards me. A presence with a malevolent will that is seeking to break down my own, and overcome me. I must not countenance this for an instant. I must use all my forces to resist it; as I have said, this presence is evil but of a superhuman quality as though allied unto powers not of earth but emanating from some antehuman twilight space unknown. Its presence, too, though unseen, seems colossal—like to tower o'er, and its [?] bulk the chambers might scarce contain, likewise of an unutterable age as to be indescribable.

Last night,—or rather about 3 a.m. this morning, a strange creeping wind seemed to pervade the place and ever rising until the house rocked as within a typhoon. And as I passed down the stairs to the floor below, a huge black clawlike hand emerged from the darkness and endeavored to thrust me down the stairs. I escaped it however, and as I passed the room where the warlocks' portraits hung, suddenly that of the serpentlike one glowed with a luminous fire (green), and the features seemed to take on a more hideous aspect; a cold chill crept o'er me as I gazed upon it, and I noticed the eyes of the wild, swinelike one were lurid with an unmistakable evil glow. Also the background had changed unto a lone bleak moor with a dirty-yellow sky, whereon grew a wretched looking black thorn bush.

- - - - -

Today within the little locked room I discovered another

painting to the likeness of a woman, or rather a she-thing of some sort for although the face and form is of a fair girl, her pale skin is greenish and scaled, and her beautiful features bear the most fiendish expression I have ever beheld.

— — — — —

There are unseen presences here as I have said, some of them so great (seemingly) the rooms might scarce contain them. There is a formula of Evocation in the old conjuring book (I found in the attic) to compel them to materialize, but I greatly fear to do this. There are also faces and forms to be seen at odd times within the dim corners of the halls and chambers, faces and forms so hideous, and loathsome as to defy description, and today when I descended into the locked vaultlike cellar beneath, I distinctly heard the menacing padding and mutterings as of gigantic things within; likewise the slithering as of a great sea-beast dragging its bulk over the stone floor. What can be contained within that locked cellar? I would not open it for worlds. The lock is old and encrusted with rust, and the evil looking hieroglyphics upon it may be graven Elder signs for they seem to be of an indescribable old age, and at times to glow with greenish hue.

— — — — —

The black clutching hands that ofttimes appear in my pathway have assumed more formidable dimensions; they appeared today from out the darkness of the cellar, and seemed to be alive with a far greater malevolent will. Also muffled reverberations emanated from behind the locked vault that seemed to echo upon the far horizon like distant thunder. What is to be my ultimate end within this place? I might not leave here now if I would, for a strange command, or rather power, holds me back.

— — — —

As I have said, the house is very, very old, and has an undeniable bad reputation. It is built in no particular recognizable style, for so many repairs have been added at different times it would be impossible to discover the original one. There are two portraits in the lower dwelling room of the warlocks who I suppose lived here at different times. One has the most disconcerting countenance I have ever beheld. It is serpentlike with great green eyes. The other has a longish face resembling a thin wild swine; the eyes are set near together and seem when evening falls to glow with a baleful light. They are cheerful companions, these two. I wonder if any murders have been committed here (or suicides)? The atmosphere of the place might well suggest these and worse.

— — — — —

There are several female presences that have dimly materialized. They are of the same hellish beauty as the portrait I found in the hall's locked room. There is one whose fell loveliness is above the rest; her poisonous charms are like a honeyed flower growing on the brink of hell.

I have found in an old trunk in the attic a book on magic and an old diary. These are very old, torn, and mouldy. The book dates back to the sixteenth century and the diary seems fully as old. It is filled with a strange crabbed writing, and a colored drawing fell out of it when I opened it. This is of a hideous creature resembling nothing so much as a squid, beaked and tentacled with great yellow eyes; yet is not such, for the human form is decidedly intermingled in its construction. For instance the head, hands, and feet . . . these are strangely clawed. It is seated upon a pedestal resembling a throne and upon this are symbols and seeming words like I have never seen before. They resemble Chinese but they are surely not such; there is a sinister atmosphere about both the writing and drawing I cannot describe, save that the evil of ages seems to be centered in the unnamable creature depicted in the drawing, and the unknown characters of writing seem to be endowed with an evil life of their own as though sentient, and fain would wrest themselves forth from the parchment and wreak a mischief upon whomsoever gazes upon them. This is a delusion but whoever depicted the strange monster wrought it with a hellish precision, and the letters with an unholy purport.

— — — —

Found today in the little locked room an old notebook evidently the property of one of the warlocks. It is in barbarous Latin and almost indecipherable. It seems to be a collection of hurried notes jotted down at random, the name Yian-Ho appearing many times within it. Yian Ho! that lost and hidden city wherein lurk secrets aeons-old! There seems to be a sort of cryptic key running through the maze of almost unintelligible sentences; perhaps this will enable me to translate the sinister writing aforementioned. Also noticed that the attic door resisted all my efforts to open, and when it at last gave way a seemingly colossal unseen shape flew or rather soared away. I could distinctly hear the beating of gigantic wings; also noted that the black [. . .] and hands appear more often now and have grown until they assume gigantic proportions. What I may not grasp is the several un-human presences here whose shadowy bulk is so vast I cannot conceive in what manner the chambers may contain them. There are terrible primal arcana of Earth that are better unknown; there are dread secrets (un-human) that none may know and have peace—more secrets that render whosoever knoweth them an alien unto the tribe he belongs to, that cause him to walk alone on earth, for he who takes pays. Likewise there are dread un-human survivals that have straggled down through the aeons, none know how, monstrous blasphemous entities that have slept or lain in secret crypts and in remote places for unhallowed ages governed (as I have said) by neither logic nor reason as we know it, to be awakened from their age-long sleep by whosoever knoweth the rites, the signs, and words, for they die not but shall be until the ending of all things.

— — — —

Upon this day of St. John's Eve I was conscious at sunset

of a distant sound coming apparently from the strange circle of stones upon the hill. It was a shrill [. . .] intermingled with a hideous hissing and haunting sound resembling no earthly music I have ever heard.

— — — — —

Today I spent several hours on the hill. There is a strange wind that whirls about the forbidding monoliths, from which emanates at times a faint cryptic utterance or whisper. These monoliths are certainly of no Druidic origin and unlike in both hue and texture any stone I have ever seen. They are neither brown nor gray but rather a dirty yellow blending into an evil green. Yet do they seem to change and ever change whilst their texture resembles that of a scaled serpent, and nauseous to touch, it being cold and clammy as a toad or other reptile.

Noticed today, Lammas day, that the whispers were unmistakably louder, angry, and humming. I could almost distinguish words of a hissing sibilant character resembling those of the unspeakable chant aforementioned and like unto a faint blink of summer lightning for a brief moment. Lit up the distant horizon whereat a sinister detonation as from out the evil cosmos seemingly from miles and miles away, yet 'twas not such for I could distinctly hear an indescribable colossal un-human terrible voice give utterance to dread hissing words which ended in a peal of gutteral laughter! Gods, what has my unwarranted curiosity evoked from out the twilight spaces? What will be the end?

— — — — —

At last my dreams are to be realized in this shunned old house. I have come across an ancient forgotten one who will show me the gateway I would enter, the lost signs and words. I wonder how long he, or rather it, has lain buried and forgotten within, one whom ones of earth no longer know, whose name is only whispered by a few who fear to utter it even in secret, or why none have ever glimpsed it in the crypt wherein it has lain?

At last I have learned the meaning of the dread symbols and have mastered the seven lost signs of terror. I have learned likewise in silence the hideous unspeakable words of fear. All that remains for me to accomplish is their chant which will transfigure that forgotten one who is guardian of the ancient gateway. I marvel much at the chant; it is composed of strange repellent gutteral sounds and hissing sibilant syllables resembling no language I have ever heard. I was tempted to read this aloud upon the hill today but my efforts were seemingly futile, for I succeeded in eliciting a strange sinister rumbling echo perhaps from the evil cosmos, along with a cloud of dust—not dust as we know it but a cloud of hideous blinding elemental dust like an evil living thing. Better luck next time.

— — — — —

Today dark ominous clouds hovered o'er the circle on the hill. I have noticed them several times before. They are smokelike and seemingly of fantastic forms; one might indeed fancy them to be evil presences, more especially by the manner in which they float in a circle about the monoliths, ever in a circle as though endowed with an evil life of their own. I could swear that an angry murmuring emanated from them. Also they never seem to stay above a quarter of an hour; then they slowly sail away ever eastward in the manner of a straggling battalion. Could they indeed be those dread ones whom Solomon knew of old--seeming like great flocks whose number is legion, whose tread doth shake the earth?

Rehearsed today the chant that will transfigure the nameless thing, yet strange fears assail me when I utter it even under my breath, and the only way to it is through the locked cellar wherein it rests amid the horrors that lurk within, and though this chant is the station [?], there is no formula for controlling what is evoked, save it be the formal signs and gestures. Also where is the key that will unlock the prisoned horrors pent within? I greatly fear for all this, yet an unknown force urges me on. I may not disobey; I must unlock the cellar at any cost.

Late this afternoon I descended to the forbidding precincts. At first all was silent; then the menacing padding began anew, this time louder and more formidable. Also the slithering as of a great sea-beast seemed swifter and intensified, as though it were striving to force its way through into where I stood. While the restless muffled pacing ever grew more restless and more sinister, suddenly began the old reverberations, but louder—increased a hundredfold. I can liken it to nothing save the roar of some dread monster of the last saurian age, when fell primordial reptiles roamed the earth. How may I bear the onslaught of these dreadful ones when I unlock it?

– – – – –

Found today in the little locked room the key. It was buried beneath a host of rubbish as though its owner sought to conceal it. It was tightly wrapped within the dried skin of some unknown reptile, and upon the inner side were written in the same crabbed characters as the diary the following words:

I shall never reveal the secrets of those monstrous primal ones whose cryptic characters reveal dread antehuman secrets, secrets of things no one of earth should learn would he know peace [any] more, for I have been to Yian-Ho, that lost and aeon-old city, and have found and borne away one from that dreadful and forbidding place, for frightful things I saw therein and shapes more dread than these. And lo! that which I have awakened and borne away with me I may not part with again, nor may we be separated [any] more as it is written within the *Book of Forbidden Things*, for lo! that which I have willed to live hath turned the dreadful shape about me as it is written, yet if I pass untimely it must abide a while for its time is not yet.

I am at a loss to describe this key; like the lock it is of a greenish metal (frosted), resembling brass tarnished with verdigris and wrought to fit the coffin-shaped opening; like the lock it is ponderous, the handle being a rough attempt at an un-human image of some sort no longer recognizable. It is passing strange that though an inert object of metal, I could distinctly feel it quicken in my hand when held there any length of time. Below the image is graven in the eternal Chinese-like characters "My vengeance lurks"--the rest of the inscription is undecipherable through age. Awakened last night to see the key glow lurid green even as the lock has done, and strange hissing whispers seemed to emanate from it, wherein these words were manifest: "The Hour Falls." It is an omen, and I laugh at my own fears. Have I not the dread words of fear and the seven lost signs of terror? The power that is coercive of any Dweller of the Evil Cosmos or darkened spaces unknown? I will no longer hesitate; there is a terrific storm coming on, even greater than the one I encountered upon my arrival three months ago. The lightning renders the fell circle of stones upon the hill a lurid green, and the menacing padding and muffled reverberations below echo upon the distant horizon louder than the dread thunder with which they are intermingled.

A Sacrifice to Science
Gustav Adolf Danziger (Adolphe de Castro)

I.

There are many people living now who will recall with a shudder the frightful epidemic which raged in the city of San Francisco a score of years ago. This epidemic was a malignant typhoid fever, which made its appearance first in the hospital of the county jail. More than fifty-eight convicts died in one summer of that mysterious disease, which manifested always the same symptoms and always ended with a fatal result. The people in the city knew at first very little of this dreadful calamity; moreover, they were quite unconcerned whether more or fewer convicts lived or died behind the massive walls of the county's penal institute. However, the newspapers soon spread the matter abroad; people became cognizant of the danger that threatened the community. Thus far, the people of San Francisco had been mercifully spared; but while some spoke in whispers about the epidemic which was raging among the outcasts of society, others spoke with pride of Dr. Clinton, the penitentiary physician, who had discovered the disease, and was the first to give a minute description of it. He had not been able to cure any of the convicts, but his fame had reached the remotest corners of the civilized world.

Dr. Clinton lived in a gloomy house at the outer end of Broadway, which stood alone in a block of land. He was not very sociable, but that did not prevent the wealthiest people from calling him to their houses.

Dr. Clinton was born in the city of New York, had graduated from the medical college at quite an early age, had gone to Europe, and after years and years of hard study at the great universities, had at last gone with a scientific expedition to study the fever epidemic and other noxious diseases among the natives of the West Indies, finally settling in San Francisco.

Some of the younger physicians were enthusiastic about Dr. Clinton's discovery (the older practitioners were less demonstrative), and adored his fine scholarship. It was a pity, they said, that he was so exclusive, and buried himself in the old house on Broadway, when society was eager to lionize him. The Doctor paid no attention to gossip, either favorable or otherwise. The prison and his gloomy house on Broadway were his world; he was satisfied.

With Dr. Clinton lived his sister, Alvira, who kept house for him, and a dismal-looking servant by the name of Mort, who had accompanied the doctor on his travels.

Alvira Clinton was wealthy in her own right; her parents, at their death, had left her and her brother enough means to live in luxury all their lives, but the Doctor's love of science had made him careless of ease.

Alvira Clinton, without being very beautiful, lacked by no means a certain attractiveness. She had big black eyes, which were expressive of intelligence; about her mouth there was that peculiar

97

expression said to be expressive of an indomitable will. But when Alvira talked she was positively handsome. There was a bubbling over of spirit, a sparkling of wit, that charmed all men. She talked but seldom now; her devotion to her brother, her tireless help in his scientific labors, occupied her time. She did not care for society, its gossip and its parties, but was seen more frequently in the houses of the poor, her neighbors and well-wishers. She went to see them because, curiously enough, the miserable Mexicans in the neighborhood were afraid to enter the gloomy house, which was surrounded by a high fence and tall eucalyptus trees.

At a short distance from the house was a large stable containing the animals on which the Doctor experimented, and which Mort called the "Clinic."

Alvira shuddered when she heard her brother give the details for the dog clinic; the whinings of the tortured animals filled her with unspeakable horror. This annoyed her brother, and he made her enter the gruesome hospital. He desired her to satisfy herself that the animals were not being tortured, and that the noise came from the dogs playing in the garden. Alvira was compelled to acknowledge that the animals in the "Clinic" were quite as lively as the dogs in the garden; there was no sign of cruelty, nor even harshness, visible; everything was kept scrupulously clean, making quite a pleasing impression. Of course, there several of the sick rabbits stretched out in their cages; the light had gone from their eyes, and they seemed to wait for the end which was sure to come. But this had to be; it was in perfect harmony with a hospital.

"Are you satisfied now?" Dr. Clinton asked his sister.

"Yes," said Alvira; "still, I think I had better keep away from your clinic."

"Suit yourself," said he, calmly. It was just as well she stayed away; he had no need of her there, and she might be in Mort's way. The latter attended to all the business in that domain.

Mort was Clinton's right-hand man. He was absolutely indispensable. He contrived to keep the "Clinic" supplied with the animals necessary for anatomical purposes and to dispose of them after that. Alvira hated him because he seemed too familiar with her brother. She shuddered when he came near her; he was so repulsive-looking. From the back of his head to his forehead there was not a hair. His head looked like a huge ball of polished ivory. He had neither brows nor eyelashes, and his nose was flattened down to a wide mouth with colorless lips and immense teeth. His body was lank and his clothes too wide. The skin of his face and hands looked like yellow parchment drawn taut. One invariably imagined that his clothes covered a horrible skeleton. And this individual, at the sight of whom dogs drew in their tails and ran away, had the fullest confidence of her brother.

"No one outside of the Doctor and myself shall see what we are about in our hospital," he once said to a presumptuous reporter. And thus they lived, secluded from the world, with nothing to disturb them. The many famous physicians and the lesser lights who had come to study the peculiar disease, and had expected to be treated hospitably by Dr. Clinton, were somewhat disappointed. Not that he did not treat them with the necessary civility, but while he took them to the prison hospital, he coldly refused to admit them to his private study or to Mort's "Clinic." They should neither see his notes nor the means he employed to check the disease.

His persistent refusal to show his private "workshop" caused the learned doctors to shake their heads suspiciously. Clinton saw it and bit his lips; but when they had gone his rage was uncontrollable. "The idiots!" he cried, and ran into the garden, racing up and down. Mort, who knew the cause of the Doctor's rage, roundly abused the "Eastern quacks." This invariably had a pacifying effect upon the Doctor. He smiled, and a defiant look came into his face. Let them shake their heads. Mort and himself, and not a living human soul besides, should enter his sanctum until the work is done.

Any person who ventured into the garden or into the house was treated most ungraciously by Mort. "What do you want? We don't receive visitors," was the stereotyped remark with which he sent away men and women.

However, one man, George Dalton, was an exception. He alone dared to enter the lonely house without being sent away.

II.

George Dalton was a lawyer who had known the Clinton family in New York, and had transacted their business there. He had asked Mr. Alfred Clinton, Sen., for permission to pay his respects to the only daughter, but was met with such harshness by the old gentleman that he did not make a second attempt. Of course, George Dalton was an impecunious young lawyer, but he was young, well educated, of a jovial disposition, and quite hopeful. When the old Mr. Clinton told Dalton that he could aspire to transact the legal business of the family, and to nothing else, George said nothing. But he no sooner left the Clinton mansion than he proceeded to the nearest barber, had his blond locks and beard cut and shaved, and went home, packed his portmanteau, and went West. In less than five years George Dalton had made a reputation and a fortune; but his early timidity never left him. He recalled the words of Clinton, Sen., and he stayed in the city of San Francisco.

Ten years more had gone by and one day George saw Alvira on the street. The hot wave that suffused his face when he saw her clearly told that the years and space had no effect upon his affections. Alvira, too, was happy to see him. She told him of the death of her parents, of her brother's great learning and fame, and their intention to locate in the city. They were indeed a handsome pair as they walked up Broadway. Dr. Clinton was favorable to Dalton, as far as he was capable of showing his regard. He spoke a word or two with the friend of his sister, and then left them alone. Dr. Clinton had no interest in anything or anybody that did not betray the symptoms of typhoid fever. But when George Dalton succeeded in getting him the position in the prison hospital, he condescended to express his appreciation, not to Dalton, but to Alvira. She was happy that he thought well of George; for, be it understood, she loved the lawyer, and would have followed him, were it not that she pitied her brother, who would have been helpless without her. Nor could she think of leaving him alone with his "evil genius," as she called Mort.

Dr. Clinton was sure of his sister. He knew that she would not leave him for any man. He did not object to Dalton's visits, which, however, were not so frequent as to cause him any uneasiness. Every Sunday evening the gloomy house, or, to be more precise, the family sitting-room, was enlivened by George Dalton's pleasant conversation; and because Alvira seemed to enjoy the lively chitchat, her brother rather encouraged the visitor. Without it, the Doctor thought she might tire of the loneliness and gloom, and—who knows?—might leave him alone—the very thought caused him to shudder—with his factotum, Mort. The latter knew that this thought upset the Doctor, and he never failed to allude to it. These allusions enraged Clinton, and he would have chastised his servant or dismissed him—if he could. But as he could not do either, he raved in impotent rage, and then consoled himself with the thought that Alvira was too sensible to entertain any such ideas. How could she?

One bright, sunny morning, it was on a Sunday, a scene was enacted in Dr. Clinton's garden that caused Alvira to weep, the Doctor to rave, and Mort to grin; and when Mort grinned, the birds in the trees ceased their chirping and flew away; everything seemed to wither when Mort's eyes glistened and Mort's mouth grinned. The scene was as follows: In an altana in the garden sat George Dalton, Alvira, and the Doctor. Dalton seemed depressed,—strange for a man of his temper; the Doctor was smoking, and Alvira was speaking rather hastily and incoherently. At some distance, but near enough for him to hear, was Mort with his dogs. Clinton had just thrown away the stump of a cigar, and Alvira, glad at the pretext, went into the house to fetch some fresh cigars.

Dalton took advantage of Alvira's absence and said, "I might as well say it now as at any other time. Dr. Clinton, I love Alvira; have loved her for years, and have reason to believe that she is not indifferent to me. In a word, I desire to marry your sister. She shall never have any cause to regret it. Give us your consent, Doctor."

Dr. Clinton seemed to think of a proper expression to couch his refusal. Dalton's speech had evidently displeased him, but it did not come unexpected. He had grown tired of the lawyer's visits. He wanted absolute seclusion. If the lawyer suffered a second rebuff, he was sure to stay away for good. He stroked his beard, and a smile of satisfaction flitted across his pale face.

"You are speaking of an impossibility, Dalton," he said. "My sister has concluded, once for all, to devote her life to such an unworthy old bachelor as I am."

"But you cannot—you dare not—accept such a sacrifice, Dr. Clinton," said Dalton. "Alvira is not the girl to spend her life in the society of that fellow Mort and his dogs. You ought to be more reasonable, Doctor."

Dr. Clinton rose from his seat. He was a shade paler than usual. His dark eyes shot flashes of malignant hatred and contempt. Dalton involuntarily stepped back as the Doctor hissed the answer into his face: "Whether I have the right to accept the sacrifice of my sister,—if to resign the drudgery of a commonplace marriage can be called a sacrifice,—this, I judge, is no business of a stranger."

"But I am—"

"A stranger for us," said the Doctor. "You could have spared yourself this explanation if your feelings had been less youthful than your age would lead one to believe."

George Dalton was astounded, but he gradually gained his balance. "We two are done, Dr. Clinton," he said. "Miss Alvira is of age, and mistress of her own action. I will ask her to decide."

"There she is," said Clinton. "I will leave you two alone, so that you do not accuse me of influencing her decision."

When Alvira returned she was astonished to find her brother and Dalton facing each other in evident excitement. Clinton cut the matter short by saying: "Alvira, Mr. Dalton desires to speak to you. I will, in the meantime, look after Mort's boarders."

Alvira took a seat and motioned Dalton to do likewise. But when Dalton was about to speak, she said, "Do not speak." Her voice was soft and sad. "Whatever changes you desire to bring about, do not count upon my consent. Years ago, yes; but now it is different. I feel it is my sacred duty to care for Alfred, who would be lost without me. Besides, I do not feel at all lonely," she added, with all the feminine tenderness she was capable of, "since you come to the house. Leave matters as they are. We have peace; do not disturb the mutual harmony."

"My dear Alvira, what you have said," replied Dalton, "demonstrates to me one fact, namely, that you appreciate my visits, and because of that I tell you, if you do love me a little, you will not refuse me. You will not cast aside the true devotion of a man tried and found loyal. I say again, Alvira, be my wife."

The girl looked at Dalton with eyes that mirrored the gratitude of her soul. She knew that she loved him, and had he taken her to his breast in youthful passion, she would have followed him. She would have forsaken her brother, if Dalton had kissed the confession from her lips. But as he appeared in a matter of fact manner, speaking friendly and sensibly, it was her duty to be sensible, too, and this demanded that she tell him where her duty lay, namely, with her brother. The reason why she would not leave him was that he was sacrificing his health and his life to science. She said it with a sigh that clearly told of her suffering.

"Then you stay with him out of sheer pity?" Dalton asked.

Alvira took hold of Dalton's hand, and with every evidence of anxiety she said: "Forgive me, George, but I cannot act otherwise. My brother believes in my faithful love and devotion, and he shall not be disappointed. On the day that he needs my life it shall be fettered by no other bonds. I must be at his side."

Alvira sank back into her seat and covered her face with her hands. Dalton saw the tears trickle through her fingers. His heart ached to see the woman he loved suffer so much.

"Your brother is ill. He ought to give up his work. Let him travel,—anything that will keep him away from his labors," said he.

"You are right," said Alvira. "His work will be his death; but he cannot live without it. You ought to have seen him when he discovered the first case at the prison hospital. He had evidently been baffled by something in his investigations, and the epidemic at the hospital had come at the most opportune moment. He suffered, nevertheless, because he believed himself responsible for every person that died,—as if he, and not God, had brought on the epidemic. The first evening—when the dread disease made its appearance—was the most horrible. I shall never forget it. He came into the house without saying a word, and ran out into the garden again, running up and down as if possessed, trampling upon flowers and the shrubbery, and laughing loudly. It terrified me, but I did not dare to speak to him. He is quiet now, and with nothing to excite him, we live quite happily. And now I see the dark clouds again. This time, dear friend, you are the disturber. For my sake, George, be friends with Alfred, and when you come again do not broach that other subject."

"My dear Miss Alvira, I am grieved to tell you that after the hard words that have passed between your brother and me it would be quite impossible for me to call at his house again; but granted I did come, it would be equally impossible for me to subdue my feelings, now more than ever, since I know how unhappy you are."

He rose and stretched out his hand, which she grasped, saying: "I know that you will forever remain my dearest, my best, friend, and because of that I ask you to promise me when I call you that you will come to me. Promise me, George!" He knew what she suffered, and without a word he pressed her hand in token of a promise, and left. Dr. Clinton saw Dalton, the only friend of the family, leave the house, but he seemed to be engrossed in some subject which Mort had shown him, and did not turn.

III.

Added to gossip that Dalton's withdrawal occasioned, was the fact that the Doctor's star was on the wane. The people became disappointed in Dr. Clinton. It is true, he had made a great discovery, and the medical journals all over the world were still discussing the subject; but suffering and death are old evils, and the discovery of one more disease was interesting, but not quite agreeable to contemplate, considering that one might become a victim to the new discovery. Dr. Clinton had not found a remedy against the epidemic, and therefore had achieved nothing.

But this was not all. He had managed to make more enemies than any man in his profession. When he had become the fashion in the city, and everyone consulted the eminent "fever doctor," he was found deficient in that one quality,—*sine qua non* to the success of a physician,—to flatter the rich, to humor their ills, especially the female patients, and be interested in the babies of fond mothers. To make matters worse, it so happened that he had some differences with one of the prison directors, who told him that he (Dr. Clinton) was merely an official at the hospital, but not the master. And last, but not least for Dr. Clinton, was the fact that the epidemic had disappeared as suddenly as it had come.

People began to lose their dread of the disease and their respect for the discoverer. Added to this was the opinion of a prominent college professor in New York, who had spent months in the city to investigate the disease.

"This disease is not a new discovery," the professor said, "and it is due to the boundless conceit of Dr. Clinton that it was given so much prominence. If Dr. Clinton had discovered a mode by which the organic disease germs can be developed and scientifically explained, if he had found the bacillus and learned to conquer its poisonous and deadly effect, let him proclaim it, and the world would hail him a Messiah. If he had not done this, he had not merited any recognition, outside of the fact that he had opened one more of the many problems which science is working hard to solve. However, the problem was not put by Dr. Clinton, but by his suffering patients. Dr. Clinton" the professor concluded, "has done nothing; he has not even attempted to save the lives of those who fell victims to the fever."

The opinion of this eminent man, being published, had the effect that not one person could be found in the city of San Francisco who would consent to be treated by Dr. Clinton. Even the poorest people were afraid to consult him, and only those who could not get the services of any other physician free of charge called him to their bedsides.

But that peculiarly malignant smile never left Dr. Clinton's lips. In the fever ward of the prison hospital he was still master; there no one interfered with him.

But one day the whole matter came to a sudden end. Dr. Clinton came home and told Alvira that he had been dismissed. Alvira desired to know what cause the Directors had for such an action.

"They at first made all sorts of charges," said Clinton. "I was too independent. I told them I would consult them in the future on all matters. Then they trumped up a charge of infidelity. One of them—the fellow is a deacon in a church—objected to an atheistic physician; and that cur pretends to be an American. I laughed in their faces at first, but ultimately promised for the sake of peace I would go to church and partake of communion, or that I would embrace any faith they pleased."

"You would not have done that," said Alvira. "I don't believe it! You would never have sacrificed your honor; because to dissemble is dishonorable."

Clinton looked at his sister with a contemptuous smile upon his lips.

"I have laid so many sacrifices upon the altar of science and investigation," said he, grimly, "that a lie more or less could not possibly make much difference. But they would not consider my proposition.

"The next charge was, that I was too extravagant at the cost of the institution, by giving chickens and wine to the prisoners.

Poor devils! I should have deprived them of the necessary nutriment, while I am experimenting on their carcasses. To hamper my work on account of such trifles! I mastered myself, and promised to let the sick starve as much as possible. But it came out at last. They told me that I do not prescribe any medicine for the sick. Not prescribe enough medicine! Ha, ha, ha!

"After this I was, of course, forced to leave. The professional honor demanded that I should leave! The professional honor! Ha, ha, ha! Do these fools think I am like those quacks who believe, and make their patients believe, that they can and will cure them? We are not here for the sake of hospitals, but hospitals are here for our sakes,—for the sake of science. But there was no use fighting; they had made up their minds to get rid of me, and I went."

His restless eyes gazed upon the instruments in the cabinet, then upon the big volumes in his library. There, upon long shelves, stood a fine selection of all the classical and standard medical works from Aristotle down to Pasteur. Alvira understood his looks. Among these princes of science, among the greatest of the great, should be Dr. Clinton's work on the origin and cause of fever germs and their conquest. Otherwise he had nothing to live for. Alvira, with the instinct of a tender woman, found the right words to encourage her brother. "You are on the road to fame already; in fact, you are near the goal, and in spite of the petty jealousy of small men, you will yet be glorious, brother. You have made all the observations at the hospital that you needed, and as the epidemic is on the wane, it would be the proper time to bring your work to a close." Clinton seemed absentminded, but at Alvira's last words he shook his head, and said, as if speaking to himself: "But three months more and I would have been done. I could have offered to the world the very greatest work of science,—a collection of deadly and of protecting bacilli."

But Alvira stayed by her argument. "Of course, I am not competent to judge," she said; "but from the information which I gleaned from your remarks made at odd moments, I am inclined to think that new cases of the dread disease could hardly make much difference, and should the epidemic break out again at the hospital, I am sure they will have to call you. Who else could fill your place?"

"The epidemic is gone. I was mistaken. It does not make its appearance where bunglers are at work," Clinton said with a hoarse laugh, while his right hand mechanically played with his golden hypodermic injector. He then took up a book and was soon engrossed in his reading. His sister took it as a good omen. "He may yet succeed, and be counted among the foremost men of all times," she said, going to her own room.

But Alvira's hopes were not fulfilled. He grew darker and moodier every day. He lost all interest in his dog clinic, and when Mort approached to make some report regarding one of the animals he drove him away.

"Go to the devil with your dog stories," Alvira heard her brother scream at the top of his voice. "I do not need dogs. I need human beings, and these were taken from me,—stolen. Not even a condemned murderer would they give me."

Alvira could not hear Mort's answer, but she heard his tuneless laughter and a cry of rage from her brother, who threatened to knock him down.

IV.

Not like a young physician anxious for practice, but like a panting deer crying for water, did Dr. Clinton look for a patient. A patient!—only one sick person whom he could study; but he looked in vain. Not a soul came to the house. Alvira went from room to room and sighed. She never left the house now, and Mort, who attended to all affairs on the outside, came and went like a shadow. No one in the vicinity or in any part of the city thought of calling Dr. Clinton.

Unable to bear it any longer, the Doctor left the house, incognito, to find a patient, if possible. He entered the huts of the poorest people and bribed them with food and wine. He gave the parents money and the children candy, until he had gained their confidence. Then he told them he was a physician, and when any one complained he volunteered his services. His life received a fresh impetus; he was happy. His science had found new material for investigation; Dr. Clinton was himself once more.

The best reason for his good humor was not so much the new and varied practice which he had found as the fact that the fever had made its appearance among the Mexicans in lower Broadway. It was as yet in its mildest form, but it was there, evidently and unmistakably. That no cases were reported from the prison hospital was probably due to the ignorance of the physicians, Dr. Clinton said. Those bunglers would not know the disease if they were laid low with it themselves. There was but one Dr. Clinton!

As the months passed, it was noticed that the epidemic had reached a very dangerous degree. None had died as yet; the Doctor's art had conquered death thus far, but the epidemic raged with frightful violence.

It was in the spring of the year that the poor people whom Dr. Clinton had assisted with food, medicine, and money grew to suspect a compact between Dr. Clinton and the Devil. This suspicion was fostered by the relentless hatred of an old Mexican fisherman whom the Doctor had had the misfortune to displease. As the old Mexican was the oracle among his kind, his words carried weight. "He is in league with the Devil," he was heard to say. "Look out for yourselves; he brings you the sickness." But there were some who laughed at the padre, and told him to consult the Doctor for the affection of the eyes. After much persuasion the old Mexican so mastered his antagonism as to send for Dr. Clinton. The latter performed an operation with so much skill and success that the populace danced with joy, and told the old padre that he was mistaken about the good Doctor. Nothing could now have shaken their faith in Dr. Clinton, were it not that the old Mexican caught the fever. In his delirium he uttered frightful imprecations against the Doctor. When Clinton made his visit the next morning, he was met by a mob, who warned him to keep away from their houses, else he would get hurt.

He tried to reason with them. He begged; he pleaded,—all in vain. "You are the Devil," they said. "You gave us food and money, and you bought us body and soul; but you shall not come here again. Wherever you go, there is death." And he was forced to retreat.

"The dogs! the curs!" he cried, running up and down in his study. "They are afraid of their miserable lives, as if their lives were worth anything, if they did not serve to enrich science. They want to live. Well, let them live, and starve."

As it was, these wretches had added their mite toward assisting his studies. The raging fever had revealed to him many new points of interest. If he could have brought one of these cases under the microscope, and if he could also have succeeded in curing a most violent case, his ambition would have been satisfied, his work done, and he would have laughed at their ingratitude. He was so excited that he discussed the subjects of his research with his sister and Mort. The latter taunted the Doctor with cowardice, to retreat before a mob of dirty Mexicans. Alvira suffered unspeakably. Why was her learned brother so haughty to everybody and so submissive to the taunts and insults of his servant? Did Mort know the *modus operandi* of the new method? and did her brother fear that his servant might reveal it to one of the many jealous physicians, who would benefit by the labors of her brother? Probably.

A few days later, Alvira and her brother were walking in the garden, arm in arm. Mort was busy tending to some plants, but his sharp ears never lost one word of the conversation between brother and sister.

"Ah! if I could only get to work again,—to work among people, and not among rabbits and dogs in that clinic over there," said Clinton.

"Are you sure, Alfred," said Alvira, "that mankind will be benefited by your discovery?"

A contemptuous smile played about Mort's lips. Alvira caught that smile, and shivered.

"Mankind is but a drop in the ocean of nature," said Dr. Clinton, "and nature refuses to be helped. She laughs and jeers at us when we are presumptuous enough to attempt to conquer her. Nature is without consideration. She is the most powerful murderess in existence, and science, in order to know nature, must be in sympathy with her."

"But where is the benefit to mankind?" said Alvira, sick at heart.

"Our science, my dear Alvira," said Clinton, with a smile, "knows of cases where enthusiastic pupils took poison to assist their perplexed masters in demonstrating its effects. You have heard of the painter's daughter who permitted herself to be crucified, so that her father might catch the proper expression for a picture of the Saviour? Natural science knows of such models who have sacrificed their lives mundane to live eternally in the sacred history of science. We live for science, not for mankind. Mort," the Doctor cried, "what do you say to the idea of advertising for such volunteers for scientific research?"

Clinton's eyes sparkled with a brilliancy and wildness that

frightened his poor sister. Mort, however, seemed to have considered the Doctor's proposition. "We might try it," he said. "But I don't believe it would be a success. You cannot rely upon volunteers. One must take his subjects wherever he finds them."

Alvira was horrified to hear Mort speak so to her brother. In the mouth of the latter those words seemed but the exaggeration of an exuberant fancy, but in the mouth of Mort they sounded like the words of a scoundrel. She was so overcome that she could hardly stand. She ran into the house, that her brother might not notice her weakness.

For days after this conversation, Alvira shivered at the recollection, and remained in her room so as to avoid meeting her brother's evil genius.

Dr. Clinton's endeavors to visit the poor were met with determined opposition. When he showed himself, a shower of stones and other missiles met his advance; once he was even shot at. Had he incurred the displeasure of the Americans in the same degree as that of the superstitious Mexicans, he would have been tarred and feathered, if not shot. But when the Americans heard one of those absurd stories about the luckless Dr. Clinton, they merely laughed at the horror that was expressed in the faces of the "Greasers" at the mention of his name. They had wisely or providentially been spared an intimate acquaintance with Dr. Clinton's philanthropy.

But the repeated rebuffs that he suffered from the Mexicans doubled his energy and his desire for investigation. He experimented on the animals, and very soon all the dogs and rabbits in Mort's clinic lay either sick or dead. Mort pleaded in vain against the total extermination of his animals; he refused to bring new specimens, in spite of his master's commands and threats. A gruesome stillness had now fallen upon the lonely house and in the garden. Bruno, the big St. Bernard dog, was the sole animal left; he was Alvira's pet, and sacred. He greeted his master with mighty jumps, and gave a joyous howl whenever his mistress showed herself in the garden.

One bright morning, in the middle of May, as Mort entered the library, he found the dog lying on the floor, with red eyes, and its swollen tongue protruding from its mouth,—the dog had caught the fever. Mort uttered a hoarse laugh as he dragged the splendid animal into his "Clinic." Alvira was very sad when she heard of Bruno's illness, but she did not give up the hope of his recovery. The dog had been her brother's pet, and he would surely cure him.

As often as Dr. Clinton came from the "Clinic," she asked him after the dog's health. On the third day after Bruno's illness, Alvira concluded to see the poor animal herself, and, mastering her dislike for Mort and his establishment, the girl crossed the garden toward the "Clinic." But she halted at the door, because of the angry words which her brother spoke to Mort. The two were evidently engaged in a violent quarrel. The door was partly open, and Alvira could look into the experimental room without being seen. Dr. Clinton walked up and down, gesticulating wildly and uttering curses at his factotum, while the latter busied himself with cleansing the microscope, but kept a vigilant eye on his master.

"Your spite and obstinacy be damned!" cried the Doctor. "You miserable wretch, you would prevent me from completing my work by refusing to bring me the necessary subjects, eh? I have asked you again and again to bring some, but you have not brought me a mouse, even. I would like to experiment day and night, but am hampered by your obstinacy."

"Ha, ha, ha!" laughed Mort. This laugh caused Alvira's heart to stop. How dared the wretch be so insolent to her brother! She listened again.

"You are experimenting! Ha, ha, ha! Well, I don't propose to go to the penitentiary for stealing dogs. If I am to hang, I want to be as great as you are, Doctor. I shall then have done my share of work by the million."

"Shut up!" cried Dr. Clinton, his voice hoarse with passion. "You miserable cur, you know very well why I desire to complete my work just now. It is the last moment. I am maddened by the thought that while I am longing for subjects to finish my work some one else might publish a book on the subject, and spoil the work of a lifetime."

"No one in America or Europe can do that," replied Mort, with a grin. "To do what we have done one must have a steady hand like you, and be without prejudice. I can rely upon you! No one else could possibly accomplish your work. After Bruno's death there is nothing left but to experiment on yourself; who else would —"

"Shut up, or—" Alvira was unable to listen any longer; the knowledge that her brother had sacrificed his pet dog was too much for her. She understood that science could not have benefited by Bruno's death; that her brother must certainly have acted under mental stress. In that case, however, he was not bad; he was only unfortunate; his work and anxiety were too much; they had undermined his health. But what could she do? Her brother, she knew, would sooner die than give up his work. She was miserable beyond expression. There was no one to help her; she was alone in the world, without a friend or relative. But no; she was not without a friend. There was her friend Dalton, of whom she had so often thought with love and longing; she would call him. Alvira was about to return to the house when the noise of falling furniture and a wild cry from her brother attracted her to the spot. Suddenly she saw Mort come from the "Clinic," a long knife in his hand, and, walking backwards, followed by Dr. Clinton, whom he sought to keep at a distance. Alvira being concealed behind the door, held on to it to support herself. The sight had made her faint.

"Keep away from me, Dr. Clinton, or I'll run this knife into you. Not one step, I say. Don't commit any foolishness. You could not kill me quick enough to prevent me from giving you away. I tell you, have a care!"

Alvira could stand it no longer. Satisfied that her brother did not follow his servant, she slipped behind a bush and ran into the house. Quickly she wrote a few lines to George Dalton, asking him to come to her house, either that very evening or the following morning. She was so excited and nervous that she frequently paused in writing. The note being written and sealed, she hastened into the street, and luckily finding a boy, gave him half a dollar to carry the note to George Dalton's office.

But all this had completely exhausted her strength. She barely managed to reach the library, when she fell upon the lounge, shaken by cold and fever. She had not been in there more than half an hour when the door was opened and Dr. Clinton came in. It was already dark, and he did not see his sister. He ran up and down, gesticulating and fighting imaginary foes. He was striking at one of those phantoms, when he was startled by a sigh. He was so scared that he stood as if rooted to the spot.

"Is it you, Alvira?" he asked, quite unnerved. But being answered by another sigh, he lighted a candle and stepped up to the lounge.

"For God's sake! you have the fever," he cried, in terrible excitement. But he soon mastered himself. Covering her with a heavy blanket, he hastened into the kitchen and made her a hot drink. When Alvira's fever had quieted down, he sat by her side, her hand in his. Once in a while his eyes became restless, and his hand moved toward the vest pocket where his "injector" was. Alvira, who felt much better, smiled at her brother gratefully.

"You have the fever," said her brother.

"Whose fever,—yours?" Alvira asked, frightened.

Dr. Clinton made no answer, but he gazed at her absently.

"This would be a fine affair for you and science if you were to find the very case you were after in your own house. You could be proud of your sister, Alfred."

Clinton stared at her with eyes wide open. "Is it possible, Alvira, that your thoughts could take such sublime flights? You, of all people, could comprehend me and my work! Alvira, I am your brother! Do you suppose I would sacrifice my own sister!"

"Keep quiet, dear," said Alvira, "I shall be all right tomorrow morning. Keep quiet, that you don't get sick yourself. I have not your fever, have I?"

Dr. Clinton had the thumb and index of his right hand in his vest pocket, where he toyed with his instrument, as was his habit.

"This would have been one of those tragic conflicts," said Dr. Clinton, still toying with his hypodermic needle, "if a loving brother could reach the highest aim of his life by the death of his own sister. Don't be frightened, Alvira; it is but one of those crazy questions which doctors are apt to ask. But why should it not be reality? Why should a girl not be permitted to sacrifice her life in the same manner as we? We sacrifice our life to science, and with our lives our pleasures, our youth, and all our desires. Every drop of blood, every fiber of our brain, labors for science, and thus our whole life is one chain of denials, abnegations, and sacrifices. Why should not a girl take that one brave step for the sake of science, which alone would place her on a level with the greatest of men?"

"You look quite tired, dear," said Alvira. "Follow my advice, and take a dose of morphine and go to bed. I feel sick. I would like to sleep a little, if possible."

"You are right," said Clinton, gathering his energy. "A morphine injection will do me good, and, come to think of it, you, too, would sleep better if you had one. You would, in fact, not be able to sleep at all without it," and drawing himself up to his full height, he continued, resolutely, "I will fetch the necessary articles from my room."

He left the room with a heavy tread.

V.

"Did you hear the latest?" said a physician to George Dalton as the two were walking towards the latter's office.

"No," said Dalton; "what is it?"

The physician handed Dalton a medical journal, which contained a full description of the peculiar disease discovered by Dr. Clinton. The writer stated that he had succeeded in discovering the germ as entirely independent of the person ill with the fever. He had brought this independent fever germ to its highest strength in virulence, and then weakened it so that it became absolutely harmless. All this he had tested by experiment on animals, and demonstrated publicly, and while Dr. Clinton had certainly given an impetus to investigation, he had achieved nothing new.

"This will bring Dr. Clinton down a peg or two," said the disciple of Esculapius, not without malice.

Dalton's heart was heavy as he stepped into his private office, and he experienced something of a shock when his office-boy handed him Alvira's note. He lost no time, but hastened to the call of the woman he had loved these many years.

"I am so glad you have come," said Alvira, after telling him of all that had transpired within the last few hours.

"And where is your brother now?" Dalton inquired.

"He has just gone down to get me a morphine injection. I think he is right. I shall not be able to sleep without it."

"And did he give you nothing else against the fever? Did he give you any medicine?" asked Dalton.

"No, he don't believe much in medicines," said Alvira. "I will be all right soon. Are you going to leave me now?" she asked, seeing Dalton rise.

"I am going to see your brother," the latter replied resolutely.

"That is right," said Alvira. "But be patient with him, for my sake, and, above all things, try and excuse your presence in the house."

Dalton left the room. He stepped down hastily, and as he turned to the Doctor's room he noticed the light coming through the open door. Dalton halted and looked into the room. At the table sat Dr. Clinton, staring into the light. Before him lay an open book in which he had evidently been writing; his right hand held a pen, and his left toyed with the golden injector. Dalton entered, and as Dr. Clinton recognized his visitor, he jumped from his chair and said: "My sister has a slight attack of fever, I was afraid she might grow worse, and concluded to give her an injection of morphine, which I had just now chemically tested. Remedies like these require the greatest care."

He had evidently forgotten how he had dismissed his sister's suitor. Clinton's words, at first full of embarrassment, grew rather mocking in tone at the end. Dalton lost all control of himself. His eyes involuntarily fell upon the book, and there, in the Doctor's large, bold handwriting, stood the date of the day, the month, and the year, and beneath it, in red ink, the words *8:30 P.M., last trial.* Clinton turned toward the door, and was about to leave, but Dalton barred his way.

"Can you give me your word of honor, Dr. Clinton, that this injection will do your sister no harm?"

Dalton said this in a hoarse voice. Clinton was stunned at Dalton's words, but he soon regained his composure and his mocking tone: "This remedy is reliable, I assure you."

But, suddenly changing his tone, he said: "May I ask the reason of your visit at such a late hour, Mr. Dalton? I had an idea that we had done with each other for life."

Dalton kept an eye on Clinton. Taking the medical journal containing the article against the "Fever" from his pocket, Dalton spoke in measured tones: "In this journal, Dr. Clinton, you will find an article which is of the greatest importance to you, and it affects your lifelong labors. Read it."

Under the pressure of Dalton's gaze, Clinton looked at the journal. He had hardly read the heading of the article when he turned deathly pale. The hand that held the hypodermic syringe trembled, and, totally unnerved, he sank into a chair. Clinton read the article, and after he had finished, he heaved a deep sigh, like one who has received a death-blow. He looked at Dalton as if he desired to read the latter's thoughts. Dalton could barely stand this look, for he felt as if he had spoken Dr. Clinton's death-sentence. Suddenly Clinton rose from his seat, stepped to the other side of the big table, so that the table was between him and Dalton. His eyes shone with radiance that beautified his face.

"You have asked me a while ago whether I would pledge my honor upon the reliability of this remedy. I will pledge my life." Dr. Clinton had taken hold of the loose skin on his neck, and before Dalton could move, injected the contents of the syringe. At first Dalton was paralyzed, but he soon ran up to Dr. Clinton and tore the injector from the latter's hand. It was too late. Clinton tried to make light of the matter, saying that he only meant to scare Dalton; but when he saw the latter's despair, his bravado gave way to a like feeling. With a cry of horror he threw himself on Dalton's breast and said: "For God's sake, George, save Alvira. I am lost, but you will spare me for her sake."

"I will," said Dalton; "and now lie down and rest. I think you will need to. I will look after Alvira."

Slowly Dalton went upstairs again, so as to collect himself, and not to frighten Alvira by his looks. He told the girl not to despair about her brother; that he was all right, and except the interruption caused by some physical disarrangement, will continue his work. However, he thought it advisable that Alvira should look after her brother once in a while, and for that purpose she must try to get well soon. He also said that he had made up with her brother, and that he would now call more frequently, after which he left her in a blissful deception, but himself heartsore and troubled.

Two days passed. Dalton came twice a day, and Alvira's reports were quite encouraging. "Her brother felt tired," she said. "He writes everything in his book of scientific notes,--his pulse, his temperature. To me he is quite tender, and he is full of praise about your manliness and worth"; and the girl smiled as a woman only can smile when proud of the man she loves.

On the third day a frightful fever attacked Dr. Clinton. His sister watched by his side during the day, and at night Dalton changed with Mort. Upon a little table near the bed was the day-journal in which Clinton wrote notes as often as he was clear-headed. During the day, while his sister was by his side, he seldom uttered a word; his power of will seemed strong enough, even in the heat of fever. He would not shock the poor girl. But it was different before the men. Now he seemed to be among the Mexicans, whom he gave snakes. "They are good; they don't bite; eat them, eat them!" he cried. Then, again, he seemed to be in the West Indies, where he and Mort were hunting patients. But he could not find them; and if he did not find them within a specified time, he would be hanged. The library seemed full of laughing and grinning doctors, howling dogs, and gnawing rats. He was looking for his great book upon the "Fever Bacillus," which he could not find. Some one of the grinning doctors had stolen it, trying to rob him of his fame.

When Dalton heard these ravings, he shuddered and disliked to stay. But when Mort came into the room, and Dalton saw that moving skeleton grin and leer at the poor Doctor, he was loath to leave him alone with that abominable wretch.

Five days had gone by. Clinton was still raving. Dalton sat by his side, contemplating the sad end of a brilliant career, when Clinton suddenly sat up in his bed. "George, promise me," he said, and his words came hard and slow. "It will be too late tomorrow. Send this book to the fellow who wrote that article. Let him use it."

"If this book is so valuable, why not publish it for Alvira's benefit?" asked Dalton.

"No, no!" cried Clinton. "I have worked for science only. Everything for science; for humanity, nothing. If you don't send it, destroy it. Another thing, George: in Mort's 'Clinic' over there, —in the glass tubes,—all the diseases in the world are in those tubes. There are the 'Fever Bacilli.' I want to rest in the grave. They will come from those tubes and destroy mankind to the last. Swear, Dalton, that you will destroy them—"

"How are the poisons to be destroyed?" Dalton faltered.

"By fire, by fire, by fire!" screamed Clinton. "Otherwise that fellow Mort is sure to come and carry the diseases and death among the people. He was always so hard against my dog Bruno,— I have no time now. I am looking for fresh subjects. I want to make my last injection. Ha, ha, ha! I am the creator of the fever! The fools did not know it,—one more"; and Clinton became again delirious.

About two o'clock in the morning Mort entered and desired to take Dalton's place, but the latter remained until daybreak. When he left he heard Clinton cry, "Burn them, Dalton, and Mort, too."

Dalton was gone about two hours, and was about to lie down to rest for a little while when the fire alarm was sounded. Looking out of the window, he saw the flames rising from the direction of Dr. Clinton's house. He dressed hastily and went thither. Dalton found Alvira wringing her hands in front of Mort's "Clinic," which was being consumed in spite of all efforts of the firemen. The house, being quite a distance from the "Clinic," was not in danger.

"Where is your brother?" cried Dalton.

"I don't know," answered the weeping girl. "I went to his room some time ago and found him and Mort gone."

In the afternoon the firemen found the charred remains of two bodies lying upon the stone floor of the "Clinic."

Dalton examined them and identified his poor friend Dr. Clinton, as well as his evil genius, Mort. In the breast of the latter was found a long Persian dagger.

The Automatic Executioner
Gustav Adolf Danziger (Adolphe de Castro)

"Mr. Giers, Feldon has gone, and left things down in Mexico in confusion. I have just received a dispatch; he has taken along all the stock, securities, and the private papers. You must go down at once and look the matter up. Get those papers at all hazards. As the scoundrel left but yesterday, he must be within reach. My private car will take you as far as the City of Mexico; there you take the narrow gauge to Orizaba. Your old friend Jackson will meet you at the station and assist you. Get ready. Steam it up; in five minutes you will have to start."

The morrow was to have been my wedding-day. I was sorry to think of the annoyance which this sudden departure would cause my beautiful Beatrice and her family. I had long learned to make the interests of my chief my own; delay was impossible; I could not even bid them good by. Duty before everything.

With feelings in which bitterness was curiously blended with satisfaction—satisfaction with the new evidence of confidence that I was giving—I said that I would be ready.

Returning to my office, I hastily wrote a note to Beatrice, took a box of cigars, and in another two minutes found myself in the chief's private car. He handed me written instructions and a check-book, and wishing me a safe journey, gave the signal to the engineer. A shrill whistle, and away we sped at a tremendous rate.

I read the instructions carefully. Special stress was laid upon the recovery of those private papers which the chief had mentioned. Being acquainted with the country, I was sanguine of success, if I could but get hold of Feldon, although I did not know him personally.

We reached El Paso almost before I knew it. On we sped through Mexico, until we arrived at Queretaro, where an accident happened to the car. Fortunately we were within twenty minutes of the night express from Aguas Calientes to the City of Mexico, which stops in Queretaro.

Having telegraphed the chief regarding the accident, I ordered the car and the engine side-tracked until the next day, and procured a ticket for a first-class compartment to the City of Mexico.

I say "a first-class compartment" because the ticket agent had informed me that the express was made up of English coaches, with doors on both sides. I don't feel myself called upon to discuss the difference between English coaches and American cars, but although there are some disadvantages in English coaches, owing to the fact that the passengers face each other, a first-class compartment, when occupied by one or two passengers, is certainly far more convenient than the American car, with its two-seat chairs. The seats, which run the whole width of the English compartment-coaches, are comfortably upholstered, with soft arm-rests and head-cushions.

I was talking with the engineer, who swore at the Mexicans in choice machine-shop terms, when the express rushed into the station. I was ushered into a compartment by the conductor; the engine gave a shriek, and we sped toward the City of Mexico.

The light in the compartment being rather dim, I did not, on entering, observe the presence of any other person. But I was made aware that I had a fellow-traveler by something like a growl. My companion had evidently been disturbed in his slumber, and did not greatly relish it. As I looked more closely, I saw that he was well dressed, of gigantic size, and evidently an American. I apologized for the intrusion, but he made no answer. I had been traveling alone the whole day, and was inclined to talk to someone, so, nothing daunted, I stepped across to his corner, and offered him a cigar; he refused, and turned his head towards the window.

I said no more, and, drawing my soft felt over my eyes, I tried to sleep. But—how shall I say it?—a mysterious power seemed to keep me awake. Opening my eyes, they met the steady gaze of the stranger. Again I closed them, and feigned sleep by a good imitation of a snore, while I looked at him through half-closed lids.

His gaze was still upon me; turn as I might, my eyes reverted to his, and the annoyance which I felt at first soon changed into horror, for suddenly his eyes took that strange brilliancy peculiar to savage beasts and the insane. The longer I looked at him, the firmer my conviction grew that I was the companion of a madman. It is literally true that this knowledge positively paralyzed me, for as I thought of rising, I could not move. The horror grew so intense that I felt the perspiration oozing from every pore in my body.

Thoughts chased one another through my brain with the rapidity of lightning; my school days, my life as a newsboy, my meeting with the chief, my first step to an honored position, my lovely affianced, my rise to the highest position in the gift of the chief, my race after Feldon,—all flashed before my mind; and there I was, my eyes spellbound by those of the madman.

I tried to recall my energy; I sought to coax my limbs into mobility. I reasoned with my fingers, asking them to move just a little; I knew if they but moved one hundredth of an inch, I should be safe. I tried to persuade them to move in the direction of my overcoat pocket, where I had my revolver. Life is so sweet (I reasoned); I am young, beloved, and well to do, and you know that I am a dead shot; move, oh, move just a little! All in vain; they could not or would not obey my will. In sheer despair I tried to scream, but while I heard the wheels roll upon the rails, and heard the beating of my own heart, I could not utter a sound. My God! Dumb and palsied in the bloom of life, in the chase after fortune, at the gate of domestic paradise! Help! Help! But no sound escaped my lips, and those terrible eyes still upon me!

Now he rose and slowly came to my side. What a tremendous fellow he was!—his head touched the ceiling. He stooped and looked into my eyes; his glance went right through me. He put his hand into my overcoat pocket, out of which he took my revolver and slipped it into his own pocket; as he did so he smiled a ghastly smile, more horrifying even than his gaze. Now he tapped me on the forehead, at the same time saying, "Get up, Mister!"

His touch acted on me like a powerful battery; I was up in

an instant. Strange to say, and as I stood on my feet, my faculties returned, but with them the recognition that I was absolutely at the disposition of the merciless maniac.

For a moment I thought he had hypnotized me, and wanted some sport, but I soon found out my mistake; he was obviously insane.

"What do you want of me, sir?" I cried.

"I want *you*!" he replied, ferociously.

"You want my money, I suppose. Here it is," and I handed him my pocket-book.

"Keep your money; I am not a robber; I am a philanthropist."

"And what do you want of me?"

"I want to show you an invention of my own; the automatic executioner."

"I shall be pleased to see it," said I.

"Shall you? I am glad of that."

With this he took from his pocket a curiously twisted cord, and continued thus: "I have worked on this for years, and am at last ready to show the world what real genius is like. As sheriff of Montreal, I have executed many criminals in my time, but their struggle was always a disgusting sight. My invention does away with all this; one end of the electro-automatic executioner is fastened to a hook, the noose is slipped over the criminal's head, and in a fraction of a second he is with the silent majority. Do you see the advantage of my invention?"

I thought it advisable to humor the trend of his mania, and said, "This is truly a great invention. I should like to introduce this among the politicians of San Francisco."

"Introduce it, eh? Why, yes, certainly; it shall be introduced, but I will do that myself!"

"And what do you want me to do in the matter?" I asked, trembling as the thought dawned upon me that he possibly wanted to try his invention on me. His answer confirmed my fears. He said:

"You? Why, you shall be made glorious by verifying the utility of my invention. I have been hunting in every country in the world for the proper person, worthy enough for that grand purpose, but Heaven bade me wait until this evening. I knew you would come, and am prepared to execute Heaven's command."

Imagine my horror! If I could have fainted, I should have experienced relief, and would have been executed without consciousness. But my nerves had grown strong during the last moments. I had perfect control over my faculties and feelings, and thought of means to escape an untimely death.

Involuntarily I looked at the bell-cord line, which, unfortunately for me, was on the other side of the compartment.

Madmen are cunning; he caught my look, and said, "It is useless to look for that rope there; this train does not stop at any of the way-stations; nor would Heaven permit this work to be interrupted. When we reach the City of Mexico, I shall be famous and you in heaven!"

For a moment I thought of jumping at the door, opening it, and saving myself; but the idea was not feasible, because, at the rate the train was moving, I would be dashed to death, were I lucky enough to escape the grasp of the powerful maniac.

"Make haste," said he, drawing his watch; "the execution must be completed before five, and it is now twenty minutes to five."

This intelligence caused me a thrill of joy; since force would only hasten my awful end, I must seek to gain time. The train was due in the City of Mexico at five o'clock; if I could divert him for that length of time, I was saved.

"My dear sir," said I, "I am quite willing that you should try your invention on me, but before I die, I ask you to grant me a favor."

"What is it? Speak! It is granted!"

"I wish to write my will, and a letter to a lady to whom I am betrothed, and would ask you to mail the letters in the City of Mexico. Will you do that?"

"Certainly, with pleasure; only be quick about it."

"I thank you very much. Ah, how provoking!" said I, searching in my pockets. "I have no paper to write the letters. Could you oblige me with a sheet of paper?"

"Certainly, sir; I have plenty of that," said he, extracting from his breast-pocket a tablet of paper and two envelopes.

While he was taking the paper from his pocket, I managed to break the point of my pencil.

"Just see how troublesome I am! The point of my pencil has broken off, and I have no knife to sharpen it."

"Oh, no trouble at all," he replied. "Just hand me the pencil and I will sharpen it for you." With this he took a keen-edged dagger from the belt under his coat and sharpened the pencil. He was evidently as well armed as he was physically powerful. Having sharpened the pencil, he sheathed his dagger, and told me to go on.

I thought of writing a lot of nonsense, but could not, for the life of me,—which really was at stake,—compose a simple sentence. In my despair I copied the alphabet. I drew the characters with care, in order to fill up time and space. Oh, my sorry fate! How slowly the moments passed by! How miserably slow the train moved on! I had often whistled a gallop to the "tac" the wheels were beating as they touched the connecting points of the rail, but now they were so slow that funeral music would have required a quicker *tempo*.

At last the sheet was full, and my executioner asked me if I were ready.

"I am ready with my will, but I have not written the letter to my affianced."

"Well, write quickly," said he, and his look was threatening.

"I should like to describe to her your wonderful invention. Can you show me how it works, so that I may write intelligently on the subject?"

"Decidedly, I will. You are a good fellow, entirely unlike those cowards in Montreal."

"Ah, but where will you fasten it?" I asked.

"Nothing easier; I slip the end through that lamp-bracket in the ceiling,—just the place for it."

So said, so done; but while he was thus occupied, I cast a glance at the window, and my heart gave a leap, for I saw the first houses of the great Mexican city. To gain a little more time was all that I needed; but my life depended on my doing so.

"Behold how it is done," said he, holding the cord in one hand.

"Ah, but you would have to engage a living executioner to slip the noose over the criminal's head," I argued.

"There is where you are at fault. You need no one at all to assist in the execution. The criminal himself slips it over his head, the automatic executioner being so charged with electricity that it no sooner touches his neck than it kills him."

He became frightfully excited, and in his rage did not hear the whistle of the locomotive. The sound inspired me with hope and courage. Now, another minute and I am safe!

"The only thing that perplexes me is how you prevent the criminal from slipping out of the noose. You would then need a man, after all, to keep the noose in the proper place."

"There is the great point of my invention. The electricity draws the noose together the instant it slips over his head and—"

"Can you draw?" I interrupted him.

"No," he replied. "Why?"

"Because, I should like to send my affianced a sketch of this wonderful executioner; she would enjoy it. But as you cannot draw, and as I, who am a first-class sketcher, could not possibly make a sketch after my death, she will have to do without it. She will be doubly sorry, because she edits a newspaper."

"A newspaper, did you say?" he cried, his eyes flashing wildly. "They refused to mention my invention in the papers in Montreal, the curs!"

"My affianced would be only too happy to do it, if—"

"If what?" he cried. "Why don't you finish?"

"I was going to say, if you would consent to slip the noose over your head, so that I might sketch you. She would publish the description only if it is accompanied by a sketch."

"This is a capital idea," said he; "and if you are quick about it, I'll do it."

"I will be quick," I cried. "Get ready."

I had hardly finished when he slipped the cord over his head; but quicker than thought I was at the door, opened it, and jumped. I fell into a crowd of people,—we were at the station of the City of Mexico. As I jumped I heard the gurgling sounds of the strangling maniac. Regaining my feet I hastened to the compartment, anticipating the horrible sight of the madman, strangled by the invention of his disordered mind. But imagine my surprise, when, on reaching the place of my late adventure, I found it—vacant.

Had I been dreaming, or was I mad? Had all that I suffered been an hallucination?

The curious crowd made such a noise that the conductor came forward, eager to know the cause of the tumult. I asked him if he knew my traveling companion,—if he had seen him leave. He looked at me in blank astonishment; he had seen no one leave the compartment except myself,—in the peculiar manner described. He said that I had been the sole occupant of that compartment from Queretaro; and turning to the crowd, said, in Spanish, "The American is crazy." This caused the crowd to disperse, panic-stricken. Seeing that I could get no satisfactory explanation from the conductor, I took my overcoat and bought a ticket for Orizaba. At the station there I was met by Jackson, who received me very cordially, and informed me that Feldon had been found. I had experienced so many shocks in the last few hours, that this news hardly surprised me. Still, I asked, "Where was he found?"

"In Jalapa," was Jackson's reply.

"When was that?" I queried.

"Last night," said Jackson.

"What has he got to say?" said I, sternly.

"To say!" cried Jackson; "the poor fellow has nothing to say; he is as crazy as a loon. I pity him. It took six men to manage him last night."

We had just arrived at the quartz mills, and Jackson conducted me into the room where Feldon was strapped to an iron bedstead, a raving maniac. As I looked into his face, I nearly fell, the shock was so tremendous. Great God! It was my traveling companion of the night before!

When I told Jackson the cause of my agitation, he was perplexed. "The automatic executioner is the very thing he raved about. We found him half dead, with a riata around his neck. This is very strange!" said Jackson.

My story met with many incredulous smiles in 'San Francisco. My dear wife alone believes it. "It is the projected consciousness, of your *Astral Body*, that experienced all this," she says.

The Tower from Yuggoth
Ramsey Campbell

I

Of late there has been a renewal of interest in cases of inexplicable happenings. From this it seems inevitable that further interest be shown in the case of Edward Wingate Armitage, who was consigned to St. Mary's Hospital, Arkham, in early 1929, later to be taken to an institution. His life had always been, by choice, the life of an outcast and recluse; for the greater part of his life outside the institution he had been interested in the occult and forbidden; and his supposed finding of incontrovertible evidence in his research into certain legendary presences outside Arkham which sent him into that period of insanity from which he never recovered, might therefore have been a seeming triviality, portentous only to his already slightly deranged mind. Certainly there were and still are, certain Cyclopean geological anomalies in the woods toward Dunwich; but no trace could be found of that which Armitage shudderingly described as set at the highest point of those strange slabs of rock, which admittedly did bear a certain resemblance to titan stairtreads. However, there undoubtedly was something more than the vast steps that Armitage glimpsed, for he had known of their existence for some time, and certain other things connected with the case lead an unbiased outsider to believe that the case is not quite so simple as the doctors would have it believed.

Edward Wingate Armitage was born in early 1879 of upperclass parents. As an infant, nothing peculiar may be noted concerning him. He accompanied his parents to their weekly attendance at the Congregationalist church; at home he played, ate, and slept with regularity, and in general acted as a normal child would. However, the house's welfare was naturally attended by servants, most of which in the manner of servants, had a tendency to talk more to children than the elder Armitages; and so it was that a three-year-old was noted to show unaccountable interest in what fell out of space on the Gardner farm in that year of 1882. The elder Armitages were forced to speak more than once to the servants on the subject of what was fitting for discussion with Edward.

A few years later, after a period in which Edward declined to leave the house except for walks with his parents, a change was seen to occur. It was in the summer of 1886 that this became particularly noticeable. He would indeed leave the house, but could not be seen playing anywhere nearby, though servants often saw him leave with a book from the house library under his arm—that library which had been partially built up of books from the inherited property of a grandfather. Certain of these books were on subjects occult and morbid, and Edward had been warned not to touch them— his father often considering their destruction, for he was a definite Congregationalist, and disliked such books' being in the house; but never did he put this idea into practise. None of these books appeared to be missing while Edward was away, but the father was unsure quite how many there were; and the boy was never met returning so that he might have returned whatever books he had taken. He invariably said that he had been "out walking"; but certain newspaper items, dealing with curious signs found scratched in the soil of graveyards, and certain peculiar erections, together with bodies of various wild creatures, found in the woods, gave the parents cause to wonder.

It was at this time, also, that the boy began to be avoided by all the children in the vicinity. This inexplicable avoidance began immediately after a young girl had accompanied Edward, or rather followed him, on one of his silent trips. She had seen him enter a grove of trees outside Arkham, where a peculiar arrangement of stones in the center, somewhat resembling a monolith, caught her eye. Characteristic of the cold-bloodedness of children in those times, she did not cry out when he procured a small rat, tied helpless near the monolith, and slit its throat with a pocket-knife. As he began to read in some unknown and vaguely horrible language from the book, an eldritch shadow seemed to pass across the landscape. Then came a sinister muffled roaring sound; sinister because, the girl swore, the roaring followed the syllables shrieked by Edward Armitage, like some hideous antiphonal response. She fled, telling her friends later but not her parents. Both the parents of the various children and Edward's parents inquired into the resultant avoidance, but could elicit no information. Only tales handed down through various families now make this tale available, and it is doubtful how much of it can be believed.

As time passed, Edward's father contracted typhoid fever. Further complications assured that it would be fatal, and in 1913 he was taken to St. Mary's Hospital (later to see another Armitage's consignment there) when, on the twelfth of May, he died.

After the funeral, Edward was left in the care of his mother. Bereaved of her husband, she had now only her son on whom to lavish affection. Edward's upbringing after this stage was much less strict; he was able to read and use whatever books in the library he wanted; his mother did not object to this, but she disliked his frequent trips at night, whose destination he refused to reveal. It was noticeable that after one of these nocturnal trips the morning paper would be missing; and Edward, who rose before anyone else in the house denied that it ever arrived on these occasions. One maid who showed a tendency to speak of certain nocturnal atrocities reported in the missing papers, was dismissed after the boy had told his mother of certain thefts which could only have been committed by this maid.

It was in 1916 that Edward left home to enroll at Miskatonic University. For a short time he gave most of his leisure up to study mathematics; but it was not long before he gained access to the restricted section of the library. After this step, his former leisure studying was eclipsed by a feverish perusal of those books residing in the library and about which so much has been written and conjectured. The hellish *Necronomicon* engulfed his attention in particular; and the amount of time which he spent in taking notes and copying passages from this tome of terror was only cut short by the repeated adjurations of his tutors to devote more time to his mathematical work.

However, it is obvious that he still found time to peruse these monstrous volumes; and toward such evidence is the curiously hinting tale of his tutor. Calling at the student's study while he was away, the mathematics tutor was constrained to enter and examine a few notebooks scattered over the bed. One of these was taken up with notes on the orthodox studies Edward was following; the tutor glanced through this, noting the care with which the notes had been prepared. A second was composed of passages copied from various sources—a few in Latin, but most in other, alien languages, set off by certain monstrous diagrams and signs. But the notebook which startled the tutor more than the cabalistic signs and non-human inscriptions was that containing certain speculations and references to rites and sacrifices performed by students at Miskatonic. He took this to the principal, who decided not to act as yet, but, since there were numerous references to an "Aklo Sabaoth" to be performed the next night, to send a party of tutors to spy on these proceedings.

The next night certain students were observed to leave their rooms at different hours and not to return; several of these were followed by tutors asked by the principal to report on that night's proceedings. Most of the students made their way by devious routes to a large clearing in the otherwise almost impenetrable woods west of the Aylesbury Road. Edward was noted to be one of those who seemed to be presiding over the strange gathering. He, and six others, all wearing strange and sinister objects around their necks, were standing on a huge, roughly circular slab in the center of the clearing. As the first ray of the pallid crescent moon touched the slab, the seven standing upon it moved to stand on the ground beside it, and began to gibber and shriek strange half-coherent ritual invocations.

It is only believed by one or two of the watching professors that these invocations, in languages meant for no human tongue, elicited any response. Undoubtedly it was a disturbing sight, those seven students yelling sinister syllables at that slab of stone and moving further from it on each chorused reply from the encircling watchers. This being so, the impressions of the hidden tutors may be understood. Probably it was simply an atmospheric effect which made the vast slab appear to rise, slowly and painfully; and it must merely have been nervous tension which brought one savant to hint at a huge scaly claw which reached from beneath, and a pale bloated head which pushed up the slab. It must certainly have been the marks of something natural which were found by the next day's daylight party, for such marks would lead one to believe that the reaching claw had seven fingers. At a chorused shriek from all the participants, a cloud passed over the moon, and the clearing was plunged into abysmal darkness. When the place was again illuminated, it was totally empty; the slab again was in position; and the watchers stole away, disturbed and changed by this vague glimpse of nether spheres.

The following day saw a terrible interview with the principal, by Edward, among others. His mother, perplexed, was summoned across the city; and after she and Edward had visited the principal's office, when the door was locked, they left the university, never to return. Edward had to be escorted from the office by two of his former, non-decadent fellow-students, during which he screamed curses at the unmoved principal, and called down the vengeance of Yog-Sothoth on him.

The cross-town trip was utterly unpleasant to Mrs. Armitage. Her son was continuously mumbling in strange accents and swearing that he would see the principal "visited." The disturbing interview at Miskatonic University had brought on a sickening faintness and weakness of her heart, and the pavement seemed to hump and roll under her feet while the houses appeared to close in on her and totter precariously. They reached their extensive house on High Street only barely before the woman collapsed in her reaction to that terrible interview. Edward, meanwhile, left her in the front room while he repaired to the study. He seemed to be bent on discovering a certain formula; and he returned in a rage when all the forbidden books in the library would not yield it.

For some days after Armitage, now eighteen years old, went about the house in a state of morbid introspection. From various hints dropped in what little conversation he had, it became obvious that he was mourning his loss of access to the blasphemous *Necronomicon*. His mother, who was fast succumbing to that heart weakness started by the unpleasant affair at the university, suggested that he should take up research into things a little nearer reality. Showing contempt at first for his mother's naivete, he began to perceive possibilities, apparently, in this system, and told her that he might pursue research "a mite closer to home."

It was perhaps fortunate that, on November 17, Mrs. Armitage was rushed to the hospital, taken with a bad fit of heart failure, the aftermath of Edward's dismissal. That night, without regaining consciousness, she died.

Freed from her restraining influence, unaffected by long university hours, and having no need to work because supported by the extensive estate he had inherited, Edward Wingate Armitage began that line of research which was to lead to the revelation of so many unsettling facts, and, finally, to his madness in 1929.

II

Christmas 1917 saw Edward Armitage's mourning period end. After the New Year holidays were ended, passers-by would notice him, now equipped with a small sports car—the only luxury he had bought with the recently inherited estate, driving in the direction of the countryside end of High Street. At such times he would start out in the early morning, and not be seen to return until late evening. When met out on the rough country roads outside Arkham, he was seen to drive at the highest speed he could drag out of the car. More than one person recollects that he turned off the road into an even more primitive driveway to a decrepit, ancient farmhouse. Those who were curious enough to inquire as to the owner of the archaic homestead were told that the old man was reputed to have an amazing amount of knowledge concerning forbidden practises in Massachusetts and was even reputed to have participated in certain of these practises.

From the notes in that capacious notebook which he always carried, Armitage's trip may be reconstructed. The drive through the brooding country, unchanged for incredible aeons before the advent of civilisation in New England, is recalled in detail in the first pages, as if Edward was afraid that something might prevent him from remembering the route. The exact position of the turning off the Innsmouth road is marked on a small sketch-map.

At this point, the biographer can only imagine Armitage's route. The walks up the muddy pathway to the farmhouse, between tottering, clawing, moss-covered trees, and the reaching of the leaning building on a slight rise, may be conjectured. One can but imagine Armitage's turning to stare back across the undulent fields, colorless under the glaring sun and first mist of morning. Far off could be seen the steeple of the Arkham Congregational church, towering over the glistening gambrel roofs of the busy town. In the other direction, unseen over the horizon, would lie Innsmouth, with its half-human inhabitants, avoided by normal Arkham folk. Armitage would look out across the lonely landscape, and finally turn to batter on the door of the farmhouse before him. After repeated summonses, the shuffling footsteps of Enoch Pierce, the half-deaf owner, would be heard down the oak floorboards of the passage.

The aspect of this man at their first meeting somehow startled the visitor. He had a long beard, a few straggling strands of hair falling over his forehead. He fumbled senilely as he spoke, but a certain fire in his eyes belied his appearance of senility. But the attribute which so startled Armitage was the curious air which hung about this primitive rustic, of great wisdom and unbelievable age. At first he tried to close Armitage out, until Armitage pronounced certain words in a prehuman language which seemed to satisfy Pierce. He ushered the visitor into the sparsely furnished living-room, and began to question him as to his reason for visiting. Armitage, making certain that the old man's sons were occupied out in the fields, turned his own questions on the old rustic. The man began to listen with growing interest, sometimes mixed with unease.

Armitage, it appeared, was desperately in need of a certain mineral, not to be found anywhere on earth except under the ice in certain sunken cities in the Arctic, but mined extensively on Yuggoth. This metal had various peculiar characteristics, and he felt that if he could discover where the crustacean beings of the black world had their outpost on earth, he could have traffick with them by virtue of the most potent incantation in R'lyehian, using the hideous and terrific name of Azathoth. Now that he had lost access to the Miskatonic copy of the *Necronomicon*, he would first be trying the surrounding country before visiting Harvard to attempt to peruse their copy. He had a feeling that perhaps the ancient rustic, with his reputed store of forbidden knowledge, might enlighten him, either as to the incantation or the location of the Massachusetts outpost of the race from Yuggoth. Could the man assist him?

The old man stared unseeingly at his visitor, as though his

vision had suddenly opened on the abysmal, lightless vacuum of outer gulfs. He seemed to recollect something unpleasant from out of the far past. Finally he shuddered, and, now and then stretching forth a bony hand to grip his listener's lapel, he spoke.

"Listen, young Sir, 'tain't as if I haven't ben mixed up in turrible doin's. I had a friend onct as would go down to the Devil's Steps, an' he swore as he'd soon have them Yuggoth ones about him, ministerin' at every word he spoke. He thaought he had words as would overcome them that fly over the steps. But let me tell yew, he went too far. They faound him out in the woods, and 'twas so horrible a sight that three of them as carried him wasn't never the same sence. Bust open, his chest and his throat was, and his face was all blue. Said as haow it was ungodly, them from Arkham did. But those as knew, they said those up the steps flew off with him into space where his lungs bust.

"Don't be hasty naow, young Sir. 'Tis too dangerous to go and seek up them Devil's Steps. But there's something out in the woods by the Aylesbury Road that could give you what you want, mebbe, and it ain't so much a hater of men as them from Yuggoth nohaow. You may've ben to it—it's under a slab of rock, and the Aklo Sab'oth brings it—but mebbe ye didn't think of asking for what ye need? It's easier to hold, anyhaow—ye don't even need Alhazred for the right words. An' it might get things from them from Yuggoth for ye. 'Tis worth a try, anyhaow—before ye gets mixed up in what might kill ye."

Armitage, dissatisfied, could gain no more information concerning the outpost at Devil's Steps, that vast geological anomaly beyond Arkham. He left the farmhouse in an uncertain frame of mind. A few nights later, he records, he visited the titan slab in the woods west of the Aylesbury Road. Seemingly the alien ritual had little effect, needing a larger number of participants; at any rate he heard sounds below as of a vast body stirring, but nothing else.

The next recorded trip is that to Harvard University, where he searched the pages of their copy of Alhazred's massive hideous blasphemy. Either theirs was an incomplete edition, or he was mistaken in thinking that the volume contained the terrible words. For he came away enraged, and convinced that he needed the R'lyeh Text, the only copy of which, he was aware, resided at the Miskatonic University.

He returned the next day to Arkham, and proceeded to call at the Enoch Pierce homestead again. The old farmer listened uneasily to Armitage's tale of his lack of success, both in raising the daemon in the clearing at Harvard. The recluse seemed to have had an even greater change of heart since his visitor had last seen him, for at first he even declined to aid the seeker in raising the thing in the wood. He doubted, so he said, that it would be able to supply Edward with the necessary incantations to subdue the crustaceans from Yuggoth; he also doubted that even two participants would be capable of stirring it from below its slab. Also quite frankly, he was slightly disturbed by the whole proceedings. He disliked to be connected with anything concerning those Armitage ultimately wished to contact, even so indirectly as this would concern him. And, finally, he might be able to tell Armitage where to procure the incantation.

Armitage, however, was adamant. He meant to call up that below the slab off the Aylesbury Road, and he would try this before following any more of the venerable rustic's doubtful recommendations and since it was unlikely that anyone else would accompany him to this ritual, it would be necessary to ask the aid of Pierce. When the man further demurred, Armitage spoke a few words, of which only the hideous name Yog-Sothoth was intelligible. But Pierce (so the other recorded in that invaluable notebook) paled, and said that he would consider the suggestions.

The Aklo Sabaoth only being useful for the invocation of daemons on nights of the first phase of the moon, the two had to await the crescent moon for almost a month. 1918 was a year of mist and storm over Arkham, so that even the full moon was only a whitish glow in the sky in that month of March. But Armitage only realized the necessity of deferring the ritual when the night of the first quarter arrived moonless, a definitely adverse condition.

These unfortunate meteorological conditions did not end, in fact, until early 1919, Armitage now being twenty years of age. Not many of the neighbors realized he was so young—the monstrous wisdom he had acquired from reading the forbidden books in his library and that at the Miskatonic—and those who knew about his real age somehow did not dare to speak what they knew. That was why nobody was able to stop him as he left the house at dusk, one night in April 1919.

The wind howled over the countryside as the sports car drew up at the end of the driveway to the Pierce farmhouse. The countryside, in the lurid light across the horizon with faint threads of mist rising from the marshy field, resembled some landscape out of hideous Leng in central Asia. A more sensitive person might have been uneasy at the brooding eldritch country; but Armitage would not be affected by this, for the sights he was to see that night were far more horrible, such as give threats to sanity and outlook. Muttering certain words at the not-yet-risen sliver of moon, he pounded on the oaken door.

The old man mumbled affrightedly at the sight of his visitor, and tried to turn him away with pleas of something to be done that night which was very pressing. But he had promised Armitage that he would accompany him, and his visitor held him to that promise though it had been made over a year before. He escorted Pierce out to the waiting sports car, in which they drove off across the grim, primeval landscape. All too soon they turned off to reach the Aylesbury Road. The drive down it was a nightmarish affair of close half-demolished lichenous brick walls, grassy verges with huge darkly-colored pools, and stunted trees, twisted into grotesque shapes which creaked in the screaming wind and leaned terrifyingly toward the road. But however morbid the drive may have seemed, it could have been no consolation to Pierce when the car drew off the road near an especially dense belt of forest.

The trip down the pathway between the towering trees may

only be imagined. But the walk through the fungoid-phosphorescent boles and path-blocking twisted roots soon widened out into a clearing—the clearing of that horrible survival from aeons before humanity occurred. Armitage waited impatiently as the moon's thin rays began to trickle across the boundary of the clearing. He had insisted that Pierce stand near the slab of vast mineral, and that person now shuddered as he watched the accursed sliver of moon creep up toward the zenith.

Finally, as that first beam of pallid light struck the circular stone, the searcher began to shriek those mercifully forbidden words in the Aklo language, the terrified farmer joining in the responses. At first, no sound could be heard except certain movements far off among the trees; but as the moonbeams progressed across the pitted grey expanse both Armitage and his disturbed companion began to hear a sound far below in the earth, as of some Cyclopean body crawling from unremembered abysses. The thing scrabbled monstrously in some black pit under the earth, and so greatly was the sound muffled that it was not until the slab began to creak upward hideously that the watchers realized the nearness of the alien horror. Enoch Pierce turned as if to flee but Armitage screamed that he should hold his ground, and he turned back to face whatever monstrosity might rise from the pit.

First of all came the claws and arms, and when Pierce saw the number of arms he almost screamed outright. Then, as these dug into the soil around that hole into nether deeps, the thing raised itself almost out of the hole, and its head came into sight, pressing up the impossibly heavy slab of unknown material. That bloated, scaly head, with its obscenely wide mouth and one staring orb, was in view for but an instant; for then the arm of the hideousness shot out into the moonlight, swept up the hapless Pierce, and whipped back into the blackness. The stone slab crashed back into place, and a ghastly shriek from the victim yelled out beneath the stone, to be cut off horribly a second later.

Then, however, Armitage, shaken by the horror he had seen but still mindful of his mission, pronounced the final invocation of the Sabaoth. A terrible croaking rang out in the clearing, seeming to come across incredible gulfs of space. It spoke in no human tongue, but the hearer understood only too perfectly. He added a potent list of the powers which he had called out of space and time, and began to explain the mission on which he had sought the abomination's aid.

It is at this point in the notes of Edward Wingate Armitage that an air of puzzlement is remarked by all commentators. He recounts, with a growing air of disbelief and definite unease, that he explained to the lurker below the slab that he wished to learn the long invocation of the powers of Azathoth. On the mention of that monstrous and alien name, the shambler in the concealed pit began to stir as if disturbed, and changed hideously in cosmic rhythms, as if to ward off some danger or malefic power. Armitage, startled at the demonstration of the potency of that terrific name, continued that his reason for wishing to learn this chant was to protect himself in traffick with the crustacean beings from black Yuggoth on the rim. But at the reference to these rumored entities, a positive shriek of terror rang out from below the earth, and a vast scabbling and slithering, fast dying away, became apparent. Then there was silence in the clearing, except for the flapping and crying of an inexplicable flock of whippoorwills, passing overhead at that moment.

III

One can learn little more about the ways of Edward Wingate Armitage for the next few years. There are notes concerning a passage to Asia in 1922; the seeker apparently visited an ancient castle, much avoided by the neighboring peasantry, for the seemingly deserted stronghold was reputed to be on the edge of a certain abnormal Central Asian plateau. He speaks of a certain tower room in which something had been prisoned, and of an awakening of that which still sat in a curiously carved throne facing the door. To this certain commentators link references to something carried on the homeward passage in a stout tightly-sealed box, the odor of which was so repulsive that it had to be kept in the owner's cabin at the request of other passengers. But nothing could be gleaned from whatever he brought home in the box, and it can only be conjectured what was done with the box and its contents; though there may be some connection with what a party of men from Miskatonic, summoned by an uneasy surgeon at St. Mary's, found in Armitage's house and transported out to a lonely spot beyond Arkham, after which they poured kerosene over it and made certain that nothing remained afterward.

In early 1923 Armitage journeyed to Australia, there being certain legends of survivals there that he wished to verify. The notes are few at this point, but it seems likely that he discovered nothing beyond legends of a shunned desert stretch where a buried alien city was said to lie. Upon making a journey to the avoided terrain, he remarked that frequent spirals of dust arose in the place for no visible reason, and often twisted into very peculiar and vaguely disturbing shapes. Often, also, a singular ululation—a fluted whistling which seemed almost coherent—resounded out of empty space; but no amount of invocation would make anything appear beyond the eldritchly twining clouds of dust.

In the summer of 1924 Armitage removed from the High Street residence to an extensive place at the less-inhabited end of the Aylesbury Road. Perhaps he had grown to hate the pressing crowds in the city; more likely, however, he wished to follow certain pursuits that must not be seen by anyone. Frequent trips to that abnormality beneath the stone in the woods are recorded; but presumably the lack of participants made the ritual useless, for no response could be elicited. Once or twice there is a rise of defiance, noticeable in the tenor of the notes, but before he actually visited the Devil's Steps and its monstrous secrets, he would always repent his foolhardiness. Even so, he was becoming desperate with the lack of that unearthly mineral that he needed. It is better not to think of what his actions and fate might have been, had he not finally discovered a route to learning that long-sought and forbidden incantation.

But it was soon after, in March of the memorable year 1925, that Armitage recollected words of Enoch Pierce before that last horrible April night in the haunted clearing. Perhaps he had been rereading his notes; at any rate, he remembered Pierce's plea that he might be able to tell him where to procure the incantation, one day in 1918. At the time he had believed that this was merely a lie to defer the awful moonlight ritual; but now he wondered if it might not have had some foundation in reality. For the rustic had known a number of people possessing rare occult knowledge. One of these might conceivably know that incantation.

The next day he drove to the homestead, which was even more decayed and tottering than he remembered. Pierce's wife was dead, and the two sons now lived there alone, eking out a meager income from the pitiful herd of cattle and few poultry. They were extremely displeased to see him, suspecting that their father's inexplicable disappearance had been effected by something which Armitage had "called aout of space"; but their fear overcame their hatred, so that they invited him into the parlor, albeit with unintelligible whisperings to each other. One, the younger, excused himself to tend the herd; the other listened uneasily to the visitor's questions. Who were the friends of his father who might have been connected with witchcraft, black magic and the like? Which, if any, were alive today? Where did they live? And, most important, which would be likely to know more than had Enoch Pierce?

The son's slow response resembled that of his vanished father. Most of the men who had aided Pierce in his forbidden searching were all gone now. He had had one who had only come after his father made certain actions and spoke alien words, and it had once been let drop that he had been hung in that all-embracing purgation at Salem in 1692. The great majority of the rest had also vanished inexplicably after the father had not returned, and his son seemed to consider that these were of the same kind as the fugitive from Salem. One who had come up from Portsmouth, however, kept house just outside Dunwich, or had used to. But he thought even he might have died, and only been present in the house at Dunwich when called by the vanished Pierce to aid him with the volumes there.

Excitement now began to take hold of Armitage. A man who had come from Portsmouth probably would have been driven to his new home by witchcraft frenzy in 1692, if this peculiar reference to his death before Pierce met him was to be taken literally. Pierce had had a startling amount of knowledge, but if this eldritch being had been called to his aid, it might conceivably be much more wise. And the references to the many tomes in the house outside Dunwich —why, this private library might even include the R'lyeh Text of nameless wisdom! So great was his excitement at the possible long-forgotten vistas that might be opening before him, that Armitage even stopped to thank the plainly hostile being before him as he hurried out to his waiting car.

But disappointment awaited him at the end of his frenzied drive to Dunwich. The house of the Portsmouth refugee was found easily enough, on the crest of a hill—or, rather, what was left of the house. Only three nights before it had caught fire. A party of men, in the vicinity for no particular reason, somehow neglected to call the fire brigade; and the ancient house, with all its rumored contents, was destroyed except for one or two incombustibles—such as a skeleton, human only as to the skull, but otherwise so unearthly that only voluminous clothing could allow its living counterpart to pass for a human being.

Bitterly disappointed and desperate, Armitage returned to his house off the Aylesbury Road. He began to search, it would appear, for a parallel formula in the books of the library. But even this could not be found; and he began to slip into a lassitude and depression born of desperation.

It is pointed out, by those commentators wishing to see a sane and wholesome explanation for that last occurrence in the woods between Dunwich and Arkham that in early 1928 Armitage began to take drugs. Previously he had been without hope of any road to the ritual he wanted; now, with the foolhardiness of his sudden addiction, came a resolve to carry out a quickly-conceived plan to enter the Miskatonic University and carry off their copy of the volume he sought. He would need a dark night, and even the March of that year had phenomenally light nights. He was forced to wait impatiently until October, when a series of heavy rainstorms all over the region forced him to procrastinate still further. It was not until December that the series of deluges ended; and on the day before he was to carry out his individual assault on the university, he happened to buy a copy of the *Arkham Advertiser*, and in so doing he became aware of the first of a series of events which were to lead to that frightful outcome.

The piece which caught his eye was in the inside pages of the paper, for the editor believed that it was so choked with hellish speculation as to be of little portent. It dealt with a hill in the Dunwich country already known for a disaster in 1925. The lower regions of the hill had been inundated in the phenomenal floods in that region, and when the hill had been revealed fully again by the sinking of the water, a tunnel into inner depths was seen. It led to a door in the rock below the soil, securely sealed so that the water had not passed it. The inhabitants of the neighborhood seemed to be afraid of approaching the place; and the reporter said humorously that it was unlikely that anyone from Arkham would be interested in investigating, so that it might remain an unsolved mystery. A rather ironic pronouncement, for Armitage, as soon as he realized what might be in that room, returned home and drove as fast as possible to the hill beyond Dunwich.

He drew up in a side road, which would have led past the hill of the revealed secret but for the lower part of the road's being covered in water. Leaving the car in the higher section of the road, Armitage began to approach the newly-found room, walking on raised ground at the side of the route, dry but slightly yielding. Soon reaching the passage into the hill, he began to walk down the twilit tunnel, which was now completely free from moisture. The door at its end swung open at a touch—for although it was completely sealed, the portal was balanced, in reality, in a manner once very well known in various prehuman civilizations.

The place was unlit, and the searcher was forced to switch on a torch which he had carried with him. The place revealed was a small room with walls of bare rock, bookcases around three of the walls, that facing the door being piled high with large and peculiarly-shaped boxes, covered with moss, charred earth and other less describable materials. In the higher shelf of the left-hand set were a large number of papers and envelopes. But Armitage's eye did not linger on this, for below were various hide-covered volumes, and in the center of the shelf was a copy of the aeons-old R'lyeh Text. He took this down, noting that it seemed as complete as that up at Miskatonic, and made to carry it out to the car. As an afterthought, he decided to include the bundles of letters and papers on the top shelf, for the private documents of such a person of wisdom might yield much of interest to such a delver into fearful knowledge. He was not seen by anyone as he entered the car and drove off—not even that party of men who arrived with dynamite a few minutes after and caused the destruction later reported in a slightly satirical half-column in the *Advertiser*.

Upon reaching the Aylesbury Road residence, he entered the library and began to examine his acquisitions. First he turned through the Text in an attempt to find the incantation he had sought for so many years. He discovered it easily—it had been underlined, and the former owner had written beside it in the margin: "for traffick with Yuggoth." It was indeed the right chant, and the reader could not hold back a shudder at the hideous cadences and rhythms which it recalled to his mental ear.

He turned to the documents. The man's name, he discovered, had been Simon Frye, and at once it became apparent that the nameless suspicions of the time of death of Frye must have been correct. For the date of that first letter, with its archaic spelling and handwriting, was 1688; and none in the pile bore a later date than 1735. One—addressed, it would seem, to England, but never sent—was dated 1723. and so much had it impressed the reader that he had put a large star in red ink at the top of the yellowed missive. It may not be amiss to quote it in full.

Brother in Azathoth,
Your letter was receiv'd by me some Days ago, and so great has been my Excitement that I could not send you a letter to tell you of my good Fortune. I have, as you well must know, a great yearning for ye Text. My half-human Compatriot in Asia has now sent me a Copy of Volume of Terror, and if it had been in my possession when Cotton Mather had tried to destroy ye Coven, he would have had some Thing call'd down on him! But I wish to go to ye Steps of ye Devil beyond Dunwich and call those from Yuggoth. So I thank you for ye Vial of Powder of Ibn Ghazi which was enclos'd in yr Letter, and send my hope that ye Box which I enclos'd some time ago will help you to invoke Yogge-Sothothe, and no Thing give your Occupation away.
Azathoth ph'nafn Ogthrod
S. Frye.

A second missive was clipped to this by Armitage, and it can be conjectured that the second gave him a different outlook on his forthcoming traffick than did the first. The latter was dated 1723, a few months after the first, and since it came from Asia, it is presumable that the writer was Frye's "half-human Compatriot."

Brother in Azathoth,
I write this as a warning, and hope that I do not send too late. You know that my Father was one of those from ye black world which you seek, and you must know how many Foulnesses have come down to this Earth from Yuggoth. But for exceeding Horror and Malevolence, those of ye shell-bodies are ye greatest. Tho' my Father indeed was one of those that was call'd long ago, and my Mother liv'd too near to ye terrible Plateau of Leng, I have always avoid'd the Things which come down from that Globe on ye Rim. I have walk'd with Abominations which come up out of ye Darkness below ye Pyramid, and have had Traffick with those that came down from ye Stars with great Cthulhut, but ye Monsters from Yuggoth are all Horrours of all ye Cosmos, and even Cthulhut did not come from so near ye Rim at first. I would have let them take you off into ye Gulf, because of my Father; but no Man should ever have Traffick with such, and I warn you not to go to ye Steps, or anywhere else which is known to be an Outpost of Yuggoth.
Azathoth mgwl'nglui cf'ayak
James M.

But later documents of Frye show that he did indeed visit the Devil's Steps though inexplicably not until 1735, after which no more is heard of him. Pierce's references to a friend who "would go down to the Devil's Steps" may be recalled. The description of his fate also returns to mind in hideous detail.

An imaginative person may imagine Armitage as he stared out of the window into the sunset over far-off Arkham's gambrel roofs, making it resemble some fabulous city seen far off in the red dusk of a crystal dream. For a minute, perhaps, he almost wished to be back among the quaint New England scenery and mellow architecture which he used to see from his window on busy High Street. Transiently, he may have felt a hate and repulsion for the frightful things in which he had dabbled, and the abnormalities he had called out of space and earth. But the dreadful R'lyeh Text lay open before him, and he thought of the legendary powers of the stone which he would gain from traffick with the trans-spatial entities. The warnings of "James M." had had no effect almost two centuries ago; and his warning was unsuccessful on this modern sorcerer.

IV

It was on a day of wailing winds and lurid skies that Edward Wingate Armitage left his house on Aylesbury Road to drive out to the Devil's Steps beyond Dunwich. The Yuletide and New Year holidays did not suit his purpose, for too many people might conceivably take it into their heads to drive in the lonely Dunwich region, and question his drive into the most secluded and shunned part of the woods. For this reason the trip was postponed until a day in early January 1929.

The hitherto invaluable information in Armitage's notebook, now gives out, for he was in no condition to note down events when he returned from that frightful experience on that last cataclysmic day which led to his insanity and entrance to an institution. One must now rely on the seeming insane ravings of a madman if one is to learn anything about the journey and its aftermath. When, finally, he was discovered, after passers-by had heard strange sounds from the house on the Aylesbury Road, he had succeeded in destroying most of the volumes in his library, including the fabulous R'lyeh Text. Only a few books of hexerei and other important tomes were left together with the documents of Simon Frye and, of course, Armitage's notebook. The man babbled of a monstrous focal point of outer-dimensional activity, and screamed that he knew how the abominations from that black sphere on the rim moved between the earth and their terrible home. Under sedatives he calmed somewhat, and began to tell his tale with a little more coherency. He was, it became obvious, hopelessly insane; and little can be believed of what he hints and recounts in his delirium.

Concerning the actual journey he is fairly coherent, and one would not think that anything abnormal had happened. He speaks of the nearing of Dunwich, where the trees rattled and cackled hideously, and pitchy streams flowed by the road and disappeared into unseen and unspeakable gulfs. The wind that dropped into a brooding silence seemed to affect him with unease, and the shrieking flocks of whippoorwills that were disturbingly silent near his destination, those horrendous Devil's Steps, made him vaguely disquieted. But this was no more than the usual disturbance of the mind of travelers in that witchcraft-haunted region.

When he came to the cross-roads near Dunwich, where certain persons had been buried with stakes through their hearts, he left the car and, began to follow a curse-muttering stream which flowed through the overgrown forest. On one side was a rough path, leading into archways of vine-entangled trees; on the other great cliffs towered up to unbelievable heights, with strange signs cut into the rock here and there. He narrowly escaped falling into the hellishly-colored stream once or twice, and it seemed an aeon before the waters plunged into a curiously aritificial-looking tunnel, the path widened out into marshy ground, and he saw the fabled Devil's Steps leading up into mist and seeming to touch the dismal, overhanging sky.

As he crossed the marshy tract of land before his destination, he noticed certain eldritch marks in the soft earth. If they were footprints, they must have been of beings of which it is better not to think. They led back and forth, but they often seemed to disappear into the pit of the stream, and most of them ended at the shunned Steps. But Armitage, determined now to find whatever lay at the top of that Cyclopean stairway of rock and overcome it with his abominable incantation, did not hesitate more than a moment. He reached the first of the strata of unknown mineral and began to climb with the aid of a pick-axe.

Only a painful memory remains in his diseased mind of that interminable climb up into space, where the only sounds were the noise of his axe and that unhealthy trickle of water far below. His mind must have been full of conjectures as to what might be seen when he reached the top of the hidden plateau. Possibly some alien onyx temple would come into view, or perhaps a whole windowless city of that trans-spatial race. Possibly a lake might lie in the center of a horizonless expanse, hiding some ghastly aquatic deity, or conceivably a gathering of the entities might swim into view. How long he struggled upward and occupied himself with speculations born of something like terror can never be known. But it is certain that what he did see was something resembling what he imagined, for he recounts that when his head came over the edge of the last step he gasped in amazement—and perhaps a little in loathing. At any rate, it is one of the last things he can recall with complete coherency.

In the center of a lichen-grown plain stood three closely-set windowless stone towers. All about the rest of the plain grew a fortunately unknown species of vegetation, which resembled nothing which ever spawned on the face of earth elsewhere, with its grey fungoid stem and long twining decayed leaves, which leaned and flapped in Armitage's direction as he clambered over the edge of the plateau.

The half-nauseated searcher reeled between the fungi and leaned over the edge of one of a few pits, gouged so deep into the rock that their lowest point was lost in tenebrous blackness. These, he presumed, must be the mines on earth of the crustaceans from Yuggoth. No sign of movement could be seen, though there were metallic sounds somewhere far down in the dark. There was no evidence beyond this in any of the other pits, either, and he realized that he must seek elsewhere—in other words, in those forbidding black towers in the center of the plain.

He began to pick his way through the fungi, doing his best to avoid passing near them, for it seemed very repugnant to him that one of those blindly reaching grey members should touch him. Armitage was thankful when the last of the hateful nodding things was out of reach, for there was an extensive cleared space around each tower. The seeker decided to enter the central steeple; they seemed alike, each being about thirty feet high, without windows, as on the lightless planet of their origin, with a peculiarly angled doorway revealing stairs climbing up into total blackness. Armitage, however, had carried a torch with him, and, shining it up the alien passage, he forced himself to enter the somehow terrible building, reminding himself of the incantation.

Armitage's steps rang hollowly on the carven stairs, seeming to resound through illimitable gulfs of space. The darkness which barred the way ahead and soon closed in behind seemed to have an almost tangible quality, and the seeker disliked the way the blackness seemed to move and twist beyond the radius of his torch-beam. He knew that the tower was windowless only because the buildings had no windows on lightless Yuggoth, but his mind would persist in conjecturing what blasphemous abnormalities the lack of windows might hide in the tower. One could never be sure what might be standing around the bend in the dizzyingly spiraling steps and those hieroglyphics and crude drawings of fabulous spheres beyond were not comforting to the thoughts of the climber in the dark.

He had been ascending the lightless stairs for some time when he became aware of a strange feeling, as if he was about to suffer some terrible psychic displacement. There was no apparent reason why he should imagine such eldritch ideas, but it seemed as though he was about to be dragged forth from his body, or fall into some bottomless charnel pit. Those strange hieroglyphic characters all seemed to be indicating something unseen around that everpresent bend in the passageway. Was it simply a trick of light or vision that there appeared to be no steps above a certain point, and nothing except a totally dark expanse which even his torch's light would not penetrate? He drew back in affright, but once again curiosity overcame disquiet, and he continued to ascend the stairs. Upon reaching the anomalous wall of blackness, he closed his eyes involuntarily and rose one more step into the unseen section of the passage beyond the barrier.

Armitage cried out as he fell on the steps at the other side. It was as if his body had been momentarily torn apart into atoms and recombined in an infinitesimal instant. The agony he had suffered had never registered on his brain, but there was a memory of unspeakable psychic torture, resembling a memory from another life. He now lay on stairs seemingly a continuation of the steps on the other side of the barrier, but different in several essential respects. For one thing, the others had been bare and worn away; these, however, were covered with mineral dust. The walls, too, were grown with small glistening fungi, obviously of a type not seen in sane places of the world, instead of the curious, sometimes disturbingly alien hieroglyphics.

When he had recovered from that indescribable sensation, Armitage continued up the stairs. Though he felt as if he had been changed physically in some non-visible way, he noticed that the torch, to which he had clung through all that unendurable instant, still lit when he pressed the stud. He held the torch out in front of him, the beam stretching out some five feet from the ground. He rounded the inevitable bend in the stairs, and shone the ray into a face.

What that face was like, and of what body it was the face, he does not dare to tell. There are certain things which are better known by no sane man. If the whole truth about certain cosmic relationships, and the implication of the beings which exist in certain spheres, were known by the world, the whole of the human race would be shrieking in terror and gibbering for oblivion. And the thing which Armitage saw at last—one of those hideous crustacean beings which had come through space from the rim-world—was one such cosmically terrible being. But even though his mind shrivelled up inside his skull at the unspeakable sight which leered and flopped before him in the light of the torch, Armitage had enough composure left to scream that painfully-sought incantation at the monstrosity. It seemed to cringe—though it was difficult to correlate the motions of something so grotesquely proportioned and abnormally shaped—and clattered off down the steps. As it reached that black barrier across the stairs, it seemed to grow infinitely huge and become something even more monstrous, before it shrank to an infinitesimal point on the ebony curtain and disappeared altogether, as the clattering claws became silent.

Reeling against the lichenous wall, Armitage attempted to forget that fungoid abomination which had burst on him around that corner. As his mind returned to equilibrium from that seething void of suspicion, he began to climb again, not thinking of what might yet lurk in the upper regions of the tower. The darkness now seemed even more material, as if at any moment it might close in on the hapless Armitage.

It was about the time that Armitage began to realize that he had been climbing the darkened stairway far longer than he should have in a thirty-foot tower, that he saw the ceiling of the tower. The nitrous, dripping rock seemed to meet the stairs with no means of exit, but almost immediately he saw the curiously-angled trapdoor where steps and ceiling met. Now came the time of ultimate hesitation. Why would a trapdoor open out onto a circular roof, thirty feet above the ground, of small diameter? What nameless terror might await the opening of the trapdoor? But, having come this far, he did not wish to pass through that barrier of agony without having glimpsed what might lie above. So he pushed the door open with his shoulders and stepped out on the roof.

Even in his lunacy, Armitage does not pretend to have a plausible explanation for certain aspects of his fantastic tale. He insists that the barrier across the passageway was not as meaningless as sanity would have it appear, but thinks it was in reality a barrier between points that should have been millions of miles apart, had it not been for some awful tampering with the structure of the cosmos. He seems to conjecture that the barrier changed him bodily. —Otherwise, according to his story, the circumstances in which he found himself would have led to asphyxiation and burst lungs with the first breath he took on that other side of the barrier. He explains that the abominations of the plateau did not capture him because he shrieked the incantation incessantly as he plunged down the tower's stairway and climbed back feverishly down the Devil's Steps. None of this may be disproved—and as for those disturbing hints concerning "bodily changes," X-ray examinations show certain modifications of the lungs and other organs for which the doctors cannot easily account.

As he clambered on the roof, Armitage wondered if the sight of that stunted horror on the stairs had already unhinged his mind. How could he not have noticed these towers which his torch's beams picked out on every side as far as its light would reach? And how could it now be black night, when he had reached the Devil's Steps well before midday? His torch shining down the side of his vantage tower, showed black streets where abominable blasphemies moved among hideous gardens of those greyish nodding fungi and vast black windowless towers.

Confused and terrified, he stared out at the ebony void of space which stretched infinitely away from him, and of the crystalline, distorted stars which shimmered in the gulf. Then he stared again in growing, horrible realization, at those far-off constellations --and their positions.

For the positions of the constellations were never seen thus on Earth; and Edward Wingate Armitage knew in that cataclysmic instant that this place of fungoid gardens and streets of windowless stone towers, whither he had come through that barrier between dimensions, was none other than Yuggoth.

The Ringer of the Doorbell
Jim Cort

Robert Priest crept cautiously toward the shadowed corner of the room, his every muscle taut. A single false step now would ruin everything. He raised his arm, took deadly aim and threw.

The mouse saw the book and dodged at the last possible moment. The book slammed harmlessly into the wall and the mouse, impelled by the noise, ran directly toward him. Priest stumbled backwards and fell as the mouse ran straight up his leg. He sat down with a thud, and the mouse bounded from his belt buckle on to a filing cabinet nearby, then down and out of sight behind it.

Damn, thought Priest as he picked himself up, *where's Conan when you really need him?*

Priest had named the mouse Uncle Ho. He had been at war with him for more than a week, ever since he had found the damage done in his basement. Several cartons of his Lovecraftian journal, the *Arkham Advertiser*, had been nibbled, torn up and otherwise treated disrespectfully. He had lost two-thirds of his supply of the "HPL's Favorite Recipes" issue.

So far Uncle Ho had eluded his every search-and-destroy mission. He had burglarized the traps, snubbed the poison bait and always avoided capture. And today, the wily rodent had staged a daring daylight raid on his Cheez Doodles (strictly to taunt him, Priest was sure of it), and yet again made good his escape.

Priest sat down and took a quick drink from the Coke can on his desk to steady his nerves. Next time, he thought, there's always next time. He pushed his glasses back on his nose, swivelled in his chair and was just about to resume his typing when the doorbell rang. "What now?" he said aloud.

The guy standing on the porch was tall, at least six-foot-six, and skinny as a stick. It was a hot day, one of the hottest in fact, but he was dressed in a long overcoat buttoned up to his chin and hanging down to the ground where the toes of his red hi-top Keds poked out from under the hem. His collar was turned up, his shapeless hat pulled down, and he had black leather gloves on his hands. All Priest could see of his face was an impossibly large nose that looked like a sweet potato. Perched above it was a pair of dark glasses; below it sprouted a moustache so coarse and unruly it looked like the stranger was eating a hedgehog.

From somewhere behind this thatch of hair came a voice that sounded like a reed instrument clogged with goulash. "Uh . . . Hmm . . . Hello?" it said. "Are you there?"

Priest looked himself over. "Yes, this is me, all right," he said. He wasn't feeling gracious. He had the crazy notion that this was Uncle Ho calling in disguise just to get his goat.

The tall stranger shook a little. "Ho . . . ho," he said, "excuse. I am addressing to Ro-bert Priss?"

"I'll probably be sorry for saying this, but yeah, that's me."

The stranger extended his gloved hand, leaning a little forward. "I am happy to shake you. I am called . . . um . . . Joan

138

Smit'."

Priest took the proffered hand. It felt like a bag of worms. "What can I do for you, Mr. Smith?"

Mr. Smith swayed as if in a high wind. "Um . . . yes . . . I . . . ha . . . am being sent from . . . hmm . . . dentist for you."

"You're from the dentist? Usually they just send a postcard."

"Ho . . . ho . . . um," laughed Mr. Smith. He wagged his leather finger at Priest. "You are pulling my nose."

"Not even on a bet," said Robert Priest.

"One moment, thank you," said Mr. Smith, "I am explaining. It is . . . ah . . . Dentist Who I am being sent from, yes? About Scroll of Blifthchx."

Priest scratched his beard as he mulled this over. "Dentist who," he said, "dentist . . . Dennis Howe! The scroll! Is that how you pronounce it?"

"Always," said Mr. Smith.

"Please forgive me, Mr. Smith," said Robert Priest. "I wasn't thinking clearly. I'm just recovering from an attempt on my life. Won't you come in?"

"Yes, I won't," said Mr. Smith. And he did.

Mr. Smith moved in a very peculiar way. The top of his body leaned forward until it seemed certain that he would topple, then the lower portion would toddle forward to catch up with the top, his red sneakers flapping. It made Priest seasick to watch it. Once inside, Mr. Smith removed neither his hat nor his gloves, and kept his coat buttoned up and his dark glasses on.

"Please sit down," said Robert Priest, indicating a chair.

"No, please, I can be upstanding," replied Mr. Smith, swaying a little.

Priest sat at his desk and said, "You're not from around here, are you, Mr. Smith?"

Mr. Smith wagged a finger at Priest and cocked his head to one side. "Ah . . . um . . . I can look you are some wise guy," he said merrily. "One cannot to pull the sheep on top of your eyes. Of course, of course, I am from someplace other being."

"Where might that be?"

"California."

"Yes, I thought so," said Priest. He was noticing that Mr. Smith's nose wobbled back and forth when he spoke. Maybe not a sweet potato; maybe a yam.

"But we must give to each other the business," said Mr. Smith. "I am here for . . . huh . . . um . . . Scroll of Blifthchx. I have know our commonly held friend Dentist Who gave you a sendings of it."

"Yes, he did," said Priest. "I have his letter here someplace." He rummaged around on his desk until he found a yellow sheet scribbled in green Flair pen. "Here it is. He says,—but I guess you know about this if you've come from Dennis."

Mr. Smith waved his hands in front of him, looking like the Pope underwater. "No . . . um . . . thank you to continue proceeding. I have compound interest in such explainings."

"Well, I suppose Dennis told you I put out this little magazine about H. P. Lovecraft,--critical articles and some fiction, too. We had done an issue not so long ago about the mythical books full of arcane knowledge that he and his circle thought up—you know, the *Necronomicon*, the *Book of Eibon*,--"

"*Yalu Pages*," added Mr. Smith.

"Well, not quite as arcane as that," said Priest. "Anyway, after that issue came out, I get this letter from Dennis along with a Xerox copy of this Scroll thing. Some translation he's made or something. The letter said—,'" and Priest peered at the yellow sheet to refresh his memory, "'. . . found something really astounding . . . not like the *Necronomicon* . . . this is a real—,' something; I can't make that out. I think he spilled something on this.

"Well, anyway, I read the thing over and it seemed pretty standard: creepy things from outer space with lots of tentacles ruling the earth in pre-prehistory. The only thing that was slightly different was a notion about these space guys going around in disguise, you know, in everyday life today, trying to keep their existence secret. I thought it might be fun to publish it, but I wanted to speak to Dennis before I did. I wanted to learn more about this Scroll."

"What more?" said Mr. Smith, leaning almost at a ninety-degree angle.

"Just some background. You have to be careful when you put out a magazine like this. People send you all sorts of crazy stuff. I've got a piece right here from some woman in Oswego on Lovecraft's toilet training. Can you believe that, toilet training?"

"So . . . um . . . ha," answered Smith. "I have much trouble training mine."

"Yeah, me too," said Priest. He was beginning to feel that someone had turned the room upside down when he wasn't looking. "I wrote to Dennis but I haven't gotten an answer yet. Is that why he asked you to come?"

Mr. Smith stood up straight again. "He has . . . um . . . altered his brain," he said.

"Wait, don't tell me. I'll get it," said Priest, holding up his hand. "Altered his . . . Changed his mind? He changed his mind? About the Scroll?"

"So," said Mr. Smith nodding. "He is confessing to myself that it is merely an invention . . . um . . . ah . . . of his making up. You know what a humorous joking person is Dentist: ho . . . ho. He says to go to his good friend Robert Priss and say, 'I am only pulling your nose, good friend. You may give back the . . . hmm . . . copyings of the Scroll I am sending you to my good friend Joan Smit', and also not to telling any person.' So thank you to do this."

Priest sat forward and lay the letter back on the desk. "I'm sorry to hear that," he said. "I had it scheduled for the next issue. I was just going to start the typing today. I'd sure like to talk to Dennis about this."

"He is bound and joked," said Mr. Smith.

"Tied up, right? Too busy. It's getting easier to understand you, Mr. Smith. I'm a little concerned about that." Whoever had turned the room upside down was now swinging it back and forth on a string. Priest tried to think of something to slow it down. He spied the can on his desk. "Can I get you a Coke?"

Mr. Smith said, "Ah, from coal."

"No," said Priest, "that's only the new Coke."

Mr. Smith wriggled toward him and bent over slowly to examine the Coke can. Priest thought of a snake moving through tapioca. Smith placed his nose directly on the can and nudged it. The can tipped over on the desk top spilling the soda and turning Dennis's letter into a streaming green puddle on a yellow background.

"Oh," said Smith, suddenly straightening. "I puke with remorse."

Priest grabbed some tissues from a nearby dispenser. "That's OK, that's OK, no harm done," he said. He blotted up the spill, taking all the green ink from the letter with him. He tossed the sopping tissues into the wastebasket and said "I'll just go get us some more."

Robert Priest went into the kitchen and closed the door softly behind him, grateful for any excuse to get out of the room. Talking with Mr. Smith made his head hurt. He went straight for the telephone on the wall and dialed Dennis's number. He was frantic to find out if Dennis had really sent this goon. He wouldn't have put it past him, but this guy was too strange even for Dennis. And how could Dennis be too busy? He didn't even have a job. A recorded message came on saying the number was out of service. Just like Dennis not to pay his bill. He hung up the phone in disgust and was just about to get the drinks when he was brought up short by a bump and a crash in the other room.

Mr. Smith was standing by the closet. Most of the stuff that had been in the closet was now scattered on the floor in front of it. A tennis racket was tangled around his gloved fingers, and he was shaking his hand trying to get it off. He looked like a spastic banjo player.

"What are you doing in the closet?"

Mr. Smith moved back toward the center of the room, still shaking his hand. He drew himself up to his full height and said, "I am . . . hmm . . . making a lookings for. Thank you to give me the copyings of Scroll of Blifthchx. My time is walking away."

"Just a minute, now," said Priest. "If I decide to give it to you, I will, but you just can't—"

All at once, the tennis racket flew from Smith's hand and clattered against the wall by the filing cabinet. Uncle Ho darted from behind the cabinet and scooted across the room. From inside Smith's coat a purple tendril about the thickness of a clothesline whipped out at least a dozen feet and snatched Uncle Ho. There was a single squeak, and tendril and mouse disappeared back into the coat with a slurping sound.

"Excuse," said Mr. Smith.

Robert Priest's knees turned to jello and dumped him into

the chair by the desk. He stared at Mr. Smith open-mouthed and pointed to the filing cabinet. "Top drawer, green folder," he said in a toneless voice. It took several tries to get the words out.

Mr. Smith undulated over to the cabinet. He stood with his back to the desk and seemed to shrink, his head and shoulders slowly descending a foot or two, as if the air were being let out of him. Priest heard the drawer being opened and papers shuffling. He could see both of Mr. Smith's gloved hands still hanging at his side, fingers near the floor now. He could also see a squirming under Smith's billowed coat. He didn't want to think about it too much.

After a while Smith grew to his full height again and twisted around. A corner of the green folder peeked from his coat, then vanished inside. "So . . . ah . . . I am thinking I have taking out too much from your time," he said. "Of course, you can look that there must not be speaking with any person about what this is. Elsewise I must returning to come back with . . . hmm . . . my friends. So? Thank you do not getting up. I can find out my way." He started to go and then turned back and said, "Have a nice day." Then he slid out of the room and was gone. Priest heard the outside door open and close again.

He sat at the desk for quite a while just staring at the place where his visitor had been. Then he turned his chair toward the desk and picked up a sheaf of papers. It looked like there would be an opening in the next issue. This article about HPL's toilet training might be just the thing to fill it. It wasn't such a bad piece after all, considering.

The Slitherer from the Slime
Lin Carter

1. Mad Horror

The weird and inexplicable phenomena on the heights of the hills near my home having driven me nigh unto the very brink of madness, I had dispatched an urgent wire to my friend, an eccentric and scholarly recluse, begging his aid.

These hills rose to the north of the sinister, ancient, decaying Massachusetts seaport town called Happydale. My friend, the scion of an ancient Dutch family, resided in the sinister, ancient, decaying city of Prudence, Rhode Island. His name was Jethro Van Snort, a deep delver into the loathsome lore and abstruse arcana of blasphemous books from elder eons. If anyone could remove the curse from those accursed hills, it was Jethro Van Snort!

Night had fallen; the whippoorwills and pond frogs began their hellish chorus. And then the doorbell rang.

"Good Gad, Jethro, it's you at last!" I exclaimed. His lean, ascetic features looked disgruntled.

"Takes forever to get here on the Greyhound bus," he grumbled. Unfortunately, I gathered that eccentric and scholarly recluses like Jethro are also very frequently impecunious. I offered him a chair and a double brandy; he accepted both with alacrity.

"Now, Smothly, pray tell what is the trouble?" he snapped crisply. "Your wire was brief and enigmatic." I told him of the uncanny slime-trails on the heights of the shunned and ill-reputed hills to the north of sinister, ancient, decaying Happydale. He thumbed his left earlobe vigorously, a gesture I knew from of old to indicate deepest thought.

"Slime you say, Smothly?" he snapped crisply.

"Yes."

"*Reeking* slime?"

"Yes, yes."

"Reeking *green* slime?"

"Yes, yes, yes!"

"Thank Heavens you sent for me when you did, Smothly," he snapped crisply. "The very world hangs on the brink of the deadliest peril . . . I don't suppose you've ever heard of that ancient, abhorrent, forbidden tome of loathsome lore, the dreaded *Geheimergunken*?"

"Of course not," I snapped crisply. "You know that's the sort of ancient, abhorrent, forbidden tome of loathsome lore known only to eccentric and scholarly recluses such as yourself!"

He eyed me briefly. Then: "Quite right, Smothly! Stupid of me; for a moment I forgot that you do not happen to be an eccentric and scholarly recluse such as myself. No, your studies lie with more wholesome and uplifting forms of literature . . . De Sade is your field, am I wrong?"

"The Master," I breathed reverently. He nodded crisply.

"Quite! To continue, then: the ancient, abhorrent, forbidden *Geheimergunken* was written centuries ago by the so-called Mad Lithuanian, Stanislaw Gunk. It is a volume of fabulous rarity; only a handful of copies are known to exist in the entire world. Even the greatest libraries do not possess the *Geheimergunken*. Naturally, I brought a copy along," he added, gesturing towards his briefcase.

"Good Gad, Jethro! Why would you risk carrying with you on the Greyhound bus a work of such legendary rarity?" I exclaimed.

He eyed me briefly. "Don't talk drivel, Smothly! Of *course* I wouldn't risk losing the only copy of this priceless tome known to exist in the western hemisphere outside of the guarded vaults of the library of the Vodkatonic University, on the Greyhound bus. I had a Xerox made, you simpleton!"

"Good Gad, Jethro!"

He eyed me briefly. "Smothly, *do* stop saying 'Good Gad, Jethro!' so frequently. You sound like a character out of P. G. Wodehouse, and we happen to be in a very different kind of story."

"Quite right, Jethro," I said briefly.

He opened his briefcase and withdrew a mouldering volume bound in rotting black leather. The palpable reek of unwholesome antiquity rose from its decaying pages as he opened the book, as well as a considerable cloud of dust and several fat moths. He thumbed rapidly through the crumbling, ancient pages.

"Ah, here's the passage!" he exclaimed. "It's in the rare Ethiopic translation made by the eccentric and scholarly recluse, Haile Unlikely. Fortunately, I mastered Ethiopic during my years of secret study in the obscure Tibetan lamasery of Slopsy-Blob. I shall translate it for you as I go along:

> an other of ye Demon-Gods from Beyond ye Universe is even ye Slitherer from ye Slime, ye hideous and repellent Ugg-Li, who slithered down from ye Stars when ye Earth was young, together with his second-cousin once removed, ye equally hideous and repellent Ghast-Li, and betwixt ye Twain be everlasting enmity, for that ye Ugg-Li be an Elemental of Slime, whilst ye Ghast-Li be an Elemental of Napalm. And ye Ugg-Li resideth in ye loathsome Slime Pits of Snott beneath ye crust of ye Earth, tended by his disgusting minions and servitors, ye Nerds; yet can ye Nerds summon him up from ye Slime on ye nights when ye Evil Star burneth above ye horizon.

Snapping the ponderous volume shut, and pinching his forefinger in the process, Jethro Van Snort sprang to his feet, crossed to the window, snapped up the shade, peered out.

"Good Gad, Smothly (sorry: you've got *me* saying it now!), the evil star Alpha Beta Gamma is above the horizon! There's not a moment to lose!"

II. *Reeking Slime*

We left my ancient, crumbling manor-house and progressed towards the shunned, unwholesome hills with Van Snort in the lead. Circling the ill-reputed Blasted Heath, going around that uncanny ring of Standing Stones believed raised centuries ago by the demon-worshipping Squamous Indian tribe, and avoiding the Shunned Graveyard, we climbed the hills.

After a time, Van Snort muttered: "Phew! You certainly didn't exaggerate on the 'reeking slime' part of your account, Smothly!"

"Breathe through your mouth; it helps," I urged. "Now aren't you glad I suggested we don gum-boots before embarking on this adventure?"

"Yes, good thinking, Smothly," he snapped crisply.

We forged on with considerable difficulty, the slime making us slip and slide. Eventually, we neared the crest of the shunned hills.

"What do you think we'll find, Jethro?" I asked briefly.

"Heaven knows, Smothly! Nerds, I should hazard a guess, busy with their grisly rites . . . pray Heaven we are not too late!"

On the crest we hid ourselves behind a grove of hideous, misshapen, *horribly suggestive* trees. They were either beech or maple, I forget which.

"Look at *that*, Smothly!" Van Snort snapped crisply.

There was a fallen stone, like an uncouth and horribly suggestive altar. About it lumbered, capered, shambled a herd of creatures who were singularly disgusting, with their uncombed, greasy hair, ripe crop of zits, thick spectacles, buck teeth . . .

"Nerds?" I whispered briefly.

"Nerds," he confirmed grimly.

Above the altar floated something like a titanic blob of green jello, dripping reeking slime. This could only be the hideous and repellent Ugg-Li, who slithered down from ye stars when ye Earth was young, to quote the Mad Lithuanian.

"Pray Heaven we are not too late to save the world!" he snapped crisply.

"Well, *are* we or *aren't* we?" I demanded; his repetition of the phrase was beginning to get on my nerves. He was so busily thumbing his left earlobe that he seemed not to notice my irritated tone.

"There is only one thing to do, Smothly! Recall that the ancient, abhorrent, forbidden *Geheimergunken* claims that eternal enmity exists between Ugg-Li and his second-cousin once removed, Ghast-Li. We must summon Ghast-Li, by the spell found in the writings of the Mad Lithuanian, page 1147, as I remember . . ."

"But you left the Xerox copy back in my ancient, crumbling manor-house!" I exclaimed briefly.

"Fortunately I have the spell committed to memory," he snapped crisply. "Stand aside, Smothly, there's not a moment to lose!"

III. *Flaming Doom*

Lifting his arms in a curiously abhorrent ritualistic gesture, Jethro Van Snort chanted a weird invocation in a language I had never heard before. It went more or less as follows:

> *Ia! Ghost-Li! Gug-gug-ghaa,*
> *Huh-huh huh, ghaa'ghaaa!*
> *Unky-dunk wunk, Ugg-Li*
> *Nov shmov ka-pop!*

(I learned much later that this uncouth sequence of vocables, when translated into English, reads as follows.

> *Hi, there, Ghost-Li, you're the best,*
> *Now we put you to the test!*
> *Come on down and fight Ugg-Li,*
> *And we surely will thank ye!*)

For a hideously suggestive moment, nothing whatsoever happened. Still the shambling herd of Nerds capered grotesquely about the ancient stone altar; still that vast and gelatinous blob of green jello hung in midair, dribbling its reeking slime.

Then sparks of light appeared from all directions, converging on the gelatinous thing. They must have burned like the devil, because the gelatinous blob shrank, withered, dried, burned, and certainly began to *stink*. I'll tell you!

The Nerds fled squeaking in all directions. Soon the heaving blob of green slime was gone. Jethro Van Snort solemnly pronounced some sort of a banishing ritual, and the flying bits of fire vanished, too. Dawn was rising in the east.

We began to descend the hill slope, slipping and sliding in the slime. Jethro looked exalted.

"Once again I have saved the world from direst peril!" he snapped crisply. Then he continued, more bitterly: "But will they give me the Nobel Peace Prize? Oh, no! Not to an eccentric and scholarly recluse, like myself!" Then he added, meditatively, "Maybe I should hire myself a press agent . . .?"

We went down to the streets of sinister, ancient, decaying Happydale, Massachusetts, faces lifted fearlessly into the glad light of a wholesome dawn.

Once again, the forces of Evil had been thwarted by the forces of Good; I felt absurdly happy. I glanced smilingly at my old friend as he trudged along at my side, vigorously thumbing his left earlobe.

"On the whole, Smothly, I *do* think a good P/R man could be of help," murmured the eccentric and scholarly recluse from Prudence, Rhode Island.

Limericks from Yuggoth
Lin Carter

NOTE: In the early summer of 19-aught-2 there were unearthed near Limerick, Ireland, a number of stone fragments inscribed in the characters of an unknown language. Their discoverer, Doctor-Professor Etienne-Laban de Marigny-Shrewsbury, eventually identified the mysterious inscriptions as being in High Yuggothic. As I am the only scholar acquainted with High Yuggothic (or, at least, the only *completely human* scholar), he turned his rubbings of the Limerick Shards over to me. I have eventually succeeded in translating the inscriptions, the first sequence of which is published here, without comment. I will leave it to future generations of scholars to untangle the enigmatic meanings buried in these baffling and gnomic verses.

I.

We hardly know aught of Shaggai,
And I find myself wondering why,
 Since it sounds rather jaunty,
 And lies so close to Stronti
That they wave as we Mi-Go flap by.

II.

The Hounds of Tindalos, I've heard,
Get about in a manner absurd:
 They move only through angles—
 But no one untangles
Just what may be *meant* by the word!

III.

A snobbish and dull Elder God
Once thought it unseemly and odd
 The Old Ones should rebel,
 When they had it so well—
But, then, he loathed anything Mod!

IV.

The twin brothers, Lloigor and Zhar,
Came as tourists from some distant star,
 And found Earth so boring
 They spent aeons snoring
In caves under Alaozar.

V.

Of Eibon of old it was writ
He possessed such a ribald, dry wit
   That when he told a joke
   To the shy Voormis folk,
They giggled for hours at it.

VI.

I would much rather stay in Sarnath
Than inhabit the Vale of Pnath,
   Since it sounds rather gloomy
   And not at all roomy—
But I'll probably move to Kadath.

VII.

I have heard nothing good of Irem,
Although I've discussed it with them
   Who have been there before,
   But they found it a bore,
And dry places give me the phlegm.

VIII.

Have you heard about Nioth-Korghai?
Well, he sounds like a wild, crazy guy!
   Zips around on a comet,
   Which would cause *me* to vomit,
And once nearly crashed into Shaggai.

IX.

I just might take a tour of Zothique
Say Wednesday or Thursday next week,
   Although those who've been by
   Found the prices too high,
And departed at once out of pique.

X.

And a Deep One I met at a party
Says the R'lyehian crowd are too arty,
   They compose in free verse
   And their sculpture is worse,
And seaweed for lunch isn't hearty.

XI.

And about sunken Y'ha-nthlei
I've often heard visitors say
   That Dagon's a riot,
   But stay at the Hyatt,
Where the nightlife is awfully gay.

XII.

The poor Polar Ones are a race
Rather dumb, for the Antarctic place
   Where they live is so frigid
   It makes them quite rigid,
And would freeze the nose right off
   your face.

XIII.

I suppose that a few will, in time,
Prefer a more tropical clime
   Rather swampy, with muck,
   Than the place where they're stuck—
As I'm stuck for a suitable rhyme!

XIV.

A shoggoth who'd had quite a few
Said quite confidentially, "Do
   You know when we cohabit
   It's like a jackrabbit,
And each then divides into two?"

XV.

A fastidious Ghoul named Kahood,
Growing bored with much wholesomer food,
   Became fond of the taste
   Of fresh stiffs, and posthaste
Ransacked every grave that he cou'd.

XVI.

Of Valusians (Alhazred informs)
They possessed such reptilian forms
   They could not dance a jig,
   But paid worship to Yig,
And lived celibately in dorms.

XVII.

Voormithadreth seems to be fun
If you happen to be an Old One
   Related to Abhoth,
   Or maybe a shoggoth,
And prefer to stay out of the sun.

XVIII.

A Nug-Soth to whom I'm related
Reports that back home they're elated
   For Shub-Niggurath decrees
   Them endangered species
And no more by the Dholes to be ate-ed.

XIX.

And since I just mentioned Yaddith,
Let me say it's a popular myth
  The Great Race came from there.
  Utter nonsense, I swear!
Look it up and you'll find it was Yith.

XX.

Of Carcosa, I've heard some opinions:
Hastur chose the worst possible minions,
  For the huge Byakhee
  Flap about noisily
On ugly, black, foul, stinking pinions.

XXI.

Of Lord Azathoth, the daemon-sultan,
I've read in *Unaussprechlichen Kulten*,
  That he blasphemes and bubbles
  Far away from our troubles,
And is colored a dark, rather dull tan.

XXII.

A Deep One is running the risk
Of being boiled down into bisque,
  For if he forgets
  About fish-hooks and nets,
He'd better swim terribly brisk.

XXIII.

And concerning the Shantaks, I've heard
They're a really remarkable bird,
  With one wing and one eye—
  How the hell can they fly?
I think the whole thing is absurd!

XXIV.

You should not fool around with the Yuggya,
For you're running the risk they might hug ya.
  Though they might have such whims
  Seems they lack the right limbs,
So the worst they could do is just mug ya.

XXV.

I have to admit all I know
Concerning the folks called Tcho-Tcho,
  They serve Lloigor and Zhar
  Under Alaozar,
And their leader's a chap called E-poh.

XXVI.

Of Tsathoggua I've little to say
Except he lives down in N'kai.
  And resembles a bat,
  Rather sleepy and fat,
And prefers not to travel by day.

XXVII.

Yuggoth could be perfect for you,
There are so many fun things to do!
  You'll spend your vacations
  With lizard-crustaceans—
A jolly and partying crew!

XXVIII.

But of Leng I've heard visitors speak
That the climate is wintry and bleak;
  The cuisine is, well, crude,
  And the natives are rude,
But the rates are *quite low* by the week.

XXIX.

And Irem is commendably high
On the list of good places to try—
  If you're catching TB
  Or have asthma—you see,
The climate's *extremely* dry.

XXX.

Now, of red-litten Yoth I've reports
That it's low on the list of resorts,
  Unless you like snakes
  And daily earthquakes,
And feel bored by the usual sports.

XXXI.

I cannot advise Yha-nthlei
Save for the most cursory stay.
  There's nothing to see there
  Or to *do*, either;
It's the pits, and that's all I can say.

XXXII.

Of Carcosa I've heard this opinion:
You'll enjoy it *if* you're a minion
  Of Hastur; and what's more
  If you're *not*, it's a bore.
In fact—why don't you try K'n-yan?

XXXIII.

Yikilth, though, is said to be nice,
If you're fond of a whole lot of ice.
  I may go there next week
  On my way to Zothique,
Where I've visited now once or twice.

XXXIV.

Rlim Shaikorth's hospitable, true.
You can surely sign on with the crew
  Of his flying ice-isle,
  But after a while
You'll likely end up in the stew.

XXXV.

As for Abhoth, I have to defer
To heads wiser than mine, as it were:
  For I've nothing to say
  Of Abhoth either way,
Not even if it's "him" or "her."

XXXVI.

Tsathoggua's not fond of conversin'
With *any* Thing, critter, or person.
  He just naps in N'kai
  All the night and all day,
And seems to improve, rather than worsen.

XXXVII.

Now Ythogtha lives down in Yhe
Which is all the way deep under sea;
  There, with griping and groaning,
  Their fate they're bemoaning—
His Dad and his brother and he.

XXXVIII.

Aphoom Zhah has his mountain of ice,
Which neither sounds comfy or nice,
  Although I suppose
  As apartment space goes
It's a bargain, whatever the price.

XXXIX.

Well, just about all that I know
Is he lives atop Mt. Yaddith-Gho
  (I mean Ghatanothoa.
  I *wish* I knew moa,
But that's every last thing that I know!)

XXXX.

Of Golgoroth, here's what I've heard,
That he often acts somewhat absurd.
  The Shantaks that serve him
  Will often observe him
Behaving a bit like a nerd.

XXXXI.

Why else would he pick the South Pole
To bury himself in a hole
  Beneath the Black Mountain?
  (There ain't no accountin'
For personal taste, I've been tol'!)

XXXXII.

When Zoth-Ommog came down from the stars
He passed up Uranus and Mars,
  Saturn, Neptune and Pluto—
  Never caring a hoot, though,
Since Yuggoth had classier bars.

XXXXIII.

Yep, on Yuggoth a cocktail they serve—
To drink one takes plenty of nerve—
  Gulp down three, the ground quakes,
  Even Yig sees pink snakes,
And, wow, all the stars you'll observe!

XXXXIV.

So Zoth-Ommog stopped off on his trip
Down to Earth just to sample a sip:
  His thirst was terrific,
  It took the Pacific
To cool off his headache, the rip!

XXXXV.

Come to think of it, this could explain
Why Golgoroth put ice on his brain,
  And found the Antarctic
  Cool, soothing and dark (hic!)
Just the thing for his hangover pain.

XXXXVI.

And Mnomquah lives inside the Moon
Rather far from the nearest saloon;
  When he's worked up a thirst
  He has to go first
Down to Ib on the shores of Lake Thune.

XXXXVII.

Where his minions keep lots of the sauce
Right on hand so whenever their boss
  Has a hankering hearty
  To have him a party,
It won't catch the boys at a loss.

XXXXVIII.

Yes, the whole darn tentacular crew
Of the Old Ones are fond of the brew,
  They enjoy some high jinks
  And a couple stiff drinks,
Then they nap for an aeon or two.

XXXXIX.

If the Old Ones stopped off at the store
There on Yuggoth to have just one more
  Before they descended,
  No *wonder* it ended
With the Elder Gods winning the war!

L.

But I don't think it makes any diff
That the Elder Gods won it—what if
  Old Cthulhu instead
  Had come out way ahead,
Although drunk as an old bindlestiff—

LI.

Why, it sure would be awfully dumb
To have the nine worlds ruled by some
  Cosmic octopi boozy,
  All maudlin and woozy,
And their boss a besotted old bum!

LII.

Yes, the Elder Gods still are some use
(At least they stay off the old juice),
  And rule with propriety,
  Loads of sobriety,
From their domain on the far Betel-
    geuze.*

*Pronounced "beetle-juice," you know.

*L'Envoi**

LIII.

So . . . if a Byakhee gives you the wink
And offers to buy you a drink
  Just thank him politely
  But say "no" forthrightly,
And never mind what he may think.

LIV.

And if you would keep a clear head
Go early (and sober) to bed;
  Yes, you'd really be wise
  To do as I advise—
And order a Pepsi instead.

*I *think* I mean "L'Envoi."

Mildew from Shaggai
Robert M. Price

NOT by Lin Carter

I

Those old Serpent-Men of Valusia
Will say anything just to confuse ya!
They spoke with forked tongue
Ever since they were young.
You can't trust their ophidian views--là!

II

There was a Deep One from Laguna
Who appeared only at the full moon-a
And his skin was so green,
As could plainly be seen,
That folks took him for Charlie the Tuna.

III

One thing about Shudde-M'ell,
Who bores up from the bowels of Hell:
While he drills like a lathe
He has no chance to bathe
So he carries one powerful smell!

IV

Those scholars who write about Yith
Do so with consid'rable pith.
But I really must laugh
Since they've made such a gaffe:
For Sotho tells me it's all myth!

V

There was an old wizard named Prinn
Who was burnt at the stake for his sin.
'Twas not for witchcraft,
But for sex fore and aft
With the comeliest species of jinn.

VI

A psychic detective named Crow
Was constantly off on the go.
His foes once said, "Titus,
You're too late to fight us.
Your Clock must have been a bit slow."

from the Crypt of Cthulhu

VII

Young Robert Blake once made a search
Of the old Starry Wisdom Sect's church.
As described by the sexton,
He discovered the hex on't,
And fled from the place with a lurch.

VIII

I knew a guy named Wilbur Whateley
Whom some called a Johnny-come-lately.
He cried out, "bugg-shoggog!"
When gored by a dog.
What a way to go; not very greatly!

IX

There was an old man named Shrewsbury
Who liked oft to drink and make merry.
He imbibed golden mead
When Cthulhu was freed.
How often? When asked, he said "Very!"

X

Oh, the thrice-holy Lama of Leng
Is supposed to be some ugly thing.
Of what's under his veil
To tell, my words fail,
But it's found in the *Tablets of Nhing*.

XI

There's a rumor about Zoth-Ommog
That has everyone here all agog!
On his home-star of Xoth
The air's like beef-broth
So no wonder his breath is like smog!

XII

A god of the air was Ithaqua
Who was thinking of switching to aqua
Till he got sentimental
Toward an earth elemental—
Now he's blowing around with Tsathoggua.

XIII

Nyarlathotep's my kind of people
Though he sits all alone in a steeple.
For while he's thus parked
He can see in the dark
With his burning eye which is lobed triple!

XIV

Y'know something has set me to thinkin'
Of Keziah's familiar Brown Jenkin,
Who showed me the path
Past Euclidean math
To angles that have my eyes blinkin'.

XV

Of Hastur this gossip is told:
That he can't stand the outer space cold.
But he does water ski
On the Lake of Hali
And I'd call that "Unspeakably" bold!

XVI

Shub-Niggurath, Black Goat of the Wood,
Can't learn to say "no" when she should;
In the morning he's gone,
And she's stuck with the spawn.
Why not look into Planned Parenthood?

XVII

Let me tell you a good one from R'lyeh!
The jokes they make up there will kill ya!
They all love to kid,
Most of all the big Squid—
You should hear him guffaw through his cilia!

XVIII

A meteor crashed in my field,
And it's caused an amazing crop yield.
But the plants that all grow
Have this unearthly glow.
Say, you're eating one now in this meal!

XIX

'Twas revealed to me by my friend Glaaki
That he spent quite some time upon Shaggai.
He was headed for Tond
Of which he's quite fond,
But found himself waylaid and shanghied!

XX

My girlfriend agreed to a fling
On the wind-swept plateau atop Leng.
But she headed for Sung
And I wound up in Tsang
So now of my lost love I sing.

XXI

Say, what can I do with this shoggoth
That I got secondhand back on Yuggoth?
I won him in a raffle
But I'm totally baffled;
The directions are written in Nug-Soth!

XXII

There once was a fellow named Jermyn,
Whose ancestry had poor Art squirmin'.
Unlike you and me,
His own family tree
Was a real one from which swung lemur-men.

XXIII

One day it popped into my head
To read that book by Alhazred.
I was feeling just fine
Till it blasted my mind.
Now I think I'd be better off dead.

XXIV

Wilmarth saw his friend's face and hand
And knew things weren't at all as he'd planned.
Was he talking to Akeley?
Or was it done fakely
After Henry was already canned?

XXV

As is writ in the *Book of Iod*
Abbie Prinn had one hell of a bod
But she met Vorvadoss
Who showed her who was boss
With his interdimensional rod.

XXVI

Once I ran across Worm-Father Ubb
While using his kin as fish-grub.
After one nasty look
He stuck me on his hook
And said, "How does it feel? Join the club!"

XXVII

If I'd just offer up the Red Meal
Nug the Ghoul said he'd make me a deal.
There'd be plenty of riches,
And my dreams plus my wishes.
All for one human life? What a steal!

XXVIII

"Lavinia!" cried the old wizard,
Her umbilical cord being scissored,
"We'll be damned for our sins:
Take a look at these twins—
One's unseen and the other's half lizard!"

XXIX

I had a grey stone made in Mnar
That was shaped like a five-pointed star.
Well the thing used to glimmer
And the lights would grow dimmer
When I tip-toed past Lloigor and Zhar.

XXX

Quite a funny thing happened this dawn
When an elephant statue was gone!
But all through the muse'em
There was spilled a blood-stream
Leading to the case marked "Chaugnar
 Faugn."

--Robert M. Price

Shards from Shaggai
Robert M. Price

I

Invited by Yogash the Ghoul,
I had trouble maintaining my cool:
When I asked of the venue,
"Your name's on the menu,"
He said as he started to drool.

II

I read *Unaussprechlichen Kulten*
And found it all highly insultin'.
It gave the right chant
For each spook, ghost, and ha'nt
—My immediate exit resultin'!

III

I will tell of my friend Randolph Carter
Whom some held to be a late starter.
With his pal Harley Warren
He searched realms strange and foreign
In quest of Nitocris's garter.

IV

Let me tell you my thoughts on Ithaqua,
The Old One they call the Wind-Walkua.
Instead of "Wendigo,"
He's just a Wind-*bag*-o!
All he does is to talk and to Talkua!

V

Of a certain Old One called Ybb-Tstl
Titus Crow recalls, "Boy, what a pistol!
At a party he'd spoil it
With his head in the toilet!
All his antics would fill an epistle!"

VI

Oh the star-headed Old Ones from space
Have cilia where we have a face!
For a head, they've a star.
But that's better by far
Than those rugose old cones the Great Race!

VII

Say, think you can give information
On a certain pink fungoid crustacean?
She's just out from Pluto
And looks kind of cute; oh,
What a figure: I'd say it's curvacean!

VIII

My pal's dating Asenath Waite.
He's hopelessly smitten; it's fate!
To me it looks bad,
Cause she sounds like her dad
And communes with those Ones past the Gate.

IX

Dick Pickman is canine of face
With pretty loose links to the race.
OK, human he ain't,
But the boy sure can paint!
He uses those hues out of space.

X

I once knew a chap, de la Poer,
Who used to be rather a bore
Till he went to the cellar
And found there a hell—or
So he said with his mouth full of gore.

XI

There once was a Burleson, Don,
Who with Lovecraft's work had some fun.
"Watch the text deconstruct
Once the plain sense I've chucked."
Black is white, left is right, when he's done.

XII

Oh this Burleson's foe was called Schweitzer,
Who responded, "Why bother to write, sir?
You fail to convince.
Worse, you cause me to wince,
But *I* know what a critic's insights are!"

XIII

S. T. Joshi corrected the texts
Of his hero Lovecraft's works: "What wrecks!
With typos abrupt
These tales are corrupt!
'Witchcraft love' for 'lore'!"? My God,
  what's next?"

XIV

You know of the works of one Cannon
Who wrote of Lovecraft with abandon.
With each tale of a ghoulie,
Dedicated "To Julie,"
He rose to more fame than he'd planned on.

XV

Stefan Dziemianowicz's name
Was scarcely a ticket to fame.
No one could be found
Who could half make the sound.
For non-human mouths it was framed.

XVI

HPL called his readers nitwits,
A description that maybe still fits:
With the role-playing games,
Endless new Mythos names,
We've ripped the Old Gent's work to bits!

XVII

The Gilman House, I'd recommend
If you're ichthyic, fishy, and finned,
They take Mastercard
Or an old Eltdown Shard.
Take the Aylesbury Pike to the end.

XVIII

Old Joe Curwen and Jed Orne were friends,
But both came to rather bad ends:
Things were going just fine,
With Saturn in trine,
Till they conjured but couldn't rescind.

XIX

When old Wizard Whateley was killed
The funeral parlor was filled.
I followed the mourners
Till they got to Dean's Corners—
And scattered, all plumb whippoorwilled.

XX

Thought I, I was in for a thrill
When the lawyer read Great Cthulhu's will.
But his death was mere seeming;
In fact he's just dreaming.
I inherited nary a bill.

XXI

I'd have to admit I was tense
On the trail of the family Martense.
Then I gaped, all slack-jawed,
When my pal's face was gnawed;
With *his* kisser, I'd say "good riddance!"

XXII

Last night I awoke to the sounds
Of a pack of those Tindalos Hounds.
They had snuck through an angle
And started to tangle
With a nightwatchman making his rounds.

XXIII

Museum inmate Rhan-Tegoth
Slipped out from beneath his drop-cloth.
He surprised one poor guard
By grabbing him hard
And reducing the guy to beef broth.

XXIV

Chaugnar-Faugn with the tentacled ears
Became the object of my fears.
He sneezed at the zoo
With a cosmic "ah-choo!"
And sent me ten thousand light-years!

XXV

Our archaeological dig
Unearthed a depiction of Yig.
Here's what we gaped at:
He was there with Saint Pat,
The two of them dancing a jig!

Famous Last Words
Robert M. Price

As fans of horror-fantasy fiction, all of us are called on from time to time to swallow greater or lesser implausibilities. After all, why quibble if Wilmarth can quote verbatim entire letters from memory in "The Whisperer in Darkness"? Even gross physiological impossibilities such as the "change" undergone by the Innsmouth folk from mammals to amphibians can be swept under the rug with only a wink. And the chances of Wilbur Whateley's ever finding clothes that fit? What the heck! But at some point we really have to draw the line. And what more needful place than at a particular device for ending stories? We refer, of course, to those which break off in mid-scream with the narrator's grisly doom. There is nothing untoward about such a device *per se*, but these narrators seem to be as addicted to writing as we are to reading. They perish pen-in-hand, their death-rattle committed to paper.

A few examples will demonstrate how horror shades unwittingly into humor:

> The end is near. I hear a noise at the door, as of some immense slippery body lumbering against it. It shall not find me. God, *that hand*! The window! The window! (H. P. Lovecraft, "Dagon.")

> Not long to go now; even the stone walls shudder to the monstrous weight pressing upon them—*The window!*—Merciful God, that FACE! Can anything that lives be so huge— (Lin Carter, "The Dreams in the House of Weir.")

> But now—something—Great God! Wings! *What beings at the window*! Ia! Ia! Hastur fhtagn . . .! (August Derleth, "The House on Curwen Street.")

> It is as if the walls of the house fell away, as if the street too, were gone, and a fog—something in that watery fog, like a giant frog with tentacles—like a—*Great God! What horror! Ia! Ia! Hastur!* (August Derleth, "The Watcher from the Sky.")

> Black marks two feet wide, but they aren't just marks. What they really are is *fingerprints*! The door is busting o----- (Robert Bloch, "Notebook Found in a Deserted House.")

> . . . too late—cannot help self—black paws materialize— am dragged away toward the cellar. . . . (H. P. Lovecraft, "The Diary of Alonzo Typer.")

Are we supposed to imagine poor Typer writing this onto the floorboards he is being dragged across? No, because according to the story's "frame," the narrative is all contained in his diary. And this is the problem with all these story-endings. They are part of *written documents*. And even if someone were writing when some horror came upon him, he would drop quill or Bic long before these narrators do.

The silliest of the bunch, and therefore the best example, is the ending of Frank Belknap Long's "The Hounds of Tindalos":

> God, they are breaking through! They are breaking through! Smoke is pouring from the corners of the wall. Their tongues—ahhh—.

Ahhh indeed.

There is really quite a simple expedient available to any writer who still wishes to use this hackneyed device. So far as we can tell, August Derleth is among the few to use it, in a scene from "The Shuttered Room": "Oh, that hand! That turr'ble arm! Gawd! That face . . .!" What is the difference? This frightened voice is being heard over the phone. The poor devil is calling for help, but it is too late. Now how much imagination could this have taken? Not much, actually, since Derleth stole the scene wholesale from Lovecraft's "The Dunwich Horror": "Those who took down their receivers heard a fright-mad voice shriek out, 'Help, oh, my Gawd! . . .'" A telephone is not even the only way to present this; there are always tape recorders and dictaphones. It can't be that difficult to work them into the narrative. From now on, let's hope that horror-fantasy writers will show a little more . . . but wait! Good God! What's that coming out of the garbage disposal—eeeeyahh! glub, glub. . . .

Screwtape's Letter to Cthulhu
Robert M. Price

My dear Cthulhu,

Though I would prefer to open, as ever, on a more cheerful note, I am afraid I cannot forestall the rather serious nature of my task in writing you. It has fallen to me to bring to your attention a very delicate, even dangerous, matter of . . . shall we say . . . security leaks? For, plainly, you have been letting a bit too much of the *truth* seep through into your patient's imagination.

Now, do not be quickly offended; Our Father Below is far from forgetting either your talent or your service in haunting the dreams of the reclusive writer. What he believes to be mere fictions have gone a considerable distance toward fostering just the dread and disorientation we are dedicated to spreading among the contemptible bipeds. And the beauty of it lies precisely in the "fictitious" aspect your patient has caused it to assume. Despite your disquieting hints to him of blasphemies lurking "beyond the wall of sleep," he remains obliviously complacent in his materialist convictions.

Yes, no one has forgotten your skill in such matters. But just here lies Our Father's anxiety. Of late you seem to have taken to brazenly flaunting the truth before your patient, in order, one supposes, to fathom the depth of his materialist slumber. Really, now; letting him hear it straight from his friend Lumley! Let me quote your patient's very own words following this meeting (you needn't act surprised—even my own efforts are monitored from Below): "He is convinced that all our gang are genuine agents of unseen Powers in distributing hints too dark and profound for human conception or comprehension. We may *think* we're writing fiction, and may even (absurd thought!) disbelieve what we write, but at bottom we are telling the truth in spite of ourselves—serving unwittingly as mouthpieces of Tsathoggua, Crom, Cthulhu, and other pleasant Outside gentry."

Need I stress the scandalous excess of such risk-taking? Yes, yes, your patient dismisses his friend as an eccentric, as the very words quoted suggest. But the simple fact is that the friend now *knows*, and your patient may surprise you. I hope you will keep firmly in mind on whose oddly-angled doorstep the blame will be laid should your patient escape Our Father's grasp. In conclusion, let me hold up before you my own example. Surely Our Father's House will freeze over before any of my own correspondence leaks out to the mortal public.

Again, please forgive the unavoidably severe tone of these lines and be assured that I remain

                        Your congenial colleague,
                        SCREWTAPE

[We cannot vouch for the authenticity of this text, as it does not appear in either of the two major collections of Screwtape's letters, yet we publish it here for its obvious inherent interest. --Editor]

Mail-Call of Cthulhu

I have chosen to reproduce primarily those letters which are mini-articles in themselves or which contributed to an important ongoing discussion of particular literary works or critical issues. The longest of these debates, and to my mind the most interesting, centered on the comparison of Brian Lumley's understanding of the Mythos as compared and contrasted with Lovecraft's. This debate began and continued in the review column ("R'lyeh Review") as well as in the letters pages. Hence three reviews of Lumley's books by Stefan Dziemianowicz are included at appropriate points in the sequence.

Now that you've run Don Burleson's article on Lovecraft and *outre* mathematics, allow me to supply a note on "HPL and Euclidean Geometry."

In "The Call of Cthulhu" the narrator Francis Wayland Thurston speaks of the "abnormal, non-Euclidean geometry" of the Cyclopean masonry on Cthulhu's island, while in "The Dreams in the Witch House" we hear of "odd" and "peculiar angles" in the construction of Keziah Mason's attic room. But in one tale, "The Shadow out of Time," Lovecraft supplies an instance of ordinary plane geometry that is perhaps just as problematical as these more esoteric examples.

In recalling his dream world, Nathaniel Wingate Peaslee describes a floor made up "of massive octagonal flagstones" and also "a cyclopean corridor" that is "paved with octagonal blocks." Now the mathematical fact is, in this or any other galaxy, that one cannot "tile the plane" with octagons. The only polygons that can tile the plane are the triangle, square, and hexagon. In order to create a continuous "octagonal" surface, smaller squares would have to fill in the gaps.

The first question is, was HPL aware that octagons do not fit together to form an uninterrupted surface? And the next is, if he were aware of it, why did he bother to use such an inaccurate geometric image?

Probably Lovecraft (despite his 92 in plane geometry in high school, according to de Camp) did not think of the matter when he wrote "The Shadow out of Time." On the other hand, if he had, he may simply have decided that it was too awkward to qualify his description with a phrase like: "paved with octagonal blocks with smaller square blocks in between." He was willing to sacrifice mathematical precision for the sake of avoiding pedantry.

Why, then, did he not employ one of the three regular polygons that do tile the plane? No doubt he dismissed the triangle and square as too prosaic, and the hexagon on account of its common association with bathroom floors. The octagon served his aesthetic intentions best, because it is a sufficiently exotic polygon and at the same time not so obvious an absurdity for plane-paving purposes as, say, the pentagon (a possible candidate since HPL did dwell on fivefold symmetry in *At the Mountains of Madness*) or any higher order

Many thanks for CRYPT I, 5. I think you do Lovecraft and Howard an injustice by classing them as "pseudo-intellectuals." The term was popularized by the politician George Wallace, who used to call Northeasterners who disapproved of his policies "pointy-headed pseudo-intellectuals." I don't know whom he considered a true intellectual; George Wallace, perhaps?

When in doubt, see the dictionary. Webster's Second International, among several definitions of "intellectual (n.)," gives one pertinent to this case: "Endowed with intellect to a high degree; fond of and given to learning and thinking; as, an *intellectual* person." This says nought about the intellectual's education or his ability to reach sound conclusions. It is enough to qualify him that he likes to think and talk about abstract questions like science, history, politics, and the arts.

This describes both Lovecraft and Howard. True, both suffered severe limitations, partly self-imposed, in their intellectual pursuits. Among these, lack of higher education was preeminent. Lovecraft never finished high school; Howard rejected a chance to go to college because he could not endure classroom discipline. But, in intercourse with each other and with others, both showed lively intelligence and keen interest in subjects of the kind called "intellectual." If they adopted positions now deemed wrong or even crackpot, such ideas were commonplace and respectable in their day.

For a true pseudo-intellectual, take a onetime student in a class in psychology taught by my wife Catherine. This young man filled his papers with recondite polysyllabic verbiage, which would have convinced many naive readers that this man had truly plumbed the secrets of the cosmos. A closer examination showed that the student did not know the meanings of the learned-sounding words he used and, in fact, was writing meaningless gobbledygook. As W. S. Gilbert put it, "If this young man expresses himself in terms too deep for me, Why, what a very singularly deep young man this young man must be!"
--L. Sprague de Camp, Villanova, PA

It's extremely difficult to improve on excellence, but you seem to have achieved that twice, in *Crypt of Cthulhu* #6 and the just arrived #7. But I shall have to write a word or two concerning the views of Colin Wilson as set forth in the Hoffman and Cerasini article, or risk an internal indignation explosion. Incredible as it may seem to you, despite my long August Derleth and Arkham House associations, the major part of the earlier, "pre-transition" Wilson was *new* to me. I've read and greatly admired some of Wilson's more recent essays, and can only hope that the transition is now even more pronounced in the Lovecraftian realm than the two authors imply.

To equate writers of imaginative genius of a high order with the brutal, sadistic killer behavior of pathological monsters like Manson and Company simply because they take a dark view of the human

prospect and their writings mirror such a view would send at least a fifth of the world's greatest philosophers, poets, and pictorial artists crashing from their pedestals to be engulfed by flames--not merely Wilson's "5%." It is good to know that the serious acceptance of such nonsense by readers is miniscule.
--Frank Belknap Long, New York, NY

I was pleased to see in #6 that you had made use of my article "The Derleth Mythos." I can't find any major point to argue about. You have honed the subject down more finely than Dirk Mosig or I did. Of course it makes no difference whether the narrator gets out alive or not as far as my main contention goes, which is that Derleth's outlook on the universe seems trite compared to Lovecraft's.

Yes, that ending to *Dream-Quest* was somewhat corny, and it undoubtedly influenced Derleth's attempts to carry on what he felt was the Lovecraft tradition.

Incidentally, I once told Derleth I thought he was an optimist whereas HPL was a pessimist. "No," he said, "I'm a pessimist, too." Whatever his Romish upbringing may have done to him down deep, I got the impression that intellectually he was an atheist or close to it. He also thought we were on this earth one time around and that was it.

Actually I've enjoyed the Derleth efforts very much, even if they are irritatingly sloppy at times (i.e., "Something in Wood," in which the protagonist immediately sounds out alien, pre-human hieroglyphs as if they were a familiar alphabet!). Whenever I've hauled the Mythos into a story I've retained most of the Derlethian additions and premises.

Back to the Lovecraft/Derleth Mythos: the two outlooks could be somewhat harmonized by remembering that Derleth's is probably that which most humans would take when confronted with the realization that monstrous beings exist, whereas Lovecraft's later tales come closer to explaining those beings' actual nature. (HPL's latest and greatest works turned out to be science fiction of a cosmic scope worthy of Olaf Stapledon.)
--Richard L. Tierney, Mason City, IA

On the Derlethization of Lovecraft's mythos, I should think the real pity (though here again one can see that he was picking up on hints in the later Lovecraft) was that he sought to systematize something whose great merit and original purpose was to suggest more than it described. Of course Lumley and I and others were subsequently guilty.

As for "Famous Last Words" [*Crypt*, No. 8], you might be amused by the telegram (in the days when Britain had such things) found by the narrator of "The Tomb-Herd," the first draft of "The Church in High Street": "To Richard Dexter. Come at once to Kingsport. You are needed urgently by me here for protection from agencies which may kill me—or worse—if you do not come immediately. Will explain as soon as you reach me. . . . But what is this thing that flops unspeakably down the passage toward this room? It

cannot be that abomination which I met in the nitrous vaults below Asquith Place . . . IA! YOG-SOTHOTH! CTHULHU FHTAGN!" (You can tell the chap's worried—I mean, using a passive construction in a telegram. . . .)
--Ramsey Campbell, Merseyside, England

In his essay "The Dream World and the Real World in Lovecraft" [*Crypt* No. 15], S. T. Joshi says the narrator of "Polaris" is afflicted with "ancestral memory." This is certainly a reasonable theory, for HPL did write tales of ancestral memory (among them "The Rats in the Walls," one of his best works). However, I don't believe this is the correct interpretation of the story. It seems more likely that the narrator is suffering from memories of a previous incarnation.
In a letter to Rheinhart Kleiner dated November 8, 1917, Lovecraft explained the theme of his poem "Nemesis" (November 1, 1917): "It presents the conception, tenable to the orthodox mind, that nightmares are the punishment meted out to the soul for sins committed in previous incarnations—perhaps millions of years ago!" (SL I.51-52).
This would serve equally well as an explanation of "Polaris," written less than a year later. The narrator's "sin," of course, is falling asleep while on sentry duty.
"Polaris" is one of Lovecraft's most autobiographical stories, reflecting his feelings of guilt, frustration, and uselessness during World War I. Like the narrator, HPL was "denied a warrior's part," for he "was feeble and given to strange faintings when subjected to stress and hardships" (D 21).
In May, 1917, one month after the United States declared war on Germany, Lovecraft applied for enlistment in the National Guard. He was accepted, but his mother and family physician persuaded the Army to reject him as physically unfit. When his draft questionnaire arrived in December, Lovecraft discussed it with the head physician of the local draft board, who instructed him to class himself as totally and permanently unfit. In a letter to Kleiner dated February 23, 1918, Lovecraft said wryly that the doctor "decided that a man who cannot stay up all day as a civilian, is not exactly a General in the making" (SL I.56).
--William Fulwiler, Duncanville, TX

I suppose, no, let's make that I am sure that a complete file of *Crypt* will become one of those items collectors of HPLiania will have to have even if the children starve, and that appalling prices will be paid at auctions for copies of it, some badly watermarked with missing pages and occasional obscene annotations scrawled in the margins, some in mint condition—unreadable due to being sealed up in blocks of plastic, true, but definitely in mint condition —and there will be indexes and concordances and scholarly references and God only knows what else, and something living in a settlement revolving around a star in Orion will stay up late because it has just purchased a complete set, the actual original, printed on paper held together with those metal things (how do you suppose

they got them on, anyhow?), and it knows it ought to dematerialize or it'll be all sticky in the morning, but it has to have one last look, one last touch of the pages, one last gloat over actually owning the legendary thing.
--Gahan Wilson, New York, NY

I was puzzled at some of Brian Lumley's remarks on Lovecraft scholarship in your interview with him in *Crypt* #19, hence I feel obliged to explain the intentions of myself and other critics. In the first place, Lumley repeats the old attack on critics--that any writer with creativity will wish to write fiction rather than criticism. In fact the best critics are drawn to criticism not through *inability* to write fiction (there are any number of examples of writers who have been both critics and fictionists or poets—Samuel Johnson, Emerson, Matthew Arnold, Henry James, Graham Greene, Somerset Maugham, Edmund Wilson, Gore Vidal, John Fowles—and Lovecraft!) but through differing *inclination*. There is just as much "creativity" in a brilliant analysis as in any work of fiction.

Lumley's remarks on textual scholarship I find particularly hard to understand—doesn't he *want* to read unadulterated Lovecraft? I for one am very concerned to know whether Homer wrote *theos* or *deos*, whether Vergil wrote *vita* or *vitta*, whether Schiller wrote *schon* or *schön*, and whether Lovecraft wrote *metal* or *mental* (an actual textual error in his work). There need be no fanaticism here: we need only understand how apparently inconsequential things such as orthography or punctuation can make a difference in the interpretation or appreciation of a work; frequently such slight errors *do* make a difference, and in any case the effect of most textual errors is cumulative—like the 1500 errors in the current text of *At the Mountains of Madness*.
--S. T. Joshi, Princeton, NJ

Crypt 22 is a very good issue. Cover by Koszowski: excellent! He has a real talent and seems to improve each time I see him. Dave Carson was round my place the other night and saw this; he called it great but he did point out that it was supposed to be a three-lobed burning eye, not a three-eyed burning lobe!

Carter, Myers, Howard, Moskowitz, Tierney and Fulwiler were all splendid, which is what you'd expect.

To answer, very quickly (I hope) S. T. Joshi's letter. Yes, I would like to read unadulterated HPL. If you, S. T., are going to do something about it (which is to say, convince a publisher he should give us a complete Lovecraft without errors) then I'm on your side. I'm on your side anyway: I never read anything by you that I didn't find interesting and informative. But each to his own: I personally *don't* think it matters whether theos/deos, vita/vitta, schon/schön. I haven't time to think it matters! Maybe that's the difference between a scholar and a writer, eh?

But excuse me if I don't agree with you when you say, "There is just as much creativity in a brilliant analysis as in any work of fiction." No way. A chicken can lay an egg, but the egg has to become a chicken first before *it* can lay an egg. Let's take

it logically and from square one:
Just assume that from this moment forward no one writes another word of fiction. What are all you critics and analysts going to do for the rest of your lives? I mean, there's an end in your "creativity"! But the *sustained* creativity of a writer, which he puts into his stories, is enormous. He's writing it out of his own original thoughts, not merely describing (or distorting) what someone else has written. He has to take the germ of an idea, play with it, plant it in his brain, let it take root there, nurture the bloody thing and finally, when it starts to put up a shoot, water it and train it and prune it until it's just the right shape. It's *all* creativity. The guy who comes along and bites bits out of it (or even, on the other hand, says, "Wow!—that's great! A terrific piece of" . . . etc.) is only *describing* what the author did—usually inadequately and *always* (where analysis is concerned) inaccurately. Whether the story is good or bad, the critic *can't* know what the author put into it, or didn't. As to *why* it was written—especially when the author is dead and can't confirm or deny—how can the analyst hope to get it right? I mean, I write a story because I want to write a story—not because when I was a kid my father screwed my cat. Or I was kept on a bookshelf til I was sixteen. Or my wooden leg has dry rot. (He didn't; I wasn't; it has not, incidentally.)

To say a story is bad is OK if you believe you could do better. To say one is superb is to admit that you *couldn't* do better—and that's a harder thing to do. As for your list of author/analyst/critics: yes, thank you, you've proved my point. For my money *they've all earned the right to be critical!* (Except maybe Lovecraft, who not understanding sex, could hardly hope to give a fair treatment to romance.) Yes, I know he was a male and proved he was a male. There's a tree in my garden that does that every spring. I've no doubt he could *do* it. I don't think my tree does either.

But it's my opinion anyway that there are a lot of critic/analysts about who shouldn't criticize and couldn't analyse to save their souls. Phil Panaggio, in his letter in #22, throws light on just such a case.

God help me, when I die, please don't let anyone start writing essays on why I wrote this or that! I write stories because it's better than humping coal or cleaning streets or being a toilet attendant. I imagine the people I take issue with have their reasons, too, but they can't be the same as mine because toilet attendant is definitely preferable.

But the truth will out. Eventually one of these Jungian/Freudian exploiters of the dead *will* smuggle a piece of fiction into print, and when that happens there'll be a hell of a lot of us punched-holes-in, berated, bruised and battered, *proven* scribblers out here just waiting to join the ranks of that long list of yours and turn critics in our own rights! (You will of course understand that the main body of these anti-characters [antibodies?] is chiefly active in the Lovecraft circle/Mythos related fields.)

To close: A writer of fiction is a man who tells lies for money. That's his job, by which he eats. The better he lies the more his readers like him. Critics on the other hand are supposed to tell the truth about what they read or the way they interpret it; but occasionally it's an excuse to glorify themselves and say "Hey, look how clever I am!" Which is to say that every now and then they are bigger liars than the writers!

A coroner carrying out an autopsy can be brilliantly "incisive"—but when he's finished carving up the body, will he ever be brilliant enough to build a new one?

Something else to think about: even your author/critics occasionally make a crap of it. One such, (in my opinion vastly overrated and dry and tasteless as cardboard on a hot day) has it that the second paragraph in HPL's "The Hound" is "an atrocious piece of writing . . . not, as one might suspect, a piece of juvenilia." Now, I'm just about ready to agree with him—*about that paragraph*! There are others in the story just as bad. But when you link them all together, including all the good lines, and *read* them and begin to feel the mood, then something quite different emerges. I *like* the story, for all that I know it's not superbly written. Even if the writing is bad, there's something behind it which is brilliant! But if I had heard only the critic's voice, why!—I might not have wanted to read "The Hound" in the first place! Heaven forbid! The same author/critic/analyst has it that "The Music of Erich Zann" is "crude." Parts of it may be, but overall it's a gem! And the same guy has written a couple of "Mythos" things to show how good he can do it. Well, I don't know if he fooled you but he didn't fool me. Cardboard! Lovecraft, even at his worst, gave me a certain *frisson*. He *may* not have been the world's best writer, but he did have one of the finest imaginations.

Genuine scholarship—like yours—I admire. Genuine criticism has to have its good points. Genuine analysis may be of value to minds that way inclined. But when critics/analysts/and scholars crit, an, and schol just to see their names in print, that's a different bag of shoggoths entirely . . .
    --Brian Lumley, London, England

Brian Lumley's letter in *Crypt* #23 is the kind of anti-critical harangue that will undoubtedly be applauded by some fans, but it doesn't really hold together. It simply isn't true that critics depend on what they criticize whereas fiction writers pluck their ideas fresh from their own unique imaginations; Lovecraft was the first to admit his dependence on Poe and Machen and Blackwood, and I seriously doubt that without Lovecraft any of you would ever have heard of Brian or myself. I can't quite tell if Brian underrates himself or is simply striking a pose of Lovecraftian humility; he writes because it's better than "being a toilet attendant," he's "a man who tells lies for money," whereas critics are "supposed to tell the truth." I must say I feel that good fiction does the same as good criticism: it illuminates. What the author put into the text or why he wrote it is irrelevant to criticism; what is there in the text, and can be shown to be there, is what criticism is all about, and whether the author meant it to be there is supremely irrelevant. I hope Brian won't be offended if I say his letter reads as though he would rather not think too deeply about why he, or anyone else, writes fiction--especially if I add that I think such enquiry into one's motives is likely to illuminate only a small part of the mysterious process of creativity.

One other point I think I have to refer to. Brian says "Carter, Myers, Howard, Moskowitz, Tierney and Fulwiler were all splendid, which is what you'd expect." In the context of his letter it seems fair to take this utterly uncritical response as his alternative to criticism, and I must say I would have expected better of him. The Howard piece he refers to is certainly of interest to anyone who reads Howard, and you're to be congratulated on publishing it, but at the same time it needs to be said that despite its interest, the piece is pernicious tripe—the kind of fiction that shows Howard's arrested adolescence at its most naked. It dismays me to realize that it's precisely this sensibility that attracts some readers to the genre.

A last thought. Brian feels that criticism is only permissible if one can do better than what one is criticizing. I've never written a note of music, and I don't suppose I ever shall, but for me to conclude on that basis that I'm incapable of recognizing or criticizing bad (banal, inept, etc.) music would be ridiculous. As to the amount of work Brian feels goes into fiction as distinct from criticism, I'm currently writing entries for the forthcoming Penguin encyclopaedia of horror, and I have to say I find writing them adequately more difficult than writing fiction—significantly more so. More power to those who devote their lives to criticism.

--Ramsey Campbell, Merseyside, England

I hate to have some sort of "Lumley-Joshi feud" soil the pages of *Crypt,* or even take up much more space; but I am compelled to respond to some of Mr. Lumley's views as to the critic's (and the author's) role.

It is, first of all, *not* the business of the true critic to declare any piece of work "good" or "bad": such judgments are entirely irrelevant to the critic's function, for these are *subjective* value judgments and based ultimately on individual taste. *Analysis* is the critic's role: why did an author write a work? how did he set about writing it? what were his literary influences? what influences in his life and thought led him to write as he did? I am utterly astonished to hear Lumley say that this task is impossible—it is done all the time, and quite accurately! Lumley falls into the error of believing that the author always knows exactly why he wrote something; but, as Lovecraft says, the greatest art is unconscious (or at least arises from the subconscious), hence it is entirely likely that the author will *not* know all the reasons why he wrote a work—unless he is extremely adept at self-psychoanalysis, as many writers are not. Don Burleson is fond of citing the example of Henry James, who declared that *The Turn of the Screw* was a "potboiler" (Machen had similar views as to most of his horror-fiction); I think almost anyone will find this a rather hasty and incomplete judgment.

Most of Lumley's attacks appear to be directed at *bad* critics;

but I could just as well attack countless bad writers without saying anything substantial about the task of authorship itself! Does the existence of thousands of bad paintings invalidate the art of painting? Like any art, criticism is practiced at its best only by a few. And there have been great critics who have manifestly *failed* at "creative" art—Edmund Wilson is the glaring example, and I know few great works of fiction or poetry ever written by Leon Edel, Lionel Trilling, Northrop Frye, Vincent Starrett, and on and on and on. Conversely, there have been any number of great creative artists who have notably failed at criticism—some of Shelley's critical utterances were painfully inept. Hence my previous list of great artist/critics does not prove Lumley's position, but shows that some writers have had the genius to combine creative and analytical faculties.
--S. T. Joshi, Jersey City, NJ

    The cover of *Crypt* 25 is one of your best ever: Fabian is, to my taste, superb. This one so reminded me of Bok that it had me searching for his sigil! F. B. Long and Carl Jacobi (long favourites of mine), CAS, REH, Cave, and Rimel formed a splendid line-up, and all extremely interesting—which is what you'd expect.
    Also, I note that your interior artwork has gone up in quality, putting your magazine on an even higher level. I hope it isn't just for this rather special issue? What's more, a bit of controversy invariably livens up the scene a little. All very entertaining.
    As a last word on criticism, I'd like to quote Samuel Johnson: "Criticism is a study by which men grow important and formidable at very small expense." Or more specifically for S. T. Joshi (because he'll probably better appreciate the Ancients) a quote from Zeuxis: "Criticism comes easier than craftsmanship." Ain't it just what I've been saying?
    As for Ramsey Campbell's letter: who pulled his chain?
--Brian Lumley, London, England

    About S. T. Joshi's piece on Robert W. Chambers, I can add a point. Chambers wrote four novels laid in Upstate New York at the time of the American Revolution: *America*; *The Little Red Foot*; and one other whose name escapes me and which I can't find in my notes. At least one of these, *The Little Red Foot*, directly influenced Lovecraft's fellow fantasist Robert E. Howard. Howard took the scenery for his Conan stories directly from that novel in "Beyond the Black River," "The Treasure of Tranicos," and "Wolves Beyond the Border," the latter two published posthumously in 1967 with substantial changes and additions by me, in the collection *Conan the Usurper*. The scenery was that of the Mohawk and Black River Valleys and the Adirondacks. Real places mentioned by Chambers, such as Canajoharie, Caughnawaga, Oriskany, Sacandaga, Schoharie, and Thendara, became Howard's Conajohara, Conawaga, Oriskonie, Scandaga, and Thandara. The Picts were the Iriquois Indians of that time, as described by Chambers and other frontier-story writers, especially those appearing in *Adventure Magazine*. We can be sure Howard drew from this particular novel because the name of the narrator-hero of "Wolves Beyond the Border," Gault Hagar's son, comes from the names of two families in Chambers' novel: the Hagers and the Gaults.

Howard may have also read one or more of Chambers' other American Revolutionary novels, as well as Fenimore Cooper's novels in the same setting; but *The Little Red Foot* is the one we can be sure of. It is always risky to say that any voracious reader like Howard had *not* read the works of some predecessor.

"Thendara" is a special case. The name is used by Chambers' Iroquois a couple of times; but I don't know whence Chambers got it. There was no place of that name in Upstate New York until the early 1920s. Then my father, who owned the tract that included the sawmill village and railroad stop of Old Forge, launched a real-estate development in the region. One of his people had an Iroquois dictionary, and the region blossomed with Iroquois names. Fulton Chain became Thendara; the Spectacle Ponds, Lakes Tekeni and Easka, &c. I was startled when I came upon Howard's "Thandara," knowing that REH had never been within a thousand miles of Herkimer County, NY. But Chambers' book revealed the source.
--L. Sprague de Camp, Villanova, PA

Re Lovecraft's "The House of the Worm": This may have been the working title for "The Shunned House." In a letter to *Weird Tales* editor Edwin Baird dated February 3, 1924, Lovecraft said he was planning to write a short novel of 25,000 words or more, "a hideous thing whose provisional title (subject to change) is *The House of the Worm*" (SL 1.295). "The Shunned House," written in October 1924 is a story of approximately 10,500 words. It isn't a novel, but it is considerably longer than most of HPL's previous tales.
--William Fulwiler, Duncanville, TX

About William Fulwiler's ingenious suggestion that Lovecraft's "The House of the Worm" was the provisional title of "The Shunned House" (*Crypt* #19)—a passage in *Selected Letters* 1.357 indicates that this could not be so:

> . . . on the northeast corner of Bridge Street and Elizabeth Avenue [in Elizabeth, NJ] is a terrible old house—a hellish place where night-black deeds must have been done in the early seventeen-hundreds—with a blackish unpainted surface, unnaturally steep roof, and an outside flight of steps leading to the second story, suffocatingly embowered in a tangle of ivy so dense that one cannot but imagine it accursed or corpse-fed. . . . Later its image came up again with renewed vividness, finally causing me to write a new horror story with its scene in Providence. . . . It is called "The Shunned House," and I finished it last Sunday night.

Lovecraft's description of "The Shunned House" as "a *new* horror story" in a letter written eight months after his letter mentioning "The House of the Worm," and having a specific locale in New Jersey as its immediate inspiration, shows that the two titles have no connection.   --Steve Mariconda, Pompton Lakes, NJ

  I must disagree with Steve Mariconda's conclusion that "The House of the Worm" couldn't possibly have been the provisional title of "The Shunned House." As indicated by these passages from *Selected Letters I*, it was not the New Jersey house alone, but also the memories it evoked of another house, that sparked the writing of the story:

> It reminded me of the Babbitt house in Benefit Street, which as you recall made me write those lines entitled *The House* in 1920. Later its image came up again with renewed vividness, finally causing me to write a new horror story with its scene in Providence and with the Babbitt house as its basis (p. 357).
>
> Riding home on the subway, I was struck with the memory of weird things I had seen at twilight in Elizabethtown, and other weird things of longer ago—and at once realised that I was about to write a story (p. 359).

  The plot germ of this story may have been gestating in Lovecraft's mind for years—possibly since 1920, when he wrote "The House." Circa 1922, he wrote the following in his *Commonplace Book*:

> Horrible Colonial farmhouse & overgrown garden on city hillside—overtaken by growth. Verse "The House" as basis of story.

  Lovecraft later crossed out this entry and wrote beside it "*Shunned House*"—indicating the idea was used in writing the tale.
  In letters written in February 1924, HPL said his idea for "The House of the Worm" was "partly shaped" (SL I.295) and had "for some time been simmering unwholesomely in my consciousness" (p. 304). I believe Lovecraft had the Babbitt house idea in mind at this time, but didn't fully develop the plot of the story until eight months later, when the sight of the New Jersey house stimulated his imagination. Therefore, there is no contradiction in Lovecraft's reference to "The Shunned House" as a "new" story.
  As Professor Dirk W. Mosig has observed, "The Shunned House" is thematically related to "The Festival" (1923). The fate of the dead wizard in the former tale is explained in the translated passage from the *Necronomicon* which serves as the terminal paragraph of "The Festival":

> "The nethermost caverns," wrote the mad Arab, "are not for the fathoming of eyes that see; for their marvels are strange and terrific. Cursed the ground where dead thoughts live new and oddly bodied, and evil the mind that is held by no head. Wisely did Ibn Schacabao say, that happy is the tomb where no wizard hath lain, and happy the town at night whose wizards are all ashes. For it is of old rumour that the soul of the devil-bought hastes not from his charnel clay, but fats and instructs *the very worm*

that gnaws; till out of corruption horrid life springs, and the dull scavengers of earth wax crafty to vex it and swell monstrous to plague it. Great holes secretly are digged where earth's pores ought to suffice, and things have learnt to walk that ought to crawl" (*Dagon*, p. 195).

I think this passage makes clear the meaning of the title "The House of the Worm."
--William Fulwiler, Duncanville, TX

Dear Robert,

In your shocking and blasphemous essay "Lovecraft's Cosmic History," you say a comparison of Lovecraft's stories reduces his secret history of our planet to an "irreconcilable shambles." This seems a strange statement for a theologian to make. Surely you must concede that Lovecraft's Cthulhu mythology has far fewer inconsistencies than any other mythology.

One should keep in mind that almost all the stories of the Cthulhu canon are narrated by persons who have an imperfect knowledge of the phenomena and events they describe. Hence some discrepancies are inevitable (and give an added air of reality to the stories).

I agree that the history of Cthulhu related in "The Mound" cannot be reconciled with that given in *At the Mountains of Madness*. However, I don't consider the former to be a canonical story. (If other religionists can have their apocrypha, then so can we Cthulhuvians!) An unbeliever might speculate that, after a year of unsuccessfully attempting to sell "The Mound," HPL concluded it would never be published. That would explain why, in composing *At the Mountains of Madness*, he did not feel bound by what he had written about Cthulhu in the former story. However, I suspect what really happened is that sometime between the writing of the two stories, Lovecraft received telepathic messages from Great Cthulhu that disabused him of certain misconceptions he had about the history of that deity.

In your essay you give three reasons why my identification of the Yuggothians in "Out of the Eons" with the elder race that inhabited Yuggoth before the Mi-Go seems unlikely. I dispute all three.

First, there is no reason to assume the Yuggoth-spawn couldn't have colonized earth much earlier than the Mi-Go. The Mi-Go were the *last* of the many extraterrestrial races to colonize the planet. They first arrived a mere 150 million years ago. Second, it's true the elder Yuggothians of "Whisperer" are not said to have visited the earth, but that doesn't preclude the possibility that they did. Third, I can't find any statement in "Out of the Eons" that the Yuggoth-spawn colonized earth for the purpose of mining.

Now let's consider a couple of reasons why it's unlikely that the Mi-Go are the Yuggoth-spawn of "Out of the Eons." First, the Yuggoth-spawn are said to be extinct. The elder Yuggothians are extinct; the Mi-Go are not. Second, the Yuggoth-spawn worship Ghatanothoa, a god opposed by Nyarlathotep. The Mi-Go are de-

vout worshippers of Nyarlathotep. All things considered, I think the elder Yuggothians are more likely than the Mi-Go to be the Yuggoth-spawn.
    In closing, I urge you to recant the heresies expressed in your essay. Open your mind to Cthulhu and all will be made clear. There is no theological problem that a little faith and a lot of torturous reasoning can't solve.
    --William Fulwiler, Duncanville, TX

Dear William,
    True theologians love nothing better than exegetical debates over the scriptures! Brother in Almonsin-Metraton, let me offer this surrejoinder.
    As for the Yuggoth-spawn being miners, I was thinking of the fact that they did bring the Yuggothian metal *lagh* with them to earth, apparently in raw form, as T'yog uses some of it for his cylinder. Admittedly, HPL simply says it was "carven," but not by *whom*, so perhaps it was a relic of Yuggothian workmanship; however, the phrase "a carven cylinder of *lagh* metal—the metal brought by the Elder Ones from Yuggoth" (*HM*, 141) seems to me to imply that simply a supply of the metal itself was brought from Yuggoth. (The subsequent phrase "found in no mine on earth" indeed does *not* imply that the Yuggoth-spawn could not find it in their earthly mining attempts; rather, it means only that humans of earth would never be able to dig any up.)
    A couple of points in your rejoinder seem equivocal to me: first, are you sure "Out of the Eons" makes Nyarlathotep the enemy of Ghatanothoa? On page 140 only "Shub-Niggurath, Nug, and Yeb, as well as Yig the serpent-god, were ready to take sides with man against the tyranny and presumption of Ghatanothoa." Of course I may well be overlooking an obscure but decisive passage elsewhere in the story. And besides, "Whisperer" also makes the Mi-Go devotees of Shub-Niggurath, so your point is still well-taken. However, we have no inconsistency, since "Out of the Eons" clearly implies that the Yuggoth-spawn *feared* Ghatanothoa and only served him to placate him, like the Muvians themselves who hoped to be rid of the Dark God's tyranny.
    Second, you point out that in "Out of the Eons," the Yuggoth-spawn are said to be extinct, and that therefore they are most likely to be identified with the elder Yuggothians of "Whisperer in Darkness," said there to be extinct, than with that story's Mi-Go, obviously still alive and active. But this is just the point at issue. My contention is that we have a contradiction between "Eons" and "Whisperer" right here. Of course, you are saying that the resultant contradiction itself is evidence that I am making the wrong identification. The whole argument, as I see it, turns on the question of whether there is enough *other* evidence pointing to either the elder race or the Mi-Go as the intended counterpart to the Yuggoth-spawn. I still lean toward the Mi-Go. Here's why.
    I think we must ask what is most likely to have been going on in HPL's mind as he sat down to write "Out of the Eons" in 1933. As he looked back at "Whisperer in Darkness" written three years

earlier, he decided to borrow from that tale the notion of a race of aliens coming from Yuggoth to colonize earth. Which race in the earlier story does this sound like? Here is where I think it decisive that the elder race is *not* said in "Whisperer" ever to have visited earth, whereas the Mi-Go *are*. It seems clear to me that the Mi-Go loomed larger than the elder race in Lovecraft's memory, especially since he had already used the Mi-Go again in *At the Mountains of Madness*.

Finally, let me mention two perhaps minor points. Though you point out that in "Whisperer" the elder extinct race is not actually said to be indigenous to Yuggoth, it seems to me assumed since they are contrasted with the Mi-Go who used Yuggoth simply as a "stepping-stone." But, ironically, if I am right, then it might count as evidence *against* my equation of the Mi-Go with the Yuggothians of "Eons;" since the latter are called "the *spawn* of the dark planet Yuggoth." This terminology, though I had overlooked it before, would imply these beings were indigeneous to, spawned by, Yuggoth. This would imply that these Yuggoth-spawn were the same as the indigenous elder race of "Whisperer." However, I remain undaunted because I believe that here we have a parallel to the kind of historical simplification we saw in "Challenge from Beyond," where Lovecraft does not wish to explain the business about the Great Race of Yith teleporting through space to inhabit the cone-shaped earth creatures, so he simply makes the Great Race indigenous to earth so as not to confuse the reader of "Challenge" who may not have read "Shadow out of Time" previously. Even so, in "Out of the Eons," I suggest that HPL merely wants to simplify things for the reader who has not read "Whisperer": why haul in all the details of the Mi-Go not being originally from Yuggoth, when they only function in "Eons" as vague background for the *background* of the story in the first place? Since they came to earth from Yuggoth, why not simply call them the "Yuggoth-spawn"?

Second minor point: I don't want to make much out of this, but we are told in "Out of the Eons" that the Yuggoth-spawn had been as afraid of the "sight" of the Medusa-like Ghatanothoa as the humans of Mu were (*HM*, 139). Does this detail give us any clue as to the identity of the Yuggoth-spawn? Alas, no. It would *seem* to rule out the elder race, because Yuggoth is bereft of sunlight (*DH*, new edition, 254), and any race evolved there would not have evolved sight. Yet the Mi-Go are eliminated, too! "Light . . . hurts and hampers and confuses them, for it does not exist at all in the black cosmos outside time and space where they came from originally" (ibid.). So neither race, presumably, would have worried about *seeing* Ghatanothoa, yet members of one of them did see him, and with petrifying results, back on Yuggoth itself (*HM*, 139). *Another* contradiction, if you will. And I think it shows how Lovecraft, when writing "Out of the Eons," was not concerned to harmonize details when he reached back three years to lift ideas from "Whisperer." The Yuggothians he lifted from the earlier story were most probably the Mi-Go.

--Robert M. Price

Brian Lumley, *Mad Moon of Dreams*. W. Paul Ganley (P. O. Box 149, Amherst Branch, Buffalo, NY 14226-0149), 1987. $7.95.

(Reviewed by Stefan Dziemianowicz)

Mad Moon of Dreams concludes the trilogy Brian Lumley began with *Hero of Dreams* and *Ship of Dreams*. It's the pulpiest of the three, and in the best pulp tradition, even as it sacrifices style for speed, it makes dwelling on its shortcomings beside the point.

Purists, be forewarned: although this story is set in the dreamland of Randolph Carter, there is nothing truly Lovecraftian about it. Rather, *Mad Moon of Dreams* reads like a story originally written for one market but revised to sell in another. In *Ship of Dreams*, Lumley rewrote Lovecraft as an Errol Flynn movie. In *Mad Moon of Dreams*, he crosses Lovecraft with a dollop of *The Magnificent Seven* and a wallop of Edgar Rice Burroughs's Mars novels. The result is an adventure tale chock full of science fantasy, universal peril, strange and wondrous creatures, miracles of rare device, cavalry rescues and villains you can hiss at, all wonderfully realized in several magnificent Dave Carson illustrations.

David Hero and Eldin the Wanderer, you may recall, are meek waking worlders who have died and awakened as master swordsmen in dreamland. (Lumley often uses annoying parenthetical asides, not unlike this one, to supply such background, or to tell you about what's on a character's mind.) They discover a plot by the horned ones of Leng, the moonbeasts and basically every bad guy they've run into for the last two books to bring Mnomquah (imprisoned in the moon at the time of the banishment of the Great Old Ones) to dreamland so he can consummate his marriage to Oorn. Together, these two Cthulhvian monstrosities will control waking worlders through nightmares.

Randolph Carter, the Matt Dillon of dreamland, is off in the nether spheres, trying to track down Etienne Laurent de Marigny. With the mad moon drawing ever closer to the dreamland, Hero and Eldin realize that men gotta do what men gotta do, and they round up a posse of all the good guys, including Limner Dass, captain of the airship Gnorri II, and Gytherik, keeper of the night gaunts (including those two faithful cayuses, Sniffer and Biffer!). The story proceeds uncomplicatedly from there, with Hero and Eldin falling into the same traps set by the same villains they met in the earlier books, and making the same escapes. All the while, in the background, the approaching moon wreaks "lunarcy" in dreamland.

Credit Lumley for one thing—he won't settle for the end of the world when he can get an apocalypse. He's quite good at describing climactic battle scenes and earthshaking fireworks, even when it's hard to believe what's going on in them. But these moments take a back seat to the discovery that a lot of the scheming is a ruse to catch Hero and Eldin with their loincloths down: it seems the boys have got a price on their heads because they're attaining a mythic stature inimical to the plans of Mnomquah and Oorn. Talk about larger than life characters—Conan, Elric, Kane, Fafhrd and the Mouser all rolled into one couldn't be *this* arrogant! *Mad Moon of Dreams* may go down as the first story of a new genre: sword and chutzpah.

Normally I could care less about what any reviewer would have to say about any particular work (most of them not being people who can write—if they could, they'd be authors and not reviewers), but Dziemianowicz's comments on Brian Lumley's Hero and Eldin trilogy are so far off the mark, they really can't go unanswered.

Sorry, Dziemianowicz: cracks like "Randolph Carter, the Matt Dillon of Dreamland" or "sword and chutzpah" are the kind of cute cracks made to make one look good at someone else's expense. You ain't making it. As for the stories not being particularly Lovecraftian—tell me, exactly what does that mean? The only person who could write a "Lovecraftian" story has been buried in Providence for a little over half a century. Lumley's style runs more along the lines of Robert E. Howard—God knows, after all the creaking monsters and half-baked tomes foisted on the reading public by clowns attempting to play at being Lovecraft, an attempt to inject slightly different elements couldn't hurt. No, Brian didn't write these tales for a different market and then revise them as Dreamland stories. They were written as Dreamland stories.
--Lew Cabos, Marina, CA

Brian Lumley, *The Burrowers Beneath*. London: Grafton, $7.50.

(Reviewed by Stefan Dziemianowicz)

When Brian Lumley's first novel, *The Burrowers Beneath*, was published in 1974, it was something for the Lovecraft community to sit up and pay attention to. In 1969, August Derleth had officially anointed Lumley, Ramsey Campbell, Colin Wilson and James Wade as the newest torchbearers of the Cthulhu Mythos by including them among the august company represented in *Tales of the Cthulhu Mythos*. Within five years, though, James Wade had all but disappeared from the fantasy scene, Colin Wilson had revealed his interest in the Mythos to be only one (and a relatively minor one, at that) of many things on his mind, and Campbell had outgrown his Lovecraftian influences and seen his groundbreaking *Demons by Daylight* published. The only remaining true believer seemed to be Lumley, whose 1971 collection, *The Caller of the Black*, had served up a generous portion of Mythos-related material.

It was with some surprise, though, that *The Burrowers Beneath* came out bound not in Holliston Black Novelex, but in wraps with the distinctive yellow spine of a DAW Books paperback. Here was not only a bona fide Mythos novel (arguably the first since *The Lurker at the Threshold* appeared in 1945, if one discounts Fred Chappell's *Dagon*, first published in 1967, as a book that goes above and beyond the Mythos), some 60,000 words long, but one brought out in a format guaranteed to reach more people than the limited Arkham House editions.

Readers steeped in Lovecraft immediately recognized the title of Lumley's book as the title of a story written by the ill-fated Robert Blake in "The Haunter of the Dark." (Coincidentally, it was also the same title Fritz Leiber had given to a 3,000 word fragment of a Mythos story he began writing after Lovecraft's death, and eventually retitled.) However, the similarity seemed something of a fluke. The true source of Lumley's novel was one of his two contributions to *Tales of the Cthulhu Mythos*, "Cement Surroundings." This story introduced Shudde M'ell, a lesser member of the Great Old Ones, who presides over his burrowing minions underneath the lost African city of G'Harne. It is told as Paul Wendy-Smith's account of his uncle, Sir Amery Wendy-Smith, the only survivor of an expedition to G'Harne. Ever since coming back from Africa, the elder Wendy-Smith has been fearful of going below the surface of the earth. He's also become obsessed enough with seismology to have compiled a history of seemingly interconnected earthquakes that have occurred around the world in different eras. It turns out that Sir Amery witnessed the destruction of his expedition by the burrowers, and that he has unwittingly brought back with him some of these creatures' rare eggs. The burrowers ultimately seek him out back home in England, destroy him during a freak earthquake, and later dispatch Paul Wendy-Smith as well.

"Cement Surroundings" is not a bad pastiche, probably as good as any story Derleth (to whom *The Burrowers Beneath* is dedicated) had written for the Mythos. It's told in a style characteristic of many other Mythos stories, that of the cautionary tale in which the narrator tells of some horrible knowledge he has gained through having observed another fall victim to it. The seemingly disconnected events he notes throughout the narrative are eventually revealed to be adumbrations of the final horror. Although there's little surprise in the way the story ends, Lumley shows a respect for the cumulative structure of the Mythos story that makes up for what the tale lacks in atmosphere.

However, Lumley's inclusion of "Cement Surroundings" as the third chapter of his novel had some readers scratching their heads in puzzlement. After all, they wondered, if Lumley had already played his Mythos hand and taken the reader to that mind-shattering point of contact with the unknown only a third of the way through the book, what was there left to write about? The answer to his question was, and continues to be, a source of controversy, one that has generated debates over such issues as Lovecraft's "intentions" for the Mythos, the proper function of a Mythos story, and what liberties an author can take in rewriting established Mythos lore.

"Cement Surroundings," it must be remembered, is preceded by two other chapters. The first is comprised of a series of letters to and from Lumley's unflappable occult detective, Titus Crow, in which it's revealed that a coal mine inspector has come across some unusual pearl-like objects during a recent cave-in. The second chapter introduces us to Etienne Laurent de Marigny, the perennial Watson to Crow's Holmes (the majority of chapters are presented as excerpts from de Marigny's notebooks and diaries), whose conversations with Crow indicate that both men are well versed in the (mostly) Derleth Mythos and Lumley's additions to it. Thus, by the time Crow gives the manuscript of Paul Wendy-Smith to de Marigny in the third chapter, it's fairly evident that he's completely on top of the situation. He has retrieved the "mine pearls"—obviously a new batch of burrower eggs—and, mindful that the parents will come after them, much as they did for the Wendy-Smiths, he's concocted a ruse whereby he and friends will keep shipping the eggs to each other at different locations around the world and hopefully put the burrowers through enough gyrations to make them dizzy.

Thus, Lumley's novel begins right at the point where a Lovecraft story would probably have ended—with a knowledgeable narrator. One could say that all of Lovecraft's narrators are knowledgeable from the outset, and that their stories are only a retelling of the process by which they put facts together for the benefit of the reader, yet where Lovecraft's tales end with characters subdued by the enormity of what they have discovered, Lumley's story begins with his characters galvanized into taking defensive action. That's because in *The Burrowers Beneath* Lumley doesn't approach the Mythos as something mysterious and unfathomable. On the contrary, he presents it as a phenomenon that has been studied and assessed by some of the most sober academic minds, men who don't reveal what they know not because their knowledge is beyond belief but because they're engaged in a war with an enemy who must not know about the concerted scientific effort that is being mounted against them.

The result is what Robert Price refers to in his essay, "Brian Lumley—Reanimator" (*Crypt of Cthulhu* 3(3):10, Candlemas 1984), as a "wholesale process of demythologization," by which Lumley hopes to make Mythos entities understandable through modern science. From Crow, for example, we learn that the imprisonment of the Old Ones may entail little more than a sophisticated form of behavioral psychology:

> The Elder Gods knew that they could never hope to imprison beings as powerful as the deities of the Cthulhu Cycle behind merely physical bars. They made their prisons *the minds of the Great Old Ones themselves*—perhaps their bodies! They implanted mental and genetic blocks into the psyches and beings of the forces of evil and their minions, that at the sight of—or upon the presence of—certain symbols, or upon hearing those symbols reproduced as sound, those forces of evil are held back impotent! This explains why comparatively simple devices such as the Mnaran star-stones are effective, and why, in the event of such stones being removed from their prisoning locations, certain chants or written symbols may still cause the escaped powers to retreat.

Lumley makes further efforts to drag the Mythos kicking and screaming from its captivity in Gothic wrappings into the post-Einsteinian twentieth century. Once Crow and de Marigny team up with Wingate Peaslee and the Wilmarth Foundation, a sophisticated research group (physics, not the Elder Gods, is their co-pilot) devoted to the eradication of the Cthulhu Cycle Deities (or "CCD," in Wilmarth Foundation parlance), the rationalizations come thick and fast. Of Azathoth, that bubbling blasphemer at the center of all infinity, we learn that "he was—he *is*—nothing less than the Big Bang itself, and to hell with your Steady State theorists!" Also, that Nyarlathotep, messenger of the gods, "is not a being or deity as such at all, but more truly a 'power.' Nyarlathotep is in fact Telepathy."

In effect, what we see taking place in *The Burrowers Beneath* is a reversal of the process with which Lovecraft generated his Mythos entities. Where Lovecraft distilled apprehensions about an undefinable and numinous "Unknown" into metaphorical creatures the human mind could just barely grasp, Lumley suggests that those entities are themselves abstractions of quantifiable, measurable forces. Roughly speaking, Lumley's Unknown is as physical as Lovecraft's is philosophical.

Purists have fumed for years at Lumley's radical reinterpretation of the Mythos, yet it was Fritz Leiber, in a review that appeared in the June 1975 *Fantastic*, who put his finger on the most disappointing aspect of the book as a piece of Mythos fiction. Quoting from Lovecraft's *Supernatural Horror in Literature*, Leiber remarked that

> . . . whatever this stuff may achieve, it does not engender in the reader "a profound sense of dread" or "a subtle attitude of awed listening" . . . The total result is certainly not a supernatural horror story. The Mythos was only *one* of Lovecraft's devices for arousing spectral fear, and he used it sparingly. Here it becomes almost the only device— in fact, the entire subject matter of the novel. It is on stage at all times, so how can the reader be afraid?

Indeed, Lumley's story owes at least as much to the spy thriller genre as it does to the Cthulhu Mythos. In place of the isolated individual who accidentally happens upon some unspeakable cosmic revelation, we have the good guys (the Wilmarth Foundation and its subsidiary institutions) versus the bad guys (the CCD). At times, it's difficult not to think of the story's cloak and daggery in terms of a James Bond film, in which the Old Ones are stand-ins for SPECTRE. (The passage in which Peaslee issues Crow and de Marigny their own star-stones—made from a real star-stone that has been pulverized, mixed in with synthetic stone fired in the kilns of Miskatonic University, and mass produced as protective talismans —even reads a little like those scenes in which Q emerges from his laboratory long enough to outfit 007 with the latest new-fangled weaponry.)

From this perspective, *The Burrowers Beneath* is disenchanting in the truest sense of the word, for in desanctifying the Old Ones Lumley has made them and their minions no more threatening than other human agents, and almost equally as vulnerable. Early in the novel, when de Marigny is having trouble comprehending the alienness of the burrowers, Crow advises him to "'try thinking in less routine terms.'" Yet routinization is what *The Burrowers Beneath* is all about. The burrowers are creatures with a "maternal" instinct, who pursue men who have stolen their young. Late in the book, a telepath who links up with a dying burrower comes into contact with a mind perfectly understandable in terms of human hopes and fears. By making them comprehensible, Lumley has put these creatures on a par with human beings, robbing them of all their spectacularness and expressing the threat they pose more in terms of their size than their meaning. When the Wilmarth Foundation routs the burrowers out of England at the end, humans have actually become the pursuers and the Old Ones the pursued.

It's easy, fourteen years after the fact, to criticize Lumley for creating a Mythos as distinct from Derleth's as it is from Lovecraft's, but it's only fair to ask why he thought it was necessary to do so in the first place. In an interview last year in *Fantasy Review* (10:5:16, June 1987) he explained his approach to the Mythos in terms as applicable to *The Burrowers Beneath* as anything he has written since:

> To stray too far from the Lovecraft focus is to bend the rules too far. But the Mythos can be used in as many different ways as that many writers can conceive of . . . Do it the way some people would, and the Mythos would stagnate. You *cannot* keep reading "The Dunwich Horror" and "Call of Cthulhu" over and over again, unless you happen to be some sort of nut who can't read anything else.

Whether or not one feels that Lumley has debased the spirit of the Mythos, one must concede that he has a point. "The Dunwich Horror" and "The Call of Cthulhu" have held up remarkably well over the last half century, better than much supernatural horror fiction written after them. But in this day and age, when science and technology have so demystified the Unknown, it's hard to write a Mythos story with the same conviction that Lovecraft put into his work. This is one reason interest in the Mythos has waned among professional writers. It's also a major reason why, with very few exceptions, so many stabs at the Mythos today read, at best, like nostalgic homages to the heyday of the pulp magazines when such stories were imaginative novelties.

The Burrowers Beneath stands as Lumley's attempt to make the Mythos relevant to the half century of scientific knowledge that has been acquired since Lovecraft first expressed his fears about man's ability to accept what lay beyond the perimeter of his knowledge. For all of his appropriations of Lovecraftian names and set pieces, Lumley does not attempt to pass this novel off as an extension of, or improvement upon, Lovecraft. His approach is entirely original, almost consciously distancing itself from the conceptual horrors of Lovecraft. The book is also something of a creative locus for him, incorporating the stories "Cement Surroundings" and "The Night the Sea Maid Went Down," mentioning scenes and incidents from the Titus Crow stories that had appeared in *The Caller of the Black*, setting up the sequel *The Transition of Titus Crow*, and even anticipating the society of telepathic espionage agents currently appearing in his *Necroscope* books. If for no other reason than that it may provoke readers into reassessing their own interpretations of Lovecraft. *The Burrowers Beneath* is a book that everyone interested in the Mythos should read.

I'd like to argue with a viewpoint expressed in the review of *The Burrowers Beneath*. Lumley is accused of putting the Mythos creatures on a par with humans. Further, humans have become the pursuers and the Old Ones the pursued. This is regarded (not just by the reviewer but evidently by many others) as a blasphemy against the orthodox Lovecraftian viewpoint.

The telepathic contact between a minor burrower (child/minion of Shudde-M'ell) and a human sensitive is chosen as an example. When I first read this episode (back in the seventies) I did not find this to be a "humanizing" of the alien creatures. In fact, I found my awe increased rather than decreased (as, I think, did the characters in the story).

Do not the Old Ones often make contact with humans? Does not Cthulhu send dreams to humans? When R'lyeh rises above the sea in "Call of Cthulhu," are not artists and madmen and other sensitives affected profoundly with visions of alien surroundings?

The Old Ones have many things in common with humans: the desire to rule (which got them into trouble), to reproduce, to dream. If part of their thinking is totally alien, it is unlikely a human in telepathic contact would be able to make any sense of that part (his human mind would filter it out as nonsense) and only the similarities would come through. But in any case, I claim that telepathic contact between Great Old Ones and humans is not an invention of Lumley but of Lovecraft Himself.

What about the pursuit of the Old Ones by humans—the hunters becoming the hunted? Is this a perversion of the pure tradition of the HPL Mythos? Invented by that St. Paul of the Mythos, August Derleth?—and shamefully adhered to by Lumley? Or did Lovecraft ever do anything like that?

I claim that HPL did this in some of his own stories. Let's make an analogy between Shudde-M'ell of the underworld and Cthulhu (and Dagon) of the undersea world. Shudde-M'ell has his minions, the burrowers. Cthulhu has his, the Deep Ones.

If anything, the Deep Ones are more humanized than Lumley makes the burrowers—the Deep Ones can even interbreed with humans and live on land as a first phase of their existence, before metamorphosing into sea-creatures.

Just as the private army of the Wilmarth Foundation attacks the burrowers (using oil-rigs to drill down to their depths and then employing appropriate weapons), the U. S. government attacks the Deep Ones, depth-bombing Devil's Reef and destroying their undersea cities (and the FBI removes the fishy-men from Innsmouth and puts them away in asylums).

The men of the Wilmarth Foundation even have the audacity to attack SHUDDE-M'ELL Himself!!! And they even hurt him, though they can't do any serious damage to a real Great Old One. Is this a heresy?

Think back to the "Call of Cthulhu" when Cthulhu is released from imprisonment in R'lyeh after the island has risen. The sailor (Johanssen?) is trying to escape, but Cthulhu is in pursuit and catching up. Desperately he turns the ship and (oh the gall of a mere human!) runs him down with the ship. He then gets away, but looks back and sees the figure of Cthulhu re-forming itself.

It isn't made quite clear why Cthulhu, having escaped, did not raven through the world, conquering and destroying. I imagine, though, that it isn't very pleasant to be run down and smashed apart by a ship, even if you are a Great Old One. He probably had to go back to R'lyeh for a few fourth-dimensional stitches in his three-dimensional carcass, and got trapped there when the island sank again.

With regard to the comments and reviews of Lumley's *Dreams* novels, may I make one or two remarks? These should not be approached as horror novels because they aren't. They are horror-adventure stories (similar to fantasy-adventure). My jacket blurb for *Hero of Dreams* concludes with "Here is . . . a blend of fantasy adventure with the much darker world of H. P. Lovecraft." Much of my advertising made it quite clear (I hope) that this was basically swords-and-sorcery, in which the sorcery derived from the Mythos.

It has been suggested that the stories read like a mixture of HPL and Edgar Rice Burroughs, as if this were shameful. That was my own impression when I read the novels in manuscript—if ever a collaboration between HPL and ERB could have existed, it would be something like this. Only I didn't think it was anything but interesting and exciting. Both authors were favorites of mine as a young man. For that matter, I seem to recall that HPL wrote a letter praising ERB as an excellent story teller in spite of his putting tigers in Africa.

For some, this idea will be repugnant. For them, I say, don't buy these books. For others, the idea may be intriguing. There are more Hero and Eldin stories (shorter ones), and one will be showing up in *Weird Tales* some time in the next year or so. Incidentally, there is another "Hero" in literature, a psychic investigator who appears in the Paul Gallico books *Hand of Mary Constable* and *Too Many Ghosts*. Alexander Hero derives his name from the French, Hiereaux, or some such spelling. Perhaps Lumley's David Hero is a cousin.

--W. Paul Ganley, Buffalo, NY

P. S. I wanted to make one other point, which I omitted above. HPL's version of "Titus Crow" was Randolph Carter. *The Dream-Quest of Unknown Kadath* is basically a horror-adventure story. Sure, Carter does not swing a sword; he's more like a spy than a warrior. He uses his friends (like ghouls and the cats) instead of fighting back with swords. But unlike many of HPL's protagonists, Carter has guts. He climbs mountains, boards alien vessels, creeps through fearsome layers of dream, and ultimately even confronts Nyarlathotep Himself—and bests him, or at least comes off even.

I know it's fashionable to consider *Dream-Quest of Unknown Kadath* as inferior work, and stories like "Color out of Space" (or Colour) as HPL's best work. But personally I never had much use for "Colour out of Space," while I think *Dream-Quest of Unknown Kadath* is one of his best three or four longer pieces.

My conclusion is: HPL did it all first. His successors may emphasize different aspects of the Mythos, but they aren't heretics.

WPG

Mr. Paul Ganley makes some very good points about Brian Lumley's *The Burrowers Beneath* in his letter, but I must disagree with several of them on the grounds of what may be a very personal interpretation of the Lovecraft Mythos (I leave it for others to decide). Do the Old Ones "contact" human beings or "send dreams" to them in "The Call of Cthulhu"? As I see it, the re-emergence of Cthulhu creates a disturbance in the cosmic-psychic continuum that is picked up by sensitive human beings, ranging from artists to madmen. The artist Wilcox isn't directly given dreams any more than the Cthulhu cultists are told to prance naked around a fire in the backwash of Louisiana. Each interprets the phenomena he experiences within his own cultural context: the "primitive" cultists transcribe their experience into religious frenzy; the more rational Wilcox transcribes his into art. I think there's a big difference between this idea and the notion that the Old Ones "contact" particular human beings. If you hold, as I do, that the Old Ones represent forces of cosmic indifference who couldn't care less (because they don't "care" in any human sense of the word) about human beings, this allows you to see the events in "The Call of Cthulhu" as examples of how human beings cannot help but react to every involuntary twitch of the Old Ones, and interpret those twitches in terms of puny human understanding and experience. This is not a very exalting picture of humanity but, to me, it's the one that Lovecraft wished to communicate.

Mr. Ganley goes on to say that "the Old Ones have many things in common with humans." Well—and here's where I expect to be savaged by other Lovecraftians—sez who? I mentioned before that persons sensitive to the "transmissions" of the Old Ones interpret their experience in purely human terms. That includes the Wilcoxes, that includes the Whateleys—but that also includes the Alhazreds, the Geoffreys, the Prinns, et al., who wrote the books that tell us all about how the Old Ones "think" and "feel" and "act." I feel one of the intended ironies of Lovecraft's fiction is that human beings always try to interpret the doings of the Old Ones in strictly human terms—which they can't help but do, since they know no other frame of reference. We infer (as Mr. Ganley says) that among the things the Old Ones have in common with human beings is "the desire to rule . . . to reproduce, to dream." Perhaps—but isn't there something peculiar about thinking of such transcendent entities in such pedestrian human terms? The idea that humans write and speak of the Old Ones through a vocabulary woefully inadequate for describing them certainly accounts for all of the black magic trappings in which the Mythos is swaddled: how typical of human beings to lock these embodiments of forces beyond human ken into a system that permits distinctions of good and evil (cf. Henry Armitage's foolish comments at the end of "The Dunwich Horror"), magical books, high priests and cults! The supernaturalism of religious belief is the human race's greatest yardstick for measuring something that transcends themselves, so its vocabulary is what men use to try and understand the Old Ones. My feeling is that Lovecraft was saying this is a step in the right direction—but that it isn't enough by half. Does this mean, then, that we shouldn't read the snatches from the *Necronomicon* & co. as gospel concerning the Old Ones? No, of course we should. But we should read them as gospel in the same sense as we read the gospels in the New Testament: with the understanding that they are the work of fallible men trying to describe the infallible—something they are ill-equipped to do since, by their very nature, they lack adequate tools for describing something that transcends themselves. I wouldn't read the texts written by men about the Old Ones as a literal delineation of what the Old Ones stand for any more than I would read the Bible as a literal delineation of the divinity of God. In the end, isn't this a very Lovecraftian idea—not only that human knowledge is a mere sliver of some greater, cosmic truth, but that because humans know so little, what they do know is inadequate at best, if not wrong?

Mr. Ganley is correct in noting the correspondence between Lovecraft's Deep Ones and Lumley's minions of Shudde-M'ell: if you prick them, do they not both bleed? If you pursue them, are they not cornered? My argument with Lumley's handling of this correspondence in *The Burrowers Beneath* is the degree of reciprocity between the humans and in-humans. In my opinion, Lumley made the burrowers completely understandable in human terms—as creatures that flee persecution and fight to save their young—in much the same way he tries to make the Old Ones understandable in terms of contemporary physics.

Lovecraft often showed a point of contingency between human beings and the Old Ones and their minions: the Deep Ones are a good example (although let's remember, we don't see the Deep Ones in "The Shadow over Innsmouth"—we see the hybrid offspring of human and Deep One breeding. Presumably, there is a thoroughbred race of Deep Ones from whom the hybrids are at one remove, just as the Deep Ones themselves are at least one remove from the entity Dagon); Wilbur Whateley is another good example. But Lovecraft used that point of contingency as a point of departure from which he went on to show how *unlike* human beings the Old Ones were. He didn't use it to dwell on similarities between humans and the Old Ones, which is what I felt Lumley did in the novel. It's very true that some of the story elements I criticized in Lumley's book—the "hunting down" of the Old Ones, the contact between the Old Ones and human beings—originate with Lovecraft. But, as I'm sure many readers will agree, the elements themselves do not a Mythos story make—it's how the elements are used. Mr. Ganley cites "The Shadow over Innsmouth" as a story where Lovecraft shows the Deep Ones tracked down and incarcerated like humans. Yes—but Lovecraft has that happen offstage, at the beginning of the story, for the purpose of creating a false sense of security in the narrator and reader alike. The rest of the story is devoted to showing how insidious "the shadow over Innsmouth" really is, and how foolish the narrator is for thinking he can escape from it.

With regard to Lumley's David Hero books, I hope people aren't assuming that by calling them "pulpy," as I did in my last review, I intended some dire criticism. (Hey, I co-edited a book of pulp fiction, didn't I?) Pulp fiction can be durn good fun. My remark about *Mad Moon of Dreams* reading like it was written for one market but then changed cosmetically to sell to another is consistent with my feelings that it has a pulp quality to it. Much pulp fiction —even good pulp fiction—was formulaic (and if you don't believe that, read some of Burroughs's sequels to *Tarzan and the Apes*), and for that reason easily convertible to another market. I found *Mad Moon of Dreams* formulaic. Why do I always mention the fact that there is nothing Lovecraftian about Lumley's trilogy? Because I assume (perhaps foolishly?) that any reader who picks up a copy of a book set in Lovecraft's Dreamland, and populated with some of his characters, is going to assume there is something Lovecraftian about the book. Brian Lumley is *not* an unimaginative author who needs to borrow from other writers' work. He has written some good heroic/sword and sorcery stories for markets like *Weirdbook* that are not set in Lovecraft's Dreamland. So when he uses Lovecraft's Dreamland, I assume it's for a good reason. If I can't see that reason, I find it necessary to ask why he chose that setting in the first place.

--Stefan R. Dziemianowicz, Union City, NJ

Crypt seems of two minds: is Lumley a wanker or isn't he? Well, I used to quite a lot . . . but I was just a boy then and soon discovered women. I'm glad Dziemianowicz (Jesus, talk about Cthulhu being hard to pronounce!) finally found something of mine that he likes. The *Necroscope* books, I mean; or more specifically *Wamphyri*! Hopefully he'll like *Necroscope III: The Source*, *IV: Deadspeak*, and *V: Deadspawn* just as much. But if not . . . well, you can't please everyone all the time. The last two will be the end of it. (And, incidentally, the first two in the series have recently been reprinted in UK.)

But it seems I should say a word or two about the *Hero* books (*Hero of Dreams*, *Ship of Dreams*, *Mad Moon*, etc.). And about *Burrowers*. First let me say that Dzie—can I call him Dizzy?— that Dizzy's review of *Burrowers* got the closest to the real me and my intentions than any other before it. It was like he read my mind. I applaud it because I know he *read* this one. But let me also say of his answer to Paul Ganley's letter that he's wrong.

The trouble with a lot of Lovecraft "experts" is that they aren't; usually they only remember it the way they want to, not the way it is. Or they've read the stuff so often that it just doesn't make any impression any more. I'm not saying Dizzy is deliberately misleading, just that his memory is faulty.

I have to hand it to the most recent Arkham *Dunwich Horror & Co.*, p. 139, a third of the way down the page:

> They worshipped, so they said, the Great Old Ones who lived ages before there were any men, and who came to the young world out of the sky. Those Old Ones were gone now, inside the earth and under the sea; *but their dead bodies had told their secrets in dreams to the first men, who formed a cult which had never died.* This was that cult, and the prisoners said it had always existed and always would exist, hidden in distant wastes and dark places

all over the world and until the time when the great priest Cthulhu, from his dark house in the mighty city of R'lyeh under the waters, should rise and bring the earth again beneath his sway. *Some day he would call, when the stars were ready, and the secret cult would always be waiting to liberate him.*

Quite obviously, Wilcox and others of that ilk, and the cultists, have heard his call. He has spoken to them in dreams. I mean, the story is called "The Call of Cthulhu," after all!

On the next page we learn that there are arts which can revive the Great Old Ones. So now we know why Cthulhu bothers to chat telepathically with mere people: to pass on the spells which can raise him up from R'lyeh. But . . . if I haven't made the point clearly enough, HPL himself makes it at the bottom of page 140:

. . . some force from outside must serve to liberate Their bodies. The spells that preserved Them intact likewise prevented Them from making an initial move, and They could only lie awake in the dark and *think* whilst uncounted millions of years rolled by. They knew all that was occurring in the universe, *for Their mode of speech was transmitted thought. Even now They talked in Their tombs.* When, after infinities of chaos, the first men came, *the Great Old Ones spoke to the sensitive among them by moulding their dreams; for only thus could their language reach the fleshly minds of mammals* . . .

And so on. Page 141 is full of it, too.

So you see, you're wrong, Dizzy. You asked a question: "Do the Old Ones contact human beings or send dreams to them in 'The Call of Cthulhu'?" Yes. But don't take my word for it, read the story. It's a reviewer's duty after all. Meanwhile, I'll condense it for you:

Cthulhu sent dreams to reinforce the spells of his secret priests and warn them of his imminence. The sensitives *overheard* his dream sendings and some cracked up (why, some were so badly affected they couldn't even remember the &*?@$¢ story!).

Now, there are those who'll argue black is white. I once saw two guys in a Sgt.'s Mess decide a heated argument by tossing a coin . . . and *then* argue that they'd both called heads! But there is no argument here. Whether my story was a good or bad one and liked or loathed isn't the point; what is the point is that Ganley is right, and no amount of waffle can disprove it. Lovecraft wrote what he wrote, and even in the "revised" or "corrected" version it's still writ. Be warned, Dizzy: even folks who try to rewrite HPL come on hard times, but people who would *un*write him get gobbled up by nameless things . . .

To write a definite finis on all this, on page 147 there's the narrator totting up all the damnable information:

"What of all this—and of those hints of old Castro about the sunken, star-born Old Ones and their coming reign; their faithful cult *and their mastery of dreams?*"

And those are Lovecraft's italics this time . . .
  About the Dreamlands books.
  Just like I loved everything Lovecraftian, I loved his dreamlands. Marvellous, fantastic creation. And others who used the setting tried (I think) to stick to the Lovecraft formula. Myers and Carter, for example. They *tried*, anyway. But I have trouble relating to people who faint at the hint of a bad smell. A meep or glibber doesn't cut it with me. (I love meeps and glibbers, don't get me wrong, but *I* go looking for what made them!) That's the main difference between my stories in that setting and HPL's. My guys fight back. Also, they like to have a laugh along the way.
  I give you an example from life:
  I did a little service in Malta. There are Crusader remains (and how!) in Malta. There are wonderful buildings, there's history, there are lessons to be learned, a lot to take in. But my mind doesn't run to learning *all* the time. HPL has Randolph Carter sitting in a tavern listening to the mournful songs of salty old seadogs. Me? I was down Straight Street (called "The Gut" by every sailor who ever was) listening to the Beatles, drinking Chisk, Hop Leaf and Blue Label and ogling the girlies!
  I was in places HPL wouldn't *ever* go. Now the dreamlands are made from the dreams of men, and it takes all types. So the background is the same *but the dream is different*! My guys hang out in the Craven Lobster or Buxom Barba's Quayside Quaress. And the things they get up to and the quests they go on *can't be too farfetched*! Hell, Randolph Carter passed from the moon to the dreamlands in a leap of cats!
  Point made, I hope.
  Headline Books UK will be doing the series in mass paperback starting in August. The jackets are quite beautiful.
  Crypt is good but expensive. If I didn't get complimentary copies I'd go broke. But there again I'd get a lot more *paying* writing done, too . . .
    --Brian Lumley, Devon, England

  My thanks to Brian Lumley for his remarks concerning my review of *The Burrowers Beneath*. Considering how much fault I found with the book, he was generous with his praise. My admiration for him extends to his defense of remarks made by W. Paul Ganley in *Crypt* #63 regarding the nature of contacts between the Old Ones and mankind in Lovecraft's work. My rebuttal to Mr. Ganley in *Crypt* #65 included the opinion that the Old Ones do not send "dreams" to human beings, thereby implying some rapport, or even interdependence, between Lovecraft's monstrosities and mankind; rather that human beings, with their limited perceptions, interpret the influence of the indifferent Old Ones upon their mental patterns as some sort of divine selection or ordination because it is the only way men can make sense of the experience. Mr. Lumley disagrees with me, and persuasively cites chapter and verse from "The Call of Cthulhu" to prove that my "memory is faulty" on this point. However, his argument only reminds me of the old saying "Even the Devil can quote scripture," and its unspoken corollary, that he makes it work to his advantage by quoting it out of context.

The first passage Lumley cites, which appears on page 139 of the corrected sixth printing of *The Dunwich Horror and Others*, says of the Great Old Ones, "[They] were gone now, inside the earth and under the sea; but their dead bodies had told their secrets in dreams to the first men, who formed a cult which had never died." This would appear to confirm Lumley's argument that the Old Ones intentionally send dreams to men, until we consider who is supplying this information to the narrator. A description of them appears in the sentence that immediately precedes the passage abstracted by Lumley: "Degraded and ignorant as they were, the creatures held with surprising consistency to the central idea of their loathsome faith." In other words, we are receiving this information from a cult of "degraded and ignorant" religious fanatics. Hardly the most reliable fact-givers in the world—but let's suspend our judgment for the moment.

Lumley goes on to bolster his argument with a passage from page 140 that speaks of the Old Ones "moulding" the dreams of the sensitive among mankind. Who is supplying the narrator with the information on this page? Lumley neglects to mention that it is "an immensely aged mestizo named Castro . . . who remembered bits of hideous legend that paled the speculations of theosophists and made man and the world seem recent and transient indeed." Mind you, that's "legend" recounted by Castro, not fact. Legend may indeed be based in fact, but it is also a distortion of fact not meant to be taken literally. That's a good thing, too, for how could we take literally the conclusion of Castro's account:

> The time would be easy to know, for then mankind would have become as the Great Old Ones; free and wild and beyond good and evil, with laws and morals thrown aside and all men shouting and killing and revelling in joy. Then the liberated Old Ones would teach them new ways to shout and kill and revel and enjoy themselves, and all the earth would flame with a holocaust of ecstasy and freedom.

Are we to take this image of Cthulhu and company partying with human beings and trading war stories at face value? I don't think so—at least if I have interpreted correctly the havoc wrought by Cthulhu on the few human beings he encounters at the end of the story.

As one of the stories of the Lovecraft Mythos, "The Call of Cthulhu" is (in Lovecraft's words) "based on the fundamental premise that common human laws and interests and emotions have no validity or significance in the vast cosmos-at-large" (SL II.150). In "The Call of Cthulhu," as in other stories in the Lovecraft Mythos, Lovecraft enunciates this premise by demolishing homocentric conceptualizations of the cosmos *and* the language used to describe them. Language is always a snare in Lovecraft's work. His educated narrators are forever telling us that the human vocabulary is inadequate for describing the cosmic horrors they have discovered. When the less sophisticated Cthulhu cultists try to describe their (false) role in a mystery beyond human comprehension, they descend

into a quasi-mystical patois rich in allusion, symbol and metaphor that cannot be taken literally. Just as Lovecraft showed in "The Colour out of Space" that it was impossible to describe a color outside the normal range of the visible spectrum in anything but poorly approximate terms, so was he constantly playing up the impossibility of using conventional human language to describe the unfathomable mysteries of the cosmos. Lumley can interpret the passages he quotes from "The Call of Cthulhu" literally if he so chooses. But by doing so I think he deprives Lovecraft's fiction of a great deal of its mystery. In my eyes, that makes him as much an "un-writer" of Lovecraft as he finds me.
--Stefan R. Dziemianowicz, Union City, NJ

In his "Call of Cthulhu" letter (*Crypt* #72), S. R. Dziemianowicz attempts to show that his (Dizzy's) interpretation of Lovecraft's meaning is more relevant than what Lovecraft actually wrote. Was HPL so illiterate, then, that he was incapable of saying what he meant? Look: Lovecraft has it that the artist Wilcox dreams of Cthulhu in his House in R'lyeh—dreams which are replete with chanting (Cthulhu Fhtagn!), Cyclopean undersea cities, the lot—and afterwards creates the 5"x6" miniature or tablet which is central to the story, showing Cthulhu, hieroglyphs, alien architecture and indeed everything which HPL so deftly describes, none of which could possibly be known to Wilcox unless placed in his head by some Other. Wilcox himself, *when* himself, knows nothing about it, can't explain it. It is Professor Angell who recognizes the tablet and what is carved upon it *in such detail* for what it really is! Now tell me, Dizzy: do you still insist that Wilcox's mind has not been touched by Cthulhu's? Do you expect *anyone* who has read the story to accept that Cthulhu's dreaming hasn't actually influenced Wilcox's? If so, then my reaction is simple . . . but unprintable. Again I ask you to ask *yourself* this: why did HPL call the story "The Call of Cthulhu"? Why not simply "Rising With R'lyeh"?
--Brian Lumley, Devon, England

In his letter in *Crypt* #74, Brian Lumley continues to take me to task for suggesting that Lovecraft was getting at truths in his fiction that the limited vocabularies of his narrators were inadequate to express; in effect, that when a Lovecraft character starts speaking of things beyond human ken, his human perspective automatically biases how he will describe them.

Lumley asks, "Was HPL so illiterate, then, that he was incapable of saying what he meant?" To the contrary, Lovecraft was perfectly capable to saying exactly what he meant, but he seemed to know that what was left to be inferred was more important in a piece of supernatural horror fiction than literal reality. Why else would the narrator of "The Call of Cthulhu" say of Cthulhu "the thing cannot be described," and then go on to describe it? If we follow Lumley's reasoning, it's because the narrator doesn't understand what he's saying. I prefer to think he understands perfectly what he's saying, but that he realizes he can only hope to approximate, through inadequate words, the unspeakable horror of Cthulhu.

But Lumley seems to be incapable of looking beyond the literal reality of what is described in the story. He says that Professor Angell "recognizes the tablet and what is carved upon it *in such detail* for what it really is." I say that you can see differences between what Wilcox carved on the tablet and how Johansen describes Cthulhu (i.e., two men saw the same thing and described it a little differently, an effective means of sustaining the ambiguity crucial to a supernatural horror story). Lumley asks, "Do you still insist that Wilcox's mind has not been touched by Cthulhu's?" I say that Wilcox's mind has been touched by *something*, but that if one assumes that an incomprehensible entity like Cthulhu has "a mind," one thinks as narrowmindedly as a Lovecraft character. Finally, Lumley wonders if I can't accept that Cthulhu's dreaming influenced Wilcox's, why was it that Lovecraft called the story "The Call of Cthulhu." Well, Brian, I've got one for you: Why did he call another story notably lacking in shadows "The Shadow out of Time"? I think it was to evoke a sense of something more going on in the story than is immediately evident from the title. Indeed, I seem to be more willing than Lumley to accept that there is *always* more going on in a Lovecraft story than meets the eye—perhaps because I credit Lovecraft with the subtlety he thought so crucial to effective weird fiction writing.
    --Stefan "Dizzy" Dziemianowicz, Union City, NJ

Brian Lumley, *Elysia: The Coming of Cthulhu*. Ganley, 1989, 190 pp. $8.95.

(Reviewed by Stefan Dziemianowicz)

Brian Lumley's *Elysia: The Coming of Cthulhu* in one fell swoop brings together Lumley's horror and fantasy fiction involving Titus Crow, his two Ithaqua/Borea novels, his Hero of Dreams Trilogy, his fantasy cycle set in Theem'hdra and virtually everything he has ever written in the Cthulhu Mythos. That's no small feat for a book that weighs in at less than half the length of a single novel in Lumley's Necroscope quintet.

It's not as though this amalgamation was completely unprepared for. In his 1978 novel, *The Clock of Dreams*, Lumley merged the world of hitherto realistic horrors found in the Titus Crow stories with elements from Lovecraft's dreamworld fantasies, and then further compounded the situation in *The Moons of Borea* (1979), by having the Crow saga dovetail with his pair of novels set in the otherworld of Borea. The motif that served as the glue to bind these diverse stories together was the clock of Etienne-Laurent de Marigny, which Titus Crow and his sidekick Henri-Laurent de Marigny (son of Etienne) used to escape from Shudde-M'ell and his minions at the end of *The Burrowers Beneath* (1974). When Crow discovered in that book's sequel, *The Transition of Titus Crow* (1975), that the clock allowed a properly sensitized person to traverse space, time and genre with impunity, it set the stage for all of the boundary-breaking that occurs in *Elysia*.

Elysia, Lumley fans will recall, is the home of the Elder Gods, a species of creatures developed by August Derleth and confirmed as the beneficent photo-negatives of Lovecraft's Old Ones by Lumley. Because he was recognized as a distant cousin of the Elder Gods, Titus Crow was allowed to reside in Elysia with his goddess sweetheart Tiania at the end of *The Transition of Titus Crow*. Crow and Kthanid (the supreme Elder God, who is the good cop to Cthulhu's bad cop) extended an invitation to de Marigny to come live in Elysia in *The Clock of Dreams* (1978), but de Marigny seemed to lack the necessary navigational skills to pilot the clock there and, in *The Moons of Borea*, wound up taking a wrong turn into the titular world, which Lumley had portrayed in *Spawn of the Winds* (1978) as being populated by Ithaqua's human abductees.

It *appeared* at the end of *Moons* that de Marigny's good deeds in Borea (which included giving Ithaqua the old heave-ho and wooing away his human fiancee, Moreen) were enough to pay his fare to Elysia. Apparently not. *Moons* concluded with Moreen slipping into the clock with de Marigny, intent on sharing his just rewards, but *Elysia* opens with the couple still in search of this ever elusive Shangri-La. The Elder Gods haven't been the most helpful travel agents either, and for a very good reason: as Kthanid informs Titus Crow, the stars are almost right once again, which means that it is nearly time for the devilish Old Ones to return from their respective exiles and wreak havoc on the space-time continuum. Elysia will undoubtedly be the first target of their ire, and for that reason the Elder Gods are taking no incoming calls—from the wandering de Marigny or anyone else. However, they do have a secret agenda for cosmic salvation in which de Marigny is to be instrumental, and they allow Crow to make contact with his old buddy to apprise him of the situation and start him on the quest that ultimately will bring him to Elysia *and* save the universe.

It may sound like one has to reread Lumley's entire backlist just to prepare for *Elysia*, but that's really not necessary. As de Marigny encounters characters like Hank Silberhutte, David Hero and Eldin the Wanderer and King Kuranes, each recalls his or her past exploits for the reader's benefit. This is a major shortcoming of *Elysia*. In fact, in *Elysia* Lumley has done little more than build a frame that can accommodate synopses of nearly everything else he has written before. Just as *The Transition of Titus Crow*, possibly Lumley's worst novel, seemed to have been written solely to introduce themes and characters that would be put to slightly better use in future novels, so does *Elysia* seem to have been written solely to create a larger context for events that take place in those novels. If *Transition* serves as a table of contents for this saga, then *Elysia* is its index. Lumley introduces virtually no new ideas through his story, except at the climax, which I won't reveal.

The biggest obstacle to my enjoyment of this book is Lumley's handling of what he refers to as the CCD, or "Cthulhu Cycle Deities." If you have been able to accept his portrayal of the entities treated with awe and terror in Lovecraft's fiction as antagonists evenly matched to human protagonists, then you will have no problem with *Elysia*. But if you have found Lumley's anthropomorphization of Lovecraft's creations and his anthropocentric view of Lovecraft's universe to be more annoying than any misinterpretation of

Lovecraft by August Derleth, you will find that *Elysia* achieves new heights—or depths—of foolishness. The book treats us to portrayals of human characters who are made out to be so much greater than gods that they can shake their fists at supernatural entities and shout, with perfectly straight faces, "We're going to teach these Hounds of Tindalos the lessons of their lives—or un-lives." *Elysia* also holds up for our appreciation a portrait of Elder Gods who can't remember how they originally defeated the Old Ones because after a couple of vigintillion years their cosmic gray matter ain't what it used to be, and it characterizes Cthulhu, Yog-Sothoth and Nyarlathotep as monsters who are about as threatening as the Nazis of "Hogan's Heroes."